FIRST BORN

BOOK 1 IN THE

LILY MOORE SERIES

TRICIA ZOELLER

TABLE OF CONTENTS

Chapter		Page

DEDICATION

For my husband Lou—"Against All Odds." Thanks for humoring me, Mr. Nonfiction. For my family and friends who have raised me up during the lowest points both in my writing and in life.

Come to the edge.
We might fall.
Come to the edge.
It's too high!
COME TO THE EDGE!
And they came,
And he pushed,
And they flew.

— Christopher Logue

CHAPTER 1

THE EDGE

"I WANT TO show you something," Phil said. He swung the BMW into the parking lot of Grady High School's empty football stadium sending Lily off balance. She clutched the door handle as the car rocked to a halt.

"I think I just want to go home," she said. He had talked about himself the entire time at dinner, but she attributed it to nerves. Once in his car on the way to get ice cream, he made some ridiculous sexual innuendos.

"Ah, Phil?" Lily called as he jumped out his side and came around to the passenger door. He yanked the door open, and offered her his hand. She didn't take it.

"Here, let me help you." He leaned in and undid her seatbelt. "I think you drank too much wine."

"I'm not feeling so good. I thought we were going for ice cream?"

"Let's take a walk and get some air first."

His smile made her stomach twist. She didn't understand why her brain was so foggy. She only had two glasses of wine with dinner. She looked past him to the empty stadium. This was not her idea of a romantic evening.

Phil clutched her arm. "Let me..." He pulled her out of the car and kicked the door closed. Once on her feet, Lily fully realized something was not right. Her legs could barely hold her. "I don't mean to be a party p—"

He pushed her back against the closed door and planted an open-mouthed kiss on her lips. The wine from dinner had made her tired, but his touch was like a Jägerbomb. The Red Bull part kicked in. His warm breath on her face smelled of booze and bad gums.

"I can make you feel better, Lily."

She squirmed against him, but he trapped her with his body. Lily couldn't bring her knee up because of her narrow pencil skirt. He jammed his beefy knee between her thighs binding her legs completely.

Her head swam as she tried to gain her faculties. "Get. Off. Me." When she looked at him, he wore a smirk, but he took one step back. Lily exhaled, realizing she had been holding her breath. She turned to the side to open the door. Suddenly, her head slammed against the window. Pain shot through the bones of her skull, sending shock waves from her temple, down her jaw to her teeth. She could not believe he just hit her. Her fear tasted of metal and bile. Her hand clung to the side mirror of the car as she knelt on one knee, her entire body weak. She managed to turn and stare at him. When he struck her face again, her vision flashed a brilliant white.

Rage. Pure unadulterated fury accompanied the blinding light and surged through her body. Her fingers throbbed. Her teeth ached. A cramping sensation fingered its way up her spine before a spinning disorientation all but consumed her. She stayed conscious, but barely. She righted herself as terror ignited her. As she tackled him to the asphalt and bit him, his screaming filled her ears. Liquid metal filled her mouth. His blood. Her vision blurred and she lost contact with him.

When things cleared, she saw him feeling along the locked steel fence that secured the field. By the Eighth Street end zone, he discovered the one open gate leading on to the field, but she had caught up with him. Cussing and screaming, he attempted to run away from her, but she tackled him at the edge of the bleachers. One swing at his head and he was quiet. She dragged him across the lawn by the collar and heaved him over the crossbar.

Dizzy, Lily collapsed on her behind at the ten yard line. Everything had changed. White chalk lines stood out in stark relief against lime green grass as if viewed through polarized lenses. Pain seared through her face and temple. Her mouth stung and her eyes burned with tears. She spit out bits of asphalt, blood, and *hair?*

A moan rumbled behind her. It hadn't come from a Grady Knight. And at twenty-six, Lily Moore was no cheerleader. She didn't dare look back. *What have I done?*

She sensed him first as she pushed her face into the warm breeze. Gun oil. Fruit. Animal. Spice. A man dressed in dark clothing stood off in the distance, watching. A cap sat low over his face. He didn't make a sound. He took one step toward her then stopped and turned his head. Loud voices came from behind the bleachers. *Teenagers.* Lily heard each sniff, cough, chuckle like they were standing next to her.

The Watcher backed away toward the parking lot and disappeared from sight.

Lily gazed at her naked body. Something was wrong with her hands, her feet. Another glance at the end zone caused her to panic. She gulped the air as she took off running. Her limbs felt uncoordinated as she ran through the lot and across the desolate street. Buildings, trees, cars looked eerily disproportionate like she'd been dropped into an alternate universe.

Did he drug me? Terror fueled her forward, but her body just wouldn't function. After a few blocks, she collapsed to the ground. As she lie on her back gazing up at the black branches of a massive tree, her eyelids slid open and shut like faulty garage doors. *I just need to rest.*

CHAPTER 2

MISSING GIRL?

DETECTIVE CALDWELL SIMMS parked his unmarked car off Charles Allen Drive in the faculty lot for Grady High School. Atlanta PD's lead crime scene investigator, Tiny Hunt, had both the Tenth Street and Charles Allen Drive entrances blocked off to the stadium.

Caldwell walked down Tenth Street to the main entrance of student parking. Power lines ran in front of the wrought iron arch that boasted the school's name. Red and black running shoes suspended over them. He doubted they were part of the crime scene.

Immediately across Tenth Street stretched 189 acres of Piedmont Park. You never knew what you would find there. People from all walks of life frequented the park, which hosted art, cultural, and musical festivals throughout the year. After dark, many a homeless vagrant found a spot to rest.

It was a good place for people watching. You may even find a Little Person on stilts. *Nah, that's just Tiny.* The moniker bestowed on their investigator as a child still fit him as an adult. Usually the sight of watching Tiny Hunt conduct a crime scene investigation while wearing his Powerstrider stilts made Caldwell smile. He couldn't summon one at this time of morning. The spring-loaded stilts helped Tiny work a scene without needing to use his metal grabber or a stool to reach items. Plus, his ability to powerbock, run and jump athletically, earned him card-carrying status in the Badass Club. His responsibilities continued to expand with the APD. Tiny often worked in more of a liaison role for them, coordinating information between agencies. His unconventional methods added to his mystique.

Caldwell signed the logbook before ducking under the crime scene tape.

When he reached the bottom of the drive, Tiny greeted him. "Simmulator, I'll walk you through in a minute. We're still marking evidence. It spreads from the BMW crossover, through the open gate on the field, to the dumpster, and out to Charles Allen Drive." Tiny's dark eyes shined under the lights. Caldwell took in the yellow numbered tents and stood back as technicians took pictures and collected blood and other possible samples to test back at the lab.

"Thankfully, we were able to reach the maintenance man at this hour and he came out to turn the lights on for us."

Five minutes later, Tiny walked, sans Powerstriders, through the crime scene. Caldwell noted the unusual scratch marks on the side of the vehicle, the shattered glass of the passenger window, the blood, and strands of silky dark hair clinging to the surface. He stepped back to allow the tech to collect it.

"We already bagged Lily Moore's purse and torn clothing." Tiny said.

Caldwell bit the inside of his cheek. This woman could not catch a break. He met her when he was investigating her boyfriend's death nine months ago. Authorities found Peter Marx dead in his car on a side street about ten blocks west of this location. Marx had injected too much insulin, had a seizure and died. They ruled it accidental, although Ms. Moore had disagreed vehemently.

Tiny's voice brought him back to the present.

"You talked to the lieutenant?" Tiny asked.

"Yeah, high school kids found twenty-six-year-old Phillip Miller at the base of the goal post and called 9-1-1. Lake said it looked like something straight from the TV series 'When Animals Attack.'"

Tiny pointed to the ground, a set of bloody prints led past the ticket booths to the open gate of the metal fence. "Never seen anything like it."

"You're thinking some kind of animal?" Caldwell asked.

"Or somebody's in dire need of a pedicure," quipped Tiny. "You gonna be okay with this."

"What do ya mean? I'm fine."

Tiny studied him. "I just know that you talked to her a lot about Marx. Kinda got under your skin."

"Give me some credit." Caldwell said.

Tiny shrugged.

On the field, Caldwell squatted to examine strange feathers as one of the techs bagged them. "What the hell?"

Tiny shook his head. "I'm as confused as a cow on astro turf."

Caldwell rubbed his face.

No sign of her. He had calls into hospitals, friends, and family. He continued the rest of the morning in auto mode not letting anything trigger an emotional reaction. He drove down Juniper Street as he scanned each house, shrub, tree, and dark corner in search of some sign of Lily Moore. Ernie Gates's Search and Rescue dogs had already started tracking. Still, guilt rode shotgun. Caldwell wasn't sure why things were getting to him. Perhaps because his gut had indicated something was off about Peter Marx's death despite the lack of evidence.

He thought of Lily Moore's green, almond-shaped eyes and all that blood. It was like being punched in the kidney. Rage kept his nausea in check. He hoped Miller regained consciousness soon so they could talk.

LILY'S EYES POPPED open as adrenaline raced through her veins. *How long was I out?* Her mind flashed to the witness at the football field. *I need to go home.* She fled past playground equipment and geese that had bedded down for the night. Looking over her shoulder, she saw the brilliant blue twin fins gleaming atop Symphony Tower, the gothic architecture standing out in Atlanta's night sky-line. Recognition bloomed as she escaped through the stone pillars flanking the Charles Allen entrance to Piedmont Park.

Dehydrated, she stopped several blocks away to drink water from a puddle. She looked again to the night sky surprised by her heightened perception of things. Cicada chirped a mysterious serenade as clouds danced across the face of the moon. She shook her head to focus. A metallic taste permeated her mouth. She ran her tongue over her gums finding the empty socket where her top canine used to be. Suddenly, a familiar scent hit her, drawing her toward home.

After a quick right on to Myrtle Street, she stopped in her tracks while her heartbeat thundered in her ears. Two police cruisers occupied the street in front of her duplex, their blue and white strobe lights spinning. Each turn of the lights sent menacing green-gray shadows to stretch then contract on the front wall of the yellow Victorian home. Lily shivered then held her breath when she saw a lean muscled figure pacing behind an unmarked Ford Taurus.

Detective Caldwell Simms? Lily crept behind the neighbor's shrubs to spy on the Atlanta Police detective. She stayed close enough to hear his side of a cell phone conversation.

"Lieutenant, we checked the house. Her brother, Seth, let us in. No sign of her or a struggle here. Her landlady, Mona Sinclair, isn't answering, although her car is in the driveway." He stopped his movement as he listened. "Bite marks?"

Detective Simms looked to the lit windows of the house. "You staying there with Miller? Okay, I'll keep you updated."

One of the officers on the scene approached him. "Detective Simms, anything?"

"Nothing of significance here. We've recovered her purse and torn clothing from the vehicle at the high school. There's blood all over the outside of the car. Lake's at Piedmont Hospital with the male victim. He has some strange bites and scratch marks."

"Some sort of animal get 'em?" asked the officer.

"No idea, but if Moore survived, she's in bad shape.

We'll continue to check hospitals."

"I'll keep patrolling this area. Let you know if I see anything," said the officer.

"Thanks. I'm going to see about rousing more neighbors."

Lily must have been unconscious for a while if the police already had been to the high school. The hairs on the back of her neck stood up as she recognized a scent. *So close.* It was the man from the field. She knew his smell now, a fact she couldn't explain. Creeping backwards into the neighbor's hedges, she peered out, scanning the street. Police, some nosy neighbors, but no man in black.

With the police all over her home, she couldn't hole up inside. No matter how many deep breaths she took, she couldn't comprehend the night's events. How would she explain things to the cops? To Detective Simms?

She slunk away and ran the streets until she came to a halt at the end of a long driveway. Instincts drove her toward a home with white columns that seemed to reach toward heaven.

She hesitated. The scene she left behind twisted her thoughts. Her left eye had started to swell shut and throbbed. Confused, she looked around with her right eye. Her surroundings felt familiar, so she continued up a tremendous flight of stairs coming to rest before a storm door. A cacophony of deep barks pierced the night. Every muscle in her body tensed. As suddenly as it had erupted, the dog quieted and stared at Lily with glowing green eyes. It raised its hind leg and began to scratch.

Much better. Relief washed over her from an itch properly addressed. *Did I just? Nah, I couldn't have.*

But she had. She glanced down at furry paws then back up at her reflection in the glass. *Fur, tail, pink tongue, bum eye.*

They say life doesn't give you anything you can't handle. Well, they could just stuff it because she was not handling this at all. She finally allowed herself to cry. Phil, the asshole, had drugged her, attacked her, and now she was on some sort of whacked-out trip with no signs of recovering soon.

She was in bad shape. And what of her date? *I hope he's not dead. Or maybe...it would be better if he were.*

The foyer light came on in the house. Its beam spilled onto the porch, dispersing her dark thoughts and suspending her whining. The door opened an inch at a time to reveal a hulking figure in dark silk pajamas.

The man turned toward someone behind him. "Larry! There's a skunk on the front porch." Lily heard a commotion before a round figure appeared before her. Dressed in a lavender paisley bathrobe, Larry peered down at her with his colossal peridot eyes. Straight from toon town, *her* Larry, was the size of the Jolly Green Giant. "Geez, Frank, don't be ridiculous."

Lily *knew* she recognized this house. If someone is going to find you bleeding and hallucinating, it should be a dear friend. Larry was her co-worker at Cartoon Network where she worked as a graphic designer.

Larry picked her up, "Oh puddin', what happened to you?"

"What is it?" Frank asked.

"It's a Shih Tzu!" Larry said, crinkling his nose as he got a whiff of her. The two men peered out into the night as if it held the answers. She wasn't sure what they expected to see. A stork, the Shih Tzu fairy perhaps?

Larry looked at her with gentle eyes. "There's no collar or tag," She buried her head in his neck and cried. The noise she made was more like a cat's tortured purr.

Frank looked at her, his eyes wide. "That doesn't sound right."

Lily held her breath and pouted.

"Frank, don't be an idiot. Maybe she has a cold or something," Larry said.

She was so confused she had to remind herself to breathe. Lily had experienced rough nights, drank too much in college, but this "trip" was intense.

"Now, now, it's okay. Are you hungry?" She knew food was Larry's solution to all of life's woes.

One ham and cheese omelet later and Lily couldn't keep her one functioning eye open. Her demonic growling precluded Larry's attempts to attend to her wounds. He must have felt sorry for her because he allowed her to sleep at the foot of the bed. Safe at last, she fell asleep.

At least Lily thought it was sleep. Perhaps it was another chain of hallucinations. *Somebody make it stop. Please.*

CHAPTER ✒ 3

REALITY BITES

LILY SHOT UP in bed, somehow catching the scream before it burst forth from her throat. Trembling, she pulled the sheet up to cover her nakedness. Just another violent nightmare like the others she had experienced since Peter's death. She heard a masculine moan next to her. *Oh my God. This isn't my bed!* She rolled off the bed and landed with a "thud" on the floor.

"Frank?" Larry asked, from the other side of the bed.

Reality sunk in. She was in Larry's bedroom returned to her original form, minus clothing. Purple bruises and red gashes mottled her legs and arms. Her left eye now opened halfway. *What did I do last night?* Had Larry nursed her through a drugged state? The thought of Phil Miller had her burping up vomit.

She distinctly remembered thinking she was a dog. She scanned the floor for something to cover herself. Spotting a throw on the chaise lounge, she crawled across the plush carpeting in order to yank it down. Just as she considered how to apologize to Larry for the previous night's indiscretions, he sat up in bed, turning toward the hallway, "Frank! Do you have the dog?"

Dog? She flattened to her stomach before worming her way under the bed. Lily heard the rattling of dishes in the

13

sink downstairs. Frank hadn't heard him. The light switch-ed on.

Larry shuffled around the room calling, "Here, puppy."

Cowering under the bed, Lily held her breath and stifled a sneeze as he explored every room of the Ansley Park home. She didn't dare move from her hiding place.

As he circled back around to the bedroom, Lily grew more anxious. Larry shuffled to the bed. His crepitus knees protested as he knelt on all fours before lifting the bed skirt.

PPPPPPFFFFFTTTTT.

"Good Lord! No more eggs for you," Larry said look-ing her squarely in the eye. Her mouth hung open in a pant. She looked down to see furry paws. *I am a dog. And a flatulent one at that.* When she panicked, she had become a Shih Tzu again. *What is happening to me?*

After he lured Lily out, Larry lifted her in the air to study her face. "Your eye is much better, but you still smell like an old sponge. We're taking you to get groomed today."

Frustrated, Lily squirmed. How could she explain to him that they had grossly different agendas? She needed to return home and lock herself inside until she stopped growling, rumbling, and panting.

Larry carried her downstairs where they found Frank standing in the foyer looking all kinds of fine in his tailored Armani suit and gelled hair. His lineage had blessed him with olive skin. Blue-green eyes gleamed in contrast to his dark complexion. A scar over his left eyebrow made him look like a rugged Greek god.

He furrowed his brow as he studied their new pet. "He's a funny little creature, isn't he?" She didn't bite him, although it was tempting.

Larry scowled.

Lily eyed the food on the counter.

"I need to tell you something," Frank said.

Larry's head turned to the TV where the morning news anchor was talking about a current story. Lily's ears perked up as she listened to the anchor mention her name and that she was missing.

"Oh my God," Larry gasped.

"That's what I wanted to tell you," Frank said looking somber. He attempted to slide a biscuit across the counter to Larry.

"I'm not hungry."

Frank sighed. "They found her car at Houston's Restaurant on Peachtree Street. The date's car was at Grady High School. It looked like...well there was some blood, apparently."

Larry's jaw dropped. "I need to call her brother."

"Good idea. And a Detective Simms with the Atlanta Police Department left his number. It's still on the machine."

"The police called us?" Larry asked.

"Well, you specifically."

"I just can't believe it." Larry snagged a bit of biscuit and stuffed it in his mouth.

"What do you think she was into?" asked Frank raising his thick black eyebrows.

"Into?"

"Her boyfriend offs himself and then she is brutally attacked. I'm thinking drugs."

"No, Frank, she wasn't on drugs," he hissed. Lily

backed him up with a snarl.

Frank stared at her with a glint of fear in his eye. "Geez Larry, we don't know if that thing's had its rabies shots."

Larry's look sent him scooting out the door.

"Asshole," Larry said. She couldn't agree more.

As Larry reheated breakfast, Lily gazed out the back sliding glass door pondering her current situation. Her nightmares over the last several months perhaps were not a result of past events, but some warning of what was to come.

A bacon biscuit torn into bite-size pieces pulled her from her reverie. Larry served it with panache on their fine china. The first taste had her stomach grumbling. The biscuit overwhelmed all her senses. Her sadness was a dull ache in the background.

As she was devising a plan of how to score more, the doorbell sounded. Larry looked at her while pulling the belt tighter on his bathrobe. Low demonic barks came from her as she charged the front door. "Easy Cujo," he said to her.

She knew before he flung the door open. *Detective Caldwell Simms.* Despite her grief, Lily had developed a schoolgirl crush on the detective. It seemed to be getting worse each day.

Larry gasped. *Oh for God's sake Larry, he's not that good looking.*

Simms waited on the doorstep, charcoal gray slacks fitting his muscular legs just right, blue oxford shirt showing off his eyes.

"Mr. Jones?"

"Yes, Sir."

"I'm Detective Simms. I left you a phone message. It's about Lily Moore."

"This is embarrassing. Excuse my pajamas," Larry said. His hands fluttered to the lapel of his robe. He blinked rapidly as splotches of red bloomed on his neck and spread to his face.

"No big deal. I just have a few questions for you."

He shook the detective's hand and invited him inside. Detective Simms stepped in, eyes immediately dropping down to her. "Wow. Did that bark come from him?"

"Oh yeah. She's a killer."

As they walked down the hall to the great room, Lily ran circles around Detective Simms's legs, wagging her tail while jumping on him.

"Oh yeah. You're terrifying," Simms said with a smirk.

"I'm so sorry," Larry said. He scowled at her while attempting to shoo her away.

Desperation pumped through her veins. She followed Simms onto the couch and looked at him with imploring eyes.

Up close, she noted his unshaved face and dark circles under his eyes. He smelled like musk, woods, citrus, spice ...and stale coffee. *You're dreamy.*

Detective Simms took a quick glance at her before absently rubbing her long ears, which set her hind leg to tapping out Morse code on the couch. "Is that a good spot?" he laughed.

Any spot's good, buddy.

Turning toward Larry, Simms pulled his small notepad out of his shirt pocket. Then, he turned back and stared at her. "I've never seen green eyes like this on a dog before," he said.

I've never seen eyes like yours!

"She's definitely unique," Larry said. "Actually, she showed up injured on our doorstep last night. I've not seen her around here before."

Simms kept looking at her eyes. Lily stared back, willing him to understand.

"Don't you wish they could talk?" he asked.

"Yeah. You get a load of her eye? Somebody hurt her," spat Larry. "Wish I knew who. I'd hunt the bastard down and introduce him to a crowbar or a tire iron or possibly a bludge..." Larry censored his murderous rant. Lily realized he was staring at the firearm on the detective's hip.

Simms flashed a good-natured smile.

Sigh.

"Dog! Hello!" Larry clapped his hands to break her relentless gaze. "Stop mooning over Detective Simms."

Mooning, I'm not mooning over him. She sat next to him, refusing to relinquish her front row seat. So what if she had memorized his left ear, his broad shoulders, and strong callused hands. She wondered what his calluses might feel like...

Detective Simms focused on his job of questioning Larry about Lily's dating life, personality at work, and her habits. He asked about her relationship with her mother, Maggie Moore, and her brother, Seth. Simms returned several times to her "relationship" with Mr. Miller. He asked why Lily got in the car with the man when she had driven herself to the restaurant.

Ice cream. We were going for ice cream. It was no use.

She knew he thought she got into Phil Miller's car for *other* reasons.

Then Simms broached another dark subject—Peter. Simms shifted forward to rest his elbows on his knees. He held his hands together and studied them. "I know you are close to Lily. I've had several conversations with her myself regarding Peter Marx. This kind of tragedy could unravel anyone." Simms's slate-blue eyes sought Larry's. "I need to make an accurate assessment of her mental state in the last several weeks. It will help us to look at things from every angle."

Lily snarled, surprising herself as much as everyone in the room. Simms turned his head to study her. He drew down his eyebrows while his mouth fought with amusement. "She sounds a bit possessed."

She chuffed softly before settling back down to rest her head on her front paws and shift her eyes to Larry. *I'm not crazy. Possessed? That's entirely possible.*

Larry adjusted his bathrobe for the sixth time while pressing his lips in a thin line. "Lily's one of the most resilient people I've ever met. I know she was depressed, but never unstable."

Simms nodded.

"I've never heard her mention this Miller guy," Larry said, nibbling on his bottom lip. "I worry because we all pushed her to be more spontaneous, get back out there, and find some joy again in life."

This isn't your fault, Larry. She jumped down from her perch next to Simms. Placing her front paws on Larry's knee, she nuzzled his hand earning her an ear scratch. Larry's eyes were wet.

19

Simms asked a few more detailed questions regarding co-workers and friends. As the detective finished up, Larry pulled himself together, sitting up straighter in his chair.

"Detective Simms, have you completely shut the case on Peter's death?"

The taut muscles in Simms's jaw twitched. He swallowed before flashing a tight smile. "Sorry, Mr. Jones. You know I can't discuss that investigation." He clicked his pen shut before putting it in his pocket along with the mini notepad.

Larry looked down. "Isn't it odd that a young man dies and in less than a year, his girlfriend is attacked?"

"We're considering all the circumstances," Simms said.

"You know I always wondered about Peter's work at that lab. He was very intense and worked crazy hours with Professor Hitomi. I mean, he was just a part-time grad assistant."

"Workaholic, huh?"

"More like fanatic," Larry said.

Simms's phone buzzed. After checking the number, he excused himself before walking to the foyer. She followed him.

"Lieutenant?" His face turned gray. "Cause?" He paced the marble floor of the foyer. "Time of death? I'll be down there in fifteen, just finishing up with Mr. Jones."

Lily followed Simms back to the great room to find Larry unblinking with worry lines creasing his forehead. Apparently, he had been eavesdropping.

"Not her," said the detective.

Larry let out a long breath.

"Thanks again for your help," Simms said as he handed Larry his card and encouraged him to call if he thought of anything else.

After the door closed, Larry fanned himself. "Goodbye, Detective Hottie!" Placing his hands on his hips, he surveyed his new pet. "Don't look at me that way. You were the one slobbering and jumping all over him."

"Wuf!"

With Simms gone, Larry busied himself with the breakfast dishes, but Lily could see how shaken he was by the tension in his face. If only she could communicate to him that she was okay.

She continued to shadow him, following him up the wooden stairs to his bedroom. It was serene with blue walls, antique walnut furniture and white linens on the bed in various textures. She hopped up on the chaise lounge, which was a coffee-colored leather.

Once Larry was in the shower, Lily scurried across the room to the mirror.

After several seconds of staring at herself, she looked at the ground. *What have I become?* She felt warm tears flood her eyes. She took another glance. Her familiar green eyes stared back at her from a black mask of fur. Her eyelashes had doubled in length. She wagged a large plume of a tail. *A cross between a miniature mountain yak and Zorro.*

Lily fought panic as it closed in on her. Crying was not an option. Panic would not dominate her. Someone, somewhere had an explanation to what had happened to her and why.

CHAPTER 🪶 4

TAKE A BITE OUT OF CRIME

CALDWELL AND LIEUTENANT Lake stood across from the Victorian house on Myrtle Street. The yellow crime scene tape was a grim reminder of the tragedy that surrounded its idyllic façade.

As Lake ran his fingers through his short hair, Caldwell chugged a Red Bull. His stomach gurgled in protest.

The lieutenant's whole face puckered in disgust. "Man, really?"

"What?"

"That stuff can make you tachycardic."

Caldwell looked down at the empty Red Bull can. "Listen Mama Lake. My real mother lives in Jersey and brushes her teeth with Jim Beam. It could be worse."

"I hear that's good for the gums."

Caldwell held his gaze for several uncomfortable seconds then burst out laughing. "Shit Lieutenant, I'm kidding. My mom's a California girl. You know, all natural granola crap."

Lake shook his head. "All I know is don't come running to me when the corpse seems to be moving. That stuff makes me squirrelly. I have enough natural adrenaline." As if to prove his point, an alfalfa stuck straight up in the back of his blondish-gray hair like an antenna.

At forty-six, the lieutenant was short by most standards, but a solid mass of muscle. After his recent divorce, he had become a health nut. Caldwell suspected his new relationship was with a Bowflex and a Jack LaLanne juicer.

In synchrony, both detectives looked up at the gabled window of the second story apartment of Lily Moore's neighbor, Mona Sinclair. After the news had broadcast the disappearance of Lily, Ms. Sinclair's sister, Sarah Clemens, had come over to check on Mona at 10 a.m. She found an officer stationed outside the house who offered support once they entered the home and found seventy-one-year-old Sinclair dead inside.

"You ready?" Lake asked.

"Third time's a charm. Marx, Moore, and now Sinclair."

"A strange coincidence," offered the lieutenant.

"Right."

Caldwell followed the lieutenant under the tape and up a flight of worn stairs. At the entrance, he signed the logbook and put on booties and gloves. When the smell of decomp hit him, he reconsidered the strength of his cool mint gum. In his spare time, he planned to invent a type of gum that worked its way through your sinus passages like Pop Rocks. His theory was that the smell of death couldn't take you hostage if your sinus passages were on fire.

Crime scene technicians were studying a brown patch on the carpeting while the Medical Examiner Investigator, Jimmy Chu, bagged a used syringe. Mona Sinclair sat on an antique couch with unfolded laundry next to her, a laundry basket on the floor. Her eyes drooped to half-mast, her cheeks sagged like deflated balloons, and her lips peeled back from her teeth. It was an undignified smile on what looked to have been a dignified lady.

Chu glanced up to greet the detectives. "Are you guys stalking me?"

Caldwell smiled. "Jimmy. You've gotta work on your bedside manner. I don't think your patient is responding."

Lake glared at Caldwell as if he'd farted in church.

"Sorry, Lieutenant." Caldwell swallowed as he studied the deceased woman. She looked like someone's grandmother.

Chu glanced up. "Mona Sinclair...my daughter and I heard her read from her latest book last week during the library children's hour."

"What's your take?" Caldwell asked.

"Found a sharps container in the bathroom. Won't know anything until I talk with her doc and the tox screen comes back. Looked like she just went to sleep in the middle of folding laundry, except for the syringe I found lodged in the crease of the couch."

"You have any idea what it is?" Lake asked.

"She had oral prescription containers for Inderal and Prevacid in the kitchen," Chu said. "I've got a call in to her doc to see if she had a prescription for an injectable medication. I'll let you know as soon as I hear back."

"Looks like she's been here a while," said Caldwell.

"The lividity indicates she was in this same spot. The flaccid stage of the body suggests it's been around thirty-six hours—rigor came and went," Chu said.

"Thanks, Chu."

"No problem. I can get preliminary findings to you in

the next day or so. Formal report may take longer depending on when I get things back from the GBI lab." The Georgia Bureau of Investigation's crime lab served as the processing plant for forensic evidence in the state of Georgia. Like any processing plant, sometimes the GBI got backlogged.

As Chu finished up, Caldwell conferred with the forensic techs as they bagged items. They informed him they hadn't found a suicide note. Caldwell took his own careful look around the apartment. Although nothing stood out, he found the timing of her demise remarkable. There was no way in hell Lily Moore's disappearance and Mona Sinclair's death were two unrelated incidents.

Two hours later Caldwell removed paper booties and gloves and placed them in the biohazard bag by the door. Lake followed him out.

At the bottom of the steps, Caldwell turned to the lieutenant. "Strange."

Lake raised an eyebrow. "Pretty ordinary to me."

Caldwell raised both eyebrows.

"Well, it doesn't jump out at you like last night's scenario," added Lake.

"True."

"You follow up on our animal attack victim?"

Caldwell nodded. "Miller is semi-conscious and very talkative with the hospital staff."

"What's your take on him?"

"Phillip *Eugene* Miller works as a used car salesman at European Dreams on Cobb Parkway. According to his Match.com profile, he's twenty-six. Record includes a reckless driving and a DUI six years ago. Co-workers describe him as a cocky, womanizing slimy bohunk."

"Nice," Lake said.

"He suffered quite a bump on the head. During his psych eval he talked about Moore 'not cooperating' and then referred to her as a 'demon woman with glowing eyes.'" Caldwell's voice cracked. He'd like to add a few more lumps to Miller's cranium.

Lake rolled his head from side-to-side, cracking his neck.

"The hospital tox screen showed the only thing in his system was alcohol. We'll need to check back with him and see if his story changes as he comes down off the pain meds," Caldwell said.

The lieutenant looked back at the house. "Tiny called before you got here."

"I wondered where he was."

"He's tracking down a forensic odontologist to examine Miller's bite marks. Maybe the expert can help determine what caused them."

Caldwell just shook his head.

Lake squinted. "So in addition to the interesting animal marks, Tiny had the same impression you did of the car scene."

"Bad date interrupted?"

"Possibly. We'll know for sure once we get results back from the lab," Lake said.

"You would think with significant injuries she wouldn't have made it far," Caldwell said.

"Unless something dragged her off."

Caldwell stopped chewing his gum. That hadn't occurred to him.

"You see Miller's claw marks?"

"Yeah. What the fuck?" Caldwell asked.

Lake shrugged as he turned to look down the street. "You gonna help me talk to Sinclair's neighbors?"

"Sure," he said, faking an enthusiasm he didn't feel. Sinclair was dead, but Moore might still be alive somewhere and in need of help. He'd touch base with Search and Rescue the moment he got back to his car.

CELINE DION BLASTED from the Bose sound system as they rode through Buckhead in Larry's convertible Mercedes. It felt so good to hang over the side of the car with her face in the breeze Lily wondered why she hadn't tried this instead of sitting for hours on a therapist's couch. *Note to self: stick Celine Dion poster on Larry's cubicle…if I ever get out of this situation.* She and Larry had a long-standing feud at work that involved the exchange of teen-age boy-style practical jokes. He would never live down Celine.

Lily didn't let the music get to her. The pink bows and matching rhinestone collar that Larry picked out for her were still giving her fits. She wasn't too thrilled with the hot pink nail polish either, but hey, he paid for it. She didn't have much say in the matter.

He had worked on his laptop and returned phone calls from the coffee shop next door while she received her spa treatment. Lily spent most of the time trying to review the latest developments in her miserable life. Guilt plagued her. At least she recognized it for what it was. How could she have been so dumb, so trusting of someone like Phil Miller?

As they pulled into the driveway of the Ansley Park home or "the Manor" as Lily had come to think of it, she noticed Frank's black Audi A-4 in the driveway.

When they entered, she ran to the front of the house to peer through the French doors of Frank's office. He was pacing while talking on a headset. He waved as Larry picked her up and held her to the glass. Confusion washed over his face followed by a eureka moment.

"A girl!" he mouthed.

"Duh," said Larry through the glass before walking back to the great room. As he flipped on the Channel 5 News, he fed her gourmet doggy treats. She didn't want to hurt his feelings so she ate them. Hungry as a pregnant elephant, she would have eaten cardboard.

Larry gasped as a familiar picture flashed on the screen. The news anchor relayed the few known details about the death of Lily's elderly neighbor as the camera panned to a picture of the duplex they had shared, now draped in yellow crime scene tape.

"Oh no!" Lily began to rumble like an asthmatic cat while she paced the floor.

Larry turned toward her. "What?"

She sat. *I talked.* This wasn't good. Lily attempted a howl, "Oroarorarara."

Larry took a sidelong glance at her, fear evident in his pupils. "What is that? Are you hurt? Did someone damage your vocal cords?"

She chased her tail before flinging her new squeaky heart toy in the air at him. *I'm an idiot dog, Larry!*

He rubbed his face and hair before shaking his head. "I have got to get some sleep." Turning back to the news, Larry reversed his steps and plopped onto the cushy sectional. She lay down with her ears wilted to the side of her head. Officials were not releasing any information about the cause of death. Of course, the reporter speculated about Sinclair's death and a connection to Lily's disappearance and the bizarre attack on Phil Miller. Lily growled fiercely at the image of him on TV.

Larry's eyes darted to her. "Pea brain, what's the big idea? I can't hear a word they're saying."

As they flashed to the crime scene again, she caught a glimpse of Detective Simms. She watched his every move on the screen.

"Dog!"

She turned to Larry. His frosted hair was heavily gelled in a faux hawk and it looked like it was standing on end even more than usual. He raised one eyebrow at her. "Did you recognize Detective Hottie?"

"Wuf!"

"You are something else." He turned back to the TV to listen to the details of a house fire in Smyrna. With a deep sigh, he clicked off the TV.

She raced over to him with the stuffed squeaky heart in her mouth and dropped it at his feet.

"Aw, thanks." He lifted the heart between two fingers, his nostrils flaring. Apparently, he had an aversion to dog slobber. He placed it on the ottoman. "Now," he said with his hands on his knees. "If you are to stay here, you need a name."

She cocked her head as Larry turned and yelled,

"Frank, come in here!"

Frank skidded into the room, hair frazzled, earpiece askew, documents in hand. "You just see the news about the neighbor?" he asked. Lily didn't appreciate his morbid interest.

"Yes, but I don't want to talk about it."

Frank waited.

"We need to name Dog."

Frank looked at her.

She gazed back.

"I'm sorry I thought she was a skunk this morning," he said, shaking his head. "I didn't have my contacts in. She did kind of smell." He grabbed the heart and chucked it her way. She stood stock-still.

Larry chuckled.

"I think there may be something wrong with her," Frank said.

"There's nothing wrong with her," Larry insisted.

"Well. Look at her bottom teeth. Why do they stick out like that?"

"It's an underbite; very common in little dogs," Larry huffed.

"Weird," Frank said, sitting down.

"You better kow-tow to the princess. The groomer said she's a *purebred* Shih Tzu. They used to live in the palaces of China."

"Yeah I read about that. They may have originated in Tibet," added Frank. "Do you know that Shih Tzu means lion? She is considered a foo dog or guardian lion like the ones that protected palaces and temples."

Impressed, she snuck a glance at Larry. He was dumbfounded.

"Let's call her Cimba—it means 'small' in Tibetan."

"Cimba makes me think of a large elephant," Larry said disgruntled.

"How about Foo Foo?"

Larry squinted with disgust. Lily snarled a deep primitive rumble.

"Scary," Frank said, eyeing her with respect. "How about T-Rex?"

Larry ignored him as he picked up the heart and threw it across the room. Lily bounded into the kitchen and returned to drop it at his feet.

Frank walked to the kitchen. Lily scurried behind him nipping his heels the whole way. Frank swung around to glare at her. She rushed back to hide behind Larry. "Did you just see that?"

"See what?" asked Larry.

"I think she bit me."

"Frank, really? She weighs eleven pounds. How 'bout I call you a waaahmbulance?"

Frank smirked as he took a sip of water and returned to his spot on the ottoman. I printed out some info on the foo dogs of China." He handed a page to Larry. Lily strained on her hind legs attempting to see the picture.

"What an ugly mug," Larry said. It was a Wikipedia blurb showing two lion-like creatures. One had a ball under its paw, representing the earth, but Lily didn't pay that much mind. She focused on their menacing, demonic faces.

"It says these fierce lions guarded against evil spirits," Frank said.

"I know that would scare me away," Larry responded.

"Tibetan lamas bred the dogs to resemble little lions. They are considered holy dogs because when Buddha came to earth from heaven he rode on a lion," Frank said, placing his glass on the side table.

Larry bent down, surveying her as if she were an oracle.

Frank chortled. "There ain't nothing holy about that dog. She sounds like Satan's hell hound when she barks."

Lily wanted to bite him. Not just nip. Take a chunk out of him.

She breathed a visible sigh of relief when they settled on "Tashi" which apparently connotes prosperity and good luck.

As much as Lily liked Frank and Larry's company, she yearned for some time alone to think. All the talk about fierce Chinese lion-dog creatures made her nervous as did the haunting image and scent of the man in black. Her sweet neighbor, Mona Sinclair, was dead. She had been a good friend to the Moore family.

Lily tried to keep out the dark emotions that crept through her mind, but she couldn't. Her father, Officer Arthur Moore, had been shot in the line of duty six years ago. Her boyfriend died nine months ago. Now Mona was dead. What was going on? She needed to figure out how to get her body back so she could function. Life as a dog was a real bitch.

CHAPTER 5

FENGHUANG CHENG, CHINA

LILING SIPPED FUZHUAN black tea from her favorite tea set decorated with a peach blossom pattern. The pink blooms brought to mind her granddaughter, her namesake, far away in the Peach State. She managed a weak smile. Another coughing fit struck, but she sipped some more tea. It didn't prevent the coughing, but it did ease her throat.

Out the kitchen window, she watched young children kicking a shuttlecock made with the handsome striped feathers of a pheasant and a lucky coin wrapped in bright material. She studied the green waters of the river as she touched the warm surface of her mother's sacred heirloom positioned next to her teacup.

After a deep breath, she arranged the jewelry in a silk-lined box and closed the cover. With trembling fingers, she traced the outline of fucanglong, the dragon of hidden treasure, engraved upon the box's teak surface. The creature assumed to undulate and pulse. But it was just her nerves bringing him to life, deceiving her eyes and ears.

Her eyes stayed locked on the dragon as emotions raged inside her. A tear escaped, accelerated over the curve of her cheek, and halted at her jaw, suspended in uncertainty. She wiped it away while whispering a blessing for Liling through dry, cracked lips, "Shangdi baoyou." Her granddaughter had already been tested, but the true crucible was yet to come.

CHAPTER 6

GOOD LUCK SHIH TZU

AS SHE WATCHED Larry reading his email messages on the computer, Lily wrestled with guilt. Perhaps she should warn him that she was not good luck, but rather the Grim Reaper in a furry costume. People were *dying* around her for God's sake.

It was hard to sit idly by while she worried about loved ones and they worried about her. There was also the constant fear that she would suddenly shift to human form, providing a peep show for her new roommates.

Just as she started to relax, she heard a loud whoop from Frank. He emerged from the hallway and skated across the kitchen hardwood floor like Olympic gold medalist Evan Lysacek in black socks. "I did it."

Larry looked up briefly from the computer. "Did what?"

Frank flashed a cocky smile. "I nabbed that big investtor."

"Holy crap!" exclaimed Larry, who jumped up from his chair to join Frank in an end-zone dance. Larry's exuberant movements resembled those of a cheerleader rather than a wide receiver. *Where was her phone?* She could have videotaped the entire episode and blackmailed Larry for months by threatening to post it on YouTube. Instead, she watched helplessly from a blanket on the floor.

"Let's celebrate!" said Larry.

They spent several hours guzzling champagne, feasting on filet mignon, and conducting Yo Yo Ma and the Berlin Philharmonic orchestra before doing something that resembled Zumba moves to Lady Gaga. Finally, at one in the morning, Lily followed them upstairs to bed. They had separate bedrooms since Larry snored. Within five minutes, she understood why he slept alone. It sounded like a Nor'easter was blowing through. She stumbled to Frank's room and collapsed next to him on the down comforter.

Frank had fallen asleep with the light on. In the morning hours, Lily felt like a little girl scared of the monsters under the bed. Panic had crept back to taunt her. To distract herself from her tragic reality, she ogled Frank and fantasized about him as James Bond.

When she opened her eyes at 5:30, she was staring directly into his exquisite face. His full eyebrows slanted down as if he were pondering something unpleasant. In the middle of the night he had divested himself of the down comforter and now lay bare-chested in silk boxers. He had an angular face and long, narrow nose. As her adoration began anew, she stretched her arms above her head. She wiggled her toes and...

Toes. She had toes again. *Holy mother of Buddha I'm butt-naked in Frank's bed.* Her leather collar was in several pieces across the comforter, a casualty to her transition. Quickly, she slunk backwards off the bed. *Clothes.* She grabbed sweatpants and a hooded sweatshirt from the closet. Keeping an eye on Frank, Lily backed out of the room.

"Aaaaachoooo!"

She turned toward the source of the sneeze. Larry. The door to his room was ajar. A shadow loomed across the threshold. After several moments with her breath held, she bolted for the stairs. She hit the top step going way too fast. Frank's sweatpants that she had haphazardly rolled at the bottom had come undone. The polished oak floor acted as a ski ramp and she caught air. After several bad bounces on her rump, Lily managed to grasp the handrail mid-flail. Her left arm was stuck at an awkward angle above her head where she clutched the banister. *Ow!*

"You okay Frank?" yelled Larry.

"Whataya mean, I'm fine," Frank replied still half asleep in his bed.

Sprawled on the stairs face up, Lily listened for the slightest sounds that would indicate the actions of her roommates. With her enhanced hearing, she could discern the slightest squeak of the mattress coils as Larry shifted in his bed. A soft rustle of Frank's down comforter indicated he was not a threat either. After several more seconds, she reassembled her limbs before tiptoeing the rest of the way down the stairs.

Dehydrated from the previous night's libations, she slurped water from the kitchen faucet. On her way out, she gazed into the front hall mirror. She looked like a deranged, hung-over cheerleader with hot pink hair bows. A swollen nose, two fading black eyes, and a raw burn around her neck, completed the look. She tore the little bows from her hair. The "Vegas girl" pink on her nails made her cringe. *Justifiable homicide.*

A thought occurred to her. She smiled, revealing a

jagged white nub in her pink gums. Her top canine was growing back. *Okay.* Things had reached a new level of weird. *I will not cry.* On a positive note, now she wouldn't need a trip to the dentist.

Stepping out on to the front porch, she felt her throat tightening as her anguish began to build again. She forced herself to close the door on her grief. With each step toward the immaculate manicured lawn, she breathed a little easier.

A primitive pull began in her stomach calling her to fling herself down and roll with complete abandon on God's emerald carpet. A quick shake of the head set her straight. *This is not my body. These are not my urges.* The birds' ethereal singing overpowered her sensitive ears as it reached rock concert decibels. She spotted a chipmunk across the street perched on the neighbor's wicker furniture. Each hair on the creature's face was discernible.

Snatching her hood over her head, she shoved her hands in her pockets before taking off at a brisk clip toward Myrtle Street. Seeing a chipmunk that close-up had disturbed her. She sneezed from the pollen that blanketed every surface like a fine layer of snow. *I will get my life back.*

Halfway to her duplex, Lily panicked. People were dying around her and her house was a crime scene. She couldn't explain her current condition or control it. Various *COPS* TV episodes shuffled through her mind, feeding her paranoia.

A blaring siren crescendoed behind her. *The cops!*

Before she realized it, she was in Shih Tzu form zooming across a random yard chasing a rabbit. She stopped herself before she yapped up a lung. Lily was even more discouraged when she realized it hadn't been a cop car, but an ambulance. She had ditched her human form for no reason and lost Frank's clothes.

I need help. She figured she could catch her twenty-two-year-old brother, Seth, at work.

SETH WORKED AS a security guard at the Colony Square, a complex that housed a hotel, office space, residential condominiums, and a retail mall. In reality, he was a glorified receptionist with the looks of a bouncer dressed as a Catholic schoolboy.

His uniform consisted of black Dockers pants, a white collared shirt and a maroon blazer with a security insignia on the front. He wore his dark blond hair all one length that came to his chin. Seth derived most of his looks from their father's Belgian side of the family with a hint of their Chinese grandmother in the shape of his eyes, although they were blue in color. At some point, he had adopted a type of swagger to his gait. Her best friend, Katie, said that the combination screamed male stripper. She had scowled at Katie, but in private had laughed at her accuracy.

Lily sighed. She was entrusting her precarious life to her flaky younger brother. This transformation apparently was decreasing her cognitive abilities.

Seth's behavior in the last several years had been erratic. Gentle by nature, he didn't make it past one year in the army. College hadn't worked out well for him, either. Since then he had sampled numerous career paths.

His reaction to her current situation was difficult to predict. Despite his macho façade, he was a latent cat lover who couldn't resist a female in distress. She was definitely distressed.

The half-mile dash to Peachtree Street went by in a blur. She crouched in the grass, problem-solving her infiltration of the complex. Doors presented a challenge when you were nine inches tall.

She dashed into a section of the revolving doors behind an older gentleman who was keeping a tepid pace. He didn't continue pushing after he cleared the entrance, which left her trapped in a claustrophobic triangle of glass. While performing a bass solo operetta, she pawed the door. It didn't budge. A woman came in behind her providing the needed shove. She shot out on her butt, skidding across the lustrous marble floor like the star in "Shih Tzus on Ice."

She recovered herself in time to spy on her brother. He was flirting with a young woman, regaling her with stories of his high school football days. He omitted the fact that he was a benchwarmer. Dad had wanted him to be the big football star, but he never had the killer instincts. From the conversation, she learned that the woman worked at the radio station situated in the next tower over.

Once the female DJ sauntered over to the elevators, Lily darted across to Seth. He was still watching the girl, a salacious grin painted on his face. She finally nipped him in the ankle to get his attention.

"What the fuck...over." Seth had been using his walkie -talkie too much.

Perhaps biting was not the best way to make her introduction. He peered down at her. She held her position at his size eleven feet. Behind the colossal counter, she remained hidden from the throng of people dashing through the lobby.

"Little Dude," he said puzzled.

She wagged her tail. "Seth, it's me Lily," she said in her gravelly voice. Seth didn't scream or run. However, he did tilt his head and look at her as if she were a monumental boil on an ogre's butt. She had a bit of a speech impediment with the underbite.

"You got something stuck?" Seth placed her over his upturned forearm as if she were a baby whose airway he needed to clear.

"Seth!"

He became perfectly still with her head held upside down, her tiny Shih Tzu body straddling his arm.

"What?" After placing her on the ground, he bent way down to study her.

Forcing herself to slow down, Lily tried again. "It's Li...leee." She realized it came out like a video on slow-mo.

"Whoa."

"That Phil guy attacked me and I turned into—"

"An Ewok!" His eyes searched the lobby to see if anyone was looking. There was a temporary lull in the traffic. His calm acceptance was unexpected. He picked up the desk phone while looking straight ahead. *What the hell is he doing, calling for back up?*

"Lily, I'm going to talk into the phone receiver so I don't look like a crazy person. Are you okay? Tell me what happened again. I can't understand you very well."

She smelled a Dunkin Donut's egg and cheese croissant. When she pawed at his leg, he took the hint and halved his sandwich. She gobbled it down. Essence of spearmint lured her to the garbage can. She perched on hind legs peering into the cornucopia of delicacies that awaited her, including gum.

When she looked up, Seth was staring at her. "Aren't you something?"

She didn't have time to be embarrassed. "Phil hit me!"

"Phil Miller?" he hissed.

Just then, he reached down to shove her further under the desk while addressing a guest to the complex. When the coast was clear, he continued. His expression had changed drastically. His nostrils flared, his mouth a tight line, he looked at her. "Lily. Why on earth would you go out with that loser?" Seth had worked briefly with Phil at European Dreams.

Lily looked down at her paws. "He emailed me through the online dating website and remembered I was your sister. He would email me funny quotes each morning or sweet poems. I didn't know he was like that..." her voice cracked.

When she looked up, Seth's mouth opened and closed as if he was struggling to ask the question.

"He tried to...but I *defended* myself."

Seth exhaled. With tears in his eyes, he patted the top of her head. "What are we going to do?" he asked.

Lily held her frustration in check. If Seth didn't stop crying, she feared she would start and she was not a pretty crier in her current form. Or in any form, for that matter. He looked scared, like the ten-year-old little boy who had accidentally broken Dad's prized gas grill. Of course, that incident had been her idea. All of fourteen, she had formed a hypothesis. Being the devious heathen that a ten-year-old boy is, he had been more than happy to follow the scientific procedure and test the two hypotheses: 1) a bottle rocket lit in a closed grill would burn a hole clean through the attached grill cover, or, 2) said lit bottle rocket would merely blow the entire lid clean off the hinges with minimal damage to the actual cover. The outcome was not what they had expected.

"Lily," Seth asked, drawing her attention back. "You okay."

"Do I look okay? I'm a freakin' wappy dog."

"Happy?" he asked softly.

"What?"

"You're *happy* like that?"

She tried to achieve a "y" with her tongue, but it wasn't working. "Wappy! Wuf, wuf, wuf."

"Keep it down someone's going to hear," he said shoving her further under the counter. He looked at her in deep concentration. "I get it already, but I wouldn't call that yappy."

"Humph," she said, quoting Larry.

"Where have you been staying? Are you safe?"

"Larry's house on one-sixty-eight the Prado in Ansley Park. They're close to Piedmont Park."

"Ansley Park?" Seth asked for clarification, every muscle in his face strained with concentration.

"Wes. And they don't know I'm a girl. I had a close call this morning. I woke up naked in Frank's bed." Seth wrinkled his nose. "Oh, and my dog name is Tashi."

Seth snorted. "Sounds like the playmate of the month."

She gave him a soft growl before relaying her predicament to him about not being able to control her body or perform the simplest task in dog form not to mention there was some weird man in black somewhere who creeped her out. She didn't know who he was or where he'd gone, but she had a feeling she would see him again. She finished with the idea that she could stay with Seth.

"You can't stay with me, *Tashi*. You said yourself that Detective Simms saw you at Larry's. Detective Simms and Lieutenant Lake have been tag teaming me with random drive-bys."

As she started to protest, Seth's buddy, Reggie, came back from his break. She nipped Seth's ankles trying to convey that Seth needed to get rid of him.

Reggie gave her a disparaging look. He was a stickler for the rules and wasn't convinced that it was okay for a pretentious businesswoman to have left a dog for them to watch while she attended a meeting.

"It has an uncanny resemblance to a transvestite that kept hitting on me at my brother's bachelor party," said Reggie. "Plus, did it just bite you?"

Seth shrugged. Lily nestled closer to his legs and whimpered.

"What the heck was that? Does it have asthma?"

"Oh Reggie, you hurt her feelings," whined Seth.

"Whatever. It can't understand me. Dude, it's a dog!" Lily watched Reggie eye Seth as if he had been doing vodka Jell-O shots for breakfast.

Curling up at Seth's feet, she snuck pitiful looks through her long eyelashes. By lunch, Reggie had come around. He plopped her in his lap then fed her chicken wings. He applauded her unladylike belches. She suspected that her malocclusion caused her to swallow a lot of air, producing belches of which a sailor would be proud.

Reggie was an immense black man with an attractive bald head. She found herself mesmerized by it. When Lily began to lick it, Reggie giggled in a guttural way. He tasted salty and sweet, like saltwater taffy. Seth yanked her away from her devotions to his head. "Jesus!" he said. She couldn't help it. Dogs explored things with their mouths.

After lunch and the licking incident, Seth relegated her to the hiding space by his feet. Feeling safe for the first time in days, she drifted off to sleep.

Some time later she woke up in a storage closet wearing her brother's maroon blazer. It came down to mid thigh. Standing up abruptly, she bashed her head on a box that was hanging off a shelf overhead. It set off a domino effect of paper products raining from the shelves. *Wonderful. My very own ticker-tape parade.* The room was about the size of her mother's walk-in closet at home with items stacked high on wall shelves.

Seth had taped a note to the blazer—just like kindergarten when the teachers would pin notes on their shirtfronts before sending them home to their parents.

Tashi, phone in pocket.

She retrieved Seth's cell phone and dialed the number on the note.

"Colony Square, this is Seth."

"Hey it's me. Where the hell am I?"

"Everything okay?" he asked.

"Yes, thankfully I've lost my fur coat," she said while yanking Seth's jacket more tightly over her chest.

"Uh huh. I'll stop by there in a few minutes. Sixth floor, right?"

Ah clever boy, now I know where I am. "I'll just hang out here and weave myself a thong out of toilet paper."

"Ooo-kay. I'll see you in a few," he said, a chuckle in his voice.

After hanging up, Lily looked around at the paper products and bottled chemicals while considering her options. Her friend, Katie, came to mind. The news team had interviewed her last night and she had been inconsolable. The two friends had graduated from the Savannah College of Art and Design, Atlanta campus together. Katie worked at an ad agency in Buckhead. She was a trustworthy friend, but Lily didn't know how she would explain herself if she called. Plus she wasn't sure her brother's cell phone was "secure." Why were the police so interested in Seth? Did they think he was responsible?

Driven by his comment about the police, she accessed the *Atlanta Journal-Constitution* online to read about the investigation of her attack and Mona's death. She was impressed she got internet on the phone inside the janitor's closet.

Lieutenant Lake stated that they had new evidence explaining the occurrences the night of the incident, but they were not disclosing details at this time. Phil Miller remained hospitalized. *Humph.* Mona had perished three days prior to Lily's attack. Lily's stomach did a somersault. She was lounging next door eating pizza and watching ultimate fighting while her neighbor had expired.

In response to the feathers and animal marks at her abduction scene, police were still waiting on lab results before drawing any conclusions. Friends and family were cooperating with the investigation. They explained that her mother, devastated by the news, planned to return from her travels abroad.

Keys jangled in the door lock. Seth slunk in, closing the door behind him. He managed to procure his phone from Lily with minimal eye contact. His body hugged the door.

"Seth?"

"Yep."

"What's the matter with you?"

"What's the matter with *you*? I just carried my naked sister up three flights of stairs after I found out she's a dog," he hissed.

"Okay, I can see how you may be taken aback by that, but don't be a butthead."

"You try carrying someone up three flights of stairs. What the hell have you been eating anyway?"

Lily gasped before pulling the blazer more tightly around her midsection. "You calling me fat is not helpful." She had the overwhelming urge to slap him so hard he'd see Elvis, but with an incredible amount of effort, she controlled herself.

Her face felt warm. "Oh dear God. Please tell me Reggie didn't see me naked."

"No one saw you except me," he said with a pained look. "One minute you were snoring at my feet like a sumo wrestler with sleep apnea. The next, you were twitching like you were having a seizure. That's how I knew to get you out of the lobby. You changed in the stairwell between the third and fourth floors. I carried you the rest of the way."

"Okay," she replied.

"No, not okay. Dis-tur-bing! It started with your toes and then all of sudden everything exploded." His eyes were enormous.

"Yuck." She attempted to strike the image from her head.

"Oh, and there was the sound." He reached past an ancient Eureka upright and scooted a tall box toward him so he could sit. She considered sitting down too then remembered she wasn't wearing undergarments.

"What sound?" Lily asked.

"Like a long fart."

"Unbelievable. I'm in serious trauma here and you're talking about farts like a ten-year-old boy." A tingling sensation crept up her neck toward the top of her head before radiating back down her spine. Seth straightened his back and cocked his head, waiting, perhaps anticipating that her next transition would be into something cool like the Incredible Hulk.

"Are you done because, Dude, I am totally serious. It sounded like a Guinness Book of World Records fart."

"Great. Like I'm not self-conscious enough that I'm waking up naked in strange places and that I have a beard. Now I have a flatulence issue to address," she retorted.

"I didn't say *you* farted. Just sounded like one."

"Thank you for the scientific analysis, Dr. Moore. Technically, it's not a fart. The sound waves created gave the perception of a fart," she said crossing her arms to mimic him. They both started to laugh, which relieved some of the tension between them.

They took a synchronized breath after their laughing jag. Lily studied Seth's face. "You're taking this animal changing thing in stride."

He shrugged.

"You don't look very surprised at all."

He shifted on his cardboard box, which made its own flatulent noise in protest. She was too intent on hearing his answer to laugh. His attention was on the nasty linoleum floor. Following his gaze, she confirmed that there was nothing interesting there.

"You better start talking Sethasaurus," she threatened. "People are dying and my life is really messed up right now. I'm walking that line between sanity and *One Flew Over the Cuckoo's Nest.*"

He cleared his throat and looked up at her.

Lily noted the worry lines on his forehead. She waited with her arms crossed, trying to look intimidating despite her inadequate clothing.

"Did anything seem weird to you when we were growing up?" he asked in a quiet voice.

"Define weird."

He sighed. "Remember the police dog Dad worked with?"

"Barney? What about him? I loved that dog. He had such human..."

"Yeah." Seth's gaze held hers.

Apprehension fluttered in her stomach. "He wasn't just a dog?"

"No." Seth swallowed. The last time she saw such apprehension in her brother's eyes was during the grill incident. He was okay with the explosion, not so much with the bomb squad and five fire trucks that showed up at their house.

"What?" she asked.

"Think about it, Lily."

She pictured the beautiful Belgian Malinois that was part of the K-9 Unit for the APD. The Malinois's head resembled that of a German Shepherd, but its body was sleeker and fawn-colored. Dad's colleague, Li Liu, was its handler, but Dad partnered with him on assignments.

"So what you're not saying is that Barney was a man." She looked over to her brother. "Who was he?"

"Lily, did you ever see Barney and Dad together?"

"Of course they were together. Dad worked alongside Li Liu often."

"Mr. Liu was the K-9 handler." Seth waited.

"No," she said, shaking her head.

"Yes." Seth said, determined.

Lily's mind raced. It was true. The times they were around the dog, it was Mr. Liu who was with them, letting them pet him. But there was a picture of the three of them together. "That picture—"

"Was most likely just another dog they grabbed to pull off the deception."

"How?"

"I don't know the specifics," Seth said. "Let's just say that as a teenager several events led me to suspect and the circumstances of Dad's death convinced me."

"Why the heck didn't you say something to me?"

Seth bristled. "Would you have believed me? Or, would you have told Mom I was cracking up?"

"Thanks for the overwhelming trust."

"Well, you know now. I'm sorry I didn't tell you. Let's just figure out what to do from here."

She didn't have time to argue with him, or create any more drama. "We need to talk to Mr. Liu."

Seth shrugged. "That should be an interesting conversation."

"I don't know what else to do," she replied.

"Fine, I'll call him."

"What about me?" she asked.

"You need to stay safe. What's the deal about the 'Dark Watcher' guy?"

Lily bit her lip. *How crazy do I sound saying I saw a man in black then he disappeared, but then I smelled him around my apartment?*

"Pretty crazy," Seth said.

"What?"

"You didn't say that out loud, did you?" Seth's jaw dropped.

"What the hell?"

"I think you just talked inside my head."

"That's not possible."

"Try it again."

Lily sighed. *You are a first class monkey butt!*

"Dude!" Seth stayed on his box, perhaps scared to get any closer.

On her feet, Lily held the blazer closed and told herself to breathe. Then she decided to sit down, modesty be damned, because she was afraid she might pass out. She sat on a box slightly smaller than Seth's, but her entire bottom sunk in since the cardboard was old and the box half empty. At least that's the reason she told herself.

Normally Seth would have laughed at her, but he looked too spooked still. "Can you...hear what I'm thinking?" he asked with a trembling voice.

Lily closed her eyes and thought about entering Seth's brain. All that happened was that she realized she *really* didn't want to know his thoughts. Expelling pent up air, she cocked her head to consider him. "Nothing." She watched all of the muscles in his neck and chest relax. "Just as I always suspected. Nothing going on upstairs."

"Ha, ha."

"Now what?" she asked.

"Don't bite my head off, but your best bet is to stay hidden until you can control your *condition*. You think you can hang in there for a while at Larry's?"

"Guess I don't have much choice." She kicked the box in front of her, sending it airborne. The force behind it shocked her, particularly because she was still sitting. "I'm eating dog food and going to the bathroom outside."

Seth grimaced. "Sorry." He looked like he really meant it. It wasn't a word he used frequently, and now he had used it twice in one day.

"I just don't understand what's going on," she whined.

"I think it's called shapeshifting," Seth said.

Lily shrugged.

He went on to instruct her on meditating, breathing, and getting her heart rate down hoping this would help her relax and learn to control her shifting.

"What the heck, Seth?"

"I used to date a yoga instructor," he said proudly. Her brother, the Yogi Lama of generation "Dude." Who knew?

Her mind strayed back to Peter as she considered how alone she felt. "Peter's dead, my neighbor's dead..."

"You need to focus on yourself right now Lily," Seth interjected. He deflected any further discussion that involved Peter. Peter and Seth had become friends, playing basketball together every Saturday morning. Seth put a wall up when anyone tried to discuss death. Wasn't just any wall. It was the Great Wall of China.

Before she let him go, they discussed her communication issues and clothing. Seth said he would add another touch screen phone to his plan and scrounge up some clothes. He agreed to leave a bag of items on the side of Ansley Park Manor behind the air conditioning unit late that night so she would have some provisions.

Seth's radio squawked. It was his boss. "Lily, I definitely have to go. I'll leave this roll of toilet paper as a doorstop so you can get out of this closet if you do change. If I don't see you sneak out as a dog, I'll check on you within the hour and we'll figure something out."

He made full eye contact with her when he stated that she needed to stay hidden in Larry's house until they got some answers. It was as if he was channeling their father, Arthur Moore, with the tone of his voice and stern look in his blue eyes. The awkward hug he extended in goodbye unnerved her the most. Was he afraid to touch her? Perhaps he thought she was cursed. She certainly was considering it.

After he left, she sat cross-legged on the floor and closed her eyes, doing her best to think of all things scary:

sharks, spiders, and the Dark Watcher. She had ascertained that being terrified triggered her hysterical Shih Tzu side; being relaxed shifted her back to human form. One memory of the man's scent and she was in canine form again.

Before exiting the room, she gazed down at Seth's maroon blazer, which she evidently slashed to threads during the transformation. Beside it was a single shiny feather. *What the hell?*

Her next thought was to flee the building before somebody found her. She peered out into the hallway before sprinting for the stairwell door that Seth had left propped open.

"Oh, look at you!"

Uh oh, single white female. A twenty-something woman was leaning down to pick her up.

She considered channeling a pit bull, but her bark was menacing enough as it was. She did froth at the mouth to improve her performance. This delayed the woman long enough for Lily to dart through her legs and make a mad dash down the stairs.

"Stop. I didn't mean to scare you. It's okay," she called to Lily.

Great. She gave full-grown men pause, but not this lady. Lily heard the clip clopping of heels behind her. It sounded like a Budweiser Clydesdale pursuing her down six flights of stairs to the lobby. Lily stopped to get a breath before darting across to Seth. It was 4:30 p.m. People packed the lobby, apparently absconding the scene before their bosses caught them in a five o'clock strategy meeting. She hid under the desk.

The woman approached Seth and Reggie at the front

desk who were busy giving a man directions to the Westin Peachtree Hotel downtown.

"Did you see a little dog?" she interrupted.

"What dog?" her brother asked, his eyes shifting from the man to the pretty young woman in front of him.

"The Shih Tzu," she said, placing one hand on her hip. The other hand hovered inches above the counter allowing her to drum her ruby red nails rhythmically on the wood.

Inspired by the voluptuous blonde, Reggie decided to be valiant. "Oh this one, is this your dog?" he asked while dangling Lily in the air for the world to see.

Seth snatched her. "That's Mrs. Brown's dog, so glad you found her. We were getting worried."

The woman looked disappointed, but flashed Seth a knowing smile. Lily had seen that smile used on her brother since he was fourteen years old. Her stalker regained her composure, chatting with the guest and security guards while scratching Lily's ears with her acrylic nails before making her departure. Seth finished giving the gentleman directions then took the dog outside "to find Mrs. Brown who he believed was sitting by the flower boxes." Once he went around the corner, he sat down on the edge of a flower box with his back to the street.

"Okay, you need to get out of here Lily."

"Weah. I wanna make sure I'm home for dinner." Larry was a good cook.

Seth snorted.

Remembering the janitor's closet, she paused a moment and thought of a delicate way to express the state of his blazer. "Uh, I left you a surprise upstairs."

Seth's face lit up. "Dude, what kind of a surprise?"

"Wour jacket looks like the Incredible Hulk got it."

"It's okay, Lone Ranger," he said laughing.

Maybe he *had* been doing vodka Jell-O shots for breakfast.

"The mask," he said as if she should have made the connection. "Oh look, you even have a little black saddle on your back." She nipped his fingertip. Her Shih Tzu markings did include a black mask and saddle, but her sense of humor was gone.

"Ow! Look for that stuff tomorrow and make contact as soon as you can," he said while nursing his finger. "I'll try to meet with Mr. Liu."

She barked in agreement and licked his face before sprinting down Peachtree Street.

"Yuck!" Seth said.

Ewww. I need to stop this licking compulsion.

As she rounded the corner on to the Prado Northeast, she saw a "lost dog" poster on the telephone pole. Larry was probably having a stroke. The thought of him worrying kicked her into turbo drive. There were no cars in the driveway when she reached the manor. She barked and scratched at the front door before running to the backyard. Plastering her face to the glass of the sliding door, she peered inside. No one was visible through the glass.

Feeling deflated, she returned to the front mat. The temperature was in the high seventies. Flowering dogwoods, redbuds, and cherry trees lined the street sending pastel blooms into the air. A slight breeze stirred, bringing with it a plethora of irresistible aromas. In her past life, this was the kind of day she would have relished. She and Katie would have gone to drink sangrias at one of the restaurants that had seating on an outside patio.

Instead, she relieved herself in the grass then came back to rest with her beard on her front paws. She fretted over the revelations made about her deceased father. Her thoughts turned to Mr. Liu. She prayed he held the answers. Lily remembered Li Liu as a quiet, but fierce individual. She guessed he must be nearing fifty years old by now.

He could be gentle as he was the night he consoled her mother over their father's murder. He never hugged or shook hands with the kids, but rather taught them how to bow in respect to their elders. The few Chinese words Lily knew, she had learned from Mr. Liu. Her mother had rejected her past, Americanizing as much as possible, even dropping her Chinese name, Chanjuan, and going by Maggie.

Lily's current condition had her reconsidering family dynamics. Her grandmother was a proud woman who Seth and Lily only met twice. The first time was in grade school when they traveled to China. The second time was when she came to the states for her son-in-law's funeral. Their grandfather was an American businessman who had met their grandmother when marketing to the Far East. He died of a stroke in his sixties. Arthur Moore's parents were both gone, as well. They had died the year before her father's death. She wondered if her grandparents had known about their son's uniqueness. *How could they not?* Lily didn't know them well, either. They had spent much of their time in Florida.

The thump of a bass drum drew her head up. Snatches of obscure voices and techtronic rhythms drifted to her along with the engine hum of a luxury car. Larry coasted down the street with the Chemical Brothers blasting from the speakers of his convertible. The pulse and thump of the music lent interesting orchestration to the blooms swirling in the wind. As soon as Larry pulled into the driveway, she ran to him. He opened the garage, but didn't pull forward. Throwing the car into park, he opened the driver's door, allowing her to leap into his arms.

"You little shit! Where did you go? I was scared to death." He looked to her expecting an answer. She buried her face into the crook of his neck and smelled him—grilled salmon from lunch mixed with his cologne that filled her nose with notes of bergamot, cinnamon, patchouli, sandalwood, and leather.

He drove into the garage with her on his lap. As soon as he opened the car door, she jumped down and waited to be let in. Larry carried his computer bag with him as he let her into the house. "You must be starving. You never ate breakfast," he said.

My hero. Some people looked to muscle-bound men with big guns for rescue, but at this moment, Larry with his pear-shaped body clad in a crisp white shirt, lavender pullover, and white slacks was a god!

Before starting his meal prep in the kitchen, Larry created a top knot with her fur and positioned a magenta bow in the middle of her forehead. "You look adorable." He snapped several pictures. The only reason she tolerated it was because she could smell the chicken on the counter.

When he began cooking his grandma's recipe for fried chicken, she almost forgot about her troubles and the latest news about her father. However, betrayal is a prolific virus. Once it burrows deep into your core fibers, it's difficult to shake. Her parents' deception was not sitting well. When she thought about her father withholding this information from her, she felt ill.

CHAPTER ✒ 7

LI LIU

THE TRANQUIL NIGHT contrasted with Seth's state of mind as he stole away from the Ansley Park home. One block east on Barksdale Drive, he slipped into his Dodge Ram truck. His hands were sweating as he started the vehicle.

For Christ's sakes, I'm not a crook. He had parked his truck one block away since he wasn't sure how to explain what he was doing at the side of Larry and Frank's house with a bag full of chick stuff. But he had promised Lily a care package and he delivered it behind the air conditioning unit as they had agreed.

The time glowed green on the dash, 11:54.

It had felt weird to be close to Lily, yet unable to talk to her. He had been tempted to peer inside the impressive home, but "Peeping Tom" was not a skill set he'd like listed on his resume.

Seeing the place in person, he now appreciated why Lily referred to it as "the Manor." *At least she's comfortable and safe.*

Seth turned on to Peachtree Street. His shoulders relaxed as he drew closer to home. Tomorrow was another challenge. Before his work shift at 11:00 a.m., he planned to visit Li Liu at his home in Kennesaw. The retired officer was expecting him.

It had been six years since his dad's death, but Seth still cringed when he heard Mr. Liu's voice over the phone. His father's colleague had always been warm and supportive, but at this point in Seth's life, it was just *too* familiar.

Mr. Liu's voice had tripped that wire, the one holding everything together. Seth had pushed all reminders of his father into a mental box, locked away. He *never* opened that box. Not ever. But tomorrow he would be forced to cope with his sorrow and anger. His sister's life depended on it.

SETH SLEPT CURLED in a ball, blankets pulled over his head while morning light flooded into his sparse Buckhead apartment. He was on the black futon in his living room. When he opened his eyes, he was convinced workers were blasting dynamite inside his skull. He squinted as his eyes adjusted. The microwave clock in his galley kitchen told him it was time to get up.

He shook his head when he noticed a half bottle of Bailey's Irish Cream left on his coffee table. *That explains the headache.* He extricated himself from the blankets before stumbling toward the bathroom.

The warm spray from the shower did little for his headache. As he sang Linkin Park's "What I've Done," he felt a sensation rush up his spine as a high-pitched sound reached his waterlogged ears. He cracked the sliding door and peered out into the steam.

"Where did you come from?"

The neighbor's cat, Cocoa, reposed on the toilet lid. She had been singing her eerie accompaniment to Chester Bennington's lyrics of erasing himself and starting anew.

"This is not my life," Seth said closing the door.

Cocoa shadowed him through the apartment as he finished getting ready. Seth donned the standard uniform of black pants and a white oxford shirt. The cat walked out the front door with him after a breakfast of tuna fish compliments of Chef Seth. He tried to prepare himself for his reunion with his dad's ex-partner. He heard Mr. Liu had renovated an old farmhouse and kept horses.

But Seth wasn't up for a pony ride. It felt more like he was hurtling down the first hill of a rollercoaster at Six Flags. Seth had been sixteen, Lily twenty, when Gerald Owens shot their father. The emotions were still so raw; they caused his stomach to drop, his body to experience a disorienting weightlessness.

Burping up banana, he leaned across to turn on the radio. Marilyn Manson's "Beautiful People" blasted from the radio. *Ah mind-numbing distraction.* He didn't need to think about the stranger who killed Barney, the police dog, and Arthur Moore. He turned up the volume, allowing the blaring guitar to clear his head as he sang along. It was a bit painful with his headache, but he preferred it to the other sensation.

His singing turned to swearing as he exited Interstate 75 by Town Center Mall. He gritted his teeth, weaving in and out of traffic until the congestion dispersed and he reached Stilesboro Road. Four miles further north, he saw red paint bleeding through the white blossoms of the Bradford pear trees. The barn told him he was in the right place as did the horseshoe archway over the entrance.

As he pulled in front of the gray ranch home, two German shepherds raced toward the car. The retired police dogs emitted that high-pitched cry a canine makes when it's identified something irresistible. The flash of white teeth sent Seth dashing across the yard like a scared little girl. He rang the doorbell just as the larger dog pinned him against the side of the house. He felt its warm breath on his neck. The screen door creaked, then Mr. Liu's round face peered out.

"Tonka. Spike. Down!"

The dogs dropped to their bellies behind Seth as their master emerged from the home.

Seth remembered to breathe. He dug deep inside to recover his pride after such a display.

"I'm so sorry. Are you okay, Seth?"

"Yeah. Don't you feed them?" joked Seth while his eyes darted behind him to check on the dogs.

"They're usually so well-behaved," Li said as he shook his head. "So strange."

They both looked at the dogs that drooled and panted.

"Please, come in."

Seth crossed the threshold then bowed to Mr. Liu out of habit.

Li Liu returned the bow. "Look how tall you are now!" he said beaming.

Seth flashed a self-conscious smile.

"Six foot like your father?"

"Yes, sir," said Seth.

The two dogs whined through the screen door. Mr. Liu peered around Seth and commanded, "Go now." The dogs obeyed.

Seth followed him across the wide-plank hardwood floor of the 1930's home. The décor was comfortable and eclectic. Above the stone fireplace hung a colorful robe that caught Seth's attention.

"That was my great grandfather's ceremonial robe."

"Cool," Seth said, his mouth agape. The red silk robe was aged, but maintained with meticulous care.

"Sit." Liu said.

Seth obeyed. Mr. Liu plopped into a worn recliner while Seth settled into the microsuede couch continuing to examine his surroundings as he gathered his thoughts. This was not your typical southern farmhouse. Atop the entertainment center was a jian in a green ray skin scabbard. Seth resisted the impulse to forget everything and go study the sword.

"So, you're retired now?" Seth asked, pulling his eyes back to Mr. Liu. *Interesting retirement.*

"Yes, I spent four years with the Marietta Police Department's K-9 Unit and then I hung up my hat." Mr. Liu pushed the armrests forward bringing forth the footrest. "I keep busy, though. I have the horses and recently opened a Shaolin martial arts studio. Both bring me tremendous satisfaction."

Mr. Liu leaned over, his eyes wide and bright. "You do kung fu?"

"Ah, no," said Seth. "Tried karate when I was nine, but I lacked discipline. I...quit."

"Ah, perhaps it was not you that quit, but the Master who quit you," said Mr. Liu furrowing his brow.

Seth smiled in appreciation before leaning back further

on the couch.

"So. What can I do for you?" asked Liu.

Could I borrow that polearm for a few days? Seth glanced at the large weapon hanging on the wall behind Li Liu's head. It occurred to him that he was in the belly of a warrior's den; surely he could summon some courage.

"I have questions about my father."

"Yes," stated Liu. "I expected to hear from you or Lily one day. I have tried to call both of you several times."

"I'm very sorry, Mr. Liu. We didn't mean to be rude. I guess we were both so self-absorbed."

"No apologies necessary." Worry flashed across his face. "Sorry to hear about Lily's disappearance. Have you learned anything about her whereabouts?"

Seth hesitated. The way Mr. Liu posed the question made it almost impossible to respond without lying. "The police haven't shared much with me. I think she's alive, but has been hurt." Seth's Adam's apple bobbed erratically in his throat as he attempted to swallow.

Out of courtesy, Mr. Liu dropped his intense gaze. "Disturbing circumstances—her boyfriend. Now the neighbor."

Seth cleared his throat and wiped his sweaty palms on his pants. "That's why I'm here Mr. Liu. I'm trying to gather information about Dad; well, about me and my family."

"You can ask me anything."

Seth stalled.

"Anything," repeated Liu.

Seth looked into the eyes of the dragon on Li Liu's familial robe. "My Dad *shifted*, didn't he?" He never met

Liu's eyes.

"Yes."

Seth didn't breathe. He hadn't expected such a quick response.

"Barney?"

"Yes," said Mr. Liu, suddenly puzzled. "I thought your grandmother explained this all to you and Lily."

"Waipo?" Seth asked, finally meeting the man's gaze. He tried to squelch the anger that ignited in his stomach. "I've only seen my mom's mother twice in my life. She didn't stay long when she came for Dad's funeral. Why would *she* know about Dad's situation?"

"Arthur insisted she was the only person who understood."

"My father never talked about my mom's side of the family."

"That's disappointing," Liu said looking troubled. "You must be so confused. Are you having some...problems?" He posed the question like they were engaged in an awkward father-son talk about sex.

It made Seth chuckle. "You have no idea."

"Oh, I have some idea," said Mr. Liu. "Remember, I dealt with your father." His eyes grew wide. "Seth, are you a Malinois?"

"No."

"Have fur?"

Seth looked at the ground.

"Or *feathers*?" whispered Li Liu more to himself.

Seth bristled. "If you don't mind, I don't like to talk about my issues in detail." A sense of foreboding crawled over his skin as he looked around the house at the Chinese prints of warriors and the sporadic display of antique weaponry.

"Sure. Why don't I let you ask the questions?"

"Thanks." He unclenched his hands. *Where do I start?* Seth finally settled on one word. "How?"

"Shapeshifting?"

"Yeah. Is there a logical explanation?"

"Logic? Hmmmm. I suppose there are a myriad of elaborate explanations or hypotheses out there. I can only tell you what I believe from my years as a witness."

"That's a start," responded Seth.

"I believe that shapeshifter abilities run in families. Your ancestry determines form and skills. Look back into your family's history and you may find stories to explain the how and why."

"Fairy tales?"

"Perhaps," Liu said. "Folklore indicates that the animal shape was based on your ancestry, lifestyle, spirit, and personality. Your needs at the time also determined your form. If you were a Native American fighting off an enemy at night in the woods, you would transform into a wolf in order to conquer your foe with the power of strength, speed and the pack."

"And my father?"

"His shift was triggered by a traumatic event. A man pulled a knife on us when we were walking to the MARTA station. We were just two seventeen-year-old boys coming back from a Braves game planning to catch the train." Seth noticed Li Liu look off to the fish tank; his eyes tracked the movements of the angelfish, his brow furrowed.

He turned back to Seth. "Your father shifted into a

Belgian Malinois, a guard dog. We were in an urban setting and we needed protection. He saved our lives."

Seth stared at him, wondering what happened to the man with the knife, but respecting that Mr. Liu, perhaps, didn't want to discuss the details.

"Afterward, we shared a tremendous trust. We were inseparable, even attending the academy together. I felt responsible for your father and he felt protective of me."

"You were a good friend."

"I tried."

"What did my mother think of all this?" Seth asked, feeling his anger flare again.

"She didn't know."

"Hard to believe."

He nodded. "You know, your mother chooses to see only certain things. She acknowledges something only if it fits into her perfect world. That's how she copes."

And that's why she no longer acknowledges me. "How did Dad keep it from her?"

"Well, obviously it was easier after the divorce and they lived apart."

"But they divorced when I was ten," Seth said.

"Yes, before then, your father did his best to control his shifting. Some days he partnered with me in human form, but changed to Malinois if K-9 assistance was requir-ed."

"How could he keep something that important from her?" Seth asked.

"He just did. He realized that she couldn't handle it. Your mother is...delicate. Once they had you kids, Arthur couldn't risk her reaction to the truth. He was terrified of losing you."

"Why didn't he tell *us*?" Seth asked.

"I think he planned to someday." The two men didn't discuss Arthur Moore's shooting. Seth was relieved that Mr. Liu didn't bring it up.

"What about Dad's parents?"

"We learned early that his parents had no idea," said Mr. Liu. "We asked funny questions trying to bait them into discussing the topic of people turning into creatures. They never showed the slightest indication they were aware of any such thing."

Seth shook his head. People behaved badly quite often, himself included. But this was major. Lily was suffering. Dad had suffered. Waipo knew. Yet no one bothered to tell them. How did his Chinese grandmother know about Dad, but his mother was left in the dark? Lily's current predicament may have been avoided if she had known.

He reined in his frustration and focused on gaining more insight. "How did he shift?"

"Initially, he could only transition at dark. After a while, he gained control through use of visualization and breathing techniques. It remained easier for him to shape-shift at night, but he mainly worked days so that he was available to you kids after school. He didn't want to miss anything."

Seth nodded. It really would have been okay if he had missed some of his football games. "How did he manage work?"

"The Captain knew. He assigned your dad to partner with me often. If a call required a K-9 unit, your dad shifted. Otherwise, he was a patrol officer. Overall, it worked. The days he took his own patrol car, I used my German Shepherd, Spike. The other officers knew that I worked with the two different dogs. They concluded that Barney was smarter than most people they knew, but Spike was more loveable."

"Anyone look in the back of the unit while Dad was in human form in the front."

"Windows were tinted, but we had some tricks we used, like a recording of a dog barking." Liu smirked.

Seth laughed. He could totally see his father pulling some pranks with the situation. It was surreal to be discussing his father in this way. He regretted that Arthur Moore hadn't confided in him. "Could he change into different creatures?"

"No, I've heard some legends tell of that, but have not personally known anyone that could."

"You know others besides Dad?" Seth asked in a whisper.

"I know *of* others. Don't necessarily know them."

"Can it be suppressed? I mean can you choose to never change into an animal again," he asked, leaning forward now.

"I think it is too powerful a force within you. Your father would get headaches if he didn't shift every day. He learned about himself and adjusted so that he could have a happy, healthy life."

Mr. Liu looked troubled. "Seth, it's best not to fight nature. We must have balance. If we do not, we become very ill."

Seth diverted his eyes.

"Your father coped with his condition in the most

healthy, natural way he could."

"I get it," said Seth, not entirely understanding why he was telling him this.

Li Liu caught his gaze, his lips pressed in a tight line. "I am so sorry for these circumstances, but very glad for the opportunity to talk to you."

Seth nodded, then looked at his watch. "Thanks for taking the time. I really should go or I'll be late for work."

"Yes, of course." He hesitated. "I am forever indebted to your father. If you or Lily ever need my help, I am here. In fact, you should come by my studio some time. I will train you at no cost."

"Thanks, Mr. Liu, I will consider it." Seth balked when he heard the two German shepherds whining outside, waiting for him.

At the door, Mr. Liu grasped his shoulder in a paternal manner. "I'll walk out with you." The male shepherd whined and paced as Seth walked past.

"What is it, pengyou?" Mr. Liu asked the dog.

Seth shrugged. Who was he to judge if the guy called his dog "friend" and talked to him. He had been singing with a cat in the shower earlier.

The retired officer put the dogs in a down-stay position as Seth climbed into his truck.

Seth turned the truck around so he could drive forward down the long, winding driveway. Once headed in the right direction, he glanced in his rearview mirror, noting Mr. Liu sitting on the front porch stroking one of the shepherd's behemoth heads while talking on his cell phone. As Seth exited the driveway, a dark SUV pulled away from the shoulder in front of Mr. Liu's property, headed in the opposite direction.

Weird.

It wasn't the hangover. Seth's gut was telling him Mr. Liu knew things. He knew things that weren't being said. Seth tried, but just couldn't trust the fatherly warmth. It made him squirm, maybe because it had been so long since he had experienced it.

CHAPTER 8

FAMILY DYNAMICS

CALDWELL SET HIS soft drink on the edge of the table while Lake donned his reading glasses. They sat in Lake's office on the third floor of the APD headquarters on Peachtree Street with the various agencies' lab reports spread out before them.

Ms. Sinclair's lab results suggested an overdose of Inderal, a beta-blocker used to address stage fright, high blood pressure, cardiac arrhythmias, and Post-Traumatic Stress Disorder, PTSD.

Sinclair's primary doctor had prescribed thirty-milligram tablets of Inderal to be taken twice daily to address her severe PTSD. He couldn't explain the injectable form found at the home. Inderal was not typically injected. However, in an emergency such as during a surgical procedure, a medical team may administer it via an IV bolus or continuous drip. People didn't inject it directly into a vein otherwise there was a chance they would suffer significant heart complications.

"Why would she procure the injectable form and from where?" Lake asked peering over his glasses.

Caldwell couldn't resist, "I don't know, professor. What's your hypothesis?"

"Piss off Simms," Lake said, adjusting the readers.

"Generally Inderal is prescribed in oral tablets, capsules, or liquid. The sharps container indicates she was injecting herself frequently."

"Taking the pills *and* injecting herself," Caldwell added. "That's overkill."

"The number of pills missing from the container indicates she was taking the oral dose sporadically."

"ME found only one injection site. If she was using the injectable regularly as the container suggests, wouldn't she have track marks or some bruising?"

Lake shook his head. "Not adding up. She has no history of swallowing difficulty; there's no logical reason for her to need the injectable."

Caldwell drummed his fingers on the table. "If it was suicide, why not just toss back the whole container of pills?"

"Wanted to be certain she didn't purge the drug," Lake offered. "And she did not mix the oral and injectable the night she died. ME only found Inderal in her bloodstream, not her stomach."

"But why have all those syringes if it was a one-shot attempt?"

"You said Sinclair's sister didn't shed any light on her situation. Neither did her literary agent, Susan Beck, who was the last person to have seen her?" Lake said.

"No. Beck flew in two days prior to Sinclair's death to have lunch with her. They strategized about the development of her next book and the agent returned to her home in New York. I checked all of her records to substantiate her story. Beck mentioned that she's never been in Sinclair's home and admitted that Sinclair came across as a bit of a loner. The woman was not familiar with Sinclair's medical history."

"What did Clemens say about the scenario?" asked the lieutenant.

"She insisted that her sister would never intentionally overdose and she was floored by the syringes." Caldwell shook his head. "Lady was genuinely shaken up. Thinks her sister's anxiety disorder was getting worse which made her more forgetful."

"Maybe it's denial. She can't accept suicide because that would mean somehow she ignored the warning signs," Lake offered.

Caldwell shook his head. The crime scene revealed a busy woman who was in the middle of writing the next book in her bestselling children's series. She had just started the promotion of the current book. "I'll keep pouring through Sinclair's internet history, email, and phone records trying to find any evidence of her getting her 'affairs in order' so to speak."

Caldwell stretched his cramped legs and arched his back in the chair. He couldn't decide if it was the case making him tired or the five miles he ran that morning. "Lieutenant, you know they're related?"

Lake took a sip of his protein drink and winced before putting it back down. "Marx and Sinclair?"

"Yeah. I pulled out the Marx file. His research work with Dr. Hitomi was on PTSD. Inderal is one of their trial medications."

Caldwell looked up at the timeline they had drawn on the board. Lake had organized photos of the victims on either side.

"That's why I want a full victimology report on Moore, Miller, Sinclair, and Marx.

Finally. "We're looking at this as a homicide then?" Caldwell asked.

"No Simms, we're sitting under these nasty vents in here just waiting for our hair to set." Caldwell smirked.

Lake walked over to the board. "Tiny's reviewing the Marx evidence to see if there are some similarities. Forensics submitted some hairs retrieved from Sinclair's clothing to the GBI lab. Until those come back, we aren't closing the Sinclair case. We're keeping her place sealed. I can't ignore the chain of events here."

Caldwell got up to stand next to his boss. He stared at Lily Moore. Homicide continued to work in conjunction with the missing persons division, but Lily Moore's trail was running cold. "Perhaps she wasn't the paranoid basket case we thought she was."

Lake's whole body stiffened. "We found nothing in Marx's car. No evidence of foul play. No fingerprints present other than Marx's."

A rap at the door interrupted the tension that was building between the two of them.

Ernie Gates entered, his jaw working overtime on a piece of nicotine gum.

"How's that for timing?" asked Lake raising one eyebrow to Caldwell.

"S'up Gates?" Caldwell asked.

"How's it going, Simms?" Gates chuckled at the officer and gave him a slap on the upper arm. Caldwell felt the jolt, but winced inside.

Gates took a seat while the two detectives wrote a few

more notes on the board on the wall next to Lake's desk. When they turned to sit down, Gates was rocking back in the chair while picking at his cuticles.

"Whatcha got?" Lake asked, leaning back against his desk. Simms went to sit across from Gates. The office was small. With the three men together, it was darn right uncomfortable.

"Lucy is frantic. Ricky is distracted, which isn't that unusual for him. He's a male bloodhound, they're more inclined to be ADD," he said.

It's like he's talking about his nine-year-old twins. Caldwell refrained from teasing him; the man took his hounds seriously. Plus, even though Caldwell had two inches on him, Gates had more bulk. The fifty-year-old was six foot and fit. Gates had retired from the Decatur Police Department ten years ago and started his work with scent hounds. Now his partners were two bloodhounds, Ricky and Lucy. Having found his true calling, he contracted with the APD on a regular basis.

"They got a hot scent around the Ansley Park area on one particular street, but they keep doing a loop. We've gone door-to-door in this area. A Larry Jones, her co-worker, lives on that street. He was her manager so she dropped things off at his house all the time so it's possible that Lucy is picking up an old scent," Gates speculated. He rubbed his gray flat top.

"I interviewed both residents, Jones and Harding," volunteered Caldwell. "They were at a charity event at the High Museum of Art the night of Ms. Moore's abduction. They arrived home around one in the morning and went to sleep. Got up around 6:00 a.m. for work. Nothing unusual according to them or their neighbors other than some injured dog at their door in the middle of the night."

"Jones didn't report any suspicious behavior by Moore that day or in the days leading up to it?" Lake asked.

"No, he just said she hadn't been feeling well. Mr. Jones was extremely upset and worried. According to co-workers they were close."

"What kind of dog?" interrupted Gates.

Caldwell turned to him confused, "Pardon me?"

"I was just curious what kind of dog they found."

"One of those fluffy, little, um...designer kinds," struggled Caldwell.

"Huh," grunted Gates, his arms crossed. "How was it hurt?"

Lake looked over at Caldwell.

"Face and head. Around its one eye." Caldwell gestured with his hands.

"Did they take it to a vet?" Gates asked.

"I really don't know."

"Well, they should have," he admonished.

"You're right," Caldwell admitted. "I'll mention it when I check back with them."

An appeased Gates focused his attention back on Lake. "By the way, we found some new evidence—a men's hooded sweatshirt and sweatpants almost two miles northwest on Seventeenth Street. Dogs tracked Ms. Moore's scent on it. Tiny mentioned he was able to pull some hair strands off the sweatshirt. He bagged it and turned it into the lab.

Lake sat up in his chair. "Thanks, Gates. Maybe we've caught a break on the Moore case."

Gates didn't respond.

"What is it?" Lake asked.

"I know Tiny sent some of the evidence from the Moore/Miller scene to that special lab in Oregon. He thinks some exotic animal is involved." Simms knew Gates was referring to the National Fish and Wildlife Forensics Laboratory.

Lake nodded.

Gates studied his cuticles. Caldwell heard him swallow. "I just. Well, you know, I am acquainted with the Miller family. That boy...I was his football coach in middle school. I know his mama." Gates lips were a tight line. His face showed disgust. "Someone hurt that boy. I know the Moore girl is hurt too. God help me, I hope she's okay, but I don't like the implications going around that he...he was dishonorable in some way to her."

Simms talked himself down. He had seen things. Things that indicated Lily Moore's head had slammed against the car window, hard. Maybe it was some bizarre animal attack, but why was Moore outside Miller's car in a deserted parking lot? Gates's face showed how troubled he was. "I hear you. We're looking at every detail. Considering all pieces of this puzzle."

Lieutenant Lake nodded.

"Good." He got up. "I'll keep tracking. Something weird's going on. I've never seen the hounds so confused."

"Thanks. Keep me posted." Lake patted him on the back as he left.

Caldwell knew his face reflected his inner turmoil.

"Spit it out," Lake said when he turned to him.

"You know who arrested Phillip Miller for drunk

driving?"

"I know. Officer Arthur Moore."

Caldwell grimaced. "And gave him the ticket for reckless driving—a separate incident, I might add."

"Keep working the connection here, Simms. I want to know all their habits, their hobbies, quirks. Let's connect the dots so we have something concrete," he said, stabbing the board with his index finger.

"Yes, Sir."

"We have new evidence. Tonight, Lily Moore's mother is supposed to ping you when she gets back in town. I want you to go out there, get a sense of things. Then go back to everyone in Moore's circle. See if there are any holes."

"Think I'll start with her brother," Caldwell said.

"Okay," Lake said.

Caldwell waited.

"What?"

"Lieutenant, what's the scoop with Seth Moore?" Caldwell only had been with the APD for a year and a half, having moved from Ohio.

Lake shrugged.

"I saw his record," Caldwell said.

Lake crossed his arms, and exhaled for at least twenty seconds. "I worked with his father briefly." He pressed his lips together until the color blanched from them. "Seth seems to have jumped the tracks after his father died. He was arrested for indecent exposure his first year at the university."

"Frat party gone wrong?" Caldwell asked.

"It's stickier than that. He woke up in the Emory

University lab with Professor Hitomi."

"What were they doing in the Emory lab?" Caldwell asked.

"Shit Simms, playing mad scientist. How the hell should I know?"

"So did they meet each other through Marx?"

"No, Seth was her student."

Caldwell shook his head talking to himself. "A sex scandal with his teacher."

Lake's face paled.

"What?" Caldwell asked.

"Dr. Hitomi called 9-1-1. That's how he got the charge."

"Sexual assault?" Caldwell felt nauseous.

"We'll never know," said the lieutenant. "Once the officers arrived, she denied that anything happened and refused to press charges."

"Part of the staff had already seen Seth. The indecent exposure charge was necessary."

"So her brother's a sexual deviant," Caldwell said, watching for Lake's reaction.

"For fuck's sake, Simms, he was just a dumb ass kid. Responding officers said he couldn't remember a thing. He took a leave from school after that and never went back."

"Some kind of substance abuse?" persisted Caldwell.

"I don't know," admitted Lake as he ran his fingers over his stubborn alfalfa. "No piss test done."

Caldwell dropped it. He could see the lieutenant was getting edgy. He'd look at the file later.

Lake and Caldwell spent several minutes outlining their next steps. Caldwell tried to focus, but in his head, he was already grilling Seth Moore and Dr. Kyoko Hitomi.

CHAPTER ✒ 9

MAGGIE MOORE

AT 10 P.M., CALDWELL pulled into the driveway of a red brick colonial in Alpharetta, twenty-five miles north of Atlanta. Ms. Maggie Moore opened the door. At forty-nine, she was a striking woman with chin-length jet black hair. Her green eyes were hard to ignore; they were Lily's eyes.

"Ms. Moore?"

"You must be Detective Simms. Come in, please."

Simms followed her into the whitewashed home. They settled at the dark farm table in the kitchen. He could tell she'd been crying by her red, puffy eyes.

"What's going on?" she asked.

"We are continuing to search. Our concern is that Lily's disappearance may be connected to the deaths of her boyfriend and her neighbor."

"I don't understand."

Caldwell took a breath. "We have reopened Peter Marx's case to rule out any foul play. Her neighbor, Mona Sinclair died from an overdose of the medication Mr. Marx was researching."

"But I thought they were both considered accidental overdoses?"

"That may still be the case, but several details are causing us to look further."

"I don't mean to be rude, but it seems like you should be focusing on finding my Lily." Her voice cracked.

"I assure you that Sergeant Samuels in Missing Persons is working day and night. I believe you spoke with him on the phone."

She nodded. Caldwell could see her struggling to maintain her composure as she swallowed repeatedly.

Caldwell reached out and touched her hand on the table. "Our Search and Rescue officer is relentless. He and his hounds will work overtime trying to find her."

She managed a weak smile.

Caldwell withdrew his hand. "I need your help. I could really use your input on some of the people involved."

She answered questions about Seth, Lily, and Peter. Her face remained expressionless almost as if she had shut down.

They took a break after they discussed Lily. Maggie Moore made tea in the kitchen and brought two cups to the table. The tea service was plain white, no nonsense. Caldwell accepted his, not wanting to be rude. It smelled strong. Not made with a teabag.

When he came to the topic of Arthur Moore, he noticed her face waver. There was some deep-seated pain there. More than death. It was something else. He didn't tarry there, but continued on to Lily's neighbor. "Were you acquainted with Ms. Mona Sinclair?"

"No, she really was an acquaintance of Arthur's."

"How did they know one another?"

"Through his father, Charles Moore. Charles and Mona worked in the Peace Corps together in Sumatra."

"Interesting."

Her eyebrows shot up. "Definitely. Arthur didn't know anything about her until after his father's funeral."

"Really?"

"She saw the obituary in the paper and came to pay her respects. After that, I know Arthur met with her for coffee. She told him stories and had old pictures of his father." She looked down at the table. "Odd, isn't it? His father never mentioned her, but Arthur seemed fascinated by her and her tales. I suppose it helped him get to know his father a bit better."

A noise from the front hall caught Caldwell's attention. A tall man with striking blue eyes hung back in the doorway. "Sorry to interrupt. I'm Emanuel Aronson." They shook hands. He went to stand behind Maggie Moore, placing his hands on her shoulders and massaging. "Just checking on my girl. We've had a long day of travel."

"Perfect timing, Mr. Aaronson. Do you mind if I ask a few questions?"

"Not at all. Whatever will help." He kissed Ms. Moore on the cheek. "Why don't you go lie down?"

She looked to Caldwell first.

"I've asked all the questions I need to for now. Please, I know it's late."

"Excuse me then."

Emanuel Aaronson had tanned skin and the relaxed air of a retired person. Caldwell immediately sensed his disapproval of both the Moore children. "Seth is a handful. I've helped Maggie realize that he's an adult. She's not responsible for his poor decisions. It's time for him to take care of himself."

When he came to Lily, Aaronson wrinkled his nose as

he mentioned how much she was like Arthur Moore.

After he finished up with Aaronson, Caldwell drove home considering the dynamic. Emanuel Aaronson had family money. He didn't seem to want any complications in his life. In fact, it was clear to Caldwell, that Ms. Moore checked out of the kids' lives a long time ago, perhaps after Arthur Moore's murder. She was concerned, but not in tune with either kid. He had studied the photographs on the living room shelves. There was one tiny picture of the Moore family together. Arthur Moore stood proudly next to his wife with their two kids. Lily looked to be twelve, Seth eight. The rest of the pictures were of Mrs. Moore and Aaronson in various travel destinations.

A melancholy settled over him. He rubbed his face trying to distance himself from their family's grief.

CHAPTER ✒ 10

FROM THE LOST NOTES OF PETER MARX

July 7, 2010

Today was the fifth week of working with Dr. H on her real research project. If I hadn't witnessed the phenomenon of shapeshifting for myself, I know I would never believe its existence, or rather, their existence—Subject T and Subject C. I can't deny what I saw today. Although, I must admit, it has me questioning if I'm of sound mind.

The lab results from the Inderal trials are promising, but I'm concerned about side effects.

That's not all that concerns me. When I dropped by her private lab unexpected, I saw someone leaving, another subject. When I casually questioned her about the male's condition, she told me to mind my own business.

Eventually, she lightened up and said he was taking part in another study of hers. It made me wonder if he was a shapeshifter.

-Peter

CHAPTER 11

TRANSFORMATIONS

NAKED ON THE laundry room floor, Lily listened intently to the whoosh of water in the pipes overhead. As soon as Frank finished with his shower, she needed to be a dog. Last night she had relegated herself to this room, far from the boys, in case she had difficulty shifting back from human form. Just as she had anticipated, she had fallen asleep a Shih Tzu, but awakened a human.

Before falling asleep, she had dredged her mind for the minimal yoga knowledge she possessed. Practicing the deep breathing, visualization, and relaxation was effective in transforming her back to human form as long as she had at least thirty minutes. Changing into a dog was easy. Apparently, abject terror was a natural state for her at this point. Relaxing back into human form was another matter.

The silence of the pipes, prompted her to close her eyes and focus on terrorizing herself. Still groggy, she took longer than usual. With no time to spare, she found herself in canine form just as she heard Frank calling for her. Lily focused on the doorknob of the closed door. She had locked herself in. *Lassie would never have done this.*

"Tashi?"

She barked and scratched at the door. Frank jiggled the doorknob.

"What the hell? How did you get...why is the...hold on a minute." Lily listened as Frank ransacked his own kitchen in search of the key. He went away briefly then returned.

Bang!

Lily scrambled back, her nails failing to gain traction on the tile floor. After the door swung open, she gazed up at Frank who stood in his silk boxer shorts, robe hanging open with a hammer in one hand, tiny screwdriver in the other. *Who needs a bump key? Not James Bond.*

"Ha!" he said, triumphant as he peered into the laundry room to study her. "What the hell?"

Lily pranced past him, through the kitchen, into the great room, and jumped up on the couch. Frank shook his head. He padded into the kitchen to prepare a culinary masterpiece while grumbling about the craziest dog he had ever met. Ten minutes later, he plopped down on the sectional with a plate of eggs and bacon. He spread the newspaper out on the ottoman. He glanced over at Lily who drooled from the smell of coffee and bacon. Frank had put some expensive holistic dog food in her pink, bedazzled dog dish. She ignored it and maintained her position on the sectional next to him, supervising his progress with the scrambled eggs.

When he got up to get more bacon, she stretched across to the ottoman, her front legs balanced just so, and took a few glugs from his oversized mug. She couldn't resist. It was Starbucks Columbian blend.

She sat back on her haunches, a foo dog, and representative of the auspicious lion. She did resemble the guardian statue, but she wasn't sure about being a protector of the home. She was adept at guarding food, though.

Frank sauntered back into the room.

"What's all over your muzzle?" He took a step closer.

She jumped off the couch and ran. When she got to the hallway, Lily flung herself on the ground to wipe her beard on the antique Persian rug. When she straightened up, Larry stood on the landing of the stairs having witnessed the whole ugly episode.

Larry furrowed his brow, creating deep indentations that resembled bat wings. She feared she was on her way to the taxidermist. Perhaps they would mount her over one of the Manor's five fireplaces.

"Dog!" The use of her generic name indicated his level of annoyance. She sat up at attention with eyes bugging out. He bent down on one knee in front of her. "You do that again and I'm crating your ass."

Yes Capitain. She shadowed Larry, her tail at half-mast, as he finished getting ready. Frank left for work with Larry following an agonizing twenty minutes later.

Alone at last! She flung herself down on the forbidden Persian rug and wiggled around on her back. She caught herself mid-thrall. *Need to work on these dog impulses.*

Back on her feet, she surveyed her surroundings. Her first goal of the day was to secure her care package. Without the ability to reach doorknobs as a canine, she would have to shift into human form then open the garage before shifting into dog form so no one would see her. No problem. *Now watch me as I pull a Komodo dragon out of my butt.*

Twenty minutes later, she stood upright, proud to be bipedal again. She pushed the button and devised a plan while watching the garage door roll up. She punched it again when she realized she was naked and may be visible from the neighbor's yard. For her second attempt, she wore Frank's button-down oxford shirt. Realizing this wasn't the best disguise, Lily darted behind the lawn mower in the corner of the garage as the door rocked at the top of its arc.

Sitting in the lotus position, she was sure no one could see her from the street. Thinking of sharks, she was able to shift into "Tashi." She bounded into action, eager to see what Seth left for her.

Rounding the corner, she slipped behind the lattice privacy fence that hid the air conditioning unit. She found a pink JanSport backpack. Lily pulled the zipper open with her mouth, rooting around with her nose until she found the latest and greatest touch screen cell phone. "Hare Krishna, Hare Krishna!" she screamed or at least her Shih Tzu version of it. She ran back and forth by the neon green phone in a frenzy.

She looked up to see the neighbor's six-year-old staring at her.

"Oh, shit!" Lily exclaimed. Thankfully, it was a girl. A boy would have snatched her, stolen her phone, and used her for a science experiment. The girl looked spooked. For insurance, Lily growled.

There was a lot of shrieking, but mission accomplished. She ran back into her house screaming for her mommy. Now Lily felt rushed. If the mother came to investigate, she was toast. She nosed the cell phone back into the bag, stood on it with her paws and pulled the zipper almost closed with her teeth. Then she grabbed a strap, dragging it across the lawn to the garage. Back behind the lawn mower, she tried to think peaceful thoughts.

She needed to shift and get back into the house before the shrieker came back with her mother, or God help her, the father, who would probably be a Ted Nugent type. Nothing happened because she was too juiced up with adrenaline. She needed to close the garage door. The broom sat upright, just the right distance from the garage door button. *Footsteps.*

"It's over here, Mommy. It said bad words to me." *Tattle tale.* Lily threw her body into the broom, sending the handle forward to smack against the white, square button. Darting for the lawn mower, she skidded behind it to watch the door close.

"Hello? Hello?" called the mother.

Lily spied two sets of feet as the door sealed shut with a "klunk." The neighbor grumbled as she walked up the pathway, shrieker in tow, to ring the doorbell.

Pachelbel's Canon in D blasted through the house each time the nagging neighbors pushed the doorbell. Ignoring the music, Lily concentrated on a visualization technique Seth had suggested. She imagined her stress had wings and could soar away. Her legs tingled as they elongated; a soothing warmth spread throughout her body. She kept her eyes shut.

Opening her eyes, she sighed with relief. Getting up, she stumbled a bit before picking up the backpack and Frank's shirt by the door. A wave of vertigo struck and she struggled to maintain balance while walking through the doorway. *That was weird.* Thankfully, the nagging neighbor had retreated and all was quiet again.

She slurped water from the kitchen faucet while reviewing her schedule for the day: read the paper; figure out her new cell phone; hack into her roommates' computer to use her new email.

She turned to the pink backpack on the counter. Examining the contents of the bag, she discovered two pairs of underwear, a bra that was not the right size, 2 pairs of flip-flops, a cotton mini-dress, sweatpants, t-shirt, a long red wig, and $50. Seth also included a pink fanny pack with a note.

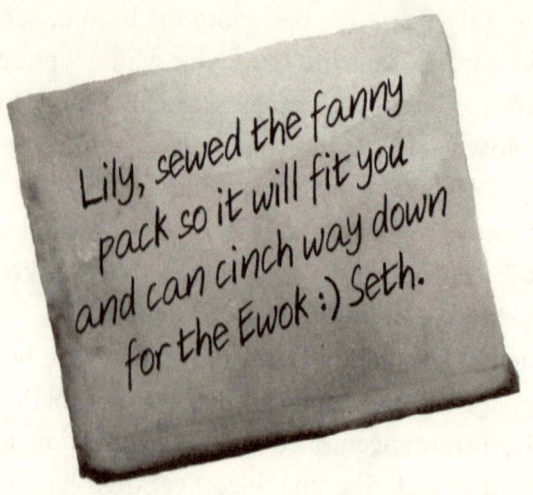

Lily, sewed the fanny pack so it will fit you and can cinch way down for the Ewok :) Seth.

A fanny pack. Lily couldn't recall ever owning one. Then again, she'd never eaten dog biscuits and now she seemed to like them.

Her new email account was ewoksrock@gmail.com. Well, maybe the Star Wars reference would help her use the force. She continued to feel light-headed with a strange itch radiating throughout her back. *Maybe it's Frank's fabric softener.* She reached back to scratch. *What the fuck?*

Something was on her back. And it was big! *What kind of critters live in their garage?* She twisted from side to side, unable to shake the thing loose. Panicked, she raced toward the front door, screeching like a Howler monkey. Something bumped against the narrow hallway walls, clinging to her in hot pursuit. Its fierce backwards pull caused her to lean forward as if she were walking into a fierce wind. She popped free as she hit the opening of the front hall. Her momentum flung her forward onto her knees.

Frazzled and disoriented, Lily panted while white stuff swirled in the air around her. Her legs shaking, she stood up. Ever so slowly, she turned to face her adversary.

Her mouth opened in a silent scream. She was so freaked out that she had lost power.

It was worse than anything she could ever imagine.

Wings.

With trepidation, Lily stared at her own reflection in the mirror. Phenomenal downy appendages extended from her bare back. Shimmering as if with diamonds, the iridescent feathers refracted colors across the wheat walls of the foyer. Her mouth hung open in a pant.

Dear God are those fangs? Her canine teeth protruded over her lips.

As she went to raise her arms, she inadvertently fluttered the wings, knocking several crystals from the chandelier overhead. She attempted to move them again more delicately. No matter how much effort she exerted, she never achieved levitation. After hyperventilating and burping up vomit, she noticed something shiny on the floor—her new cell phone.

With trembling hands, she called Seth, attempting to ignore the fact that her fingers were longer and she was sporting some crazy long nails.

"Hello?"

"It's me." Her voice was tremulous as she stared aghast at the creature in the mirror.

"Hold on one second," he said.

In the time it took for Seth to step away from the front desk at work, she had discovered that in turning from side-to-side, she could serve as an adequate disco ball, light beamed from every direction.

He came back on the line. "Okay."

"Not okay, Seth!"

"Lily? You sound funny."

She opened her mouth again to talk, but was fighting tears, so only produced a benign squeak.

"Lily? You're worrying me. Where the hell are you?"

"Wings!" she cried.

"You have to calm down. I can't understand a word you're saying."

"Fucking wings!" she screeched.

She could almost hear the gears shifting in Seth's head as he attempted to process.

"Coming out of my back. Enormous freak show kinda shit."

"Dude," Seth whispered. He cleared his throat, "Ewok, too?" Underlying his concern was an edge of excitement.

"No...not dog with wings...just self with wings...don't even work!" she continued to gulp for air.

"Wow. Okay, don't panic," he said. Then he was silent. Next, she detected ragged breathing. Clearly, he wasn't taking his own advice.

Lily bent over to get the blood back in her head. With a

death grip on the phone, she managed, "Gotta call you back." Once disconnected, she focused on her breathing.

Wings aren't so bad. She tried to rationalize that her new cartilaginous body parts were not any different from ears. These were just on a grander scale. *Breathe. I just need to breathe.*

Some masochistic force within her drew her back to the mirror. She couldn't stop looking. Her eyes were the color of Bartlett pears with a darker green ring around her enlarged pupil and there was no white part. She blinked and drew closer. A membrane stretched and retracted across her eye horizontally—a nictitating membrane or third eyelid. Goosebumps surfaced on her arms as she examined herself more closely. The wings captivated her at first glance, but enchantment turned to revulsion as she looked at the tendons growing out of her back. The eyes while lovely in color were nonhuman without the sclera. Fainting seemed imminent if she didn't calm her breathing. She refused to acknowledge the funky teeth.

Think, think, think. She started down the hallway, eventually turning sideways as she realized that in this manner she didn't knock anything else off the wall. There was a shattered photograph on the floor of Frank and Larry vacationing in Colorado. She picked it up and brought it to the garbage can. After dumping the shards of glass in the garbage, she hung the frame back up. Maybe they wouldn't notice that the glass was missing.

She settled in the great room assuming the lotus position with Larry's blanket across the front of her. The wings had a life of their own. She tried to press them in toward her body so she wouldn't break anything, but they kept popping out. Unfortunately, she had beheaded one of Larry's expensive sculptures. *Note to self. Look for Super Glue.*

Thinking of all her past night terrors, she triggered a shift. She was low to the ground with her tongue hanging out of her mouth. All good signs. After dashing up the stairs to Larry's room, she skidded to a halt in front of the full-length mirror.

"Oh. No," she huffed. She had fangs along with claws on her Shih Tzu body. She shook her whole body several times, now fully understanding why dogs did that. It was like pushing the reset button on her internet router.

Lily breathed a sigh of relief when her reflection showed a normal Shih Tzu again—decent-sized canines, regular nails. However, she needed to be in human form.

Sweating, she attempted normal breathing. The wings flashed through her head. After twenty minutes, she managed to shift. A quick glance in the mirror confirmed the return of her own body, sans avian vestiges and creepy eyes. Shaking so hard her teeth chattered, she wrapped Larry's blanket around her as she walked downstairs in a daze. She retrieved the cell phone from the hall table.

"Seth speaking."

"Okay. I'll meet you at the park at noon."

"I'll be there."

SHE HAD TWO hours before going to the park. Looking at her sweat-drenched body, she headed for the shower. *This is what normal humans do. I'm human.*

Frank's bathroom belonged in the pages of *Architectural Digest*. Large off-white tiles were inlaid with smaller black diamond-shaped tiles. The enormous glass shower enclosure offered a stone bench for enjoying James Bond's steam system consisting of two showerheads, and ten hydro -massage jets. The early morning sun trickled in through the window overhead. With all jets going, she allowed the water to hit her from every angle.

Forty minutes later, her tiny voice of reason broke through her shower utopia, forcing her hand to cut the water. She smelled like Frank's Versace Pour Homme hair and body shampoo. If she had a shower like this at home, she'd never need a boyfriend.

Once the steam dissipated, the cold air brought in reality. With much chagrin, she tried the red wig. The shiner on her one eye had faded, but was still visible. With the wig and a new fat lip that she obtained from chasing her tail and bashing into the glass door earlier, she looked a bit rough. *This will not do.*

She felt guilty as she rummaged through Larry's things, but she suspected he owned some cosmetics. It wasn't a perfect match, but she used his concealer to hide the purple-green marks. A touch of his clear lip gloss and she felt like a woman again. Studying her image more closely, she realized her eyelashes had grown longer and thicker. *No need for mascara now.*

Lily focused on her agenda as she walked downstairs. The shower had helped clear her head. She first retrieved the spare key from under the Buddha in the back garden. She could get a copy so she'd have access to the house. Frank's study was next.

She surveyed his CD collection while stretching her fingers. She rocked back in his leather desk chair while considering his computer screen. Just as she was reveling in his scent, something caught her attention on the desk top. A business card—George Clemens, Sarah's husband, Mona's brother-in-law. The temperature dropped as if a ghost had walked into the room.

Before Lily realized, she had eaten half of the Ferrero Rochers in Frank's candy dish as she read and reread the information on the card. She felt bad about her gluttony, particularly because she assumed Frank would blame Larry for the missing candy.

Why the hell did Frank have George Clemens's business card? When she turned it over, she noted Sarah Clemens's and Mona's name written in blue ink on the back. It wasn't so unusual that Mona Sinclair's family was using Frank for investing or banking or whatever exactly it was that he did. Her stomach lurched as she realized she didn't know anything about Frank or Mona Sinclair for that matter.

Frank's locked computer screen substantiated this. The odds were better that she could figure out Larry's password. Larry used the kitchen desk. Lily sat in an upholstered chair staring at his laptop screen. She attempted words related to cartoons and musical references. Nothing was working, not even "Celine." Just for kicks, she typed "Tashi." *Bingo. What a dear, sweet man.*

She perused the articles online to find out the latest information on her case. Mona's obituary caught her eye. Mona Sinclair had freelanced for several children's magazines including *Spider Magazine* and *Wee Ones*. Her picture books were about various jungle animals. She won the Mulberry Award for her book titled *The Littlest One*. The police were still investigating the circumstances of her death.

Lily scrolled back to the article about herself. Police had recovered her laptop from her silver Volkswagen bug. A warm blush spread across her cheeks when she thought about someone seeing her emails.

How much more humiliation could she withstand? Everyone knew she had "parked" behind a high school with a guy she met online. She continued down the article. Rage made her see black. A scraping like nails on a chalkboard drew her eyes down to the desk surface. Long claws dug into the wood. Her claws. She closed her eyes to bring her heart rate and breathing down.

Peeking through one eye, she looked down to see her regular, slender hand hovering above deep grooves in Larry's desk. *WTF?* She swept curls of wood shavings into the wastebasket. The etchings in the mahogany looked like someone had used an awl. Guilt wouldn't fix the blemish. She grabbed a notepad to cover the spot.

Lily breathed and relaxed the muscles in her body so she could look back up at the screen.

Phil Miller smiled from the pages of the *AJC* online. The headline: "Miller Tormented by Gruesome Attack." Phil had suffered a concussion, lacerations to his chest and three broken ribs. Investigators stated that he had fallen from the crossbeam of the uprights of the high school goal post. Doctors noted injuries could have been more severe if he had tensed during the fall. He hadn't since he was unconscious. He was under the care of behavioral health specialists. At the end of the article, the writer speculated whether or not Lily was somehow the cause of this vicious attack and questioned her mental stability after the death of her boyfriend. Lily took five deep cleansing breaths so she wouldn't punch the screen. Glancing at the clock, she realized it was time to leave.

She left the house with the red wig in place. Her anger fueled each step she took. When she was halfway to Piedmont Park, it occurred to her that she had walked out of the boys' front door as a human. She prayed no one saw her. How would her two friends explain the strange redheaded woman?

Her mind, reeling with images of Peter, Phil, and her monstrous wings, she almost walked past Seth. The look on his face snapped her out of her funk. The muscles of his face froze in alarm. When he sat on the park bench, he chose the very edge like he feared she carried the Plague. "What's your problem," she growled.

He exhaled, before scooting closer to her.

"Nice disguise," he said.

She glanced down at her pink mini dress and clear plastic flip-flops. She wasn't winning any fashion awards.

"Yeah, thanks for all the stuff, except the dorky fanny pack."

"It was the best I could do. You should be more appreciative. It took me forever to sew through that thick material and I pricked my finger a gazillion times." He turned his head suddenly, looking behind him, in front of him and from side-to-side again.

"Geez Seth, don't have kittens!"

He whipped his head back toward her. His eyes

squinted in disgust. "I think someone is following me." He kept his head still this time as his eyes scanned the park. A cool chill slid down Lily's back. She followed his gaze, surveying the tennis bunnies running back and forth in their pastel skirts. A renegade black lab pissed on a Trek bike that leaned against a Dogwood tree.

"Cops?" she asked.

"I don't think so," he said. His mouth hung open.

Her long exhalation of frustration finally brought his eyes back to hers.

"I think we might be in danger." He stretched his arms in front of him, splaying his fingers before planting them on his knees.

Lily rolled her eyes. She had dealt with the dead boyfriend and neighbor. She had been assaulted and turned into a mutant. Now she was dealing with her brother whose possibly well-warranted paranoia had taken control of him.

"Okay, Seth why are we in danger?" He stared at her, silent. She heard the tennis balls bouncing across the way followed by the ping of the racquet's contact. Cries of joy and toddler woe reached them, but Seth held her captive.

"I think someone killed Peter and your neighbor."

"Thanks for clearing that up, Miss Marple," she replied.

"I know you always suspected there was more to Peter's death. That it was no accident. But now with your neighbor, it's just too much of a coincidence," he said.

"And?"

"And just from a proximity standpoint, you're next." He bounced his left knee, shaking the bench.

"Well if it was Phil, then we don't need to worry. I'm

hoping they keep him in the looney bin for a while," she said with genuine malice.

Seth looked skeptical, "I don't know if it has anything to do with him, Lily." He chewed his bottom lip. "By the way, they showed pictures from his attack. You really do that?"

She didn't look at him. "I'm afraid so." She had always been a nonviolent person except for her recent fascination with cage fighting.

"Seth, I need some help here. Please tell me you talked to Mr. Liu."

He nodded.

"So?"

"He was okay." Seth looked down at his legs stretched out before him.

"Okay? You want to elaborate a bit?"

"I'm not sure he is trustworthy."

"Dad trusted him. As far as we know he's kept that secret for years."

"Yeah, Dad trusted him, but Dad is dead. And that *secret* should have been shared with the people it affected most."

"What are you saying?"

"I don't know. He just gave me the creeps. He started out all friendly, but he was examining me." Seth squirmed on the bench.

"Well if you were acting anything like you are now then I don't blame him."

Seth caught her eyes and didn't blink.

"Perhaps he didn't know what kind of animal he was dealing with. For all he knew, he was sitting across from the elusive Big Foot. You're not Sasquatch are you, Seth?"

"Don't be ridiculous, Lily," he said folding his arms across his chest. Paranoid, she stared him down. He wouldn't meet her eyes.

"Then what's your hang up with him?"

"He initially wanted to help, but I got the feeling he wasn't telling me everything. He wants me to train with him at his martial arts studio in Kennesaw."

"Good."

"Good? Do I look like the Karate Kid?"

"You can earn his trust and learn about this shifting," she said, exasperated.

"Maybe you should do it!" he said.

"Gee, I don't know Seth. I think that might blow my cover."

Edgy, she wiggled her flip-flops back on to her feet before standing up to walk away. Seth followed, but then hung back; perhaps suspicious she may pop out a wing in the middle of the park.

The seething look she sent him pushed his legs to do double time to catch up with her.

"What did he tell you?" she probed.

"Waipo knew about Dad, Mom doesn't," he blurted. Their grandmother had always been a mystery to them.

"Weird. How is that even possible?"

"No idea," he said. "He thought Waipo talked to us at Dad's funeral about his condition in case either one of us had a similar situation."

"It would have been helpful for someone to have clued us in," she quipped.

"I explained to him that we really didn't know Waipo

and that Mom told us she was crazy."

"Maybe Mom's the crazy one," she retorted.

"I'm starting to think you're right."

"Did Mr. Liu tell you anything we haven't already figured out?"

"Dad had an easier time shifting at night and he shifted on a daily basis, otherwise he got headaches. He used deep breathing and relaxation to control it," he offered. Seth glanced at her, apparently reluctant to be the bearer of bad news in her current state.

"What?"

"It's permanent, Lily."

"I know." She looked off toward the Atlanta skyline. Symphony Tower seemed to be mocking her as it had the night of Phil's attack. Two glass fins topped the forty-one story skyscraper and lit up at night redolent of Gotham City. Today they looked like wings.

She could feel his eyes on her. Looking anywhere but at him, she gazed up at a bronze statue looming about fifteen yards in front of them—it was the Civil War monument of the winged goddess, "Peace," announcing the South's surrender and ordering a Confederate soldier to lay down his weapon. *I'm surrounded.*

Blowing out a stream of hot air, she plopped down on a nearby bench. "Seth?"

"Yeah."

"The wings really petrified me this morning." Her voice was quivering and she began to sniffle. He searched his pockets for a tissue, but came up with a gum wrapper.

"Mr. Liu said he didn't know of anyone that could shift into multiple creatures," he mumbled while shoving the wrapper back into his pocket.

"But he was aware of others out there like Dad and me?" she asked in surprise.

"He was very elusive about that, but yes, said there were others."

"I know one thing; I'll never look at a dog the same way again." She tried to laugh.

"Or a bird," said Seth staring at the statue. He stretched his hands out in front of him as if admiring his manicure. Lily noted that he had finally stopped biting his nails.

"I wasn't a bird, I just had wings," she said, hoping to avoid the maelstrom of emotions threatening to take hold of her. She couldn't bring herself to mention the fangs.

He was silent.

She stood up again. "Let's get away from here," she said, shaking her arms as if they had been asleep. Lily walked down the path with Seth in tow.

They came to a stop on the bridge overlooking Lake Clara Meer. The view was straight out of a Monet painting. Pink and white petals from dogwood trees swirled ethereally on the sparkling blue surface. A group of ducks swam and sunned themselves on the bank. *Great, more wings.*

As they approached, the ducks went into a quacking frenzy. One duck hissed their way before launching into the sky, pulling the whole flock with him.

Seth gasped while stretching his neck up. "Remind me not to take you duck hunting."

"Go piss up a rope."

"I don't know why you're so upset. It seems like you're making progress."

Nostrils flared, she turned to him, "Progress?"

"Let's face it, a Shih Tzu is kinda wimpy, but a *flying* Shih Tzu is sic."

"Are you baked?"

He stretched his fingers again before rolling his neck. She hadn't noticed this nervous tic before.

"Sorry, Seth. I shouldn't lash out at you. I just want my normal body back. And for the record, I was not a dog with wings, just me with wings."

He chewed his lip while he considered her.

"Maybe I should go to the police," she said.

"I don't think that's a good idea." His pupils dilated.

"I'm desperate Seth. What's the worst that could happen?"

"Really bad science experiments!" His face flushed. His hands curled into fists.

"Okay. Chill. I wasn't going to turn myself in, just make a phone call to that Simms guy."

"I'll go train with Mr. Liu," he said, "ask him more questions. We'll figure something out."

"Okay." For the life of her, she couldn't figure out why he looked terrified. They had circled back by the tennis courts. "I'm hungry."

Seth seemed to recover from his anger. "I have enough time; why don't we grab some pizza? Reggie will cover me."

CHAPTER ✒ 12

CLOSE CALL

WITH THE WINDOWS down, they cruised up Piedmont Avenue bobbing their heads to Seth's Ludacris CD. He took her by the Walgreen's Pharmacy first and waited in the car while she ran inside. She snatched a big Sweet Leaf iced tea/lemonade from the fridge and Twizzlers from the candy aisle. The underwear aisle was her next destination. With a sigh, she added the high-waisted granny panties to her stash. Seth ran into Ace Hardware next door to make a copy of the key and find Super Glue.

After splitting a carnivore pizza between the two of them, Seth drove the car back to the Manor. They shared the tea and gorged on Twizzlers as he drove. Lily let out a belch that rattled the windows. Seth swerved, barely missing a minivan.

"What the heck was that?"

"Excuse me," she said giggling.

Eyes bugged out, he stared at her as if trying to gauge what kind of creature lurked within. His hair stood on end. Honestly, having her brother regard her with fear and awe was the ultimate ego boost.

When he turned the corner on to the Prado Northeast, he slowed the car. A white minivan sat out front. Lily gasped when she saw a dog handler with a bloodhound searching the periphery of the Manor's front lawn.

"Fuuuuuuuck," Seth said. "Get down." Seth pulled into the driveway of a house about five houses down and across from the Manor. Lily's knees hit the glove box when she slid down in the seat.

"What's going on?" she whispered.

"I can't see from here," he complained.

"Let's not panic," she said, tasting the carnivore pizza again. Her stomach gurgled.

Seth looked at her. "Don't. Burp."

Her brother checked the side mirror and rearview mirror. He put his cell phone to his mouth and pretended he was talking to someone. She caught on and handed him a map from the side pocket of his truck door. Hopefully no one was looking out the windows of the home in front of them. If they were, Seth was just some guy lost in Ansley Park with a map spread out on the dash.

He stopped talking suddenly and swallowed. "Oh, fuck me running."

"What?" Lily grabbed the truck handle for leverage as she lifted her head.

"Don't. Move," Seth gasped.

She sunk back down.

"It's that detective."

Lily sat straight up. "Where?"

His death glare sent her back down in a slouch. *Detective Hottie is here?*

"What?" Seth asked.

"Nothing. Mind your own...*mind*, please."

"Geez, Lily. I knew you were crushin' on that dumb cop."

You're dumb. He's not dumb. He's smokin' ass hot.

"Shut up, Lily. I'm trying to focus on what's going on."

Lily stilled. "Put the windows down. Maybe I can hear."

Seth cocked an eyebrow, but did as she said.

"Anything, Gates?" Lily definitely knew it was Detective Simms's voice.

"No, Simms. Lucy got nothing. It was worth another shot since the hounds showed some interest yesterday."

"Well, thanks for rechecking for me. I really appreciate it."

"No problem," said the dog handler.

Lily held her breath as she heard the two cars drive away.

"Let's go. I'm taking you back to my apartment, but you have to pretend to be my dog," Seth said throwing the truck in reverse.

"Whoa. I'm not going anywhere. This bought me some time. The dogs indicated I wasn't there. They won't check back for a while."

"Are you crazy?"

"Seriously, Seth. Let me at least get my stuff together. I'll stay one more night and see what's going on. Any sign of trouble, I'll get out." Plus, she planned to break into her duplex tonight to get a few things. She really missed her Victoria's Secret underwear.

"I don't like this, Lily."

"It'll be okay."

He drove around the corner and Lily walked down the street, red wig in place. She let herself in the back door of the garage.

CHAPTER 13

FENGHUANG

INSIDE THE HOUSE, she focused on what to do next. Seth had handed her an apartment key. The sight of the bloodhounds had made her heart stop. With no signs of divine intervention, she couldn't waste any more time. It wasn't Seth's life. It was hers. She didn't tell Seth, but she did not intend to stay with him. It was too dangerous. People around her were dying. And she didn't want him to be next.

It was time she grew a set and took control of the situation. A phone call to Mr. Liu may give him too much time to think and possibly call in the authorities. *Surprises are always nice.*

With that thought, she peeked into the corner of the boys' four-car garage. The sound of operatic sopranos in an "Ahhhhhh!" filled her head as she lifted the tarp to reveal Frank's scorching red Honda Fireblade. There was no little brother to get her into trouble. *Borrowing* Frank's motorcycle was solely her responsibility.

A twinge of guilt hit her, but what could she do? She needed wheels. Nothing licentious about it. The keys were easy to find in Frank's top desk drawer. He'd understand, wouldn't he?

Lily packed the pink JanSport backpack with provisions and strapped it to her back. Her suspicion was that Seth's subconscious chose pink to assure him that his sister was indeed still a girl.

She opened the garage door feeling nerves flutter in her stomach. It couldn't be much different from the dirt bikes she and Seth rode as kids. She had dressed in sweatpants with a t-shirt under Frank's black leather jacket. At the last minute, she ditched the flip-flops and slipped on a pair of Frank's loafers that were by the back door. Two pairs of his socks from the laundry seemed to secure them.

With the helmet in place, she attempted to breathe with the visor down as the garage door closed behind her with a definitive thump. Determination drove out the images of her father scowling at her from above for getting on a donor cycle.

Leaning on her left foot, she swung her right leg over the seat to straddle the sport bike. Sitting back, she reviewed all the parts: throttle, front brake, rear brake, clutch, shift pedal. *No problem. I can walk and chew gum at the same time.* She turned the key, engaged the clutch and pushed the start button. The bike roared to life and so did her adrenaline causing her to wonder why she hadn't gotten herself a motorcycle. The same euphoria crept over her that had struck her when hanging her Shih Tzu head over the side of Larry's convertible.

With a twist of the throttle, she rocketed down the driveway doing a wheelie. It would have been impressive if it had been intentional and she hadn't run over the neighbor's burning bush. The good news was that she only grazed their mailbox and set the bike down on grass with no major damage, except to her ego.

Survival skills kicked in. She manipulated the throttle much more gingerly the second time and got out of there before anyone saw what had happened.

Playing with the controls, she figured out the basics and lurched on to the highway. After the first mile on Interstate 75 north, she understood the bike's moniker, crotch rocket. *Everything* tingled.

She was as coordinated as a horse riding a unicycle at 70 mph. By the time she reached the exit for Mr. Liu's, she had lost Frank's left loafer, making shifting gears a challenge.

Once on Stilesboro Road, she breathed a sigh of relief as she passed cookie cutter subdivisions transitioning to more spacious individual lots the further north she rode. She cut the engine at the end of Mr. Liu's long driveway before pushing the bike behind the gnarled trunk of a white pine tree. Uneasy, but determined, she decided to approach Mr. Liu as a dog to gauge his reaction. She stripped off her clothes, stashing them in her backpack. Sitting on the ground next to the bike, she managed to shift into Tashi.

That's when they struck.

Pinpricks of white dappled her vision as her lungs struggled to expand. Paralyzed from the neck down and barely conscious, she was flat on her back with a German shepherd's jaws clenching her throat. Crying pitifully earned her release. She wheezed for a while before her brain calmed and her body found its rhythm. She did a full body shake only to discover the other shepherd's hackles raised and its snout up her Shih Tzu backside. Well she wanted surprise and she got it.

A whistle off in the distance caused the welcoming

committee to let up. They loped down the driveway toward Mr. Liu and she followed them.

"What have you found?" he asked the shepherds gently. *My colon.* He stopped stroking their heads and noticed Lily fifteen feet away sitting in his driveway. Seth had failed to mention the dogs to her. The fanged sentries would make a quick escape impossible should she sense danger.

Except for the fact that Mr. Liu was Chinese, Lily felt like she was in a Western standoff. He stood with his feet apart hands at his hips. She stood with her paws apart a whole nine inches tall. This wasn't like a Western at all. One command from Liu and she was a Chinese dumpling to the two guard dogs.

"Xiaoyi?" He called her "little one," a term he had used since she was a small girl. She bolted down the driveway and leapt into his arms, licking his face and crying pitifully into his neck. He reminded her of her dad. Of course she could trust him. What was wrong with Seth?

He placed her on the ground then looked down gravely. He bowed. She attempted to return the bow, which put her in a "down" position. He giggled, catching Lily off-guard. She smiled with her tongue hanging out.

He became serious quickly. "Come Lily. I fear you are in great danger. There is much to discuss."

Lily hesitated, cocked her head, and eyed him. *Maybe I shouldn't be here.*

"I assume the young man in the hospital with dog bites and deep gashes is your work?" He stood with his legs together, his head slightly down and his brows elevated, assessing her, but not judging.

"Wes," she grumbled.

"I may be the only person who can help you. What choice do you have other than to trust me?"

She didn't entirely agree with his reasoning, but she'd come this far, she'd see this adventure through to the end. She trotted toward him with her black and white tail swinging in the air and followed him toward the house. The horses in the fenced corral nickered at her as she barked and leapt against the railroad ties.

"Lily, control!" ordered Mr. Liu. She snapped back to his side. They turned the corner of his ranch house and headed for a separate building, a new addition built in the back of the main home. It matched the gray siding of the ranch house. The front was predominately composed of glass.

"Welcome to my studio," he said, as he opened the sliding door. She walked in to find a padded floor like a yoga studio. However, a yoga studio wouldn't have glass and metal cases containing various martial arts weapons lining the walls.

He took her behind a bamboo screen where he handed her what looked like blue-gray pajamas. "It's a Shaolin uniform," he said. "Better communication if you are a person," he smiled.

She was pondering how to warn him about the peculiar sound she made when shifting, when he walked to the glass door and stepped outside, providing her privacy. The room was rather tranquil despite the lethal weapons surrounding her. After shifting, she donned the Shaolin gear and opened the glass door for him.

He walked to a teak cabinet in the corner. He pulled

several documents, books, and a box from the shelf and brought them to the one small table in the room. Here the soft floor ended and bamboo floors continued. She sat down in the chair across from him.

"Only dog?" he asked.

"Wings too," she whispered.

"Ah, flying Shih Tzu," The corners of his mouth turned up. One look at her face halted his mirth. He cleared his throat and became somber. "We'll talk about your shifting in a minute. First, I must tell you about your grandmother. She is fading." If Lily had known her grandmother, it would have been devastating. As it was, she still felt like someone had punched a small hole in her chest.

"I am sorry for you and your brother that you did not know her. The urgency of your situation makes my directness necessary. Your grandmother sent you an invaluable package for me to keep in my care. She included a note stating that she trusted I would know when to give it to you."

He grabbed the wooden box and tilted it to reveal a combination lock. Mr. Liu rolled in each digit on the lock until it clicked open.

"It is your mother's date of birth."

"I can remember that," she said, leaning in closer. Inside the box was a blue velvet jewelry case.

After placing it on the table, he pushed it across to her. "It should keep things in balance."

Her palms became clammy.

"I need you to open that, Liling." His face was stern, yet sorrowful at the same time, making her want to cry.

Prying open the lid, she gasped as she gazed upon an

exquisite locket on a thick gold chain. A beautiful bird was intricately engraved in the gold. The surface appeared to glow. She reached across to touch it.

Whoooooooossh.

When she woke up, she was flat on her back. *This is becoming redundant.* Lily vowed to herself that the next time she was in this position it would be for something pleasurable. The back of her head throbbed where it had struck the floor. All she wanted to do was close her eyes to make the pain go away, but she made herself stay awake.

"Good Lily. Good," Mr. Liu encouraged from above. His head appeared inflated like a balloon at the Macy's Day Parade. As his face came into focus, she heard him exhale loudly. Beads of sweat had formed on his forehead.

I've walked into some Chinese terrorist's lair. Which part of psychotic did I not pick up on? Instead, she had admired the lethal weapons like they were a seashell collection.

He helped her sit up. Dazed, she stared at him.

"Xiaoyi, you have done well," he said with tears in his eyes. Then he bowed to her as he never had before. She knew it was disrespectful not to return a lower bow, but her butt stayed glued to the floor, her whole body heavy.

A tingling sensation caused her to glance down at her chest. She was wearing the necklace. The feeling was similar to Vick's vapor rub and the more she inhaled its essence, the better she could breathe.

"What just happened?"

"Thank Buddha, you passed the final exam," he said perching a pair of reading glasses on his nose.

Panicked, she looked to him for an explanation. She

hated not being prepared for a test. "Mr. Lui, what would have happened if I had failed?"

He shuddered, "Oh, no matter now. See, you and the crucible are in balance."

"Crucible?" she asked.

"Very few can wear it. It's sacred. There has not been balance in almost a century. At least that's what the letter said." He pulled her to her feet. After uprighting the table, he pulled out another chair for her. Her thigh muscles trembled as she sat down. He plucked a loose document off the floor and placed it in front of her.

"I'll go get us some tea from the kitchen." He walked down a short hall and ducked into a doorway on the left. There were now three functioning wooden chairs. The one she had originally been seated in was shredded into teak splinters, which were scattered about the room. A scorch mark the size of her body bruised the wood floor.

Still woozy from the blast, her eyes had difficulty focusing when she turned her attention to the Chinese characters on the paper with singed edges. *This must be Waipo's letter*. Too bad Lily couldn't read Chinese.

Mr. Liu returned to the room, paying no mind to the pulverized chair. "Have some dark rose tea that your grandmother sent. You'll feel better."

Screw the tea, I need a drink. She studied him then with his black exercise pants and loose-fitting white t-shirt. The great Kung Fu guy serving her rose tea certainly gave her pause.

"It's black tea from Hunan Province. Try it," he said.

She did drink the tea. He was right.

"Most of what I know is from this letter. Your father

seldom spoke of your mother's family, but when he did, they were always interesting stories." He pushed the letter aside and opened a worn leather book to a page with a bird on it. "Fenghuang."

"Is that a phoenix?" she queried.

"No. Different. It is two birds. One male, feng and one female, huang. They are often shown together facing each other, representing the balance of yang and yin."

"Fenghuang. Isn't that the city where Waipo lives?"

"Fenghuang Cheng is the name of your grandmother's village along the Tuojiang River. The legend tells that two of these birds flew over it and found the town so beautiful that they hovered there, reluctant to leave."

"I remember seeing gardens."

"Yes, and mountains," said Mr. Liu wistfully. He poured more of the reddish-brown tea that filled Lily's senses with smoky malt and roses before focusing back on the story. "Chinese tradition says that the fenghuang nests far away from humans in the Kunlun Mountains, in wutong trees. It only comes out during times of peace and prosperity. Unlike the West's version of the phoenix that dies and is reborn, the fenghuang doesn't die, but is immortal. Pictures depicting the male and female together are symbolic of eternal love."

Waiting patiently for the punch line, Lily rolled her head and shoulders to pop her neck. The tingling continued to radiate from the crucible into her chest, spreading warm rushes through every cell of her body. It wasn't an unpleasant sensation, just foreign.

"Modern times have merged the bird into one female who is paired with a dragon, which represents yang."

Thinking of her wings, she asked, "Do you think I'm like this."

"No, Lily. You are something different. Perhaps a hybrid of some kind due to your father's genes."

"What kind of bird am I?"

He shrugged. "You are a protector, almost like a warrior. That is why you had the reaction when you touched the necklace. The fenghuang is, well, a myth. A good story. I don't know that such a shapeshifter exists. But it symbolizes so much. That's why it's engraved on this powerful...necklace."

Swell.

"Will the necklace blow me up every time I touch it?" she asked staring cross-eyed down her nose. Was she wearing a live grenade around her neck?

"No, it knows you now and has established balance." At that moment, the locket emitted a red glow. "Ooooh." He looked surprised by the light.

"Uh, what's it doing, Mr. Liu?"

"Interesting," he responded.

"I—I think there's something inside this locket."

"It's impossible," he said.

"What's impossible? Mr. Liu, I'm trying to keep it together here. Am I going to explode again?"

"No. No, I don't think so."

"What does the red mean?"

"Red? Why red means happiness and good fortune."

"Really. 'Cuz my thought is that red can be seen as anger," Lily said, her voice trembling.

"Oh, no. Even in ancient times, red was used to drive off evil spirits. It's okay."

"No, no," Lily said shaking her head. "Darth Vader had the red light saber. Hello, he was evil." The pulsing sped up, vibrating her breastbone.

"Hmmmm."

Lily looked to Li Liu in utter astonishment. *Is he going to just sit here and let us explode?* She couldn't take it any longer; she grabbed the locket and closed her eyes. A jolt hit her, followed by a warm rush that flowed through her veins.

The red light went out.

"Im-poss-ible," Liu said.

"What the hell is going on!?"

Mr. Liu reached across the table to the worn wooden box with the combination lock. He slid it in front of Lily. She hadn't paid attention to the top of it before.

"Fucanglong, the dragon of hidden treasure," he said.

Lily glanced down at the painted dragon. Something in her stirred.

"Your grandmother sent you a priceless gift. Guard it with your life."

Lily exhaled. Now she wanted to open the locket. She turned it over in her hand, studying the crease.

"I wouldn't try that just yet," he said.

Now you finally look scared! "What happens if others touch it?" she asked.

"According to the letter, regular humans won't have any problem, but shapeshifters with the wrong essence could be blown to bits."

Silently outraged that he had risked her life for his sheer curiosity, she grimaced at him.

He patted her hand. "I knew it would be okay Lily,

before I gave it to you."

"Oh, that's a relief. How did you know?"

"Gut feeling," he said jovially. His black reading glasses remained slightly askew.

She let it go. He was her elder and he seemed so pleased with himself that she would feel like a scoundrel if she protested. "Do you have a picture of what I am?"

"Oh no, no Lily," he said, brusquely closing the book. "No pictures for you. We will have to wait and see."

"Mr. Liu, you said that I am in danger. What kind of danger?"

"I thought we established this. Someone is obviously trying to kill you."

"Well, people around me. No one has specifically targeted me."

He waited.

She told herself to breathe. She had come to him for comfort, protection, reassurance.

"Sorry Lily, but people are terrified of the unknown. They will want to destroy you out of fear. Second, you have power. There will always be corrupt individuals that want to exploit it then kill you. Finally, there are those who are competitive and threatened by your abilities. They will kill you for this."

"Swell." *Thanks for the pep talk.* Looking down at the crucible, she had a strong desire to remove it.

"You must not take it off Lily."

"Even when I sleep and shower?"

"If you don't wear it, keep it close."

"What's happening, Mr. Liu?"

"Honestly, I don't know. It appears someone is

attacking people close to you. It is imperative that you stay hidden."

"You think Peter and Mona were killed because of me?" she asked.

"There is a strong possibility, but I don't have the answers."

"Do the police?"

He shook his head, his dark eyes sad. "Unfortunately, I don't believe this is something they are equipped to handle."

"What do you suggest I do?"

"Train with me."

"So I should stay here?"

"Sorry Lily, but that would be putting us both at risk. Stay where you are."

After everything she had been through, this final blow to her fragile ego was almost too much. Nobody wanted her near; she was a liability. She didn't mention the Manor or the hounds sniffing around her hideout.

He handed her his card. "Tomorrow you come back here to train."

"I'm not sure that I can keep sneaking out with the motorcycle I borrowed."

"I can pick you up at ten in the morning," he said. "You name the place."

"The children's playground at Piedmont Park."

"Perfect," said Mr. Liu.

Lily wrote down her dog alias and new cell phone number for him. He walked partway down the driveway with her. Tonka and Spike darted to and fro trying to entice her into a game of chase. Apparently, to them, she was a dog whether walking on two legs or four.

Mr. Liu insisted she keep her Shaolin uniform. It would be her uniform during training. He looked down at the ground as if struggling with something. "Take care of your brother, Lily. He needs your help."

"Seth?"

"Yes. Go now." He gestured with his hand. She felt like a dog that had been shooed away.

Numb, she obeyed. Still in her Kung Fu pajamas, she donned her wig, leather jacket, helmet, and backpack. Her journey home on the bike wasn't as eventful as her visit with Mr. Liu, except for losing Frank's other loafer.

At 3:30 in the afternoon, she canvassed Ansley Park Manor to see if the coast was clear. After waiting for some neighborhood children to go into their backyard, she pulled into the driveway and parked the bike. She ran around to the back door, unlocked it with her new key, then opened the garage door. Her strength was growing each day. She had no difficulty maneuvering the bike back into its designated spot and pulling the tarp back in place.

After returning the backpack to its hiding spot behind the dryer, she shifted back to Tashi and waited for the boys to return. Seth came to mind several times, but she wasn't ready to talk to him. Now she understood his misgivings about Li Liu. He was a puzzle. She had never been good at puzzles.

Lily fretted over her ill grandmother's gift. Necklace was really a misnomer; it was a kickass tazer. If only she knew how it worked and what the heck was inside it.

CHAPTER ✒ 14

FROM THE LOST NOTES OF PETER MARX

July 21, 2010

Subject T is experiencing limited response to oral Inderal and Dr. H. suggested a trial of injections to improve the response. I adamantly disagreed and let her know. I also let Subject T know that I thought this was dangerous. She is so desperate for some relief from her condition that she would do anything. She is such a sweet lady, I just want to help her.

Subject C is doing well on Inderal although he complains of periods of blackouts. This concerns me, again, I'm questioning the efficacy of its use in these shifters. We don't know the long-term effects.

—Peter

CHAPTER ✒ 15

CALDWELL'S DREAM

THE FIRST THING he noticed was her pretty smile. The second thing he noticed was that she was naked. Okay maybe he noticed the nudity first. Lily sat on the bleachers of Grady High School's football stadium. She reached out to touch his cheek, but he felt a scratch.

She looked at him in distress as she pulled her hand away. Caldwell noticed something wrong with her fingers—they were longer with claws.

"Sorry," she said. Her cheeks flushed pink.

When he looked again, her hands were normal. A tear travelled down her cheek.

"He hurt me."

He followed her gaze down the field to see a crumpled Phil Miller in the end zone.

"I know," he said.

She jumped up. Suddenly, she was wearing the clothes they found torn to pieces at the crime scene—a black skirt, sandals, and a green knit top. "He's here. Make him go away."

Caldwell bolted to his feet in time to see a tall man in a black ball cap, black shirt and pants dart around the end of the bleachers. Caldwell sprinted down the stairs, but when he got to the bottom, the man was gone and so was Lily Moore.

CHAPTER 16

FINDINGS

CALDWELL LOOKED IN the mirror. He had nicked himself twice shaving. He was having fantasies about a woman who he feared was dead.

"What kinda shit is this?"

His reflection didn't answer. At least he wasn't completely delusional. Nightmares and exotic dreams had plagued his sleep. Nightmares were not unusual since he worked homicide, but the exotic dreams—

He shuddered. The dreams had been explicit. At thirty-two years of age, he took most things in stride. He was well-seasoned in remaining collected, methodical and analytical. So why was his heart racing?

Struggling to focus, Caldwell took several deep breaths. His conversation with Maggie Moore the other night ran through his head. Ms. Moore kept her married name purely because she liked the Americanized sound of it. The Moores had shared joint custody of their children until Seth turned eighteen. Emanuel Aaronson kept her preoccupied travelling the world, spending his inherited family money.

Caldwell hoped today's interviews would shed even more light on the players involved. In pouring through Ms. Sinclair's phone records, he had found Professor Hitomi's number.

Dr. Hitomi currently headed up the Laboratory of Neuropsycopharmacology at Emory University. She had held the position for the last seven years in addition to teaching undergraduate and graduate psychiatry course work. He had spoken with her briefly after Marx's death, but at the time the nature of her work didn't come in to play as Marx's accidental overdose of insulin didn't seem to relate.

Now, Caldwell held an intense interest in her work. In one particular study, her team of researchers was comparing the effectiveness of three classes of drugs in treating PTSD: monoamine oxidase inhibitors, anti-anxiety drugs, and beta-blockers. The MAOI was selegiline, Emsam, in a patch form, proving to have less severe side effects than previous oral MAOIs. The anti-anxiety drug was lorazepam, brand name, Ativan. The beta blocker they were using was propranolol hydrochloride—known by its brand name as Inderal, the same drug Ms. Sinclair allegedly used to kill herself, whether it was intentional or by accident.

The other link he found between the two women was their membership in the Southern Writer's Association. Hitomi's profile in the group indicated that she was a published poet. Hitomi intrigued him. She presented as a complex individual with varied interests and behaviors. *And Lieutenant Lake thinks she took advantage of a young Seth Moore. Interesting dossier.*

Caldwell finished up and hustled to his silver Toyota Camry. He and the lieutenant were meeting at 7:30 at the office in downtown Atlanta then heading northwest to the town of Vinings to catch Hitomi in her home.

Twenty minutes later Caldwell sat in the driver's seat of the unmarked car when Lake yanked open the passenger door, clutching a cup of coffee in his other hand. He nodded to Caldwell as he climbed into the car and continued his cell phone conversation. The scent of stale coffee hit Caldwell.

He pulled out into traffic and headed toward the interstate passing the MARTA train station on Brotherton Street. A homeless man stood next to his shopping cart on the edge of the parking lot facing into the street. He smiled and stood like he was waiting for something. Men of all ages walked the lot, some waiting for rides after their release from the men's detention center connected to the APD campus.

The lieutenant finished his conversation as Simms pulled on to the interstate. "That was Tiny," Lake said. "He got some results back on the hooded sweatshirt found on Seventeenth Street. DNA from the long hair is Lily Moore's. Pulled a short strand of chemically-treated dark hair off as well. No tissue attached to test DNA. We still want to obtain hair samples from suspects involved to see if there is a match, at least we can narrow down whose hair is dyed and see if the chemicals match.

"Also, identified dog fur that is similar to the kind found on Miller after his attack. Paw prints from that crime scene are another matter." The lieutenant blew out air. "Tiny's working with the veterinary forensic experts in Oregon on the prints. One paw print is that of a very small canine. Another is of a human-like footprint with claws."

"So our suspect either is a male or female with short dyed hair?"

"Uh huh," Lake said, digging his fingernails into the dashboard. Caldwell knew he got carsick when he rode shotgun.

"And another suspect possibly barks and another is...I don't know, what does Forensics think?" Caldwell asked.

"There is the possibility that our alleged kidnapper is the owner of a toy breed," said Lake putting his foot through the passenger side floorboard as Caldwell screeched to a halt, almost rear-ending the minivan in front of them.

"For fucks sake, Simms. You drive like a soccer mom on Ritalin!"

"Sorry." Caldwell couldn't help Atlanta traffic. The lieutenant would just have to cope. "We've established that the Grady Knights didn't play any teams that weekend with some kind of bizarre mascot, right?"

"Real cute," Lake quipped.

Caldwell smirked. "Hitomi have a dog?"

"We shall see."

"How about a jackal?"

Lake shook his head. "I'm glad you're entertaining yourself. Your driving makes me nauseous."

As they pulled up to Hitomi's grey, stucco, two-story home, Caldwell began to feel the first tinge of optimism. His detective radar had a hard-on.

He rolled up the sleeves to his white oxford shirt. It was in the high seventies and the humid air already was oppressive.

As Caldwell leaned in to ring the doorbell for a second time, the door flung open, making both of them step back. Hitomi wore a satiny pink robe and high-heeled slippers.

People really wear those? Her short hair looked still damp from the shower. She had almond-shaped eyes of a remarkable citrine color and exquisite cheekbones.

"Dr. Hitomi, sorry to interrupt your morning. I'm Detective Caldwell Simms with the Atlanta Police Department. We spoke back in August about Peter Marx. This is Lieutenant Lake. We have a few questions for you if you have the time."

"I remember you," she said. "What is this about?"

"We're here to speak with you about Lily Moore's disappearance and how it may relate to two other cases we are working on."

"This is about the Moores?" she asked, lips pursed.

"Yes ma'am," Caldwell said.

"Guess I don't have much choice." She turned and sauntered past the staircase and down a narrow hall that led to the back family room. Caldwell and Lake entered the house and followed.

Caldwell noted the two-story foyer, peach-colored walls, and framed black and white nature photos. Hitomi sashayed in front of them, showing absolutely no insecurities in her lack of clothing—no nervous tugging at the V of the robe or the ends of the belt. Simms caught the boss studying her backside in the thin satin. She was a striking Japanese woman in her forties, but could have easily passed for thirty.

She came up to Lieutenant Lake's nose when she abruptly stopped and he almost ran into her. He looked wide-eyed into her unfaltering gaze. Caldwell saw something transmit between them. Recognition of a sort on both parts. She tilted her head to examine him. They stood staring, until Caldwell cleared his throat and the lieutenant took a step back.

"Perhaps you would care for some coffee?"

"Uh, no thanks, Dr. Hitomi," Caldwell responded from behind Lake.

"Please, call me Koko." She pirouetted and continued into the family room where she sat back to lounge in an off-white leather recliner. She carefully crossed her legs then impatiently peered up at them. Lake and Caldwell sat in the black leather couch across from her. Lake sat upright with both of his black loafers planted squarely on the floor. In synchrony, the men reached into their pockets and pulled out hand-sized notebooks.

"Aren't you two charming with your matching note-books," she laughed. Lake remained motionless while Caldwell chuckled nervously with her.

Caldwell initiated the conversation since Lake seemed to have fallen into a stupor.

After she confirmed her basic information with them, Lake snapped out of it. "We're investigating two deaths that have occurred in the last nine months, Peter Marx and Mona Sinclair," he said.

"And how this could relate to Lily Moore's disappearance," interjected Caldwell.

"I see," she answered. "I don't know what this has to do with me, but shoot." The corner of her pretty mouth rose, apparently amused with herself.

"How long did you work with Mr. Marx?" Caldwell asked.

"Let's see. I would say about two years." She clasped her dainty hands on her bare knee that was peeking out from her robe. "Why are you investigating Peter's suicide?"

"We're looking more carefully at his *accidental death* in conjunction with the recent events. Even the minutest detail may seem useless to you, but could be significant to the case," offered Lake.

"So sad, Peter's situation. I mean I sensed he was troubled, but it was still so upsetting. He was invaluable in the lab."

"You weren't surprised by Peter Marx's death?" Caldwell asked.

"Well, I wasn't surprised that he committed suicide, no."

"What makes you so certain it was suicide?" he asked. "The Medical Examiner ruled it accidental."

"Peter was a perfectionist and a nice guy. He lived with the Moore girl and I know that couldn't have been easy."

"What do you mean by that?" Caldwell asked, irritated.

"I'm sure you know the Moores' reputation. The father was killed, the wife and poor Seth went off the deep end, and that Lily is troubled, strong-willed, and controlling."

"You got along well with Peter?" Lake asked, giving Caldwell a sideways glance.

"Sure. Peter got along with everyone. He was harmless."

"When did you last see him?" Caldwell said.

Hitomi drummed her nails on her knee as she thought. "It was the night before he was found. We had just finished preparing lesson plans and lecture ideas for fall quarter. I offered to buy him a drink."

"Anything unusual about his behavior strike you at the time?" Lake asked.

"He looked worn out, like he was stressed and hadn't slept for days. He spent about five minutes venting to me about Ms. Moore and her anxiety and paranoia."

"Did he describe this paranoid behavior?" asked Caldwell.

She shifted her jeweled gaze to him. "She was a nag, wanting to know where he was every minute of the day."

"Was Mr. Marx hiding something from her? What specifically did he say?" Caldwell persisted.

"Oh, I don't know. I didn't live in that house," she said. Her eyes were piercing into him. He held her gaze.

"You just said that he had vented to you about her paranoid behavior," Lake said. "Give an example of what he was complaining about."

"She questioned his every move, like she thought he was cheating on her."

"Was he?" Caldwell asked.

Hitomi laughed. "Peter? Really? No Detective, he was a boy scout."

"So a pretty responsible person then?" Caldwell asked.

"As responsible as *men* can be," she said raising an eyebrow to Lake.

Lake ignored her. "Did you know anything about Peter's diabetes?"

"Sure, but we didn't discuss it much. He had it since he was a kid. He really took it in stride since he had been managing it so long." Caldwell watched as she tilted her head and stared at the lieutenant like she was propositioning him with a single gaze.

The lieutenant looked down quickly. "You mentioned that he was responsible. Wouldn't it be odd for him to accidentally give himself too much insulin?" Lake asked.

"Why would that be strange? People do it all the time," she said.

"I'm just trying to understand. You said that you thought Mr. Marx's death was a suicide," Caldwell said. She swung her head toward Caldwell and pursed her lips.

"I said no such thing. I said it wouldn't surprise me."

Caldwell relaxed back against the couch and surveyed her for a moment. She didn't squirm or fidget like most individuals would. "What happened after the drink?"

"You know this, Detective. You have your little notes from my friends. I left around 7:30 and joined my neighbors for a dinner party."

"Did you know any of Peter's friends?"

"Some fellow students and coworkers."

"What about Seth Moore?" Caldwell asked. A slight crease appeared in her forehead.

"They were friends, apparently," she said, casually.

"You had some interaction with Mr. Moore. Did he seem like an aggressive individual?" Caldwell asked.

"Seth?" she asked in alarm. "Seth is a lamb." Koko Hitomi's face flushed as she returned Caldwell's stare.

So now we know how to ruffle your feathers. "You talk to Seth much?" Caldwell pushed.

"Why would I talk to him?"

"It's just, ironic, you referring to him as a lamb when you called the authorities on him just a few years ago." Caldwell leaned forward, eyes set on her.

"That was a silly misunderstanding," she said looking down at her manicured nails. "Listen, I'd love to stay and chat with you gentlemen all day, but I really must get dressed at some point. I have work to do."

"Of course," Lake said. "We just have a few more questions. Thanks for your patience." Hitomi leaned back in her chair and slowly recrossed her legs.

Caldwell looked at the floor.

"Did you know Mona Sinclair?" Lake asked.

"Sure. She and I were in the same writer's association."

"How often did you speak with her," Caldwell asked.

"Well, it varied. At first, we saw each other once a month at the writers meetings. Sometimes she called to chat."

"Was it writing advice she wanted or medicine for her PTSD?" Caldwell asked.

"You're talking about Inderal?"

Caldwell waited.

"She did confide in me about her anxiety and depression. We discussed her medication. I'm sure you know that I'm a researcher. I spoke with her from a scientist's perspective. She had a primary care physician for her medicine. Gentlemen. I conduct various studies using different medical protocols, pharmaceutical drugs. I'm sad about her death, but I have no idea why you're here questioning me."

The lieutenant tapped his pen. "Did you know Lily Moore?"

"No."

"No university functions brought you together?" Caldwell asked.

"Honestly, other than an occasional lunch or drink, I didn't socialize with the student researchers. I'm busy. They're busy with their projects and studying."

"Except for one student, Seth Moore," Caldwell said.

Hitomi got to her feet. "Let's not beat a dead horse. You have all your notes about that night. Seth had too much to drink or smoked something and was out of it. I didn't pursue charges. I suppose I panicked at first because I was a woman by myself in a lab at night."

They got to their feet.

"Couple things," Lake said. "Please take a look at your calendar for us and let us know where you were on these dates," he handed her the dates and times of the Sinclair murder, and Miller/Moore assault.

Dr. Hitomi grasped the edge of the paper as if it were a bag of dog waste.

"We're just checking everyone's alibi within the circle of friends and acquaintances," Caldwell said, cocking his head as she had at them. Lake gave him a pained look.

"We'll also need a sample of hair for DNA evidence," said Lake. Caldwell leaned in to give her his card. "Call this number to set up a time to meet with our forensic expert."

"Why would you need my DNA if I had nothing to do with these incidents?" Hitomi's eyes flashed with anger.

"That's just it. We don't know that you had nothing to do with these incidents. DNA will help us to rule you out as a suspect. You knew and interacted with all the victims."

"I see."

Both men were quiet as they returned to the car.

"She's watching us from the window," Lake cautioned.

"Yep," Caldwell said.

They waited until they were out of the subdivision before reacting.

As Caldwell rolled through the first stop sign, Lake turned to him. "What the hell was that?"

"A serious wack job!" responded Caldwell. "Did you notice she didn't blink?"

"That's not all I noticed," Lake said. "I can't believe she had nothing on under that robe and kept lifting her leg and crossing and recrossing and crossing and recrossing..."

Caldwell snorted. "Talk about evasive maneuvers."

They quieted down as he pulled on to the interstate. "She sure had an opinion about Lily Moore despite her claim that she never met her." He realized he sounded a bit like a protective boyfriend. "And strange reaction to Seth's name. No offense, Boss, but I think he tapped that."

Lake shrugged. "I'll see if we can get a warrant to search her lab, home, phone, and computer records. Maybe we will find something related to Sinclair."

Caldwell reached for his cell. "I'm calling Mr. Moore. We need to feel him out. See what he knows."

Lake nodded.

Caldwell studied him out of the corner of his eye. He knew the lieutenant had a protective streak when it came to the fallen officer's son. He scheduled an interview for the next morning.

CHAPTER 17

THE STALKER

CALDWELL STUDIED MR. MOORE, rather *Seth*, as he insisted the detective call him. His faded jeans looked like he had retrieved them from a pile on the floor. Skin lighter than Lily's, eyes blue, but the same shape as hers. Those eyes held a deceptive calm, but his jittery fingers betrayed his true state of mind.

The detective needed to take control of his own state of mind. It was difficult to maintain objectivity when fantasizing about a suspect or victim. Caldwell's feelings about Lily needed to be tucked away like a photograph of an old girlfriend shoved in the sock drawer.

He knew what he needed to do; play hardball with Seth like he would any other person of interest in a case that had him in its jaws; shaking him like a dog does a bone.

"Thanks for coming in this morning," Caldwell said. Lake sat in his office observing the interview from a closed circuit feed.

Two people had corroborated Seth's alibis for the nights Marx and Sinclair perished. But no one confirmed his whereabouts the night his sister disappeared. His story was that he was asleep at home, by himself. Caldwell didn't think he hurt Lily, but he guessed he probably knew something. He couldn't ignore Seth Moore's involvement with

Professor Hitomi and the connection to Peter Marx.

"We're looking at a connection between Ms. Sinclair's death and your sister's attack and disappearance," Caldwell said.

Seth straightened in his chair. "How does the neighbor's suicide have anything to do with Lily?"

"We're not convinced the neighbor killed herself."

"The news said a big animal attacked Lily and her date. I don't understand what that has to do with her neighbor."

"Don't believe everything on TV," Caldwell said. He looked at the surface of the metal table and breathed. "We'd really like your help. There's some common thread here. If we can identify it, it could mean the difference between finding your sister dead or alive."

Seth didn't blink, but nodded. "Okay. Whatever will help Lily."

"How well did you know Ms. Sinclair?"

Seth shrugged. "Pretty well. I mean I saw her a lot once Lily moved into her building. I knew my dad always checked on her so I guess that made me think of her every time I saw Lily or Pete. He jiggled his leg. The vibration shook the conference table, jacking up Caldwell's nerves.

"Did Mr. Marx ever talk about her?"

"Well sure, he took her garbage out to the curb and that sort of thing 'cause she's old, you know...*was* old." Seth's face blanched.

"You overhear any of their phone conversations?"

"I don't get what you mean?"

"Records show that Mr. Marx made frequent calls to her."

"Maybe he was worried about her," suggested Seth.

"Perhaps," Caldwell said, unconvinced. He twirled his pen around his thumb as he stared at him before looking down at his notes. "Did your friend Peter say much about Dr. Hitomi?"

Seth's lips pressed in a tight line. "He talked about Dr. Hitomi and their work together."

"What about their work—he mention any of their patients having reactions from the clinical trials?"

"I'm not aware of that. Pete was professional. He didn't breach confidentiality about patients. He was getting his degree in psychiatry because he wanted to help people. He would never continue something if it was harmful to someone." Seth yanked at the front of his red polo shirt.

Caldwell realized he'd struck a nerve. "Dr. Hitomi insinuated that Peter was anxious, stressed, hiding things from your sister. You know what it was, don't you?"

Seth looked at the surface of the table before meeting Caldwell's gaze. "I know Pete loved my sister. He wouldn't do anything to hurt her. I told you before that he wanted to marry her. He had a ring."

During the investigation into Marx's death nine months ago, Seth had told Caldwell about an engagement ring. Although Caldwell traced a receipt from Zimmer's Jewelers in Atlanta, he never discovered the ring.

"He may have loved your sister, but the question is, was he *hiding* things from her?"

"I really don't know."

"So he killed himself, then?"

Seth sighed. "I know it sounds like denial, but I agree with Lily. Pete was too careful. He wouldn't inject too much insulin by accident or on purpose."

"Any enemies?"

Seth shook his head. "Everyone liked Pete, but he did deal with people with emotional issues at that clinic."

"A friend insinuated that he worked long hours with Dr. Hitomi. What were they working on that warranted such extreme dedication?"

He crossed his arms. "I didn't work there. I don't know what went on at that lab."

"Sure you did. You were there that night with Koko. I have a police report that says as much."

Seth pursed his lips as color seeped into his cheeks. "I was drunk and don't remember everything."

"You see much of her lately?"

He shrugged.

Caldwell leaned in. "You call her, Seth?"

"*I* don't call *her*."

"You still have a thing going with the professor?"

"No!"

"I know that for some reason she really likes *you*, but showed distaste for your sister who apparently she hasn't met. I'm trying to get the dynamic here."

"She likes to mess with me."

"What do you mean?"

"I don't know—she calls me incessantly. She started after that night. At first I tried to be polite particularly because Pete's my friend and I didn't want to piss off his boss."

"What happened that night?"

"God I wish I knew." He looked down at the table. "She asked me out for a drink. I went. I swear it was like I was drugged. I didn't remember anything until I woke up naked in the lab."

"You think she drugged you. That's a serious accusation. Why didn't you tell the police?"

"Who would you believe, Detective?"

"So you have yourself a stalker. That doesn't explain her animosity toward Lily."

"I don't think she's altogether stable. I mean she's wicked smart, but really intense. Pete mentioned he thought she had Obsessive Compulsive Disorder."

"And there's no possibility that Mr. Marx was her new obsession?"

Seth ran his fingers through his hair. "I know he would have told me."

"Okay, let's switch gears to Phillip Miller." Seth stiffened. "Did you know your sister was involved with him?"

"No. I can't believe she went out with that loser."

Caldwell raised his eyebrows in question.

"I worked with him at European Dreams. He's just... not someone I would let my sister go near."

"One of those guys?"

"Yeah, always on the prowl."

"Did Mr. Marx know Phillip Miller?"

"Sure. You know Phil went to grad school for a while. I think their paths crossed. And then—" his brow furrowed.

"And then?"

He shook his head.

Caldwell dropped his pen on the table and leaned forward. "Look Seth, two people are dead. Your sister could be as well. You need to tell me if you know something."

Rattled, Seth's eyes widened. "Peter mentioned that

Phil was a roid user."

"When was this?"

"When I got the job at the car place. He was being a jerk to some customer, completely over the top, and I told Pete about it and he made the comment."

"Did Lily know Phillip?"

"Honestly, I don't think so. She may have come into the car place to see me once and he was there."

"So you can't see any reason he would want to hurt her."

His nose wrinkled. "I don't know why anyone would want to hurt her."

"You've had no contact with your sister since that night?"

"No. That's why I'm here. I hope you can find her."

"I know we've been through this before with you, but have you thought of anything new related to your sister and her behavior leading up to her disappearance?"

"No, Sir."

"Okay. Please call us if you think of anything else."

After Seth Moore left, Caldwell sat back with his feet on the table as he reviewed his notes. Seth made Hitomi almost sound like a predator.

Lieutenant Lake leaned his head in the room. "He knows something about his sister."

Caldwell brought his feet down to the floor and sat up. "I know. So it wasn't just me?"

"No," Lake said.

"As close as he was to her, he strikes me as the type who would be bawling like a baby thinking about her dead or injured or someone hurting her."

"So if he knows something, why isn't he telling us?" Lake asked.

"I don't know," Caldwell said. "Maybe he's hiding something."

CHAPTER ✒ 18

THE WATCHER

SETH DIDN'T RESPOND to phone calls, texts, or emails. Lily's brain was a cesspool of anxiety full of Seth angst, grandma worry, and Kung Fu dread.

The previous night she had prayed for her grandmother, the one she had never known. That dynamic had her wide awake as did the fact that she would be attempting martial arts training the next morning. She spent half the night reading *The Art of Shaolin Kung Fu, the Wong Kiew Kit* that Mr. Liu had handed to her before she left the previous day. The other half of the night, she spent fighting the urge to open the locket. She didn't have her grandmother's phone number. She had never contacted her. Now seemed like a good time to try. Maybe Seth could help. She had been so preoccupied that she forgot about sneaking out and attempting to retrieve items from her condo. *Oh well, I'll have to deal with the granny panties a while longer.*

As the mild morning light filtered into the kitchen, she sat on guard with the utmost foo dog patience, waiting for the boys to leave for work so she could do something. *Must be nice keeping banker's hours.*

Larry turned from the doorway of the garage and looked at her, his top lip curled as he considered her.

Lily backed up. *He did not just hear my thoughts!*

He studied her another moment before yelling into the house. "Frank!"

Frank strode into the kitchen carrying his briefcase and dressed for the day sporting aviator sunglasses. His demeanor was a calm spring breeze to Larry's hurricane gale winds. "Yes?"

Larry's raised hand trembled. "What is this?"

Lily trotted to the door with Frank. Leaning into his legs, she peered out into the driveway. There was a ten foot skid mark down the length of it, leading right to the Hudson's pitiful looking burning bush. Highly impressed with herself, she ran out and inspected it, wagging her tail violently. *How in the name of Buddha's belly did I manage to avoid the mailbox?*

Frank took off his aviator glasses while sucking in copious amounts of air. In slow motion, he turned to look back at the Fireblade. Larry followed his gaze. The bike was still under its tarp.

Her tail paused mid-wag while she waited.

Frank waved a hand at the bike as though dismissing it, then turned to Larry, "I didn't do that! I haven't ridden the bike in weeks."

"Well, who the hell did?" Larry asked. "Mrs. Hudson was over here complaining about her bush!"

Frank's mouth twitched. "Well, she's certainly consulting the wrong men if she wants advice about her bu—"

Larry glared at him before reconsidering the black mark on the pavement. "Maybe it was one of the neighbor's kids." He laughed as he surveyed Frank. "Like you would know how to do something like this."

Frank's healthy ego must have taken a hit. He

grimaced before repositioning his aviator glasses, which seemed to replenish it. He sauntered out to his Audi and blew her a kiss good-bye.

"Humph," was Larry's response. "Dog. Inside, I'm late for work."

Thinking about the time he put a poster-sized childhood picture of her with braces and a bad perm up on her cubicle, she ran around for a good ten minutes while he attempted to catch her. After Larry spewed a satisfying amount of swears and sweat, Lily pranced into the house. She could hear him exercising his vocabulary with creative concoctions of her breed name as he huffed out to the convertible.

When the coast was clear, she shifted to human form, grabbed her fanny pack and Shaolin uniform, and walked out the back door naked. At least the heavily landscaped backyard offered her privacy. Only the shirt fit into the fanny pack with the crucible, phone, and her underwear. She stowed the pants behind a bush realizing she'd have to borrow another pair from Mr. Liu.

After shifting to dog form, she couldn't figure out how to get the fanny pack on so she carried it in her mouth to the playground at Piedmont Park. Contact with it made her mouth tingle since the crucible rested inside. It was an unpleasant sensation, like licking the end of a battery.

Scanning the park, she noted that Mr. Liu hadn't arrived. She wandered around the playground equipment, stopping at the double and spiral slides. As kids, she and Seth had always fought over the slides. Thoughts of her father buzzed into her mind, but she swatted them aside. He had always let her go first. Her head needed to be clear, not crowded with past woes. At the crunch of sneakers on the mulch, she slipped under a bench where she wasn't so conspicuous, but could keep an eye out for Mr. Liu. A father positioned himself at the foot of the slide as his little girl slid down squealing with glee.

After fifteen minutes, Lily hid under some shrubs, used her mouth to unzip the fanny pack and checked her cell phone for any missed calls. None.

Forty-five minutes passed and she had finished another circuit of the park. With her nose on the touch screen, she found Mr. Liu in her Favorites. She called, leaving him a message on his voicemail. Perhaps he wouldn't understand her words, but he would recognize the gruff voice.

Grabbing the fanny pack in her mouth, she ran for home. As soon as she made it inside as a human, she tried Seth's work number. Reggie answered.

"Is this Katie?" Reggie asked.

Using a strong southern accent, she managed to find out that Seth went home sick. Reggie wasn't stupid, though, he hadn't heard Seth mention a "Tashi" before and he tried to pry information out of her. To get him off the line, she told him she had another call. *Katie? Is Seth talking to my friend, Katie?*

Her life was now too confusing and complex for her liking. She couldn't worry about one more person. Lily's head hurt as she walked to the garage in a pink sundress and flip-flops. *Screw the blue pajamas.*

She pulled the tarp off Frank's Fireblade. No voices sang in her head this time. She did let out a groan, however, when she looked down at her feet. "Flip-flops, so not a good idea on a motorcycle." Of course, neither was the dress, but she was in a hurry. Maybe she'd run by the Target store on the way.

Priority number one was checking Seth's apartment, which was a ten-minute ride on the bike. Acid gurgled up her throat when she didn't see his car in the parking lot. "Where the hell are you, Seth?"

Maybe he got one of her messages and went to Mr. Liu's. That was no easy ride. She knew that traveling on the bike was a risk. If a cop stopped her, she would have a lot of 'splaining to do.

Her mind made up, she rode to the Target in her pink dress and Frank's leather jacket. The crucible, now fastened around her neck, sent little shocks of energy throughout her body. She ran inside wearing the jacket, dress, red wig, pink JanSport backpack, flip-flops and Larry's Elton John sunglasses. She emerged five minutes later with a pair of slip-on tennis shoes.

After sliding the new shoes on, she put her clear flip-flops in the backpack with a new black sundress. She decided that as a shapeshifter she needed to start carrying spare clothing. Sitting on the bike in the parking lot, she attempted Seth's phone one more time. Mr. Liu did not answer either. Cold panic seized her stomach. Her thoughts vacillated between anger and fear. Perhaps Mr. Liu had changed his mind about helping her. Something told her it wasn't that simple.

Interstate 75 took her north toward Kennesaw. Distracted, Lily didn't notice someone tailing her until she pulled off the highway. As she changed lanes, a white Range Rover changed lanes. She had seen a similar vehicle in the Target parking lot. *But was that one silver?*

As she got further down the road, the vehicle pulled up next to her. It was difficult to discern who was driving because of the tinted windows. It looked like a shorter man in a ball cap and shades. When the light turned green, she twisted the wick and attempted to put some space between herself and the car. Unfortunately, he was up for a drag race and accelerated and braked with her down the crowded street.

Thankfully, as she approached the Cobb Parkway intersection, a cop pulled up behind the Range Rover. She watched with glee as the officer hit his lights and pulled the white vehicle over. *Poetic justice.*

As she turned on to Stilesboro Road, ominous black storm clouds rolled overhead. A fine mist fell as she pulled into the ranch. Mr. Liu's silver Nissan pick-up sat in the driveway. However, no dogs greeted her.

Following her instincts, she detoured to the rear of the property, parking the Fireblade further back in the woods. She stuffed the jacket in her pack, which she leaned against the bike with the helmet before heading for the studio. Her tentative steps quickened into a run when her hyper-sensitive ears detected an eerie scuffling noise.

Where are the dogs? Hopefully, they'd recognize her scent and not attack her. She approached from the side of the building. As she rounded the front, she saw one of Mr. Liu's teak chairs on its side in the grass. Looking up, she saw the jagged remains of what used to be the sliding glass doors.

Broken glass crunched underfoot as she reached down and procured one of the split chair legs. She leapt up one step to peer inside the studio. A trail of blood snaked across the floor, drawing her eyes back toward the kitchen area. Mr. Liu's scent mingled with the Watcher's. Wielding her makeshift staff, she crept carefully across the debris. The weapons cases were shattered. The door to the teak cabinet hung askew and items had cascaded out on to the bamboo floor.

A noise came through the kitchen wall. It sounded like a bird flopping into surfaces. Hesitating, she considered other weapon options. Attempting the use of a three-sectional-whip as a novice would amount to disaster. A knife or spear was much more promising.

She dropped the chair leg and daintily plucked a ji, a Chinese polearm, from the debris on the floor. The significant spear felt natural in her hands as she raised it. Her heartbeat was deafening in her ears.

Taking in a deep breath, she started forward, but stopped. The Watcher wore a black mask and stood across the room at the opening of the narrow hallway leading to the kitchenette. He held a gagged and bound Mr. Liu captive in a one-armed strangle hold. In his right hand, he gripped a gun.

Blood oozed from Mr. Liu's chest. His eyes rolled back in his head. Lily could sense his attempt to focus. *Does he know I'm here?* She winced at the swelling that distorted his facial features. Her body trembled, aching to shift, but she didn't know how long it would take or the outcome.

"Mmm, mmm, mmm," Mr. Liu said through the gag.

"Shut up," the man said in a raspy voice. His blue eyes glared at her. "Throw your weapon away from you!" When she hesitated, he turned the gun butt and bashed Mr. Liu's temple. She flinched. Mr. Liu made no sound.

"Don't hurt him again," she said, gritting her teeth. Lily threw the spear to the side with a clang as she snuck one step forward. Holding her hands where the man in black could see them, she talked to Mr. Liu, "It's going to be okay." No response.

The crucible under her sundress pulsed, causing her sternum to throb. It was promising her something, perhaps rescue. She looked to his gun then Mr. Liu, trying to assess the situation. If she shifted, the man could shoot Mr. Liu, although he hadn't yet. He stayed nine feet from her with the gun trained at her head.

"Dumb freak," the man said. He dropped Mr. Liu with a sickening thud as her wings unfurled and claws extended. The first shot missed, but the second hit her shoulder. An object in motion stays in motion...she crashed into him in the narrow hall, sinking her claws into his chest. The gun popped free of his hand and skittered across the floor. Lily sat up and considered the gun as fangs filled her mouth. She straddled his body, attempting to pin him to the ground. He was strong. She went to claw at his face to remove the mask, but froze.

When she began to twist toward the new scent, a female scent, she was struck from behind. Pain blinded her as the force flung her top half against the sidewall. As she clawed at the wall and air, her opponent bucked underneath her.

She sensed more movement from the female behind her and turned to ward off another assault. The blow hit Lily's shoulder and she fell sideways over the Watcher who yanked at her hair while scrambling to pull his legs out from under her. She dug a claw in one retreating leg. Her vision blurred from so many knocks on the head, but she heard him bellow in pain so she was confident she'd done some damage.

Unable to focus her eyes, she localized to his ragged breathing overhead. The female kicked her in the ribs. Lily felt the air whoosh from her lungs.

"I thought you were supposed to be stronger. You're the first born." He spoke with a genteel southern accent that clashed with his appearance and actions.

Something wet oozed down her cheek. She realized it was blood. Both of them wore masks, that much she could tell despite her dizziness.

She shut her eyes in pain and curled into a fetal position. The crucible pulsed violently. She opened one eye just as the large shadow of the metal weapon came down once more and then it was dark.

CHAPTER ✒ 19

DOWN AT THE RANCH

CALDWELL SPED UP the highway toward Kennesaw. Storm clouds hunkered down on the horizon. The temperature hit the mid eighties and the pollen count broke history records for the month of May. God willing, the rain would bring some relief.

The weather change caused sinus pressure in his head. He squinted. Maybe it wasn't the impending rain. Li Liu had called him just before his interview with Seth Moore. In a sullen voice, Liu had asked Caldwell to come by because he had information on Lily Moore. He refused to talk over the phone. With the body count surrounding Ms. Moore, Caldwell couldn't blame him.

Lake stayed back at the office working on search warrants and going over forensics with Tiny. Caldwell felt pulled to Liu's with an inexplicable urgency.

When traffic congestion slowed his progress, he called Barbara Miller. He needed to see if Phil Miller was coherent enough to answer questions. Seth insinuated that Miller used steroids. His hospital labs were clean, but they hadn't tested for roids specifically. When he got her voice-mail, he left a message.

Exiting the highway, he flashed his lights to get through a jam by the mall. Thunder rumbled in the distance as the first large drops of rain fell. Caldwell found the ranch no problem—hard to miss a horseshoe archway over the driveway. To his left he noticed the old red barn. Horses huddled in the light rain behind a weathered railroad-tie fence.

He thought he heard something in the back of the house, but couldn't be sure as thunder boomed in the sky. When he went to knock, the front door swung open.

"Mr. Liu?"

A light shone in the back of the house. He stepped inside peering through a great room to the kitchen. He called again and got nothing.

Through the sounds of the thunder, he heard another noise. Outside on the front porch, he looked off to the barn. It sounded like a car engine. One step in that direction and suddenly he heard screaming off in the woods. He turned his attention away from the barn and rounded the side of the main house. Shards of glass and broken furniture littered the lawn in front of the second building.

"What the hell? Liu!"

Shots pierced the air along with screams loud enough to carry over the sound of the rain. He ran to the side of the building, gun drawn. When he turned the corner, he saw two German shepherds down on their sides.

Adrenaline pumping, he left the dogs and followed the sounds into a wall of trees. Caldwell grabbed his phone from his hip and called to request backup.

Wet from rain and sweat he frantically attempted to find the source of the gunshots, but they died off and he almost lost his way. Liu owned a significant amount of acreage. When the sirens wailed in approach, he started his return to the back building, breaking from the edge of the trees with his gun drawn. He heard cops getting out of their cars in front of the main house. He started to walk toward the dogs to check for signs of life before touching base with the Kennesaw Police. *When did that back door get open?* Lightning slashed through the blue-gray sky. He turned toward the flash of light above the tree line. *Lily Moore?*

LILY AWAKENED TO the distant sound of firecrackers. After a moment of lying on her side while her breath hitched, she heard it again, but her eyes wouldn't stay open.

The next time she was conscious, she heard a radio. She pushed up to sit, causing the room to spin. She surveyed the sea of glass across the studio floor. Her red wig lay in the middle of the floor like some kind of carcass. Pieces of her dress mixed with broken glass and splintered wood. Despite her injuries, her animal senses came back on line.

The crucible pulsed, sending energy through her aching chest. The slightest turn of her head sent white dots to dance in her vision.

She heard several car doors slam. There was the radio again, sirens. She drew on the crucible's energy to stay sitting. When she pulled to her knees, her head swam. Her shoulder protested with each movement. It hurt just to breathe.

She used her right hand on the wall to pull herself up to a standing position in the hall. When vertigo struck, she leaned her face against the wall's coolness.

Police? Her head hurt so terribly that thinking only

increased the throbbing tenfold. If she could just get her wits about her, she could think of what to do. What to tell them about the blood, the masked man, Mr. Liu, and why she was naked. But her brain kept short circuiting. It was too busy persuading body parts to follow orders.

She leaned her right shoulder against the wall for support and put one foot in front of the other, staggering to the back door.

Excited voices cut through the rain. *How many are out there?*

She pulled the back door open as she heard the crunch of shoes on shattered glass from the front. Gruff voices mingled as they coordinated their plan. Her adrenaline kicked into turbo when she stumbled over the shepherds sprawled on the back step. Pink tongues lolled out the sides of their mouths. She heard their snores as she focused on the copse of pine trees about twenty feet out. *The Watcher must have drugged them.* After stumbling once in the yard, she made it. White spots danced again in her periphery. She leaned her head against the rough bark of a tree while inhaling the invigorating pine scent and trying to gain control over her body. More car doors slammed, but she had slipped away.

"Don't move!" Simms's adrenaline-charged eyes met hers as he leveled his gun. He stood just to the side of the dogs at the back corner of the building.

"Don't," she cried.

She sensed his confusion and fear as he studied her. "You've been in my head," he said.

The comment was unexpected. Had she walked through his dreams? Speech eluded her as her mind raced.

When he turned his head ever so slightly to yell to the police, she turned and attempted to run. Pain pierced like an electric shock striking the apex of her shoulder before traveling in a current down the length of her arm as she shifted to a Shih Tzu.

She heard him yell, "Stop," but didn't look back. She disappeared into the maze of trees. In her smaller body, the pain dulled. Thunder and lightning crashed, announcing the deluge that washed over the ranch—a blessing from above.

Pandemonium broke out behind her. She didn't wait.

The Honda Fireblade waited where she'd left it like a faithful steed. Lily heard screaming as she shifted to human form. She swallowed bile as she managed the spare sundress and backpack, but left the helmet.

The bike started easily and she shot through the woods. Just holding the handlebars caused a crippling pain up her left side. Each jolt traveled up to her wound, causing her to bite the inside of her cheek to ground herself.

Then all she knew was the rev of the bike, breathing, and pain before she popped out of the forest on to a country road. Cars honked at her. She had no idea how fast she was going. At one point, she pulled over on the shoulder to vomit. Up ahead she saw a familiar sign to a small gas station where they used to buy boiled peanuts. The building lay vacant now. She brought the Fireblade to a stop, skidding into the dumpster and falling on her side. She managed to get off the downed vehicle. Her head lay in a puddle, but she didn't care. The gloom enveloped her as the rain fell in sheets.

Her thoughts were muddled. She clutched the crucible while pleading with the heavens that she just wanted to go home. Her mind flashed on Li Liu's battered face and then suddenly she heard her father's voice encouraging her as she climbed to the top of the slide at Piedmont Park, her small hands clutching the cool metal rails before plunging down. "You've got it, Lily." She felt her stomach drop as she fell through a spinning hole in space.

CHAPTER 20

SETH

SETH BOLTED UPRIGHT with a stiff neck and an awful headache. He had left the Atlanta Police building in a stupor. He had called in sick to work because he didn't want to explain anything to anyone, not even his good friend, Reggie. He meant to just rest on his futon, but he slept for over an hour.

He took his phone off the charger and powered it on. When he saw several missed calls from Lily, he felt terrible he had let his battery die. As he retrieved the first message, he stopped in his tracks. *Why the hell was she so stubborn?* He had told her not to go out to Mr. Liu's, that he would do the training. But apparently, she had set up a meeting with him. He listened to the rest of her messages. If he had known she was riding a motorcycle and Mr. Liu had "no-showed" at the park, he wouldn't have fallen asleep.

Each time he tried her number, it rolled to voicemail. "Shit!" He felt like the walls were closing in on him. Something was wrong. He ran out of the house to gray spitting skies. Broken branches littered the path to his car. Yellow rivers of pollen flowed down the galley of the curb. Exhausted, he hadn't even heard the storm.

Seth drove by the Ansley Park Manor. Larry stood at his mailbox with the front door ajar behind him—no Shih

Tzu in sight. Seth drove past without the guy even noticing. When Lily's phone rolled to voicemail again, Seth broke out in a cold sweat.

Driving too fast, he entered the interstate headed toward Kennesaw. His heart thumped inside his chest as if he were hooked up to an amplifier. He cursed himself as he pulled off the exit ramp. The phone rang. With a wave of relief, he picked it up to answer, but noted the number. *Koko*. He tossed the phone back down on the seat. The headache hit him with sharp spasms at his temples. He breathed through it as he passed Town Center Mall. Ten minutes later, he headed up Stilesboro Road. As he approached Mr. Liu's property, he saw flashing lights. His stomach muscles knotted. Officers directed traffic around Mr. Liu's driveway, which they had blocked off except for law enforcement personnel. Seth slowed to a stop next to the officer.

"Move along, sir."

"Mr. Liu?" Seth asked.

"Sir, this is a crime scene, you need to move along."

"Is the man who lives here okay?" insisted Seth.

"Move along, sir," commanded the officer.

CHAPTER 21

THE STORM

ONE MINUTE SHE stood naked and bloody, the next, she had disappeared into the trees. When Caldwell viewed the blood spatter inside the studio, he tasted bile. They knew that at least two shots were fired. They found one bullet in the wall by the sliding door. The other met its mark—Lily Moore. At least it had looked like a bullet wound. The whole scenario had been chaos.

What did Li Liu know and what the hell just happened?

There were blood smears in the galley kitchen where a fight had taken place. The CSI team looked at the disarray of the kitchen and analyzed the marks in the kitchen cabinets, presumably made from a foot kicking the wood. They surmised it was Liu making tea when he was surprised from behind. The front studio had been vandalized— the property damaged by the use of an archaic Chinese halberd. There was no sign of Li Liu on the premises. However, unique feathers were all over the main studio floor and walls. They looked similar to the ones found at the Miller scene. Instead of footprints, they noted an almost human print comprised of slightly longer toes with claws according to Tiny's analysis. He'd been learning a lot about paw and claw prints lately from the experts consulting on the case.

Caldwell now surveyed the property damage and blood while the CSI team sifted through rubble. He had never met Mr. Liu, but had seen his picture in Arthur Moore's file. He was one of *them*, and that made it so much more personal. Caldwell tried to keep his rage down to a simmer. Lieutenant Lake was inside the studio, combing over the scene for the hundredth time. Lake had been uncharacteristically quiet.

The KPD's forensics team was working on collecting blood evidence to see if there was a DNA match for Moore and Liu. Tiny showed up to consult. When he eyed the mud and puddles, he forewent his fancy stilts.

Caldwell looked off into the gray haze of the woods. The trees stood as wrinkled silent witnesses to what had transpired. He had been the only one who had gotten a visual of Lily Moore. One of the other officers claimed to have seen a dog. This was only partially comforting to Caldwell who insisted that he had seen Larry Jones's black and white Shih Tzu dart through the trees. He never saw the bike, just heard it. If he hadn't been preoccupied keeping the adrenaline-charged Kennesaw cops from going into the woods Rambo-style, things may have played out differently.

After he calmed everyone down, he briefed them on the young woman, conveying that she had been attacked recently and could possibly be suffering from amnesia or a head injury.

Officers took Li Liu's dogs to the Cobb Emergency Clinic for examination. Caldwell remained at the scene while the Kennesaw Police Department's trackers spread out in grid formation, attempting to pick up Lily Moore's or Li Liu's scent.

The rain had stopped now, leaving behind a mess for the CSI Unit to decipher.

Officer Ernie Gates came around the corner of the studio with his two bloodhounds. Gates had been in the house and studio talking with Lieutenant Lake. Both men had worked with Li Liu. Caldwell could see they were shaken, but determined. Gates wore a permanent scowl as he encouraged his hounds to pick up a scent from a shirt found in Liu's bedroom.

Caldwell scanned the woods as his cell phone buzzed at his hip. He ignored it. Two seconds later, it buzzed again. He pulled it out to see it was Seth Moore.

"Simms."

"D-Detective Simms? It's Seth Moore."

Caldwell paced in the driveway of the Liu residence. "Seth, I'm working a crime scene. Could I call you back?"

"You're at Mr. Liu's?"

Caldwell paused. "Where are you?"

He heard Moore sniff like he was crying. "Tell me he's okay."

"Where. Are. You?" Caldwell's eyes scanned the property including the crepe myrtle trees by the railroad-tie fence, the overturned rain barrel, shoeing stool and empty hobble by the barn door.

"I'm in the road, out front. Please tell me he's okay."

"What the hell are you doing here?"

"I came to see Mr. Liu. Is he okay?"

"I can't discuss anything at this point," Caldwell said, flustered.

"Oh, God."

"Seth?"

Nothing. Caldwell ran down the driveway, wondering why Seth was here. Did he have his sister? Climbing under the crime scene tape and passing the barricade, Caldwell looked left before turning and spotting Moore off to the right of the driveway, standing in the Georgia red clay on the shoulder of the road. Seth bent at the waist while sucking in air.

Caldwell approached him slowly.

Seth straightened up. "Mr. Liu was my dad's best friend. I need to know he's okay."

"This is a crime scene. I want to know why you're here."

Sighing, Seth put his hands in his pocket.

"Well?" Caldwell asked.

"I, I spoke to Mr. Liu after Lily's disappearance. He's known me since I was a kid. I wanted to talk to him about Lily and my dad. I was coming back up here to discuss classes with him."

"What classes?"

"He teaches Shaolin Kung Fu and he told me he'd train me," Seth said. "He wasn't answering his phone. I'd taken the day off so I thought I would come by. That's what I did last time."

Caldwell analyzed his every word and every move. He was trying to determine if Seth knew that his sister had been on the property.

"Mr. Moore?" Caldwell heard the Lieutenant step in behind him.

"Lieutenant." Seth nodded.

"What's going on?" Lake asked. Caldwell turned to fill

him in on Seth's visit to Mr. Liu.

"You see your sister lately?" Lake asked.

Seth took a step back, "What?"

"Did you know that your sister would be here?" Caldwell asked.

Eyeing Lake first, Seth Moore stood still, his eyes blinking rapidly. "Lily? You found Lily?" Tears started to roll down his face and he clenched his jaw. "Why didn't you say you found Lily? Is she okay?" he shouted.

Both detectives stepped forward to block him as he charged forward. He elbowed Caldwell's chin as he flew past and knocked over Lake. Lake grabbed his leg and Seth spun around, backhanding the lieutenant who flew back on the shoulder of the road.

"Stop!" barked Caldwell. Seth spun around and put his hands out.

"Jesus, Son, calm the fuck down," Lake said while getting to his feet.

"I'm sorry! I'm sorry! I just...where's Lily? Is she hurt?"

Seth was still, but his eyes were not. Caldwell shook his head to get his bearings after the blow from his elbow. *My God, this bastard's strong.* "Don't Move!" Caldwell repeated.

Lake approached him. "Keep your hands out. We're going over to my car to have a chat. Got it?"

Lake darted his eyes toward Caldwell before guiding Seth by the arm under the crime scene tape and out of the line of media scrutiny. Caldwell opened the back door of the Taurus parked off the side of the long driveway.

Moore looked like a scared four-year-old as he kept

apologizing for knocking Lake down.

"Shut up, Seth," Lake said. The right side of his face was splotched red from Seth's hand. Caldwell knew he was already upset about Liu and that Seth's appearance and outburst had unhinged him.

He watched as Seth scanned the front and side windows taking in the crime scene. Caldwell rubbed his chin. "Mr. Liu was attacked. Your sister was sighted escaping the scene with a bullet wound in her shoulder-chest area."

"You shot her?!"

"No! She was wounded before we arrived on the scene," Lake said.

Caldwell's throat felt tight. "She ran, Seth. From the back door of the studio, I saw that she was injured. When I went to follow her, she disappeared." He shook his head because he still couldn't believe it. "But then we heard a motorcycle start up."

"You know anything about a motorcycle, Seth?" Lake asked.

"Lily doesn't own a motorcycle." He glanced out the side window. His eyes followed the two bloodhounds running in the trees. "You haven't found her?"

"No, we haven't found her. That's why we're shooting the shit with you!" Caldwell said.

Lake seemed to have calmed down from being whacked. "You need to tell us right now where Lily's been."

Seth was ashen. "I'm going to be sick." Caldwell hit the unlock and jumped out to open the passenger door, allowing Seth to vomit on to the driveway rather than all over the back seat.

"Shit," Caldwell said, looking at the spittle hanging off Seth's chin. As Seth leaned out of the car, Caldwell handed him a napkin from the stash in the center console.

"Sorry," he said pitifully as he sat back in the seat. Caldwell returned to the front seat and sighed. He felt sorry for him, but he couldn't completely forget that the kid was holding back on them. He turned his body around so he could look at him.

"We don't have any information for you about your sister at this time. You need to tell us if you have any idea why the hell she is running from us," Lake said.

"Someone wants her dead," Seth answered, his voice cracking. He was watching Ernie and the hounds out the window again.

Caldwell sighed. "We didn't shoot her, but someone else out there did. She won't be safe until she comes in. You were with us this morning, but I know you're not telling us something."

"I don't understand any of this," he said putting his head in his hands.

Lake sighed.

Caldwell's temples felt like someone had put his head in one of those fancy apple corers. Part of him wanted to shake the kid, the other part wanted to hug him. His eyes were huge, his face tense, completely devastated.

"Can I go?" Seth asked.

"Stay accessible. We may have more questions. We want to know immediately if Li Liu or your sister makes contact. Got it?" Caldwell said.

He nodded. Caldwell dropped him off at his truck. "If

we hear anything, we'll inform you."

"Thanks," Seth said.

Ten minutes later the two detectives headed to Decatur. The hospital had discharged Phillip Miller that morning. No one was answering the phone. Time to pay him a visit.

CHAPTER 22

IN SEARCH OF LILY

I CAN'T BELIEVE it. Where is she? As soon as he pulled away from Mr. Liu's neighborhood, Seth checked his phone. Nothing. Next, he called his mother. Emanuel answered. Seth grimaced. He knew the guy hated his guts. "Hi Emanuel, I need to speak to my mom."

"Well she's not here."

"I guess I'll try her on her cell."

"No you won't."

"Excuse me?" Seth was pissed.

"She's in route to China. Her mother is very sick. Maggie doesn't need your shit right now, Seth."

"As always, thanks for your help," Seth said, gritting his teeth. He hung up and tried his mother's cell. He felt bad leaving her a message about Lily's situation so he told her to call him, that it was urgent.

Emanuel made his blood boil. The *only* thing he had going for him is that he seemed to take good care of Seth's mom.

Seth weaved through traffic with his phone in hand willing it to ring. He almost dropped it when it did. Koko. He was in no mood, and let it go to voicemail. The headache hit him hard causing him to squint, making his eyes sensitive to the light.

He drove erratically back to town, daring any cop to pull him over at this point. Once in the city, he hit Peachtree Street, which was a nightmare due to the earlier rain. Finally, after an hour of driving, he pulled into Peachtree Place Apartments. As he got out of his car, he knew he wasn't alone. His problem was standing in the parking lot five feet away, smoking a Marlboro. She was wearing a tight black knit top, jeans, and high heels.

"Where ya been, Seth?" Koko Hitomi glared up at him. Even in high heels, she came up to his chest. He instinctively took a step back. She emitted a raspy laugh as she closed the gap between them, and her brow crinkled. She must have caught a whiff of the vomit, despite his spearmint gum.

"You used to be so much fun, but now you act like you've been neutered."

Seth clenched his jaw. He reminded himself that indifference was the best way to cope with her. So instead, he riled her up, "Wow, does the clinic know you've escaped?"

"Come on. You know you wanted to see me." She attempted a girlish pout, but her intense eyes deflected any softness in her face.

"Have you been following me?" He stared at her while taking a threatening step forward. She tilted her head, stood her ground, unfazed.

"Aren't you paranoid? No, I haven't been following you." He actually believed her. He looked over and saw her familiar white Range Rover. He would have noticed if that car had been following him. While he hadn't seen a vehicle in his pursuit, his instincts never lied. Someone other than

Koko was stalking him.

"Look, I don't have time for this. What do you want?"

"You don't have time for me?" She put her hand on her slender hip. "I'm the only one that *gets* you. You'll make time for me."

"Or what?" he asked.

"Well, perhaps I'll fill the police in on what your true nature is like." She did have some dirt on him, which was the only reason he tolerated her bullshit.

Yes, Seth. I know all *about your sister.*

He grabbed his head. Koko had communicated to him telepathically. He really didn't want her in his head, but when he fought it, the headaches struck. She took another pull on her cigarette, which repulsed him. He usually didn't have trouble blocking her out. She exhaled smoke at him.

"What do you know about my sister?"

"Everything," she spat. Smoke streamed out her mouth and nostrils. It made Seth think of a dragon, the evil kind that ate knights. "She offed her little twerp of a boyfriend then the pathetic sickly neighbor, and now she's in hiding."

He stepped toward her, studying her carefully. "Did...did you hurt her?"

No. But I could if I wanted to.

"Go to hell, you crazy bitch." Seth squeezed his fists, feeling his nails dig into his palms.

"I'm already there." She threw her cigarette at him and flounced to her Range Rover. A minute later, Seth stepped back on to the curb as she drove by him, rubber squealing.

There was definitely more to Koko than she was sharing. Her fascination with Lily disturbed him.

Seth turned back to his apartment. A quick search

proved that Lily hadn't been there. He headed over to Ansley Park Manor going fifty in a thirty-five. He tried to steady himself in order to think logically. He parked in the driveway and headed straight to the back. Lily had mentioned Frank and Larry stashed a key under the Buddha. At 7:30 at night, he wasn't sure if Larry was home.

As he turned the corner of the house, he saw broken branches and debris scattered across the yard. "Lily!" he called.

The fading light cast dark shadows across the yard, but Seth followed his instincts and saw subtle movement in the huge shrubs that clung to the house. He dashed to the hedges to peer behind them. Lily lay in Shih Tzu form, covered in blood, barely able to move. The sour smell of vomit hit him.

"Lily!" Her body twitched ever so slightly. He could hear her ragged breathing.

With extreme care, he swaddled her in his shirt. She didn't move.

She was breathing, but it was weak. "Hold on, okay."

She needed medical help, but he couldn't take a Shih Tzu to a doctor. Lily had been to regular doctors all her life, but they wouldn't know what to do with her in her different forms. Where had Mr. Liu taken Barney the night he was shot? *The vet at Cobb Central Animal Hospital.*

Seth broke land speed records driving north on I75. *I should have protected her. I should have insisted she stay with me. I should have...* His phone rang. He ignored it. *Fucking Koko.*

CHAPTER 23

THE MILLERS

A SMALL STRAND of saliva clung to the corner of Phillip Miller's mouth. Caldwell counted to ten as he waited for the man to answer their question. Mr. Miller now lived with his mother in a ranch home in Decatur. He listed to the port side of a 1970s olive-green La-Z-Boy recliner and stared blankly at them.

"See I told y'all," said his mother standing with a dish towel on her shoulder and hands on hips. She wore her bleached blonde hair in a frizzy pile atop her head.

"How much Lithium is he on?" Lake asked, looking exasperated.

"'Nough for him to stop screaming about that demon woman."

Miller didn't blink, but his eyes widened when his mother mentioned the demon woman. "He's not been right since the attack. Look at 'em. You put his brains in a bumblebee, it'd fly backwards."

"Where were you and your son this afternoon?" Caldwell asked.

"Well he just got back from the hospital this morning. Since then I've been fielding phone calls, scheduling outpatient therapy and follow-up appointments with doctors. I had to call off work at the Big Lot just to get him settled. Oh, and I had to run out and get his prescription filled from the pharmacy."

"You have anything that can substantiate that?" Caldwell asked.

"What's this all about, anyway?"

"We had an incident today and we need to verify Mr. Miller's whereabouts," Lake said.

"What kind of incident?" she asked, narrowing her eyes.

"An attack that could relate to the crime committed at Grady High School," Caldwell answered.

"That Moore girl again!" she spat. "Look what she did to my boy. She's trouble. Alls I know is that y'all said he hurt that girl. I don't care what you say about blood spatter and DNA under his fingernails, it was self defense."

Caldwell bristled. He had heard enough about Phil Miller from acquaintances to believe otherwise, but it was definitely a "he said/she said" scenario and "she" wasn't around to plead her case. Lily Moore was somewhere bleeding to death because he wasn't quick enough and his communication with the Kennesaw Police sucked and... well the whole thing was a cluster-fuck.

Lake cleared his throat. "Discharge papers from the hospital, receipt from the pharmacy. Anything with a date and time stamp will suffice."

"Yeah, okay," she said. She walked over to the couch close to Phillip and rummaged through her purse while mumbling. "Don't know what the heck you could do. You're wetting and drooling yourself. Let me check my room."

She was gone for a few minutes. Caldwell stared at her

son. Mrs. Miller returned with forms from Piedmont Hospital and the pharmacy receipt with the date and time stamped on it.

"Thanks for your time, Mrs. Miller," Lake said.

"Uh huh. I hope you officers find her before she hurts someone else."

Lake grabbed Caldwell by the bicep preventing him from spinning around and putting Mrs. Miller in a similar state to her son.

She showed them to the door.

CHAPTER ✒ 24

A VISIT TO THE MANOR

CALDWELL SAT IN the passenger seat as Lake headed to
Ansley Park to check on the dog. It was 9 p.m. They had
spent the early part of the evening hashing over details and
adding Li Liu to their crime board. The Missing Persons
Unit continued to interview Liu's circle of neighbors,
friends, and family. The lieutenant had sighed when
Caldwell insisted it was Larry Jones's Shih Tzu in the
woods. To shut him up, Lake finally agreed to ride with
him to their home.

I did see that dog. I'm not a mad man. Although he
had been losing sleep and thinking disturbing thoughts
about Lily Moore since the case began.

As the lieutenant swung the Taurus on to the Prado,
Northeast, Caldwell drummed his fingers on the passenger
door. *What's the protocol for taking a dog into custody?*

"Caldwell!"

Caldwell stilled his fingers, realizing it was putting
Lake on edge.

Lake parked in the driveway. Caldwell puffed air like
he had just bench-pressed three hundred pounds. It sure felt
like he had.

"S'up with you, Simms?"

He breathed out long and slow. "It's just, you didn't

see her, Lieutenant."

"Not your fault Simms."

"She...someone had worked her over."

"She's alive. We'll find her. Can't blame yourself. Whoever is doing this is smart. Li Liu was a master in Kung Fu. He let the perp into his studio. This guy knew his weapons. You gotta pull it together or you'll get reassigned."

Caldwell whipped his head around.

"Not my decision, so don't look at me like that."

"What? The captain wants to pull me off?"

Lake didn't look at him. "Just stay focused. Now let's go talk to these gentlemen and get DNA from their dog, okay?"

"Okay."

They walked up the lit path to the Jones/Harding residence. Lake rang the doorbell and waited. Frank Harding opened the door wearing plaid pajama bottoms, a white undershirt, and a serious shiner.

"Mr. Harding?" Caldwell asked.

"Yes?"

"Sorry to disturb you at such a late hour. I'm Detective Simms and this is Lieutenant Lake. May we come in for a moment?"

"Sure." For a fleeting moment, Frank Harding looked like he had been blind-sided, but he quickly regained a calm demeanor.

The detectives stood in the grand foyer. "I'll just let Larry know you're here. He's already in bed." Mr. Harding went upstairs calling for Larry Jones.

"Nice place," Lake said, looking toward the double

chandeliers in the dining room to the right.

"Yeah," said Caldwell, distracted. "Where's the dog?"

"What the hell happened to his face?" Lake added.

Jones came down the stairs, eyes averted. He clutched Kleenex in his hand and wore the same lavender paisley bathrobe from when Caldwell initially interviewed him. When he raised his eyes, it was evident he had been crying.

"Why don't you officers come into the great room." He walked down the hallway before getting an answer.

The detectives sat in black upholstered chairs across from Harding and Jones on the sectional. Behind the sectional, an abstract painting in shades of blue spanned half the wall. Caldwell could make out the moon and...a wing.

"You'll have to excuse my appearance. I don't know if Frank told you we've lost our Tashi." He blew his nose, which sounded like a trumpet blast.

"What happened to her?" Caldwell asked.

Jones shook his head.

"We don't know," said Harding. "She's a little Houdini. She's gotten out by herself before, but she always comes back. I've tried to tell him that she'll probably be crying at the door again in the middle of the night."

"She was inside when I left for work this morning," Jones sobbed.

Lake leaned forward. "I'm real sorry about your dog, but we've had some new developments in regard to Lily Moore. We have a few questions for you."

"Lily?" Mr. Jones asked. "Have you found her?"

"No, not yet. Were you gentleman here all evening?" Caldwell asked. Both men looked at each other.

"No detective, we were at dinner at a tapas place in Buckhead with some friends," Harding said.

"I didn't want to leave because the dog was missing, but *he* insisted. We were with potential clients," said Jones obviously still upset.

"Do you have a receipt from dinner?" Lake asked.

"Of course, I do. It was a business dinner. Why?" said Harding.

"Where were you both this morning?" Lake asked.

"At work." Jones wiped his eyes.

"Larry works at Cartoon Network and I work at Bank of America," added Harding.

"This is standard routine. We're just checking your activities to rule you out as suspects in today's events."

"Suspects? What events?" Jones asked, his hand clutching his throat.

"Don't suppose you saw the news?" Lake asked. Both men shook their heads. "Lily Moore was spotted this evening and appeared to be injured. A retired police officer was attacked as well and is missing."

"Oh my God!" Jones exclaimed.

"So as strange as this sounds, we are interested in the whereabouts of your Shih Tzu," Caldwell said. He had used his best "don't fuck with me" cop tone, but the two still looked incredulous.

"I'm confused." Jones leaned forward. "I thought this was about Lily?"

"It is," Lake said. He uncrossed his legs. "Witnesses have given a description of a dog at the scene that matches your dog."

Jones had a look on his face like the lieutenant had

perhaps tapped into some contraband in the evidence room. "You're here because you think our little Shih Tzu is involved with what happened to Lily?"

"Precisely," answered Caldwell, fixing hard eyes on Jones.

"Okay," he yielded. "What is it you need from us?"

"Picture of the dog and sample of her fur," stated Caldwell. "If you have a dog brush, great. And, it would be helpful if you have a bone or something she has bitten or chewed on."

Harding walked toward the chef's kitchen complete with state-of-the-art stainless steel appliances. Caldwell watched him. *Is he limping?* Harding returned with a photo and the receipt from dinner. "Will this do? I'll need the receipt back for tax purposes."

Lake walked over, slipped on his glasses, and examined the picture. "Perfect. Simms, get some gloves and evidence bags from the car."

"Her dog brush is in the laundry room along with a Nylabone," offered Jones, starting to get up. Lake put up a hand. "We'll let Simms retrieve it."

"Oh," said Jones sitting back down.

Once back in the house, Caldwell bagged the photo, dog brush, and bone.

Jones and Harding looked stupefied. Their faces were almost comical, but Caldwell didn't laugh. "We believe Lily Moore is seriously injured and in tremendous danger. If she tries to contact you, notify us immediately."

"Of course," Harding said.

"We also need some DNA from the two of you. If you don't mind coming down to the station to see our forensics expert, Tiny Hunt," Lake said.

Harding's thick eyebrows scrunched down in a furry line.

"We're collecting samples from her entire network of friends and family," Caldwell explained. "Until we check your alibis, no leaving the state." He knew there was no law keeping them in place, but most people didn't realize this.

"Of course not," Harding said. "We'll do anything we can to help Lily."

On the way out Caldwell stopped next to him. "That's quite a shiner."

Harding grimaced and touched his eye. "Tashi and I went for a toy at the same time."

Jones stood behind him pressing his lips together, confusion apparent in his eyes.

LARRY RETREATED TO the kitchen. Frank returned from showing the detectives out and pointed his finger at Larry. "That's it; put your paws where I can see 'em."

He burst out laughing. "You do a really good impression of Detective Hottie."

"You think he's hot?" Frank asked.

Larry squirmed. "No, but Tashi seemed to like him a lot so I gave him that nickname."

"Uh huh," said Frank.

"Lily's hurt," he said, clutching his stomach. The empanadas from dinner were starting to revolt.

"Well at least this is an indication that she's still

alive," offered Frank, patting him on the shoulder.

"Yeah," he sank back into his melancholy. "Lily's hurt and my puppy's gone."

"Tashi will come back. I'll check the backyard to see if she's there." Frank flipped on the back floodlight. "I'll be right back."

Larry looked down at the floor where some of Tashi's toys were scattered. Frank returned a few minutes later, holding some kind of wet rag and a pink backpack.

Larry cocked an eyebrow.

Frank put the items on the counter; his face contorted. "Is there something you need to tell me?"

"What?" He approached the items as Frank backed off. He pulled the dripping rag up by his index finger and thumb. "What is this?" Since it was dripping everywhere, he dropped it in the sink where he could see the run off was a red color. Confused, Larry focused on the backpack. Pulling its contents out one at a time, Larry swallowed a huge knot in his throat. There was Frank's leather jacket, a pair of pink panties, a change purse, and clear flip-flops. He remained eerily calm as he took inventory.

"Where is she Larry? Why didn't you tell me?" Frank shook with rage.

"Where is who?" Larry asked.

"Lily Moore. You've been hiding her, haven't you?" Frank's eyes were huge and a tad scary.

"What the fuck are you talking about? Where did you get this stuff?"

"In the backyard, hung up on the crepe myrtle tree!" he shouted.

"I don't know what's going on here. Maybe we

shouldn't have touched all this stuff. Do you really think this is hers?" Larry asked.

"You tell me. You're the one at home during the day."

He couldn't believe Frank was being such an ass. "Okay. You've got me. I've got her tied up in the garage."

Frank looked at him. Something changed in his eyes that caused Larry to swallow. "I can see you believing some sob story and sheltering her. You really don't know where she is?"

"No!" Larry said. As he turned to the bloody dress in the sink, he felt cold and queasy. "You really think this is hers?" His voice rose in pitch. "This...this is her blood?"

The implication of his findings crept slowly upon Frank's face. "We shouldn't have touched this stuff."

They both backed away from the counter. "I'm gonna sit down for a minute," Larry said. He grabbed a bag of Twizzlers from inside the pantry before walking into the great room. He sat on the couch in stunned silence, chewing on a piece of licorice while his jaw clicked loudly.

Frank followed, but stood nearby. "Was that her dog?"

"Lily didn't have a dog," said Larry unblinking.

"I know she was your friend, but she's involved in some criminal activity."

"Shut up, Frank." Larry hiccupped and began to cry again. It was all too overwhelming. "Weird things were happening. I didn't tell you because I didn't think you'd believe me. I thought someone had been into my makeup the other day. And then there was the really long hair I found in my brush on the sink."

"And the Ferrero Rocher candies," added Frank. "You're allergic to hazelnut so I knew you didn't eat it. A dog couldn't unwrap candy like that and then politely discard the wrappers in the trash can."

"There was blood on my sink after the first night we took in the dog."

"She used my shower," said Frank. "I came home one day and I swear I smelled my body wash and it seemed like someone had gone through my stuff. And my favorite shoes disappeared from the back door."

"It seems that she gained access to our house and used it when we were gone during the day. That's the only explanation I have," Larry said, his mouth full of licorice. He stopped mid-chew and glanced at the licorice twist in his hand. "When did you buy Twizzlers?"

"I didn't buy them."

Larry threw the licorice on the coffee table. "Is she here now?" He looked around, frantically trying to fathom where his friend could be hiding.

Franks eyes darted around. "What if the killer's with her?"

Larry's mouth snapped shut.

"Come with me," Frank said. He retrieved his enormous golf umbrella from the corner of his office and began to search the house. Larry only screamed once when they opened the front hall closet and a tennis racket fell out.

"Quick, call Detective Hottie, you've been assaulted!" Frank said.

Larry pinched the back of Frank's arm, hard.

"Owwww."

They made their way back through the kitchen to the laundry room. Frank flipped the switch on. Detective Simms had been in there, but hadn't noticed something pink trapped beneath the dryer.

With some effort, Frank moved the dryer diagonally revealing a plastic flip-flop. "Those are kind of tacky, don't you think?" Larry asked. "That's not like Lily at all." He peered further behind the dryer to spy something else pink. He was afraid of Frank's reaction, but curiosity got the best of him. He shoved the dryer over a bit more and attempted to reach for another pink object. He sighed. He couldn't fit back there.

"What are you doing?"

"I can't fit. There's something else back there." Frank squeezed a leg in between and stretched to retrieve it. He held a hot pink fanny pack.

Frank's nostrils flared as he shoved it into Larry's chest. "This lady's stuff is all over our house. Her blood is everywhere and we don't know where she is. She's been missing for almost a week. Do you think anyone will believe we don't know anything about anything?"

"Whataya mean? We are two upstanding members of this community." He looked over to see Frank's eyes widen as he frowned.

"Aren't we? Why do you have that look on your face?"

Frank yanked open the door to the garage and flipped on the light switch. "No! No! No!" When Larry peered into the garage, Frank had a homicidal sheen to his features.

"Uh oh."

Franks hands tugged at his hair. "My bike! The bitch took my bike!"

"Lily wouldn't do that unless it was life or death."

"This is bad. I don't want to go to jail." Frank rushed past Larry into the kitchen.

"Don't be ridiculous. Of course we're not going to jail," Larry mumbled while performing a forensic study of the pantry. Things were clicking into place. The Funyuns bag on the top shelf, the Blue Diamond almonds... Why hadn't he noticed Lily's favorite snacks in his house? When he closed the pantry door, he was alone in the kitchen. "Frank?"

He followed the rustling noise to the office. Frank was fastidiously packing up paperwork along with his computer.

"What are you doing?"

"We're going on vacation. Pack your computer and suitcase," he said while jamming fistfuls of paper into the shredder. "I knew there was something suspicious about that old lady."

CHAPTER 🪶 25

AT DEATH'S DOOR

SETH'S PHONE CALLS kept rolling to Dr. Gladson's answering machine, but he remembered that the veterinarian lived in a ranch home adjacent to the clinic off the South Loop in Marietta. Leaving Lily in the front seat, he approached the red brick house and rang the doorbell. Two large dogs barked in warning. The door creaked open a crack with the chain still in place. "Who is it?"

"Seth Moore. You knew my father, Arthur."

"Moore? What do you want?"

Seth shifted his weight to his right leg. "I have a badly injured Shih Tzu in my car."

"Then take her to the emergency clinic on Cobb Parkway."

Seth swallowed the lump in his throat. "Please," he pleaded. "I'm taking a huge risk here, Dr. Gladson. You used to treat a police dog named Barney, a Belgian Malinois. She's...she's like him. I think you may be the only one who can save her." He looked back toward his truck, thinking he should have carried Lily in his arms. Once the vet saw her, there was no way he would refuse.

"You're Arthur's son?" he asked.

"Yes."

"Show me some ID," he insisted.

Seth reached into his back pocket for his wallet and produced his driver's license. Dr. Gladson handed it back to him.

"Bring her in."

Seth ran back to the passenger side of his truck, and retrieved Lily. *God is she dead?* Her tiny mouth gaped open, her tongue hung out the side. The vet unchained the door revealing a man close to Seth's height with shoulder-length gray hair, a mustache, and round wire-rimmed glasses.

Two black Labradors converged on him having made their mad escape through the open door. "Back!" he said.

With one command, Dr. Gladson had the labs back in the house. His brown eyes shined, inquisitive, yet calm. "They seem to like you," he noted as he motioned Seth to follow him next door to the clinic. The keys jingled in his pocket. He unlocked the doors and turned on the lights. The place smelled of nervous animals, pet food, and antiseptic. Seth followed him through a small reception area to an exam room. "What's her name?"

Seth paused, "Tashi."

"What's her real name?" he asked gently.

"Does it matter right now?" asked Seth. "Can't you just treat her?"

"If she has any connection to that Malinois then it would be pertinent to the care I provide," said the vet as he efficiently pulled supplies on to the table.

"She's related to the Malinois."

Lily lay on her side. Seth watched for a breath. He breathed a sigh of relief when he noted the slightest movement of her rib cage.

Dr. Gladson went to work using Seth as his technician for holding and retrieving items. He removed a beautiful necklace from around Lily and placed it on the counter, before x-raying her neck and shoulders. Then he started an IV for fluids and pain medication.

"The wound has already healed a bit." Dr. Gladson studied the exit wound. "That's strange," he said.

"What?"

"I'd say the bullet went clean through the shoulder muscle, but...usually the exit wound is larger than the entrance." He stared at it almost as if he was waiting for it to confess under his pressure.

"Is it still inside her?"

"No. It just occurred to me that perhaps her body rejected it on its own and the wound is closing. I would have liked to clean all her wounds before they closed, but I don't want her to start bleeding again. I'll do the best I can and administer an antibiotic to stave off infection. Her head wound may be trickier. Thankfully, her lungs are clear and I don't detect any signs of internal organ damage."

"Does she have a concussion?" Seth asked.

"Yes, a severe concussion. Her body seems to have gone into its own hibernation state so it can heal."

Dr. Gladson glanced at the necklace on the counter. "That's unusual."

"Yeah," said Seth, eyeing it. He could swear it vibrated and emitted a high-pitched frequency. He sure as hell wasn't touching it.

"I'll put it back on her now," said the vet looking at Seth. Seth wasn't sure that was a good idea, but stepped back from the table. The vet carefully lifted Lily's head to slip the necklace in place. Her body twitched and her eyes popped open, glowing a brilliant green.

Seth touched her gently, "You're okay." Her eyes shut. The hair on the back of Seth's neck stood at attention as he looked at the locket now glowing red.

LILY HAD FELT tremendous pressure pulling her body in every direction. Then spinning and plummeting down, down, down. She didn't understand how one moment she was behind the old abandoned gas station, the next she was sprawled on the damp earth of Frank and Larry's backyard. The house was empty.

Pain had made her shake and vomit violently. Her body naturally shifted into a Shih Tzu. In this form, the pain had dulled slightly. Noting the crucible lying in the mud, she had squirmed over to maneuver the chain around her neck. She remained prone with the crucible underneath her ribs. Warm waves of energy surged through her skin and traveled up her body to her shoulders and head.

The next conscious moment, Lily recognized Seth's scent. Wrapped in his shirt, she felt safe and secure as they sped down the road in his truck that smelled like Abercrombie & Fitch Woods cologne mixed with sweat.

Then bright fluorescent exam lights seared her eyes. She caught glimpses of the man working on her. Seth seemed to trust him, so she did too.

Detecting Seth's anguish, she wished she could let him know it was okay, but the crucible took her away to a place so tranquil that she wasn't sure she cared to find her way back. She stepped off into another's dream...

Lily stood in the middle of a narrow wooden bridge, a fine mist rising up around her from emerald green waters. The evil triumvirate: Blood, Violence, and Pain had fled. Fishermen sang their songs to her from flat-bottomed shanban while women washed laundry in the Tuojiang River. In the distance, the verdant Nanhua Mountains imposed their majestic presence. To the south of the river stood the ancient city wall composed of mauve sandstone. Two watch towers loomed one to the east and the other to the west of the Great Wall.

She was in Waipo's dream. In her village. She walked across the bridge and down the narrow flagstone alleys between the high-gabled wooden houses on stilts. Upon these diaojiaolou or buildings with hanging legs, red lanterns bloomed like poppies in a vertical field.

She felt compelled to walk through town greeting everyone, instinctively knowing their names and faces. Stopping in front of one house, Lily sensed a mystical breeze beckoning her inside. The first floor was a storage area for firewood and gardening supplies. Climbing up the stairs to the second floor, she passed through a front room to the rear where she found an ornately carved kitchen table in front of a fireplace. On the table, steam rose from a cup of tea. Lily sat down on the bench and leaned her face forward allowing the warmth to kiss her face. She enjoyed the aged fuzhuan black tea with lonyan honey. The tea brought to mind sweet red dates. She began to smile, but stopped when her eyes drifted to the corner. A red votive candle flickered in front of a memorial ancestral tablet.

There was no sense of time, no feeling of urgency. When she felt ready, Lily ascended to the third floor, traveling down the hallway to a small room at the end. A bird more magnificent than any she had seen in her life caught her attention. It did not see her gazing upon it from the doorway, but continued a haunting song of wutong trees, warm springs, and mountains.

Before she knew it, she had crossed the threshold and settled upon a twin bed dressed in plain white linens. Mesmerized by the bird's song, she studied it. Although it was the size of a blue heron, it was more elegant than a peacock. Its head and body was that of a pheasant in various shades. The tail consisted of the five sacred colors: red, blue, yellow, white, and black. The fenghuang's story lulled her into a deep sleep. The lightest touch woke her.

Again, she had no knowledge of how much time had passed. Lily gazed up into Waipo's amber eyes saying good-bye to her. Then her grandmother was gone. The bird disappeared. The bed disapparated from underneath her.

When Lily opened her eyes, grief overcame her. Torn from the utopian place that felt as comforting as the womb, she felt cold and naked. Actually, she was naked. She was in a different bedroom. A small lamp illuminated the corner, allowing her to discern the outline of Seth crumpled in an armchair. Warm blankets covered her, but that was all, except for the crucible around her neck. As she went to move her hand, she noted clear tubing tethering her to an IV pole. Using her free hand, she reached up to feel a bandage on her head. She took a moment to allow the silent tears to flow. Her chest tight, she dried her face with a corner of the sheet.

"Seth?" He stirred, knocking his jacket to the floor. "Seth!"

He jerked upright, "Dude!" He focused his eyes on her. "Lily?" Seth stretched his long legs in the process of getting to his feet. She watched his slow approach, each footstep cautious as if it might send a jolt through her frail body.

Good Lord, how bad do I look? "Where are we?"

"Dr. Gladson's. I brought you here last night. How do you feel?"

"A little wonky in the head. What time is it?"

Seth looked at his watch. "Eleven o'clock in the morning. He has blackout drapes. Do you want me to open them?"

She shrugged.

He stepped over and drew the cord. Involuntarily, she held her breath. Despite the closed blinds, daylight filtered into the room displaying dust moats as they swirled in the sunbeams.

"Open the blinds," she said.

He did. Outside, she saw buildings, but they were not diaojiaolou.

Seth's eyes were teary when he turned from the window. "God Lily, I thought you were going to die." He came over and sat on the edge of the bed. He seemed afraid to touch her for fear she would scream in pain.

"I think I'm okay. Nothing really hurts anymore. I just feel weak and extremely stiff."

He nodded. "Your wounds healed before our eyes."

Lily touched the crucible. Seth's eyes followed her

hand. "Where's Mr. Liu?" she queried.

"The police think he's been kidnapped. He didn't do this, did he?" Seth asked, bolting to his feet.

"No. Some man took him."

"What man?" he asked gently.

"The Dark Watcher. He wore a mask."

"You're sure it was the same guy?" Seth asked, settling back down.

"I smelled him."

Seth's eyes flew to the necklace again.

"It's Waipo's. She sent it to Mr. Liu to give to me. It's a crucible. Supposedly, it balances things. Not everyone can touch it."

"Dr. Gladson touched it," he said.

"Shifters are the ones who need to be wary of it."

Seth wiped his eyes. "I'm going to get the doc, let him know you're awake."

Ten minutes later, Dr. Gladson stood over her checking her vitals. *I never thought I'd need a vet, for myself.* She studied his gray hair, young face, and small hoop earrings through each ear and couldn't guess his age.

"Amazing. This is like a month's worth of healing in one night," he said as he checked her head and shoulder wound. "How do you feel?"

"Hungry."

Both men looked at each other. "I'm thinking we should start you on a liquid diet." Her stomach protested. Dr. Gladson looked worried. "What do you feel like?"

"A fourteen pound steak, loaded potato, salad and a chocolate mountain lava cake covered with raspberry sauce."

Dr. Gladson blinked. "Why don't we start with some broth?"

She capitulated since he had saved her life. He redressed her wounds with smaller bandages then went back to the clinic. Seth made himself useful in the kitchen, making Lily a cup of chicken broth that lasted two seconds.

"Easy, Lily!"

"My body needs some fuel. Now go see if this man has bacon, eggs, and biscuits. I'm starving."

Thirty minutes later, she wiped her mouth with a napkin and belched ceremoniously, setting off Seth's car alarm in the driveway. The low rumble didn't alert the humans in the next building, but the dogs barked no doubt hearing it and feeling the vibration.

Seth grimaced, "Must you do that?"

"I was paying my compliments to the cook."

"Dude, that's really not normal."

"Sethasaurus, we passed normal weeks ago."

"Yeah, but if you keep doing that someone's liable to call the cops!" He fished the keys out of his jacket in order to deactivate the alarm.

Returning to the wood-paneled bedroom, he pulled a shaker-style oak chair up to the side of the bed.

"What happened, Lily?" he asked, using a stern Dad-like voice. She wondered if he was even aware of lowering the pitch of his voice.

"Well Seth, someone slapped me so hard I saw Elvis," she said, lowering her pitch like his.

He folded his arms across his chest then stretched out his legs, crossing them at the ankles. "I'm aware you got knocked upside the head."

"Were you aware that it was Mr. Liu's ancient halberd that's been in his family for eons?"

Seth sat up, "But you said it wasn't Mr. Liu?"

"No, some evil man. Actually, a man and a woman. Someone came up behind me." She eyed the IV needle stuck in her arm. "Hey, do you think he can take this shit out; it's really bugging me?"

"Two? Lily. Focus. He'll take the IV out once he sees you tolerated breakfast okay and you've finished that bag of fluids. Now please tell me what the hell happened yesterday or I'm going to lose it."

Pulling the blanket more tightly around her first, she turned to fluff the pillows. Once she was settled in comfortably, she began.

"Waipo passed away." She watched him squirm. "I had tea in her house."

Seth's eyebrows shot up in question.

"Before she passed, I went to her guest room to listen to her pet fenghuang sing me to sleep."

"Fenghuang?" queried Seth.

"It's a sacred Chinese bird whose head is the sky, her eyes the sun, her back the moon, her wings the wind, her feet the earth, and her tail the planets."

"Lil' hon'. You have major narcotics still in your system."

"Seth hon' come look at this crucible!"

He scowled.

"Listen to me. Nothing is as it seems. Our father was part dog. I'm part dog-bird creature. Mom's still out to lunch, most of the time. Grandma held some sort of sacred family secret related to shapeshifters. Mr. Liu was beaten and abducted because of his knowledge of our family. You gonna listen now?"

"You need to calm down!"

The tingling in her back started as a slight tickle. Exhaling slowly, she regrouped and told him the previous day's events ending with Detective Simms seeing her in the woods. He then relayed his ordeal with the police interrogation, explaining that he had to describe the Koko Hitomi incident. Lily had a strong feeling he had edited the version he relayed to her about Hitomi.

"What the hell is the deal with that lady anyway?"

"She has some kind of obsession with me," Seth said.

"Yeah, Peter mentioned that, but I didn't know she still stalked you. Can't the police do something about it?"

"That's the least of their worries right now. They suspect I'm aware of your actions. They were trying to lean on me to see if I knew your current whereabouts. In fact, I'm waiting for a call from them today. I'm sure they will want to follow up."

"What else? Did they say anything about Peter or Mona?"

Seth averted his eyes. "They are investigating Peter's death as well as Mona's in conjunction with your disappearance."

"I want to know what's going on, Seth!"

"What do you mean?"

Before she could answer, Seth's whole body stiffened and he swung his head toward the door.

"What?"

"Stay here Lily. Lock the door!"

With that, he moved faster than she imagined he could,

leaving her to fend for herself with the darn IV pole. Some yelling at the door had her frantically ripping the tape off her arm, pulling the needle out, and applying pressure to the site with a bare hand. Rifling through the dresser drawers, she found a man's large Georgia Bulldogs shirt. She got her head through, but only her right arm due to the soreness in the left shoulder.

As she tiptoed down the hallway, she grabbed a walking stick from the corner of an office to use as a weapon.

"You can't come in," hissed Seth to someone at the door.

"What is she, Seth?" asked the voice.

"Stay away from her!"

As Lily entered the living room, something broke through the doorway, sending an explosion of feathers into the air. It was the most surreal experience. Having been frightened and vulnerable, Lily shifted into a Shih Tzu, losing the stick. Suddenly there was a soft body covering her and growling. "Leave her alone!" boomed a voice overhead.

The pressure on top of her lifted in a flash of fur and cat squalls. Her instincts kicked in. She wanted to chase the kitty. When the scent of another bird wafted to her, her body wavered toward it directionally, like a divining rod to water.

The beast was in her territory. Tashi leapt over the sofa heading for the commotion of feathers and fur. Mid-flight the voice screamed at her, "Lily. No!" That's when she identified the voice. It was Barry White. She recognized that deep baritone anywhere. *But, Barry White is dead.*

Distracted by the voice, she crashed against an end table coming to rest on her back with her paws in the air.

Her shoulder and head throbbed. A laugh erupted overhead followed by a whoosh of feathers. Something grabbed her feet and she felt weightless as she flew through the air upside down. The cat tackled the bird, digging in its claws.

CH-CHK.

Lily fell on her back. Looking up, she watched as feathers and fur swirled slowly down, coming to rest in the living room like fall leaves on a forest floor. Dr. Gladson stood in the doorway with his cocked shotgun trained on the scariest looking bird creature Lily had ever encountered.

"Don't shoot," said the cat sitting oddly with his left paw up in a wave position. The cat was talking like Barry White. *What the hell kind of narcotics did Dr. Gladson give me?*

The cat did a free-running move involving a back flip over the couch. Two seconds later up popped her brother pulling on Calvin Klein boxers.

Lily was stunned.

"What the hell?" Dr. Gladson asked. Lily wasn't sure which scenario was more bizarre: the free-running, talking cat or her gun-slinging hippy vet.

"Koko is leaving. Aren't you?" Seth directed.

Koko?

Dr. Gladson kept his gun on Koko the bird. For some reason that made Lily think of cuckoo birds and she started to chuckle.

She had to give the vet credit. When Koko the cuckoo

bird shifted back into a hot naked woman, he kept it together. Unlike Seth, Koko was unfazed by her nakedness. She stared at Lily like a hawk does its prey. *Don't worry, I just want to talk.*

She had spoken in Lily's head and she sure didn't look like she just wanted to talk.

Dr. Gladson kicked her clothes to her. She shimmied into the dress then slipped into her heels. Seth handed the purse to her like a perfect gentleman. He had managed to slip on torn jeans, but his shirt lay shredded on the floor from the violence of his shift.

"What is she, Seth?"

"She's a dog, that's it."

"Bull shit." Koko Hitomi glared at Lily who cowered by Dr. Gladson's legs.

"She's guarding something. Whatever it is, it makes my skin crawl."

They all watched from the doorway as she backed her Range Rover out of the driveway. The front door hung askew on its hinges. Dr. Gladson rested the gun against the wall so he could attempt to fix the door. It creaked and squeaked as he tried to force the splintered wood back into the space.

He was a determined man. After he shoved it in somehow, he turned to them. "I should call the authorities, but I have no idea what the Sam hill I'd tell them." He looked over at Lily. "You all right?" She limped over to him in order to lick his hand. She had new wounds on her legs from psycho bird's talons. They both stopped to stare at Seth.

"Dude, I told you she's crazy!" He laughed while

raking his hands through his hair. Deep gashes across his back oozed blood. "I'll be fine," he said in response to their shocked faces. "I heal almost as fast as Lily."

Lily scurried past Seth to the back bedroom, dragging the t-shirt in her mouth, her Shih Tzu tail between her legs. After she found a baseball bat and beat him, they were going to talk, but she needed to shift first. Returning a few minutes later in the Georgia Bulldogs t-shirt, she walked in on Dr. Gladson reaming him out.

His tirade ended with, "You should have told me, Seth. You need to leave now!" He looked at her. He meant both of them.

CHAPTER ✦ 26

FROM THE LOST NOTES OF PETER MARX

July 28, 2010

Dr. H's secret side project relates to shifters—she is attempting to trigger the condition in dormant subjects she refers to as Vestiges.

Vestiges are individuals born into shapeshifter families who don't exhibit the ability to shapeshift. According to her, the phenomenon triggers during adolescence. I continue to refer to this as a phenomenon because scientifically, I cannot differentiate the difference between shifters and humans at the cellular level.

For Subject T and C, she is attempting to suppress their shifting with Inderal because they are having difficulties controlling their condition.

For the Vestiges, she is utilizing anabolic steroid injections in the hopes of activating the dormant condition.

Subject T and C are dear friends. I'm concerned for their well-being. The Vestiges worry me as well. I assume they came to the clinic initially to receive care for PTSD. This doesn't strike me as an efficacious treatment protocol. At this point, I'm keeping such thoughts to myself in order not to jeopardize my graduate work. Dr. H doesn't involve me in the work with the Vestiges. She doesn't even allow me to meet them or review the notes. What I know, I've garnered piecemeal from her pedantic lectures while working together.

    —Peter

CHAPTER 27

LUCKY CAT

LILY AND SETH pulled up to the McDonald's drive thru. They were both wearing some of Dr. Gladson's old clothes. He had actually gotten them in decent shape, attending to their wounds and providing them with pain meds, antibiotics, and a first aid kit before sending them on their way. Lily didn't feel so much like an ejected house guest, but a kid whose mother has packed her things and sent her off to summer camp.

She removed her seatbelt so she could lean in to read the menu. Neither stress, nor death threats, nor crazy homicidal cuckoo birds hindered her voracious appetite. She ordered enough food to feed a football team.

Seth stared at her. "A Big Mac and a Quarter Pounder?"

Lily shrugged then winced from her wound. "What'll you have kitty—a Filet-O-Fish sandwich?" she asked.

Scowling at her, he placed his order which included a Filet-O-Fish sandwich. He pulled into a parking space while she gorged.

"Don't you dare belch," he warned as she dipped the French fries in the shake before eating them.

Once Lily put herself in a food coma, she reclined back in the seat. They both stared out the windshield watching children on the playground. "We used to be innocent," she said more to herself than Seth.

Seth cleared his throat, "I'm sorry I didn't mention my issues."

He did not sound sorry, more like someone inconvenienced because he'd been busted.

"Listen, I'm letting my food digest. Otherwise, we'd have a throw down right now," Lily said. She looked around the parking lot. "We need to get out of here. Do you have to use the litter box before we get on the road?"

"Quit with the cat jokes!" he said.

"All right. All right. Geez, don't be such a pussy."

Seth jerked her across the truck by the neck of her shirt. His eyes changed to a lighter blue color, dark aqua, with deeper clouds of color surrounding his slit pupil. "Lily, if you hadn't almost died last night, I would be kicking the Shih Tzu out of you."

"Bring it!"

Lily felt the crucible burn and throb with the change in her mood. Her fingertips and spine tingled in response to his physical threat. They maintained a stare-down for two minutes. Then he let go of the t-shirt. With her good arm, she attempted to fix the stretched-out neckline.

"What am I going to do with you?" Seth asked. He wore Dr. Gladson's Greenpeace t-shirt that was tight enough to reveal his sinewy torso.

"Do with me? You're the lying, sneaking, philandering SOB!"

His hair stood on end. She watched him take deep slow breathes to relax his body while distracting himself with the kids on the playground. She was impressed how quickly he decompressed.

"Take me to mom's—I can hide above her garage," she suggested.

"Yeah, because that's not the first place they'll look. Besides, Emanuel would rat you out in two point five seconds."

"Let's think of places we used to go as kids," Lily said.

"Right. You know what, why don't you let me do the thinking since you suffered some brain trauma," he griped.

"Listen, just 'cause you have a psycho bird girlfriend and you're possessed by the feline version of Barry White, doesn't mean you need to give me shit!"

"She's not my girlfriend," he seethed.

"Fine, but there's no way you can deny that you're a cat."

He sighed, putting his fish sandwich down on the dashboard. "Lily. I think I was adopted."

Lily groaned. She couldn't handle any more drama. Boring had been such a nice state of being. "Seth, you were not adopted."

"I'm serious. My point is I am a cat. Not a dog like Dad. Not a ferocious lion, but a lucky cat."

"What do you mean by lucky?" *I don't like the sound of this.*

"From what I can tell, I resemble a large Japanese Bobtail. Now they apparently originated in China, but it's got me wondering if I'm Japanese."

"Seth, for God's sake, what are you talking about? I almost died last night. Let's just focus on the issues at hand and we can explore random adoption accusations later, okay?"

He glared at her.

"Sorry, but sometimes you're just a bit paranoid. Why the hell would you be adopted?" asked Lily.

"I don't know."

"Okay, just explain to me what you are."

"I'm a maneki neko, a beckoning *Japanese* lucky cat. I'm supposed to bring good fortune. The figurines in Japanese businesses have their left paw up to beckon customers into their stores. I think the Barry White voice comes from an instinctual urge to seduce or lure people to me."

Suddenly, his cat rescuing, girl chasing and obsessive sushi eating made sense. Lily knew her mouth was hanging open, but she couldn't seem to make it work.

He looked to her in challenge.

"You're not Japanese, Seth."

"Why do you say that?"

"Because everything is made in China. Let's turn you over. I bet it's written in red on your butt."

"You're not a nice person," he grumbled.

She sighed. "Am I even a person?"

He shrugged.

"You're really comforting, Seth."

"Right back at you."

Lily watched the little boy on the playground maneuver across the monkey bars. "What's with your crazy acrobatics?"

"Oh, I have some mad free-running skills in both forms," he said, beaming.

"Cool," she smiled back. She wanted to keep him off the adoption crap. In between slurps of chocolate shake, she considered her brother's feline status. "So, does Koko want to eat you?"

"No," he stated firmly. "But she sure was fascinated with you and that damn necklace. I've never seen her that weirded out."

"She's one scary creature." Lily shuddered. "I guess the whole unrequited love thing will make a bitch crazy. So she has the hots for you and you like someone else?"

Silence.

That's when the proverbial light bulb went off in her head. "Seth?"

"What?"

"Do you have a thing for Katie?"

His ears flushed crimson. "I've been *seeing* her."

"How much of her have you been seeing?" she asked.

Silence.

Now she was seething. Was she not a trustworthy enough person that he could tell her things? What the hell was wrong with Katie that she lied to her, too? They grew up together, played together, spent summers at camp and at her parent's cabin.

"My love life is none of your business," Seth said.

"Katie's dad is in Sedona this time of year."

Seth looked startled. "Dude, I haven't met her parents or anything. We're just dating, casually."

"No, I'm not...listen Sylvester, I don't care if you're doing my friend and her pet cat, too. I think the couple of knocks on my head did me some good. Katie's father and stepmother are not in this state. They're in Arizona. Their cabin in Helen is empty. Now let's get going. That couple on the motorcycle is staring at us."

"Katie never mentioned her parents had a cabin," Seth said, his mouth in a pout.

Lily stared back at him. "It backs to the Chattahochee National Forest—very private."

He threw the truck into reverse and navigated toward the highway. Helen was about an hour and a half northeast of the city.

"I'm not sure about this," Seth said. "How do I check on you?"

"It's called a phone."

They looked at each other.

"Buddha's butt!" exclaimed Lily.

"Lily—"

"Watch the road!"

"No reason to freak out."

"We just left all of my stuff at Larry's," she said.

"The phone is in *my* name," Seth said. "Fuck!"

"Wow. They might think you offed the old lady and then came after me," she reasoned aloud to herself.

"Thanks," Seth said, his mouth flat in a grimace.

"Huh. On a positive note, now Frank may blame *you* for what I did to his Fireblade."

Seth's eyebrow rose. "What happened to the Fireblade?"

"There's a possibility it is still crashed by the dumpster behind the old Stewart's gas station."

"In Kennesaw?"

Lily fidgeted with Dr. Gladson's Georgia Bulldogs t-shirt.

"Stop stalling and tell me."

"I was in one place. Then, suddenly I was pulled apart

and hurled into another."

Seth's mouth dropped open. "Okay. I get it. You don't remember from the brain trauma."

"No. I'm certain I got sucked into thin air in Kennesaw and spit out in the Manor's backyard in Ansley Park."

"Like you thought about it and you poofed there?" suggested Seth.

"No poofing. Feels more like being swallowed, digested and hurled out."

"Nice."

Since she already sounded like a raving nut, she figured she'd disclose all. "In addition to that and the mind diarrhea, I've been...in other people's dreams."

"I don't understand." Seth said. He regripped the wheel and exhaled a long slow breath.

She knew he felt stressed out of his mind after the night they had. "Dreams. I walk...I talk to people in their dreams," she said, her voice shaking. "I think that's how I saw Waipo."

Seth reached across, found her hand, and squeezed. "Let's just get you situated at the cabin."

Lily fought back tears. Her body had been on autopilot due to the shock. Now the reality of it all exhausted her. "Thanks for saving my life, Seth," she said. "I'm sorry I've made a mess of yours."

"You haven't made a mess of my life. I take full responsibility for that."

They traveled in silence for several minutes.

"You sure this won't be an obvious place?" Seth asked.

"Katie told me once that it's under her stepmother's

last name, Hughes. Her parents own a townhouse in Buckhead, this cabin, and a place in Sedona. No one really comes out here until July."

"Okay," Seth said.

Leaning her head back on the seat, she gazed out at the lush Georgia foliage. The trees reminded her of Waipo's village. Her head, shoulder, and Koko gashes hurt, but she had taken a painkiller at lunch so things were down to a dull throb. She could almost be at peace if the police and a killer weren't chasing her. Melancholy set in as she considered her brother's secret life. Her father's and Peter's death had sent her into a narcissistic world. She hadn't been available to Seth. *What kind of sister am I?*

"Sorry that I wasn't there for you Seth." She turned to look over at him while palming the crucible. The warm tingling crept up her arm and into her shoulder, soothing its ache.

"What?"

"You didn't trust me enough to talk to me."

"That's not it, Lily," he said swallowing. She watched him stretch his double-jointed fingers before repositioning them on the wheel.

"What happened, then?"

His shoulders tensed. He turned to her with a sardonic grin, "Oh, so you want to know about the Moore curse, do you?" He raised his eyebrows up and down.

"Go ahead."

"Where to start—"

"With Dad," she demanded.

"Remember how Reggie and I used to go back in the field behind the house and practice ball?"

"Yeah. That was a great place, private. No one ever came back there," Lily said with a smile.

"I don't even want to know," he tucked his hair behind an ear. "You're right. No one ever came back there, but Barney did. Shit. I was standing there holding a joint that Reggie and I got from Ronnie Oaks. They were with me. I hadn't even lit it."

Lily's jaw dropped. "What the hell were you thinking?"

"The damn dog growled and went after us like criminals. Reggie and Ronnie ran all the way back to Ronnie's house. I had put the joint in my pocket and ran back to the house with the crazy dog nipping my legs. I thought the darn beast had lost it.

"Mr. Liu was there. He didn't even call the dog off. He just told me to go in the house. Five minutes later, Dad walked in. He made me empty my pockets then proceeded to toss my room. Dad grounded me for a month and threatened to drop me off at inpatient rehab if I ever touched the stuff again. He insinuated that he had ways of knowing. There are more stories like that, Lil. I finally pieced it all together after his death. I wished I had known when he was alive." He shook his head, his nose wrinkled. "I hadn't even lit it."

Lily laughed so hard tears streamed down her face.

"It's not that funny."

"It is. Can you see Reggie going home to Mama Green worrying the whole time that Dad's gonna rat him out to her?"

He smiled. "I don't think he did. I would have known." Seth cracked the windows as they continued down the highway. The warm breeze streamed in, blowing her hair. Lily savored the feeling of it lifting the stray strands from her neck and tickling her cheek.

Under normal circumstances, she would have been on her lunch break. Instead, she sat next to her brother, the cat, while pondering her life as a fugitive.

"I changed the first time in college. My metamorphosis was not triggered by anxiety or fear, but rather another emotion." His ears tinged red again.

"Okay. What happened?"

"Date. Thankfully, she went to the bathroom to slip into something more comfortable. When she came out, there I was in cat form. I was starting to talk to her when she came at me. I realized immediately something was wrong when she picked me up. I saw us in the mirror together. Like you, I thought I was hallucinating.

"The good news was that my date loved cats. She thought it had been sweet that I left her a present. We had been drinking so she fell asleep which allowed me to slip out the window. I'd like to say that it was the strangest night of my life, but things got a lot stranger when I met Koko."

The mention of Koko got Lily's ire up. She turned to the window again to calm herself. Everything seemed exaggerated: sharper, greener, bigger, smaller, fresher. She wondered if she would ever get used to her new intense senses. It took great resolve to pull herself back and listen to Seth with an open mind.

"What happened with Koko?" Her legs throbbed at the mention of her name. *Honestly, the bitch tried to kill me.*

"I don't think she was trying to kill you, Lil."

She clenched her teeth. More of her mind diarrhea.

"Koko is more interested in studying things. She was curious, trying to establish dominance, and possibly sensed the power of the crucible."

Her poor brother had been dealing with Koko so long that he was impervious to her craziness.

"This is where we have differing opinions. She threatened me inside my head!"

"She did?"

The reminder of the threat triggered her hyper vigilance. "You don't think she's following us, do you?" Lily checked the sideview mirror.

"I don't think so," he said. He wasn't convincing, particularly because he glanced in the driver side mirror.

"How did you even get involved with Koko?" It felt strange to refer to the terrifying bird lady by a name that was more suitable for a fluffy kitten.

"I was in her class. One day, she asked if I wanted to get a beer." He shrugged. "I'm not gonna lie. I thought she was pretty hot. One thing led to another. I had less control over *everything* back then. We went out several times—the whole time without me knowing she was a tengu, a shapeshifter. I hadn't met another one. I didn't know what they smelled like. I just knew I was drawn to her. Things became weird. She started communicating in my head, reading my mind, and entering my dreams. I never felt so violated. She was the reason I left school. I woke up naked with her in the clinic lab. She called the cops. There was a big hullabaloo and I've been trying to get away from her ever since. She's not bad really, more obsessive...about her research. About certain people."

"What's a tengu?"

"My laptop's in the backseat. I'll show you when we get to the cabin. It's a creature from Asian folklore. It's a very strong warrior bird. Some stories describe them as goblins of the forests and mountains."

"Lovely," Lily said, the sarcasm keeping her voice from trembling. Buddha's belly, she prayed she wasn't a goblin. "Okay, you think possibly I'm some kind of goblin. Never mind, I don't want to know anymore about the tengu right now. Just go back to your story. So the police came and you were naked with Koko. I'm asking the obvious, but why didn't you shift into a cat before the police got there?"

"I couldn't." He became very quiet.

Her patience had run out. "Seth, you really need to tell me everything. Things have gotten to the breaking point. We can't afford to have secrets."

He took a deep breath. "I was drugged Lily."

"What do you mean?"

"Peter—"

"What about Peter?" she spat.

"See this is why I could never tell you anything."

She counted to ten allowing the tingling to subside on her back. Popping out wings right now would be painful.

"Peter and Dr. Hitomi were using Inderal in their research, a common drug used to control blood pressure, heart palpitations, and Post Traumatic Stress Disorder. Also, some musicians have used it to control stage fright."

"Yes, I'm aware." *Like I didn't know about my boy-friend's research.*

He took a deep breath. "She slipped some in my drink that night to see if it would help suppress my shapeshifting.

I blacked out, but then the Inderal did control my shifting for a few days. It was so nice not spending every waking moment concentrating on being in control. Other than the initial rough twelve hours, it seemed like the miracle drug. The oral dose took even longer for its full effect—twenty-four hours. And it had a more pronounced side effect. Don't ask me why this causes blackouts in shifters. It certainly isn't a side effect of the medication in humans."

"She drugged you? And you don't think this lady is capable of murder?"

"Lily, I don't know what's happening. I tried to stop participating in her study. She's been on my case ever since."

"God, Seth. I'm sorry. Why would any shapeshifter take that stuff?"

Silence.

Lily felt a sick pull in the middle of her stomach. "How long, Seth?"

"I quit after Peter died, but fell off the wagon after you were attacked by Miller. Haven't done it since the night before I went to see Mr. Liu."

She couldn't look at him. In fact, she had to remind herself to breathe.

"Peter brought syringes of Inderal to me and your neighbor every Saturday when we played basketball."

Not judging. Not judging. Not judging. Not judging.

"I don't know what happened to them Lily. Honestly. It wasn't until Mona died that I got suspicious that one thing had anything to do with the other."

"Pete?" She couldn't believe that she lived under the same roof and slept in the same bed with her brother's drug dealer.

"Lily, it's not what you think. He and the professor thought they were helping us. Inderal does not normally have an addictive quality. There was no way for them to understand what truly was happening to me or to your neighbor."

It was all too much to process. The geriatric neighbor next door was a shapeshifter?

"You know what's really screwed up?" he asked. "I truly didn't realize how much the medicine had impaired me until you started to shift."

"What do you mean?"

"You're so strong. You can...well broadcast in people's heads. You can dream walk, like Koko. My life's consisted of wandering in and out of a fog. I wonder how I would be if I hadn't been taking this medication all along. Would I actually be a more substantial creature?"

"Uh, Seth, did you miss the turn?"

"What?"

"Never mind, it's just, we could have taken Alternate 75 and gone around Helen."

"No way, and miss all this?" he asked. She managed a weak smile.

"What was Mona?"

His eyes widened. "A tiger," he whispered.

They rode along in silence after that. Lily looked out the window at the roadside signs for Georgia mountain honey, mescadine cider, and sorghum syrup. Every five minutes they passed another handwritten sign for boiled peanuts. Her stomach growled. As they made their way through Cleveland, Georgia, she breathed a bit easier, just another twenty minutes to the cabin. Thunderheads dominated the sky. One looked like an ominous man's face with his mouth open in a silent scream. She averted her eyes to cast off the nasty vision. Down below was a trio of vultures palavering on a low fencepost of a barren field. *Blood, Violence, and Pain, incarnate.* Her hackles rose.

Ten minutes later when they were outside Cleveland, she exhaled in relief as the granite face of Mount Yonah ghosted through the clouds. Trees whizzed by in a blur. She couldn't shake the unease, though; it crept over her like a cold sweat.

Who is this stranger in the seat next to me? Yesterday had been terrifying, but this moment wasn't much better. She didn't know who her brother was anymore. The urge to shift to Shih Tzu mode and hang her head out the window was overwhelming. Anything to cleanse herself. *Better yet, I'll hang him out the window. It would make me feel so much better.*

"I'd like to see you try it," he laughed.

"What?!"

"Hang me out the window."

"Get out of my head!"

"I'm not doing it. You are," he said, his hair bristling.

At the next light, Seth swung the truck into a Walmart shopping center. Lily stayed in the truck pondering her new world while Seth stocked up on supplies. Nobody was who, or rather *what*, she thought they were. A wave of nausea hit her. She didn't think it was the pain meds, but the latest influx of information. She was in a worse mood when Seth returned to the car with scissors and hair dye...for her.

CHAPTER 28

CALDWELL'S DREAM/INTERROGATION

LILY SAT ON top of the metal table in the interrogation room wearing a pink mini sundress with little daisies on it and white platform sandals. As she crossed her legs, she studied the shoes. Her eyebrows rose. "Stripper shoes?"

Caldwell paced back and forth in front of her which was no easy feat considering the size of the room. He grinned. "What's wrong with the shoes?"

She twirled a strand of her hair then stopped. "Hey, it's your dream. Who am I to judge? Knock yourself out."

Before he knew it, he had closed the space between them, grabbed her jaw in his hands and kissed her soft wet lips. She kissed back. He caught himself sliding his one hand down her arm to rest on her bare thigh. With a jolt he remembered who and what he was. He removed his hand from her thigh and placed it on his forehead. "Sorry. I have no idea what's the matter with me."

Lily sat up. Her pouty mouth was open and her eyes gleamed. "Why don't you sit down in the chair."

He sat down. The sensible cop in him surfaced from somewhere. "Where's Li Liu?"

She bit her lip. Her eyes were wet. "I don't know. They took him."

"Who?"

223

"I couldn't see their faces. They wore ski masks."

"They?"

"Man and woman. The man was big, maybe as tall as my brother. He had blue eyes, gruff voice. The woman I didn't see at all. She bashed me in the head with a metal weapon."

"Jesus." Caldwell looked her over. There wasn't a scratch on her. "Am I hallucinating?"

"No. I'm here. Kind of."

"Why did you run?"

"That's complicated."

"I need to know where you are?"

Lily's head turned to the side. A dark figure stood in the doorway holding a gun.

She screamed.

CHAPTER 29

EVIDENCE

CALDWELL WALKED PAST a new recruit on his way in to the office. He shook his head at Tiny who was telling the unsuspecting victim about the time he had been an extra in the *Lord of the Rings* movies. As Caldwell stepped on to the elevator, he heard Tiny delivering the punch line, telling the female cadet he had hairy feet, too.

The doors closed, but Caldwell knew there would be a pregnant pause while the unsuspecting nube considered whether or not first, if there were any black hobbits and second, did he really have hairy feet. Tiny had a vice all right. He loved to make people squirm.

Caldwell tried to shake off his night of distressed sleep. If anyone knew the head case he'd become, they'd send him to a shrink. *I just need some coffee.*

Ten minutes later Caldwell sat in Lake's office at his round meeting table ready to go over forensic reports. Tiny sat across from him on the edge of the chair, his legs dangling.

"Tiny," acknowledged Caldwell. "You borrow those glasses from Mr. Potato Head?"

Tiny looked at him. It dawned on Caldwell what it might sound like to Tiny. "I meant the color, not the size." They were bright yellow. Caldwell's cheeks burned.

Tiny laughed. "I know what you meant, Simmulator."
He breathed a little easier.

"You look like you're makin' three tracks in the dirt," Tiny said.

He shrugged. "Losing some sleep over this case."

"Tell me about it." Tiny glanced toward the lieutenant. Lake's eyebrow rose in question.

"Okay, for starters. The scene at Grady High School turned up dog fur and these weird feathers. Despite running the information through the GBI lab and Fish and Wildlife, there is no match with any known bird species," Tiny said.

"What about some exotics from South America, Africa, or Asia?" Caldwell asked.

"Nothing in the world," Tiny stated. "The morphologists from the wildlife laboratory say the closest DNA match would be to a peacock, but color and size varies greatly."

"There isn't a question in my mind that these scenes are linked. The same unique feathers were found all over Liu's studio," Lake said. He stepped up to their victim board and pursed his lips. His face looked like he'd tasted something sour.

"True, Lieutenant. But I don't get it. This guy comes in packing a forty-five and a bird on his shoulder?" Tiny asked.

"Say hello to my little friend," Caldwell said in his best gangster voice.

"Hello," said Tiny mimicking a parrot. They both doubled over cackling. They stopped when they realized Lieutenant Lake was glaring at them.

"You guys done?"

"Yeah, sorry Lieutenant," Caldwell said.

Tiny cleared his throat and stifled an unmanly giggle with his hand.

"You two are totally inaccurate. You see the size of those feathers? This ain't some parrot." Lake smirked. "So, I've put out feelers to animal shelters, dog grooming places, and pet stores to track down the Shih Tzu and mysterious bird connection. I'll check the exotic bird websites as well," Lake said.

"Thanks, Lieutenant," Caldwell said.

Lake nodded before looking to Tiny. "Do we have the results back yet on the human hair from that sweatshirt found in Midtown?"

"It doesn't match Hitomi. I haven't seen anything from Harding or Jones yet."

"When will we get their results?" Lake stood by the corner of his desk squeezing the stress ball.

"I don't have their samples." Tiny looked over his yellow frames at Caldwell.

"They didn't show?" Caldwell held his breath.

Tiny shook his head and darted his eyes to Lake.

"Shit!" Caldwell put a hand to his head, trying to massage out the knot that had just formed at his temple.

Lake tilted his head and stared at Caldwell.

"Ewww. They gonna run?" Tiny asked.

Caldwell and Lake locked eyes.

"We better check in with those two," Lake said, tossing the ball back in the middle of his desk.

Caldwell stood up, grabbed his cell phone from his pocket, and shuffled through the file in front of him. He attempted every number he had for Jones and Harding, getting no response. He pulled his things together getting ready to bolt.

Lake put a call into an Atlanta patrol officer to go over to the Ansley Park house.

"Stay put," commanded Lake. "Wait until we get word. No sense going off like a blind bird in a hail storm."

Caldwell froze. They all had birds on the brain. And dogs. And sexy Asian chicks—okay that might just be him.

"Let's talk about the Liu scene," Lake said, not blinking. "Tiny?" Caldwell sat down on the edge of the office chair.

"We've been coordinating with the Kennesaw PD. The rain and chaos compromised the scene. Still working on the tire tread pattern for the perp who according to Caldwell fled from behind the barn. It was mud soup back there and there were so many previous tracks from tractors, farm equipment Liu used—we'll have to see what we can get. We were able to decipher tread on the motorcycle presumably used by Lily Moore to flee. It's consistent with a sport bike," Tiny said.

"What about the blood in the studio?" Lake asked.

"Blood type matches Moore's and Liu's but it will be at least a week before we get full DNA results. There were cast off and drips of blood, consistent with stabbing, in the kitchen area which we believe are Liu's. Can't be sure if Liu was shot as well. We just recovered one bullet from the wall by the sliding door. There was some blood spatter in the hallway of the studio. Not enough trajectory to indicate gunshot. Could be from blunt force trauma.

"Ballistics come back?" Lake asked.

"Bullet found went through a thick tapestry on the wall

so it was remarkably intact. No blood found on it, just fibers. Ballistics identified it as a .45 caliber hollow point. Markings on the bullet suggest it was fired from a polygonal barrel. No casings were retrieved from the scene. There is GSR on the clothing and wig that we suspect belonged to Lily Moore. Long dark strands of hair on the inside of the wig are most likely hers. Blood all over the items matches her blood type."

"The wig definitely Moore's?" Caldwell asked. He tried to control his voice from cracking.

"Looks that way," said Tiny.

"GSR on Moore's clothing could indicate she fired a weapon," Lake said.

"She wasn't holding a gun," Caldwell said.

"You don't know she didn't have one on her," Lake said. "Or threw it off into the woods before you saw her, and we haven't found it yet."

Caldwell looked at Lake. "Sir, she didn't have a gun on her. She was naked."

Tiny shook his head. "Lieutenant, there's a bullet hole in the torn dress. I doubt she shot herself in the shoulder. Besides, the angle of trajectory suggests a taller person; at least six foot. Moore is five foot six. Someone else was firing in the woods. Same bullets found lodged in a tree match those pulled from the studio wall. Between Kennesaw and Ernie's hounds, that area was covered five times over. No weapon was found."

"I don't understand why an innocent woman is disguising herself and running from the authorities?" Lake said.

"She was injured sir. Could be amnesia, or kidnapping," Caldwell said, his mind racing.

"The team noted size twelve *and* size nine men's boots with Liu's size eight and a half. The pattern suggests the perp dragged him out the front door. Moore's trail of blood is out the back. Team says that there is only one set of footprints by the bike suggesting she was alone." Tiny looked over at Caldwell.

There went his kidnapping theory.

"We've narrowed the shoe tread down to Timberland men's work boots," he added. "They're as common as..."

"Tits on a Hooter's girl," Caldwell blurted.

Lake threw his pen down on the table. "What the hell did this girl get herself into?"

Caldwell suppressed an impulsive retort that would have gotten him in trouble. He'd reached his quota for the day. "I bet Liu knew," he said.

"And her brother," added Lake.

"We need to pay him a visit," Caldwell said.

Lake nodded.

"Anything else, Tiny?" Lake asked.

"We've got two perps here according to footprints. Not much in the way of fingerprints left behind. We've matched fingerprints on a pair of sunglasses found in the woods to Lily. We were able to lift *another* set of prints from these glasses as well. We didn't find a match with anything in the database or from the evidence collected from suspects."

"Thanks," Lake said.

With that, Tiny returned to his office. Caldwell sat still in the chair, stewing. According to his dream, one of the perps was a woman, but he had no evidence to support that. The size nine Timberlands could have been a man's.

"What are your thoughts, Simms?" Lake asked, pulling into the round meeting table.

"Just trying to figure out the second perp. We could have a man and woman working together."

"It's something to keep in mind. Anything else?"

"Got the search warrants for the Hitomi house, office, and lab. We need to check emails, phone numbers, lab equipment and logs. Maybe we'll find syringes like the one at the Sinclair crime scene," Caldwell said.

"Why don't you follow up regarding the Jones/Harding household and Seth Moore? I'll go into Hitomi's with the warrant team."

"Will do," said Caldwell.

Lake smacked him on the shoulder as he headed out of the office.

Caldwell dialed Seth Moore's cell phone and left him a message. The Patrol officer, who Lake asked to check the Jones/Harding residence, beeped in to let him know there was no sign of anyone at home. Caldwell called all their numbers including work numbers again. Neither man had shown up for work yesterday.

He called the patrol officer back. "Hawkes. You mind staying put? I'm on my way over. We need to take a quick glance at the property."

"No problem," he said.

They didn't have a warrant yet to search the property, but both men looked along the periphery of the yard to see if anything stuck out. Caldwell leaned against the back of the house and studied the setting. His eyes scanned the stonework on the patio, followed the purple blooms of the vine climbing the arbor, took in the pink lilies on the koi pond, and stopped at the Buddha sitting resolute at the back wall. The property told of meticulous work and patience. He tried to imagine Larry Jones fleeing town. It would take a lot for a person to leave this environment.

Caldwell's eyes travelled across the lawn once more coming to rest at the base of a purple crepe myrtle. An unnatural green glowed against the pine mulch. Two seconds later, he stood above a blood-spattered cell phone. After a quick trip to the car, Caldwell carried the bagged item with him preparing to check in with Lake. At the garage, he heard a tapping sound.

CHAPTER ✒ 30

SANCTUARY

THE HUGHES/QUINN COUNTRY property backed up to the Smithgall Woods Wildlife Preserve just outside of Helen. It took Seth and Lily several attempts to find the correct road off Alternate 75. They passed Hootenanny Hills Drive as well as Goats on the Roof Restaurant. Finally, after they turned around twice, they found Horton Creek, a narrow gravel road marked by a handmade sign that read, "Pat's Place." Unlike them, apparently Pat *wanted* to be found.

They drove slowly over the gravel, passing a dilapidated trailer with a propane tank. The next lot looked vacant. A green John Deere tractor sat abandoned in the center, surrounded by four weathered school buses parked helter-skelter. Wildlife had claimed the vehicles. Bird poop dotted the rusted paint. Ivy and kudzu snaked through shattered windows and out holes in the roofs.

"Crrreeeepy," whispered Seth.

They passed eight more abodes ranging from "cute country cottage" to "scary inbreeding zone."

"Are you sure we are on the right road?" he asked.

"Yep."

They drove up a steep hill coming to a fork of two driveways. The addresses were not visible. "Stay left," she

said.

Seth slammed on his brakes before three deer leapt across the road and disappeared into the woods. She could smell them. The pungent odor made her cough.

At the end of the quarter-mile drive Seth let out a low whistle as their hideout came into view. The cottage consisted of natural wood siding, enormous picture windows, a stone chimney, and wrap-around deck.

"Why didn't you tell me about this before?" Seth asked.

"Gee I don't know. Maybe because breaking and entering my best friend's family's house just isn't something that occurs to me normally."

"Point taken," he said agreeably. Seth had been manically happy since he had purged himself of all of his secrets. She was flip-flopping through emotions faster than a politician changes platforms.

"The key may not be where they used to keep it," Lily said.

They got out of the truck and walked alongside the house, glancing up at it as if it were watching them. They took the quaint stepping stones engraved with various quotes on them down the incline to a cement birdbath. Smiling cherubs and lambs decorated the pedestal holding the flower-shaped basin.

They stopped on either side of it.

"Cherubs always seem evil to me," Seth said. "Look, their eyes are telling us 'run, run away from the Quinn house.'"

She gave him a withering look. "In the last week, I've been attacked by a date rapist, shot, almost blown up by a necklace, and you're scared of a bird bath?"

"Demonic bird bath covered in Georgia's finest pollen slime."

"Say a little prayer." She tilted the bowl of the birdbath sloshing the yellow-green soup on to the ground. Reaching her hand between the bowl and the pedestal, she found salvation.

The silver key was old and chipped, but to Lily it looked like the rarest diamond sparkling in the sun. Seth let out a whoop. Lily did a happy dance involving a lot of butt shaking. She halted when her shoulder protested.

Seth ran back to the car while Lily dashed up the rear stairs leading on to the deck. *A hot tub!* She forced herself to run past the hot tub and around the porch swing to un-lock the front door. Next to the door was a cute plaque decorated with ivy scrolling around painted letters that read, "The Quinns." She hesitated a moment before reaching up to turn the plaque over. *There.* Now it was just a blank white plaque.

She pushed the front door open and flipped on the lights. Huge glass windows let in shafts of sunlight. Vaulted ceilings and exposed beams accented wide-plank hardwood floors. She let out a sob as she realized no more sleeping on laundry room floors or having people praise her when she took a crap.

"Dude!" Seth almost barreled her over as he came into the house carrying Walmart bags. "This is a total party pad."

After plopping the bags down on the granite counter tops, he opened the stainless steel fridge, which was empty except for a six-pack of beer. "Thank you, beer gods," he said as he looked up to the heavens. She just shook her head and ran down the steps to retrieve the rest of the items from the car.

When she returned, Seth sat with his shirt off downing a Fat Tire. "Are you sure they're out of town?"

"They go every year for months. Do you see a car in the driveway?"

"No. I don't." He took another swig and burped. "You bring up a good point. How are you supposed to manage out here by yourself without a car?"

She scowled. Then she remembered her visits with Katie. She crossed the room to the Quinn's junk drawer, yanked it open, and procured a garage door opener. "Aha."

Seth followed her out the back door and noted the hot tub. "Sweeeet!" he proclaimed.

She pressed the button. "Open sesame." The door went up. There was the ancient red Jeep Wrangler. She opened the driver's door and sat down. Seth stood in the driveway, arms crossed, looking through the windshield at her. She felt under the driver's floor mat, retrieved the keys, and started the car. Problem solved. Mrs. Quinn always hid keys for when friends and relatives used the cabin.

When they got inside, Seth pulled out his laptop. "I want to show you a few things."

She sucked down an entire two liter of Coke and belched. He raised his eyebrows at her. "That is really unnerving to me, Lil. It doesn't sound—"

"Human?" she finished for him.

"Yeah."

"One of my new Super Shih Tzu powers."

"That will be helpful in a fight," Seth said. He typed in

tengu and turned the laptop toward her. "I think you should read this."

She leaned in to learn more about her fate through deciphering Asian folklore.

Tiangou or "celestial dog" is a creature of Chinese legend. The Chinese describe the tiangou as a meteor or black canine monster that devoured the sun during an eclipse.

Holy crap, that's me. I'm a canine that will eat anything.

The dog made a noise like thunder and was a harbinger of war. In Japanese culture, the tengu is a supernatural creature resembling a bird of prey. Buddhism long held them as harbingers of war.

There was a picture next to the text. Seth attempted to pull the computer away, but she latched on to it. In the picture, the creature had an old man's face with a long red nose, not unlike that of a Proboscis monkey. "Not encouraging! My God Seth, I do not want to look like that!"

"Lily, you control your outward appearance to some extent. Koko doesn't look like an old man. She has a magnificent beak."

"I don't want a beak either for crying out loud." She turned back to the screen and continued to read.

Tengu or tiangou are considered masters in shapeshifting. They have the ability to speak telepathically and to enter dreams. In addition to flying, they can travel via teleportation. They are famous for their skill in Kung Fu and their love of the arts, particularly poetry. Over the years, their reputation has softened. However, people still consider them spirits or monsters of the mountains and forests.

Frantic, she looked at Seth. "Is this supposed to allay my anxiety and misery? I'm not a monster!"

"Of course you're not," he said as he sat up. "You're a heavenly dog!"

"Teleportation? Beam me up Seth. I've surpassed my threshold for weird." She looked over to see his huge eyes. He was beyond excited.

"This, this is what happened," he stuttered. "There's no other way you could have made it over twenty miles in the condition you were in."

"Well Captain Fuzz Face, next time I'll take you along for the ride. Trust me. It sucked. I don't ever want to do that again."

He frowned. "Wish I could teleport."

She huffed. "Mr. Liu didn't mention me being a tiangou. He talked about the fenghuang and Dad's genes."

"At this point anything is possible. But keep in mind. You are in control of yourself. It does not mean you are evil, or bring war and destruction."

"Oh really, take a look at my boyfriend, neighbor, and Mr. Liu. I was the harbinger of some wicked events."

"None of this is your fault. I'm not sure whom to blame at this point. Part of me is angry at Dad for never telling us anything about himself."

"Being angry at him isn't going to change our current predicament, Seth."

Seth continued to look dejected.

"What's the matter?" she asked.

"I don't feel right leaving you here, but it won't help if I disappear too."

"What are you going to do?" She didn't feel right just

throwing her baby brother under the bus. This made her think of the school bus graveyard and then *she* didn't feel right about him leaving her either.

"I guess I'll go back and face the music," he laughed.

"What are you going to do if they arrest you?"

"Get a lawyer and pray," he said. "You stay hidden. If you get in a real bind, you should call your vet."

"I don't think he wants anything to do with us."

"*Me*. I don't think he wants anything to do with me...or Koko." Seth just grimaced.

Lily felt tears sting her eyes. "You can't go back! They'll put you in jail." This was her baby brother, and despite all his faults, she did love him.

"I need to go back. Maybe in some way I can help them figure out who this killer is." She tried to control the tremble in her lips. "Don't cry," he pleaded.

She pulled herself together so she could think logically. Once they found her bloody cell phone and connected it to him, there was no way he would walk. "Seth, I don't want you in trouble because of me." She felt herself starting to hyperventilate.

"I find my own trouble whether you're around or not. At least now I feel like my actions are for a good cause," he laughed.

They hugged. He didn't pull away. She realized before the confession he had always avoided close contact with her. She wondered if it was because he feared she would discover what he was.

"Call me and let me know you are okay," she demanded.

"Don't worry about me. You need to focus on

controlling your situation. Learn what you are. What type of things you can do."

"Okay," she said, kissing his cheek.

She waved from the door while he turned the truck around to head down the driveway. Glancing at the clock, she noted it was already 3:30. Hopefully, he wasn't returning to squad cars in front of his apartment.

TO BE ALONE for the first time in weeks felt good. She was used to living alone after Peter's death. She could walk around naked, singing at the top of her lungs if she wanted. Scanning through the Quinn's CDs, she found old school Sarah McLachlan "Building a Mystery" and sang off key while eating two PB & J sandwiches chased down by another liter of Coke. The shapeshifting definitely drained her strength. Perhaps, that's why her new metabolism was that of a teenage boy.

Sitting in her underwear and a tank top on the brown leather couch, she stared at the two-story fireplace considering her options. Built-in oak shelves flanked the fireplace. The Quinns' book collection was much more alluring than the shears and hair paraphernalia Seth had grabbed from the Walmart and neighboring Sally's Beauty supply store. She was avoiding the inevitable; she needed to chop off her long hair then dye it. And according to Seth, she would need to use the hair bleach first before the dye or she'd wind up looking like Carrot Top. Having a brother who was a serial dater of blondes apparently had some advantages.

As she made her way back to the CDs, she noticed a wine rack in the corner. She diverted from her path to pluck out a bottle of Pinot Grigio. "Thank you, Bacchus."

Feeling empowered, she continued to the music selection. Katie's stepmom had a majority of country CDs. This seemed appropriate for getting drunk while feeling suicidal. Martina McBride? Lily blasted "Wrong Baby Wrong" while she started to cut. A half bottle of warm Pinot Grigio was necessary to get her to read the directions on the tub of Clairol's Extra Strength Basic White hair bleach. She stared at the Caucasian woman on the front of the box of L'Oréal's #9, Natural Blonde. Two hours later, she was woozy from fumes and alcohol. But she was a blonde. *Nothing natural about it.*

When she was in a bad way, she sang "I Like It I Love It" along with Tim McGraw. But she *really* didn't like it or love it. After covering every mirror in the house with a towel so she could avoid looking at herself, she dressed in a purple sundress with clear plastic flip-flops.

Once back downstairs, she sat on the couch, the bottle of Pinot cradled lovingly in her lap, glass forgotten. With a southwestern throw draped over her feet, she clicked on the TV. Breaking news flashed across the screen. Paramedics ushered a man into the back of an ambulance, his eyes looked tragic—particularly with the bloody gash over his left brow. They posted the picture of their Most Wanted on the screen then—armed and dangerous.

Warm tears fell. Numb, Lily turned off the TV and drank the rest of the wine.

CHAPTER ✒ 31

BAD LOVE

LARRY'S HANDS WERE numb from being pinned behind his back and handcuffed to a chair in the garage. He passed delirium hours ago. He had cried, screamed until he was hoarse, pissed himself, prayed, and cried some more.

Three years he had been with Frank. The house, the vacations, the cars, the laughter, and good food. Now where was he? Sitting in his own piss in the four-car garage wearing a Budweiser drinking helmet filled with two water bottles. *Bastard!* Frank had started to gag him then decided that he might die if he didn't have water. He figured by the time someone heard Larry, he would have put some distance between them.

Frank had anchored the chair in place with a bungee cord so Larry couldn't scoot over to the garage windows or throw himself over to attempt breaking the chair.

Larry was semi-conscious when he heard the men talking in his backyard. At first, he considered the voices were in his head or perhaps from another realm that would suggest he go further into the light. Either way, screaming seemed like a good idea.

Unfortunately, when Larry went to scream, all that came out was a raspy croak. He had gone completely hoarse. Frank had tied his feet to the chair, bungeed the chair to the wall, and cuffed his hands. That only left his head. He attempted to rock in his chair, but he was perfectly tethered. That's when he went ballistic. He truly couldn't take much more.

Frantic, he looked around him. The pooper scooper rested against a post approximately two feet away from his chair. About three feet away was the metal garbage can.

Larry heard the men walk past the garage doors. Frank had positioned him by the Mercedes front bumper, out of sight if anyone peeked inside the square garage windows. *Bastard.*

In desperation, he leaned over from the waist and grabbed the handle of the scooper in his mouth. His head hurt from where Frank hit him over his left eye. He barely had strength left to keep his head up with the freaky helmet in place. He bit down as hard as he could, swung the scooper sideways and made contact with the metal trashcan. Thwack! He had hoped for more of a reverberating gong sound. Thwack! Thwack! Thwack! Through his Mercedes's front windshield, he saw a face in the window. He dropped the scooper between his knees and attempted to scream again. Nothing.

He picked the nasty pooper scooper up in his teeth again and bashed away at the garbage can. He didn't know Morse code. That would have been very savvy. Instead, he kept flinging the pooper scooper while remnants of dog doo flung in the air.

"SOMETHING'S GOING ON in there!" Officer Hawkes

said.

"Call for backup!" Caldwell said, drawing his gun. He peered into each window of the garage door, shining his flashlight. He caught a glint of red through the Mercedes windshield—something red and moving. Then he heard the sound again. Thwack. He spotted the side of a metal trash-can as it shook from some force.

"I'm going in," he screamed to Hawkes who was returning up the driveway. "You cover the front." Caldwell made his way to the back door of the garage then tried the knob. Locked. It took three kicks, but he got the door open. When he did, the sun streamed in on Larry Jones with some kind of contraption on his head. As Caldwell drew closer, the scene perplexed him. Jones held a pooper scooper sideways in his mouth and wore a beer drinking helmet. His arms and legs were tied to a chair.

Larry Jones dropped the scooper from his mouth, "Don't shoot," he rasped.

Caldwell checked that the room was clear. "Anyone else here?"

Jones shook his head. Caldwell examined the contents of the water bottles in the slots on the helmet to ensure that they were not some kind of bomb. "Hang tight," he said as he proceeded through the house, calling for Hawkes first. After they made sure the place was clear, they returned to the scene in the garage. Drenched in sweat, Jones was barely keeping himself alert despite the water. The temper-ature had been in the nineties in the last twenty-four hours, and was even hotter in the garage with no ventilation.

They called for paramedics then extricated him from the kitchen chair. Caldwell removed the helmet to reveal

Jones's sweat-drenched hair plastered to his head.

"You okay?"

Jones just shook his head and whispered, "Frank."

"Mr. Harding?" Caldwell asked.

Jones nodded his affirmative.

"He do this to you and take off?" Caldwell asked. Jones nodded. "I know you don't feel well, but I really need your help here. Was Frank armed when he left?"

Jones nodded. "Sig P220," he whispered.

"You know where he's headed?"

Jones shrugged, "Out of the country."

Caldwell called the office to put out a BOLO on Frank Harding, which notified airports, customs, the GBI and FBI.

"He didn't kill anyone," Jones said.

"Mr. Jones—"

"We found all her stuff."

"Ms. Moore's?"

"She had been staying here...using the bike. We didn't know. Never saw her...just the dog."

"What did you find?" Caldwell asked. His stomach dropped. Lily was hiding there the whole time. *How the hell did I miss this?*

"Backpack, clothes, *blood*," he said. Caldwell squinted as he concentrated on hearing him better.

"Where?"

"On the dress and backpack."

"Where is she now?" Caldwell held his breath.

Jones looked at him blankly, "I don't know. Frank didn't know. He looked surprised by it all. He was worried about the papers."

"Papers?"

"He was shredding them. When I asked about them, he hit me in the head with his golf umbrella. Bastard!"

"You don't think he hurt Ms. Moore or had her tied up somewhere?"

Jones thought for a while before shaking his head. "He was genuinely surprised by Lily's things, but more worried about the papers."

"What was on the papers?" asked Caldwell.

"Don't know, but they belonged to Mona Sinclair. Apparently she was a client."

"You realize how this looks?"

"I love Lily. She's the bratty little sister I never had," he said, starting to cry. "I understand how this looks, but I wouldn't harm a hair on her head."

Hawkes escorted paramedics into the garage. After ten minutes of their attending to Jones, Caldwell checked in with them.

"I need to take him to the hospital, get his head stitched, hydrate him, and make sure all his feeling comes back in his limbs," said the EMT.

Caldwell nodded. "I'm sending Officer Hawkes with him."

Caldwell took a few more minutes to wrap up questioning. Jones volunteered all of Frank's favorite exotic countries to offer some leads. He denied knowing Hitomi, Li Liu, or Mona Sinclair.

Once the CSI Unit showed up and Jones was on the way to the hospital, Caldwell headed back to the office. He needed to check in with Tiny to see if the bullet retrieved from the Liu crime scene could have been fired from the barrel of a Sig Sauer P220.

CHAPTER ✒ 32

LAKE UPDATES

CALDWELL STOOD AT the board in Lake's office, but he wasn't looking at it. Instead, he peered out the one tiny window at the full moon. He worked Lake's American Heart Association stress ball with his left hand. As much as he tried, he could not accept that Lily Moore was involved in these crimes. He feared the lieutenant disagreed with him.

Caldwell placed the stress ball down on the corner of Lake's desk which was empty except for one file folder organizer, a calendar and his phone. No matter how busy he was, Lake kept everything in its place. The wall furthest from their crime board housed Lieutenant Rocky Lake's awards. There were plenty. Caldwell had earned some awards, but nothing like this. He glanced at his 2008 Outstanding Service award. The plaque held the Atlanta Police Department's logo and motto, "Resurgens, Rising Again." The embossing consisted of a phoenix rising from the flames. Next to it was the 2005 Medal of Honor Lake earned the year he chased down Arthur Moore's killer.

"Did you eat anything?" Lake asked from the doorway.

Caldwell startled, but recovered. "No." He couldn't remember the last time he had.

Lake placed two Cokes and subs down on the round

meeting table.

Caldwell took a seat. "Thanks. I got completely wrapped up with the Jones/Harding scene."

His jaw fixed, Lake unwrapped his sub.

"I got Moore coming in tomorrow for additional questioning," Caldwell said.

"Good."

"What happened with Hitomi?"

"Dr. Seduction?" Lake asked.

Caldwell grinned.

"Too bad she's a mad scientist, otherwise I think she and I could have something," Lake said.

Caldwell almost spit out his Coke.

"Good to see you laugh, Simms. You look like shit."

"Right back at ya."

Lake's mouth twitched. "Kennesaw police pulled over Hitomi for reckless driving several miles from the Liu crime scene yesterday."

Caldwell stopped eating.

"Yeah, time period fits. Her house and lab were interesting. I believe she had cleaned up the place before our visit. But I got all kinds of info from her neighbors this time. She definitely had people coming to her home. My guess is that she held her own side projects out of her home lab that she has in the basement. We seized syringes, logbooks, files, and her laptop as well as office equipment."

"Anything of significance?" Caldwell watched Lake. He was building to something important. His tell was the slight extension of his neck, the elevated position of his chin—*totally pleased with himself.*

Lake wiped his hands on a napkin and pulled out an

evidence bag from his briefcase. "Really interesting stuff in there." Wings dominated the cover of a Japanese mythology book.

"Thanks Uncle Wocky, you brought me a present. Is this my bedtime story?"

Lake took a sip of Coke before wiping some lettuce off his white shirt. "Got her in lock-up."

Caldwell put down his sandwich. "What's she doing there?"

"Gee Simms, I don't know, entertaining the guards."

Caldwell smirked. "You're enjoying this, aren't you?"

"Steroids. We found a large stash of steroids in her basement. No Inderal, but at least we've got her on something."

CHAPTER 33

SOMETHING OLD, SOMETHING NEW

CALDWELL REMOVED HIS tie and stuffed it in his pocket. He rolled up his sleeves, before donning booties and gloves. Breaking the seal, he entered the Sinclair duplex with Tiny bobbing along behind him in his Powerstriders.

"You think I'm crazy?" Caldwell asked.

"Yeah, 'bout a half a bubble off plumb," quipped Tiny.

Caldwell glared at him.

Tiny cackled. "Ooooh, you scary!"

"Thanks for the vote of confidence, Tiny," Caldwell said. He turned to look at him. "Thanks for coming back in here with me."

"Not a problem. Ya gotta follow your instincts," he said.

Caldwell turned and bashed his head on the pendant light in the foyer. "Damn! Sorry."

"Don't apologize to me. You can't help it you're vertically challenged."

Caldwell rubbed his head and looked at Tiny.

"What? Ask me if I *ever* hit my head on things. That would be 'no.' Don't give me that look, Simms. You do all right for being slightly brain damaged."

"What?" Simms asked.

"Think about how many times you hit your head in a month. Seriously, that has to have some accumulative effect." Tiny grinned.

Exasperated, Caldwell closed his mouth and continued to make his way through the thousand-foot condo. The off-white carpet in the living room was worn, but clean. The astringent odor of strong cleaners mixed with decay. The six plants in the bay window had succumbed to their abandonment.

"Cool photos," Tiny commented, looking at framed photographs of Sumatran villagers and wildlife.

"She led an interesting life." Caldwell worked his way from the living room to the spare bedroom that Ms. Sinclair used as an office. The antique desk appeared neat and orderly. Tiny checked the drawers and closet, as well as in and under the pull-out sofa.

As they entered the master bedroom, Caldwell stopped to survey the décor. The four poster bed was dark walnut. Green and tan cushions covered every surface coupled with earth-toned fabric cascading from windows and walls to create a womb feeling.

"Almost overwhelming, isn't it?" Tiny asked.

"Yeah." He hadn't noticed before with the slew of people in the space the day Clemens discovered Sinclair.

They searched the room, looking behind cushions, fabric, prints. Caldwell noted the reading material stacked on the nesting tables by her bed: *National Geographic Magazine, Utne Reader,* Sudoku puzzles, *Selected Poems* by E.E. Cummings, *The Oxford Book of Fantasy Stories,* and Dr. Seuss's *Are You My Mother?*

Tiny shifted the mattress, checking the corners and

feeling along the box spring. The sound was barely audible—soft like the scuff of a shoe heel on a wood floor.

"Stop," Caldwell said with his hand up. "You knocked something loose."

He approached the intricately carved headboard while shining his flashlight on the wood. The corner of the center square inlay appeared offset. *Is it an illusion?* Caldwell dislodged the square to reveal a hidden space in the headboard.

"Good night!" Tiny whispered, cautiously shifting the mattress back in place.

Caldwell let out a loud breath as he surveyed the space with his flashlight.

"Well go on Petunia, we ain't got all night," coaxed Tiny.

Caldwell flipped him the bird before reaching in and drawing out a stack of papers including a yellow padded envelope.

"Elvis has left the building!" shouted Caldwell, startling Tiny. "What's the matter, I scary now little man?"

Tiny grimaced. "It's late. You're lucky I have a sense of humor or I'd knock you into Tuesday."

"I guarantee this is the same type of envelope and label found at the Hitomi lab. And that the ink matches the Hitomi computer printer," Caldwell said.

Tiny sauntered up to examine the seal on the envelope. "You lucky SOB. I bet we can get DNA from the saliva on that seal."

Caldwell hardly heard him. He was too busy reading the love letter from Charles Moore to Mona Sinclair. The notepaper was yellowed and wrinkled like jaundiced old skin. "This is from Arthur Moore's father." Tiny looked over his elbow to scan the print.

"What's the deal with the envelope?" Tiny asked.

"This, obviously, is more recent. My guess is that Dr. Hitomi was sending her syringes of Inderal in these padded envelopes. No return address, but as you noted, someone licked the envelope to seal it."

"You're reaching."

"It's all I got—my gut."

"Let's get back," Tiny said. "I'll send it off right away."

CHAPTER 🪶 34

MOORE TROUBLE

SETH MANAGED TO get back into town much later than he anticipated. He got stuck in traffic on Interstate eighty-five. Detective Simms had called to schedule another interview tomorrow at ten. His body felt clammy when he considered how that would go.

He looked around the parking lot. No one was around other than a single mom toting her two children and groceries into the redbrick apartment building next to his. He saw the stray cat he had been trying to care for in the last several weeks slink low beneath a parked car, seeking refuge from the Atlanta heat. "Oscar, that is not a safe place to rest." He sighed. The stress from the last twenty-four hours hit him suddenly. "I am so screwed!"

He had no idea how he was going to make it through tomorrow. He hadn't slept much since Lily's attack. Push-ng the car door open, he stretched his legs and breathed in the hazy Atlanta air.

He carried some comfort with him—a large anchovy pizza. He chuckled to himself when he considered Katie's look of disgust the first time he had ordered one. His humor vanished as he approached his front door and smelled Koko. That wasn't what upset him. It was the unfamiliar scent at his threshold and the door's appearance that had the hairs on his neck at attention. His pulse quickened as he swallowed. Someone had kicked in the door. He listened. Whoever had been there was gone now. He could actually see a footprint on the surface of the door.

Seth shoved the door open the rest of the way. Someone had tossed his place. His headache felt as if it were taking on a life of its own, strong tentacles grasped the sides of his head and squeezed. Instead of shutting his eyes to block it out, he made himself look. His belongings spilled from drawers and open cabinets. Seth waded through the living room, kitchen, and into his bedroom. Nothing appeared missing except for his Inderal. It didn't surprise him that Koko had been in his apartment. However, someone else had been in his apartment as well.

He didn't want to call the police. He needed more time to devise an exit strategy. They most likely would discover the cell phone with Lily's blood left at the Ansley Park Manor and tie it to him. His explanation of things would only land him in the looney bin. Besides, he had more questions than answers.

Only an idiot would walk into the situation in the morning without a lawyer, but he couldn't remember the man's name that his mother used. *Looks like tomorrow I'll be facing the firing squad.* He didn't clean up his apartment. He was too damn tired to care anymore. As he inhaled his pizza, he flipped on the TV. That's when he saw the news coverage about Larry Jones.

Could this situation be any more messed up? He stretched out on the futon and put his head down to rest his eyes.

Seth awoke in the middle of the night and grabbed his

car keys off the coffee table. He closed the door with its bent frame the best he could. As he drove out of the complex, his thoughts went to Katie and what she must think. He hadn't been talking to her much. Lying was not his favorite thing, although he'd done a lot of it lately. When he returned home an hour later, he felt better. He had taken some steps toward a plan. The plan was a crazy one, but it gave him hope, albeit a false sense.

The next morning his alarm roused him from a miserable sleep. For breakfast, he took a bite of cold pizza but was too nervous to eat. After a quick shower, he started to head out the door. As an afterthought, he exchanged his ACDC t-shirt for a white polo shirt. On the way to the station, he let Lily know what was going on with his apartment. He advised her to call Dr. Gladson if he wound up in jail. He disconnected when she began to rant.

LAKE, CALDWELL, AND Tiny had a quick pow-wow in the lieutenant's office before Seth Moore's arrival.

"So, the hair matches Frank Harding. We're ninety percent sure the Sinclair syringes came from Dr. Hitomi. The footprints at the Liu crime scene could be Harding's— shoe size matches. Hitomi was a mile from the Liu crime scene about the right time period, but there's no evidence placing her there. She wears a size five and a half shoe. Tread pattern is consistent with a bigger person. Don't think she could pull off wearing a size nine boot," Lake said pacing the small space in front of his desk.

Caldwell stood by the crime board. "Lily Moore was at

the Ansley Park residence. The bloody cell phone belongs to Seth Moore and his fingerprints are on it. Hitomi's in custody. The drug charges will stick. Hopefully we'll get results from the saliva on the envelope seal and any trace evidence on the package found in Sinclair's house. May be a match with Hitomi. May not."

"Anything else?" Lake asked.

"Found the mystery bullet," Tiny said.

Both detectives looked at him.

"In the Harding/Jones backyard, we retrieved a bullet matching the one pulled from the Liu studio wall. Looked to be covered with DNA material." He looked to Caldwell. "Blood type matched Ms. Moore's."

"Harding?"

Tiny shrugged. "Ballistics says the bullet markings indicate it was shot from a polygonal barrel. From the gun receipt found in Harding's desk, we know he owned a Sig Sauer P220 which has a *traditional* barrel."

"Harding could've used another gun we don't know about," Caldwell said.

Lake nodded as he crossed his arms and leaned against the desk. "We need to pressure Jones some more. See if we can gather anything useful on Harding. Still can't believe he doesn't know anything about Lily Moore's whereabouts, either."

"I can't believe her brother doesn't," Caldwell said.

The Lieutenant blew air, puffing up his cheeks. "We have the security tape from Colony Square showing the Shih Tzu with Seth Moore from over a week ago."

"And we know Mr. Jones had the dog as well. Those sunglasses found at the Liu crime scene have Jones's fingerprints on them as well as Lily Moore's. What are we gonna do with him?" Caldwell asked.

"Lean on him like you said," Lake spat. "He's in this crap up to his neck."

They both looked at each other, catching the lieutenant's choice of words at the same time. Lake cracked a quick smile. Caldwell knew he was thinking about the image of Larry Jones in the beer helmet holding the pooper scooper.

"We get the search warrant for Seth Moore's phone records, computer, and apartment?" Lake asked.

"Got the call. The team's going in as we speak. They'll call me ASAP with any interesting info," responded Caldwell.

Carrie, the receptionist, poked her head inside the door. "Seth Moore is here."

"Thanks, Carrie. Show him into the interview room," Lake said. He collected his paperwork while downing the rest of his Coke.

Seth Moore sat behind the table bouncing his knee. His eyes were puffy with dark rings around them. Lake and Caldwell exchanged looks concerning his appearance.

"Mr. Moore." Lake nodded at Seth.

Caldwell sat across from him while Lake took the chair to the side of him.

"How have you been holding up?" Caldwell asked.

Seth flashed them a half smile, almost a grimace. "Not real well."

"Honestly, you look like shit," Caldwell said. "There something you want to get off your chest?"

Moore rubbed the palms of his hands on his jeans. "I

know Larry Jones didn't hurt my sister. I saw the news last night."

"Why do you say that?" Lake scrutinized him over his reading glasses.

"I just know that Larry never hurt Lily or knew her whereabouts."

"Now how could you know that?" Caldwell asked.

"Because Lily told me she was hiding at their place."

His confession seemed to suspend time. Caldwell held his breath as he turned his head toward Lake. Lake licked his lips and swallowed. When Caldwell turned back toward Seth, the kid wasn't blinking.

"So you've been withholding information from us?" Lake asked.

"I'm protecting my sister."

"Do you really believe that?" Caldwell asked.

Seth was quiet.

"Wouldn't Arthur be proud," sneered the lieutenant.

Seth stared back at him, a crease formed across the bridge of his nose, his mouth set in a snarl.

"Did your sister assault Phil Miller and kill Peter Marx and the Sinclair woman?" asked the lieutenant.

"Do *you* really believe that?" Moore asked turning toward Caldwell. Caldwell stared at him. Seth Moore's eyes made him hesitate. *Something's just not right about him.*

Seth interrupted Caldwell's thoughts, "Somebody is trying to kill her. That's why she's been running."

"You're not telling us everything. Why the hell wouldn't she come to us?" Caldwell asked.

"That's complicated," he said, folding his arms across

his chest.

"She was shot then she ran from me! You want to explain that?" barked Caldwell.

"She's terrified."

"Of whom? Is it Frank Harding? Li Liu? Dr. Hitomi?" Lake asked leaning toward Seth.

"I don't know who it is. She—"

"She what? We know you've been talking to her. We found the phone. A team's searching your place right now as we speak," Caldwell said.

Seth turned to Lake, his brows furrowed. "Well, your team may find the fact interesting that it's been ransacked."

"What do you mean?" Caldwell asked.

"I got home yesterday to find someone had tossed my place."

"Did you report it?" Caldwell asked.

"No."

"You got something in there you don't want us to see?" Lake asked.

"Honestly, I was just too damn tired last night."

"I need to call the team," Caldwell said as he excused himself from the room. He got a hold of Crime Scene Specialist Maura Reeves to let her know they needed to treat the place like a breaking and entering. It could be a ploy, but he wasn't taking any chances.

Returning to the room, he found Lake questioning Moore about the dog. "The employee on the sixth floor at Colony Square said you were adorable and really had a way with animals," said Lake. "In fact, she mentioned a toy dog you were watching for a woman named Mrs. Brown. Your bud, Reggie, confirmed this story. When we looked at the visitor's log for that day, there was no Mrs. Brown."

Caldwell stared at Seth's eyes again.

"Mr. Moore, you listening to me?" Lake asked.

"Yes, sir."

"Where's the dog?" Lake asked.

"I don't know."

"You don't have the dog?" Caldwell asked, settling back in across from him.

"No, sir. I thought Mr. Jones had the dog."

"You told Reggie Mrs. Brown had the dog," Lake said.

"Yes, but last I heard Mr. Jones had the dog, but then it ran away."

"Screw the dog, Seth," blurted Caldwell standing up. "What the hell has your sister gotten herself into?" He was standing over him, fists clenched.

Seth wiped Caldwell's spittle from his face.

"My sister hasn't gotten herself into anything. She's in grave danger."

"You're gonna be here a while," Caldwell said. "You may as well start talking."

"Shit!" Seth said, standing up. Lake jumped up as well. Seth looked at them as if sizing them up. He quickly sat back down. "Sorry," he said, while raking his hands through his hair.

"What the—" Caldwell said.

"Geez son, what the hell you got going on in that head?" Lake asked.

"You guys been following me?" He looked straight at Caldwell.

Caldwell made himself sit back down. *Bastard's gotta know where his sister is.*

"We ask the questions," Lake said.

Seth looked like he was trying to figure out some complicated calculus equation.

"You have a tracking device on my car?" he asked.

"What's with the paranoia, Seth?" Caldwell asked.

"People are dying and someone's attacked my sister and Mr. Liu."

"Who?" Caldwell asked.

"Lily said it was some big guy with blue eyes in a black mask. She said he knew Mr. Liu."

"When did you last talk to your sister?" pushed Lake.

"Yesterday."

The two detectives looked at each other.

"Listen. I really need to know if someone's been tracking me or following me from your department."

This guy's either really stupid or he has the cojones of a Right whale. Caldwell looked over at Lake.

Lake stood up and smiled. Caldwell hadn't seen this smile on the boss before and that in and of itself was frightening. "Seth. I've lost all my patience here. Where the hell is Mr. Liu?"

"Lily said some masked man took him."

Caldwell sat across from him with his mouth agape. "Where's your sister?"

"I think in a lot of danger," cried Seth.

"I'll be right back," Lake said. He placed his back toward Moore and mouthed "car" before exiting the room. Caldwell knew he was looking at Seth Moore's car hoping to find it unlocked so he could check for drugs. Moore's behavior was erratic and Hitomi's phone records indicated that he had a lot of communication with her.

Caldwell allowed silence to pervade the room. He watched as Seth's eyes bounced around the space eventually coming to rest back on him. But the detective continued the silence. He would wait him out. After several minutes, Caldwell leaned forward. "Where did you go after you left Li Liu's the afternoon he disappeared?"

"I think I'm going to be sick!" Seth started to gag.

"Not again!" Caldwell said, turning his head toward the garbage can in the corner.

Caldwell didn't have enough time to process the flash of movement in his periphery. The heavy metal table rose up smacking him in the head with so much force that he flew back, crashing into the wall.

When his vision cleared, he scrambled out from under the table to find Seth's clothes on the floor. Caldwell yelled as he stumbled from the room. Officers came running.

"What happened?" asked another officer.

"He kicked the table, then I don't know..." Caldwell said. "Son of a bitch. Didn't any of you see him run past?" Caldwell felt something wet on his face. He put his hand to his temple where the table had struck him. Blood.

Grabbing his cell phone from his belt, he called Lake.

"Simms?"

"Lieutenant. Moore just escaped."

"What!"

"I'd stay by his vehicle in case he heads your way." Caldwell pushed past people as he headed down the hall.

"I'll call to lock down the building," Lake barked before hanging up.

Caldwell secured his phone in his belt and took a napkin one of the detectives offered him. The napkin did little to staunch the bleeding from his head, but Caldwell kept it in place as his eyes scanned cubicles and offices. Fellow officers joined him in searching every inch of the work space. His head hurt like hell, but he felt certain they'd find Moore.

"What an idiot," he mumbled under his breath. His thoughts were of Seth, but they applied to himself as well. He felt woozy from the knock to the head and even worse when he considered having to answer to the lieutenant. "Where the hell did that bastard go?"

CHAPTER 🪶 35

HELP FROM SOME FRIENDS

"AWWW, WHAT'S YOUR name, kitty?" Tiny asked while scratching Seth's ears. He almost didn't have to bend down to reach Seth who was a large Bobtail.

"You're sho are a big sumabitch. What you been eating...midgets? Hee, hee, hee."

"Meoooowww."

"'Long as you don't eat the black ones," Tiny laughed as he sat back down at his desk to finish his lunch. Seth eyed his tuna fish sandwich.

"Oh, I see how it is. You want my food!" He broke off a piece and placed it on the floor for him. Seth gobbled it up all the while keeping an eye on the elevators.

They both heard the code for lock down called overhead.

"Oh Lord, it's gonna be one of those days."

Ding.

Seth took off like he was shot out of a cannon, darting into the elevator just before the doors closed.

He heard Tiny yell, "Hey," but nothing else as the door shut and enclosed him in the strange elevator world.

The machine lurched then whirred as it descended. Seth stood at the seam of the doors willing the metal box to move faster. Tom Jones crooned "What's New Pussycat?"

through the speakers. *Really? Ya gotta be kidding me.*

It stopped with a gentle bounce as Seth's body quivered. He crouched low to the ground, his bobbed tail twitched impatiently. The doors opened and he dashed through the lobby, following the exit signs to a back hall-way. The smell of a lit cigarette led him to a young main-tenance worker who happened to have the back door prop-ped open with a cinder block. Seth launched past him down the alley toward Peachtree Street.

He heard choking sounds behind him as the young worker was startled from his moment of nicotine Zen. Seth sprinted north on Peachtree Street toward Colony Square and Reggie. It was not a short trip. Once in front of the building, he waited at the revolving glass doors, scooting inside with a young businessman.

The clock read 11:30, which meant Reggie would be taking lunch soon. Seth stalked behind two guys who were talking about Italian food. He crouched in the shadows, waiting at the column of elevators. When he darted inside with them, one man sneezed and the other voiced his strong dislike of cats.

Reggie's red Pontiac Grand Am was in the corner of the parking garage. Seth knew it would be locked so he waited.

Crouched under the car, he felt useless, having no way of warning Lily that she was in more immediate danger than he initially thought. Twenty minutes seemed like two hours. Finally, he heard Reggie's familiar whistling in the parking garage followed by the click of the doors unlocking remotely. Seth considered shifting and opening the door, but didn't want the security cameras to catch his naked form slipping into Reggie's car.

When Reggie popped the trunk, Seth used the opportunity to throw his Barry White voice, "Mr. Green!"

Reggie turned toward the elevators seeking the source of the loud, authoritative voice. Seth leapt into the trunk, maneuvering himself under Reggie's work blazer.

"Huh," Reggie said before closing the trunk.

Over the hum of the engine and thrum of tires, Seth listened to his buddy's rendition of Luther Vandross's "Here and Now." He concentrated on breathing to stave off a panic attack. He never liked closed spaces.

Eight minutes into their ride, Seth flailed as Reggie swung the car left. The car swerved left again and Seth bumped his head on the top of the trunk as he bounced along with the car over several speed humps. They came to a halt in what Seth assumed was a parking space. Reggie finished singing "Dance with My Father."

While Reggie was distracted, Seth launched his attack, kicking down the back seat with a tremendous "Meeooow!"

"What the—"

Seth jumped through the front bucket seats and landed as his passenger.

Reggie flung himself against the driver's door. Alarmed and suction-cupped to the window, he attempted speech, "Wha, wha, wha—"

Seth waited for Reggie to catch his breath and purred to try to put him at ease.

Reggie pulled his arms down and turned from the window, managing to look over at Seth with a wide-eyed crazed expression. If he had hair, it would be standing on end.

"What kind of demon...cat, animal...how'd you get in here?"

Seth looked at the car keys swinging in the ignition.

Reggie's chocolate brown eyes magnified three-fold as he looked at his uninvited passenger. Seth tilted his cat head while staring back at him.

"You're one big mo fo. You know that? What the heck are you, some kind of bunny/puma crossbreed?"

Seth laughed.

"What kinda noise is that?" Reggie asked. "I never heard a cat make a noise like that?" Seth inched closer to him.

"Whoa, uh, niiice kitty. You stay there. You had all your shots and stuff?"

Seth leaned forward to bite down on the keys. He pulled them out of the ignition before leaping into the backseat.

"You slinky sonuvabitch!"

Seth growled.

"Damn. You got rabies?" Reggie asked, just the top of his head and eyes visible at the side of the seat.

Seth attempted to look innocent. *This isn't going to work.*

"Listen. No offense, but I'm not a cat person. Now give me back my keys and I'll let you out of the car," Reggie negotiated.

Seth stared at him—willing him to exit the car.

Reggie turned back around in his seat, placing his forehead on the steering wheel. "No one would believe the week I'm having."

"Try me," Seth said, having dropped the keys and

maneuvered his body on top of them.

"What the—!" Reggie lifted his head up to glance in the rearview mirror. He waited a moment. "Shit, I just thought you talked to me," he laughed.

"I did."

Reggie spun around so fast he must have wrenched his neck. "What?"

"Reggie. Your friend, Seth, needs to borrow your car. Leave now, have lunch. Tell people the car wouldn't start. Get a ride from Mama Green. Then you can say the car was towed by the time you came back to get it. By tomorrow, you can come to the conclusion that it must have been stolen."

Seth was sure Reggie was going to pop out his contacts. His nostrils flared and his pupils dilated.

"Breathe," Seth suggested. "Your friends are in danger. Now I'm commandeering your vehicle." This was one thing the two friends had discussed. If Reggie went into law enforcement, he'd have the authority to commandeer a civilian's vehicle. Seth had suggested he make sure it was a Mercedes S Class.

Reggie went back to resting his forehead on the steering wheel with his eyes closed. Seth watched him gulping in deep breaths. "I swear to God I need to get more sleep."

"Why don't you go have a beer and relax? By the time you come back, I'll be gone," suggested Seth the cat.

Reggie's bald head popped up, slick with sweat. "Shut up!"

Seth screeched. It was the kind of cat noise that had inhibited man and larger predators for centuries.

Without a second glance to his back seat, Reggie clambered out of his car, not even bothering to close the door. Seth watched him bend over in the middle of the parking lot like he was trying not to puke. Then he jolted forward like a man shot with adrenaline, almost running over two women as he entered the microbrewery.

Once Reggie stepped inside the restaurant, Seth jumped down on the floor to shift. In human form again, he reached back into the trunk to retrieve Reggie's workout clothes.

After slipping the clothes on in the back seat, he hopped out of the car to feel the undercarriage. The package was still taped there from last night's covert op. It was a risk, but he had to know. After ripping it free, he slid into the driver's seat clutching the package to his chest. Ten minutes later, he was traveling north on Georgia 400 wearing Reggie's Educated Black Man t-shirt, black bandana, and workout shorts. He knew Reggie would be pissed about his Nike Air Hoops in addition to the loss of his car.

CHAPTER ✒ 36

LILY AND SETH

IT WAS DUSK as the steam rose up around her. From the hot tub, Lily surveyed the deciduous broadleaf and evergreen trees. She preferred this skyline to any one made of glass and metal. With her improved vision, she could see a hawk perched thirty feet up. They watched each other. After thirty seconds, it let out a call and flew away. Its cry sounded as if it were sitting next to her on the ledge of the hot tub.

There was no longer silence in her world. Everything hit her ears then bounced inside her brain like a pinball trying to find a place to land. She was practicing filtering out the barrage, but it didn't always work.

While she soaked, Seth paced the cabin like a caged tiger. His distressed movements were hard to block out. He had arrived mid-afternoon the day before commanding that she evacuate the cabin. He explained that someone had ransacked his apartment and he was sure had been tracking him.

She understood his concerns, but she wasn't going anywhere. There was nowhere to go. Instead, she had showed him the arsenal that she uncovered locked in the garage: a Remington 700 youth rifle, a Winchester 20 gauge shotgun, a Glock 36 handgun, and a .38 Special. She also found a camouflage field pack containing shotgun shells and three boxes of rounds for the other guns the Quinns used for hunting.

"If he comes here, I'm shooting his ass!" Lily had said.

"This isn't a game," Seth said.

She was far too aware that this was no game. All of her injuries healed in a matter of days. The residual scars were emotional, not physical. She remembered the crush of fear, pain, and failure that day at Mr. Liu's house. Her anger remained coiled in her stomach like a snake raising its head at any reminders of her ordeal over the past week. She was tired of being a target.

But they were both targets now. The news organizations were speculating about the Moores, suggesting that it was such a tragic story of a good cop's kids gone bad. Seth, in particular, made for some excellent sensationalism. The public remained divided about her. She tried to block it all out. Her main concern was the Dark Watcher and his bitch of a sidekick finding them. The police concerned her as well, but hopefully they didn't want her dead. Their backpacks, full of supplies, waited for them at the back door so they could be ready at a moment's notice.

The low rumble of the old sliding door interrupted her thoughts. Seth stepped out on the deck, holding a newspaper he had borrowed from the neighbor's driveway. He extended his arm, avoiding the water.

"I realize that you're relaxing, but I have some news." He stood over her, frowning. She waited. "They are keeping Larry in jail along with Professor Hitomi. Your buddy Frank is MIA."

She nodded. These were all things she knew, but

couldn't do anything about.

"Oh and we have a new status. We are considered dangerous persons of interest. Some individuals speculate that a serial killer is responsible. Others think that we are delusional drug addicts on a brother-sister killing spree."

She knew the drug reference exacerbated his self-loathing. He had gone from blaming everyone else, their father in particular, to shouldering all the strife in their lives. According to Seth, his behavior had been the catalyst for all the trouble raining down on them. Sometimes she thought this too.

"Anything in there about Reggie?" she asked.

"Yes. They believe I stole his car. So far, no one is blaming him. Witnesses saw him pull into the parking lot alone and walk into the restaurant. There were no security cameras in the parking lot."

"Sorry."

"Couldn't be helped. I'm relieved that they don't suspect any involvement on his part." Reggie's red Grand Am remained in the garage. They kept the jeep combat-parked outside so they didn't have to open and close the garage door. No one could see them from the road, but they didn't want to take a chance by displaying a stolen vehicle in the open.

Her moment of peace destroyed, Lily climbed out of the hot tub as her stomach began its familiar grumbling. Seth stayed on the deck looking at the forest while she went inside. After drying off and changing clothes, she grabbed a can of Chef Boyardee Beefaroni out of the pantry for dinner. Looking outside, she noted that Seth had shifted. He perched over the hot tub, pawing at the bubbles with his head cocked to the side. She admired his fuzzy white fur, one dark ear and one red ear. His stunning blue eyes stood out above a pink nose. *He really is a cute kitty.*

"Bunnies are cute!" he bellowed at her.

Crap. Her mind continued to leak information telepathically when she was unaware. "Sorry. You are a ferocious feline. Hear you roar!"

His head hung in dejection as he studied the bubbles. She knew he was ashamed of shifting into a cat. He had told her that he was going to confide in her, but then she had sprouted wings, diminishing his already tenuous self-esteem.

When her gourmet dinner began to bubble in the pot, she checked out back for Seth. He sat on his haunches watching the birds splashing in the birdbath. He sat still with his beckoning leg up. She gasped when a blue jay flew over to perch on his paw.

How was it that her brother was the Gandhi of the feline world while she was eyeing the birdbath as if it were nature's fondue pot?

When she opened the door, she watched the birds with a salacious thrill as they took flight. Seth scowled at her for disturbing his bonding time. He emitted a funny fur ball laugh then launched into his free running—kicking off the side of a tree, landing on the deck, and leaping over the hot tub. He waited for her to turn her back so that he could shift and pull on his pants.

After dinner, they modified a well-used Chutes & Ladders board game that they found in the built-ins. Their version involved beer. Before they knew it, they were laughing together, something they hadn't done since Peter died. She almost felt like her old self, not the stranger she had become.

The next morning her body reminded her that she wasn't her old self and never would be. She was sitting at the kitchen counter when the news started. She took her coffee into the family room, positioning herself a foot from the TV screen.

Lieutenant Lake updated the public on the latest findings on the case. The GBI and FBI were now involved due to the nationwide manhunt for Seth and Lily Moore, and Frank Harding. She cringed when they flashed Larry's mug shot. His eyes were two endless holes of sadness.

When Detective Simms began to speak, she plunked her coffee cup down on the end table. His blue shirt brought out his amazing eyes and accentuated his broad shoulders. Her fingertips touched the screen, increasing the force as if to feel his skin. She sensed Seth watching her from the kitchen.

The flaming warmth enveloped her again as it traveled from her head down to her toes sending waves of yearning to her center and lower. Her mouth opened in a pant while her eyes focused telescopically on the fine hairs of his eyelashes then the coarser hairs of his eyebrows and the stubble along his jaw line. An inexplicable ache pulsated through every neuron of her being.

"Lily?" Seth said, his alarm evident in the high pitch of his voice.

She meant to respond, but she was riveted. As Simms began to talk, his voice drowned everything out. His voice was like the singing of the fenghuang, haunting her with its timber. Each inflection tantalized her. Tuning into his eyes, his mouth, his fingertips as he gestured, she felt the arousal in her breasts as they pressed against the thin cotton of her sundress.

"Lily!" Seth persisted. He was like an annoying mosquito, droning in her ear.

When she turned to him, she could see his energy field in colors of green and orange. She watched his sinewy movements as he approached.

"Your eyes are changing," he warned.

She continued to pant as she turned back to the TV. As the detective raised a strong hand to wipe the perspiration from his forehead, she lifted her own hand. Her hand stroked a soft caress from her forehead to her cheek. She continued to her chest where the crucible rested. It beat rapidly in sync with her heartbeat. As the camera drew into a close-up of his eyes, Lily's breath caught in her throat.

Seth grabbed her upper arm, pinching hard. "Lily, stop it!"

The rage pierced her temples, tightening the cords of muscle running down the sides of her neck. She backhanded him. Seth landed on his feet with a growl.

"I can smell it on you, Seth. You big freaking liar. Don't tell *me* what to do!"

He hesitated.

"Yeah, that's right. I can smell the Inderal," she spat.

Turning back to the TV screen, she was devastated to see that Caldwell was gone. He needed to know that she hadn't hurt anyone. She wasn't bad. *Other than bitch-slapping my brother just now.*

The anger uncoiled. Seth had told her about taping the package of money to the Grand Am's undercarriage the night before his police interview. His foresight impressed her, but not the residual Inderal scent that permeated the bills and plastic bag.

"I thought they stole your stash of Inderal," she said.

Seth looked down. "I had some in my car that I transferred to the Grand Am's undercarriage with the money."

"Why?" Lily asked.

He didn't move.

"*This* is the reason we've been targeted. Peter, the professor, Mona, and you! It's about the Inderal," she said.

"I didn't know what to do. Who to tell. My body was out of control," Seth said drawing closer. "And it's gotten worse. Thanks to you."

"Me?"

"That," Seth said, pointing to the crucible. "Does not create balance. It's evil. The only relief I've been able to get is from the Inderal. I have one syringe left because someone stole the rest when they tossed my apartment."

She shook her head.

"Don't judge me," he said. "My God, look at yourself; you were going to hump the TV."

She palmed the crucible. It sent thrills of warmth through her. "You're evil." He flinched as if she had struck him. "Waipoi's dead. Mr. Liu, the only person who could help us, is most likely dead too. There's no one left."

"Right, Mr. Liu would have saved the day. Lily, I know you've had quite a beating, but get a grip. He almost killed you with that damn necklace. You call *me* evil? Where is the great Kung Fu master now? How was he supposed to teach *us* about power if he had no power himself?"

"He took care of Dad. He—"

"Are you kidding me? Dad is dead, Lily. Who was with him when he was killed?"

"No. Waipo trusted him. Dad trusted him."

"They're both dead you stupid, clueless girl!"

"Don't call me stupid. You're nothing but a weak, sniveling addict!"

Seth's eyes widened, his fingers stretched and his hair stood up. The air inside the cabin smelled of metal, like lightning had struck.

She broke the stare as her skin prickled in a wave down her spine to her feet. Sweat dripped off her onto the floor. Her nails grew into claws. *Breathe, Lily.* She shouldn't have looked up at him. When she did, she saw his eyes glow with challenge.

Before she knew it, Seth had shifted then crashed through the screen door. Lily tore through the foliage after him, diving off a ten-foot drop, landing in the lush green Georgia flora. He had taken the rocky route with deep ravines and cliffs.

She didn't know who or what she was. Her body was human, but her vision was sharp and her toe nails lengthened to dig into the mud. As the itch prickled along the sides of her back, she gave in and released all the tension. Her wings unfurled.

They saw each other at the same time. Seth launched himself from a tree. They collided mid-air in a ball of fury. They wrestled, scratched, and bit. She finally stopped when she had him pinned. His rapid neck pulse beat under her clawed foot. As she glared down at him, his fear-filled eyes jerked her back to her senses.

She released him then tore through the woods, her wings catching on branches. The colors swirled around her as if the forest were pulsing. Reaching a clearing in the trees, she felt her wings retract. She plucked her torn dress from the ground and threw it over herself. As she walked forward studying the patterns in the air, her personal storm shifted from rage to overwhelming grief.

She plopped down on the cool earth. Examining her body, she noted inflamed cat engravings on her legs and back. She cried deeply for everything and everyone she had lost, including her baby brother.

The grass rustled behind her and she smelled him; his scent was like a sunny meadow.

When she summoned the courage to glance up, her heart sank from the despondent look on his face. He had found his torn shorts. Blood oozed from his head and neck. Her butterfly hair clip rested in the palm of his hand. She had never worn her hair short before. For some reason, wearing Katie's rhinestone barrette made her feel like she was still a girl.

She pushed herself up to stand in front of him. He grabbed her in a hug, his eyes flooded.

"Sorry," he said. His body quaked with emotion as he finally let go of his hell.

"I know. I know," she whispered. They stood there for a minute, afraid to break the bond.

"Lily?"

"Yes?"

"You're one scary bitch." He smiled at her with the blood coagulating on his forehead. "You should have seen yourself!" It wasn't anger on his face, but respect and awe.

She was exasperated. *Boys.*

They made it through that morning without tearing each other apart. By the afternoon, they were both edgy as they laid out plans to address Moore Armageddon. They knew it was coming. There was no way they would survive if they didn't pull together.

CHAPTER ✒ 37

THE CAT'S OUT OF THE BAG

WITH THE DOOR closed, silence hung between the three men like a thick fog. Each one was afraid to venture forth as if blinded by the unthinkable. Caldwell wiped his sweaty palms on his pants.

Lake stood up, shoving his hands into the pockets of his black pants. He came around the wooden veneer desk to lean on the edge and face Caldwell and Tiny.

"I think we need to address the elephant in the room," he said.

Tiny fidgeted in his chair.

Caldwell stared down at his shoes.

"We all know what we saw on the Seth Moore videotape. In addition, the forensic evidence is pushing us to look at something unique, bizarre even. But at some point, we need to discuss openly what's going on."

Lake cleared his throat. "I want a blood oath from both of you that what we talk about right now goes no further until we figure out how to manage things."

Tiny nodded as did Caldwell.

"Just listen." Lake sighed. "It's about the night Arthur Moore died."

Caldwell found it difficult to swallow. He didn't dare look at Tiny. His stomach fluttered. They were at the edge.

Once Lake's words came out, Caldwell knew there'd be no going back.

"There had been a disturbance at a construction site of loft apartments in Midtown. Myself and my partner, Randy Lucas, got split up while pursuing two perps. I got lost in this maze of machines and building materials. As I turned around, I heard a shot. Lucas was down."

Lake swallowed. Caldwell watched him take a breath to steady himself.

"By the time I worked my way back, Officer Liu was there with his dog, Barney. I took off in the direction of the suspect, not paying any attention to Liu's protests. I knew he'd take care of Lucas. I just wanted to hunt the bastard down who'd shot him."

He shook his head. "Damn dog. Always was smarter and faster than me. Flew past me. The perp fired and Barney took a bullet in his back leg. I checked the dog. I swear, he, I just thought it had grazed him. If you could have seen his eyes. It was like he wanted me to keep going. I got my quarry. Gerald Owens raised his gun, but I was quicker. Got him right between the headlights." Lake looked down as he chewed his bottom lip.

"When I made it back to that location, the dog was gone—I mean no body, disappeared. In that same spot lay Arthur Moore on a crash board, bleeding to death, too far gone for the paramedics to help."

Caldwell snuck a peek at Tiny and saw he was studying the floor.

"Bullet fucking severed his femoral artery. He bled out," spat Lake.

Lake's eyes were wet, his nostrils flared. The room

remained silent. Caldwell looked at him.

"I questioned Liu over and over about when the hell Officer Moore got there and how he was shot and where was the dog. Liu was just numb, but before we returned to the station, he grabbed me by the collar. He said 'Arthur Moore was killed in the line of duty. Barney has been taken to a veterinary clinic where he will be pronounced dead from a gunshot wound. You should not be so impulsive.'"

Lake huffed. "I was pissed. I just couldn't figure it out; all I was sure of was that I had royally fucked up."

"Man," Tiny said.

"Lucas recovered. I was a hero. I chased down the cop killer, according to my friends. But I knew better." He shrugged. "Liu blamed me. He always has. Shortly after the incident, he transferred to the Marietta Police Department. I wanted to pursue it, but I just couldn't look Liu in the eye."

"Arthur Moore was a special man," Caldwell said. He thought he understood the scenario from that night.

"Very special. I worked with him and Li Liu for years. Officer Moore was any *man's best friend*," Tiny said, staring straight at Lake as if to challenge him.

Seth Moore was another matter. Caldwell had watched the videotape of Moore's interrogation over and over with Tiny.

"I think I saw a pooty-cat. I did. I did see a pooty-cat," was Tiny's response. Caldwell had given him a dirty look while he nursed his injured head. Eventually, the lieutenant insisted he go over to the hospital where he got eight stitches for the damage Seth Moore had done flipping the metal table on him.

Caldwell shifted in his chair.

"So you see, it wasn't so strange for you to have seen Lily Moore change into a dog in the woods," Lake said.

"Yeah Simmulator, don't take it too hard that a kitty kicked your ass in the interview room, either." Tiny's nose crinkled. "I gave that little shit my tuna fish sandwich."

Caldwell looked from one man to another. He didn't have the words to describe his dreams. The different crime scenes shuffled through his head. All the pieces still didn't fit together.

Lake exhaled. "So we all have the same idea about the Moore family's situation."

Tiny whistled the music to the X-Files sending a chill down Caldwell's back.

"You don't think they are..." Caldwell couldn't say the word.

"Some genetic mutation?" Lake offered.

"But what about the feathers and the weird footprints?" Tiny asked.

"Someone or something is targeting them or those close to them because of this," Caldwell suggested. "You think that Miller guy knew what was up? What really happened at that field?"

"I don't know if any of this is even connected," Lake said, trying to smooth down his hair. "Maybe we're trying to piece together stuff that's just doesn't go together."

All three men were stumped.

There was a knock at the door. "Detective Simms?" Carrie, the receptionist peered inside the office. "There's a Sarah Clemens here to see you."

Lake's eyebrows rose.

"She tried to call, but couldn't get through to you. She

has something of her sister's to show you."

Caldwell rose from the table and followed Carrie out.

CHAPTER 38

SECRETS

CALDWELL HAD INTENDED to talk to the Moores' family and friends and then pay the Millers a surprise visit. Instead, he had to go sympathize with a grieving old lady. He took several breaths to calm himself and tried to put on a pleasant face as he entered the conference room. Mrs. Clemens looked up at him with a tight smile. Her eyes were red from crying and she held an intricately embroidered handkerchief in her hand. She wore her white hair swept back in a bun.

Ah hell. "Hi Mrs. Clemens, I'm Detective Simms. We spoke briefly over the phone the other day about Charles Moore."

"Yes, yes. I remember," she said fiddling with her hands.

Caldwell walked to the table and sat down next to her. "What can I do for you?"

"I found this in my attic as I was going through some of Mona's things."

Caldwell looked down at a worn leather-bound journal then back up at Mrs. Clemens. "What is it?"

"One of my sister's old journals," she said wiping a tear.

"I can see how upset you are Mrs. Clemens," Caldwell

said.

"Wait until you see what's inside." Some alarm fired in Caldwell's head.

"Where was this?

"In a trunk in my attic. You know it's been there a while. We stored some things for her when she first moved back to the states before she bought the house on Myrtle Street. I think we both forgot about it. I thought it just had some old photographs of us as kids. I was feeling nostalgic today and opened it."

"It's definitely Ms. Sinclair's?"

"Yes, it's her handwriting."

"I understand." Caldwell sighed. "Because of our ongoing investigation of your sister's death, I have to treat this as evidence."

"You're not going to look at it now?"

"There's something important in there?"

"Something dreadful," she whispered.

Caldwell nodded. "Let me grab some gloves and an evidence bag and I'll look through things."

She nodded.

Caldwell left the room and grabbed the items from his desk. He waved his hand through the glass at the lieutenant who was on the phone. It was the best distress gesture he could muster. Lake held his hand up indicating he'd be right there.

Caldwell sat back down with the items. "Lieutenant Lake is on his way," he said.

"Thanks," said Clemens, biting her lip.

Lake entered a minute later. He shook Mrs. Clemens hand before sitting down next to her. She gave him a weak smile and swallowed hard. It was an odd arrangement, but they flanked her on either side in order to study the book. Both men wore gloves.

Caldwell opened the book. The writing looked familiar. He'd seen it from the Sinclair crime scene. They would get their expert to verify it.

Mrs. Clemens cleared her throat. "There are some things here that I will not speak of to you. I just can't." Her lips trembled. "I brought this for you to read, but I'm not comfortable with my sister's issues being public knowledge."

"We understand," Lake said.

"That said, it appears that my sister became pregnant when she was in Sumatra with the Peace Corps. At the end of her service she stayed on for three more years."

Caldwell nodded. "I remember you telling me that."

"It was the sixties and she was kind of a free spirit. I'd like to say that there was a boyfriend, but I think the fact of the matter was that she was with a group and there were *friends.*"

She looked at Caldwell who nodded to reassure her.

"I was aware of her having a baby, but was told that it died from a terrible infection. I chalked it up to the living conditions in a third world country. I couldn't believe she stayed over there. Anyway, my sister returned to the states and made a new life for herself writing children's books. She never would give me the details of her son's death. She has suffered in the past several years from poor health. She said she had some depression. I had no idea it was extreme anxiety and *delusions.*

"Mona had twins. After the one died, she gave the

other baby up for adoption to a family in the states. It was a closed adoption. As far as I know, she never attempted to make contact with the surviving son. I never understood why. Apparently, the twins were born two minutes apart. The first born was strong and healthy. The second one weak."

Caldwell shifted in his chair then asked the million-dollar question, "Do we know the name of her son?"

"There's a Hindu name mentioned here." Her brows dropped down, her lips pursed in disapproval. "Ankur. I don't know how adoptions work if the adoptive family names them...or..."

Caldwell slowly turned a few pages, "I know this is difficult for you. Thank you so much for providing us with this—"

"Detective, there's more," she said. Caldwell held his breath.

"My sister's child did not die from an infection. His younger brother killed him."

Caldwell stopped his page turning and paid closer attention to the woman next to him.

"Apparently, the bigger one became very ill with a fever. She left the boys with a neighbor to go into town and get some medicine. When she returned, the neighbor held his lifeless body and wouldn't stop crying. Ankur wasn't hiding. He had been waiting on the front step for her. He admitted that he put a pillow over his brother's face." Clemens gulped. "Mona writes here that 'his eyes were not an innocent child's.' The Medical Examiner stated cause of death as respiratory distress secondary to infection. Mona states clear as day that Ankur, at three, smothered his brother with no remorse." Frown lines creased her forehead. "I don't know that a three-year-old can be evil. Do you? I mean, he wouldn't have known any better."

Lake patted her hand.

"She couldn't look at the child. She gave him up for adoption."

"Mrs. Clemens, I know I asked you before about Charles Moore—"

"Yes, I remember, but I've never heard of him. My sister was rather secretive. Why?"

"We just wondered if he was the father," Lake said.

Mrs. Clemens daintily wiped her nose. "Who knows? Maybe the father was an Indian."

Caldwell nodded. "If you don't mind, just a couple more questions, Ms. Clemens."

"Yes?"

"I know we talked briefly about Dr. Hitomi's research over the phone. Were you aware of any kind of relationship Ms. Sinclair had with her."

"No, again, I have never met that woman. Mona never talked about her."

"Did she ever mention Frank Harding to you?"

"Who is that?"

"Someone who may be connected to this case. He knows the Moores. I just was seeing if you were aware of Ms. Sinclair knowing him."

"No, I don't recall my sister ever mentioning that name. But again, there's so much I didn't know about my sister."

They gave her some time to collect herself and asked if she needed a ride, but she assured them that her husband was waiting on her to drive her home.

Once she left, Caldwell and Lake poured through the book more thoroughly.

"Let's give this to Tiny," Lake said. "Then I'll call the US Department of State's Vital Records department to track down the name from the original birth certificate."

"Hopefully that'll work and we won't have to wait for Clemens to petition the court for the adoption record to be opened," Caldwell grumbled.

"Tragic story, no wonder the lady had PTSD," Lake commented. "But a three-year-old is still just a baby."

"Was a baby. Now he may be one pissed-off, traumatized adult."

CHAPTER 39

DOES A CAGED BIRD SING?

AFTER LUNCH CALDWELL and Lake stood side-by-side working on the crime board in Lake's office when Tiny knocked. He placed a manila folder on the meeting table before coming to stand by them, his bright yellow glasses perched on his head. He rolled up the sleeves of his pink oxford shirt. "It's hotter than stew fire in here."

"Yeah, I already complained," Lake said. He had an oscillating fan on top of his desk. "Tell us some good news, Mr. Hunt."

"The envelope in Sinclair's secret agent bed and the one found in Seth Moore's car both contained traces of Inderal. The saliva on the seal was Hitomi's." Tiny leaned against the gunmetal gray wall while twirling his yellow glasses by the arm.

Caldwell marked in the info under Hitomi's name. He drew a line from Hitomi to Mr. Moore. "So Seth Moore was most likely using Inderal or delivering it to private test subjects. It would explain Seth's continued contact with her."

He contemplated the information. They found Hitomi's fingerprints at Seth's apartment, but she denied breaking into his place. The footprint on the door matched the size twelve imprints found at the Liu scene. He wondered why the perp didn't wait on Seth and attack him. Had he only wanted the Inderal from Seth's apartment? Had it been Harding? The shoe size matched. They had no leads on Harding's location or the Moores for that matter.

"We gonna talk to Dr. Seduction again?" Caldwell asked Lake.

Tiny's dark eyes gleamed in amusement against his brown skin.

Lake cocked an eyebrow. "Maybe I'll let you handle her."

"Chicken," Tiny said as he excused himself from the room.

Ten minutes later Caldwell and Lieutenant Lake sat across from Hitomi at the Fulton County Jail. She wore a prison-issued orange top and pants that looked like scrubs, white socks and flip-flops. "My lawyer says not to talk to you."

"We know you were at Seth Moore's apartment. We also know that you provided him and Ms. Sinclair with syringes of Inderal," Caldwell said.

"We also know you provided anabolic steroids to young men. What exactly does that have to do with PTSD?" Lake asked.

She leaned in, her brilliant eyes piercing. "Did it ever occur to you gentleman that I'm not the bad guy here? Perhaps I've been trying to help. Perhaps, my interactions with Seth were of a protective nature."

"So, trashing his place and giving him drugs is a protective measure?" Lake asked.

When her attention turned to Lake, she smirked. "So you liked me better in my pink satin robe?"

Caldwell glanced at Lake who had a hand on his forehead. "Answer the question." Caldwell said.

"Only if he does," she said with a smile.

"Fine. I don't think orange is your color," Lake said.

She smirked.

Then the boss's demeanor changed. "You were the last person to see Peter Marx. We found your fingerprints inside Seth Moore's house. You were very close to Li Liu's ranch the day he was attacked. Things aren't looking so good for you, Professor."

"Things don't look so good for *you*. It occurs to me that Li Liu knew his assailant. I've never met the man in my life, but common sense dictates that he wouldn't let his guard down around just anyone."

Lake placed an object on the table in front of Hitomi. "You ever seen this before?"

Hitomi's eyes widened and her nostrils flared. "No."

The lieutenant left the feather in its clear evidence bag in front of her. Caldwell watched her. Her posture was relaxed, but her eyes were not. She was fascinated.

"Do you know what kind of bird that came from?" Caldwell asked.

"No."

Lake placed the mythology book in its clear bag next to the feather. "Are you sure?"

"Lieutenant, I didn't know you were into fairy tales."

Lake nodded at Caldwell to continue the questioning. Caldwell sighed. "So you don't know Mr. Liu. How about Frank Harding?"

"According to my attorney, I don't have to answer anything you ask me."

Lake removed the evidence bags from the table.

Caldwell propped his ankle on his knee and leaned back studying his notes. "But you are here, Dr. Hitomi. You look worried. I believe you're being protective. But is it of Seth Moore or yourself?"

Hitomi studied each of them separately. "I'll reiterate my point. I'm not the bad guy. I don't know Frank Harding."

Back in the car, Lake chomped on chicken fingers while Caldwell downed a cheeseburger. "You know, Gates had his hounds all around Hitomi's property. He attempted to use Liu's shirt, see if they picked anything up—nothing," Lake said.

Caldwell nodded. "None of her records indicate any contact with Liu. Not seeing Harding's number come up, either. So was it coincidence that she was so close to Liu's property the day he was attacked?"

Lake downed half his Coke in one gulp.

"You okay, Lieutenant?"

Lake stopped chewing. "That lady read my mind."

"Nah, she was just messing with you."

The lieutenant was adamant. "Swear to God. I was absolutely picturing her in the pink robe and now my head hurts like a bitch."

CHAPTER 40

FLYING SHIH TZU

THE FIGHT IN the woods had been the turning point for Lily and Seth. Afterward, they had agreed to wake at sunrise each day and walk through the woods, venturing further each day to condition themselves and study their surroundings in case they needed to make their escape. They followed game trails during off hours to avoid people.

At night, Lily practiced shifting. She had the dog form down and could even transform without making any uncouth noises. But Seth insisted that she was holding back and that without finding out entirely what she was, they would never stand a chance of surviving.

The term tiangou was a difficult one; she refused to add it to her vocabulary. Bird was okay, but she refuted even the slightest suggestion that she was a mountain monster that brought war. She preferred to think of herself as a fenghuang hybrid although that would have made her a peace-loving herbivore not an aggressive carnivore.

They didn't want to be defenseless so they practiced shooting the guns a few times. The preserve was a wildlife management area where hunting was allowed, but it was restrictive as far as how many hunters were permitted at a time and which areas could be used on what day. The sound of gunfire in an undesignated region would draw the warden's attention.

On their fifth day at the cabin, they waited until twilight to walk into the woods. She promised that tonight she would trust and just let go. It was early June, but the temperatures made it feel like July.

Seth turned his back to provide her some privacy.

He had suggested that she wrap her dress around her neck like a scarf so that she would have clothing handy when she shifted back. It was a great idea, if not disturbing, since she knew he had seen Koko do it. She had learned a system of rolling the dress tightly so that it even fit her Shih Tzu neck and didn't drag on the ground. Seth was to remain in his human form so her "bird-creature," as he termed it, wouldn't war with his cat. He still thought she was a tiangou or tengu. Lily knew he did, but wouldn't voice it because any inference to that point made her cringe.

Seth's speech reminded her of a flight attendant's just before takeoff. She knew it was important information in case something went wrong, but she didn't register the words. The night sky engaged her; doing its best to romance her. Seth was spewing accolades about Koko's poetry. She wished he'd stop talking about that woman. Lily's rage surged, flowing forth from a tingling in her toes to a monstrous throbbing at her temples.

There was an "umph" then a "thud." She disregarded those sounds as she allowed the sensory overload from the earth and sky to wash through her. Her wings unfurled in the breeze as her eyes followed every movement of the leaves and the bugs. She glanced down at her body to see white and black fur covering a heavily muscled canine body the size of a Saint Bernard. Her feet had formed large paws almost like a dog's, but more claw-like allowing her to bear down to root more firmly in the soil beneath her. Her teeth suddenly felt like they overflowed her mouth, but she told herself not to focus on that. Instead, she embraced the tremendous rush of having wings. Just as she was planning to launch into the heavens in answer to the night sky—

"Ohhh."

She turned around to see Seth semi-conscious on his back, moaning. Apparently, he had been standing too close.

"You okay?" Lily asked.

His eyelids fluttered. A rivulet of blood trickled from his nose in a diagonal toward his ear. His breathing was labored and his eyes cloudy as he peered up at her. Once he sensed what she was, the hairs on his head and arms stood on end.

"Dude!"

She'd like to think that the vision of his sister with kaleidoscope wings would have evoked something more deep and meaningful, but she was satisfied to hear "Dude" since it meant she hadn't bludgeoned her brother to death.

"You're...not what I expected!" he said. She wondered what she looked like. For once, she felt powerful.

"Easy," said Seth as she moved toward him. "You need to get your bearings. And no, I don't believe my nose is broken." He sat up slowly and held his shirt to his face, trying to stop the bleeding. Her intense stare at the blood on his shirt caused him to hiss.

"Don't take this the wrong way, but when you hiss like that it just provokes me. Don't worry, I won't eat you," she said with a laugh.

"So. Not. A bird," he said. The expression on his face caused her to pause.

"What do I look like, Seth?" He hesitated. She looked down at her four, large furry legs and claws. "I'm a monster?"

"No. No. No," he said. "You are...impressive."

That's what he said about a wild boar the first time he saw one. "Why won't you tell me what I look like?" She plopped her furry butt down on the pine needles and began to sob the sputtering and backfiring of an old VW Beetle.

"Shhhhh. Settle down now. Someone will hear you."

Lily began to tap her front paw on the forest floor, impatiently waiting for him to say something right. Something to talk her off the ledge.

"You have very big eyes," he said. "They're so... green."

"Uh huh. Fuck this. I'm going back to the cabin to see for myself." She took off at a lope headed for the cabin. The speed impressed her. Before she knew it, she was clambering up the front steps. She sat in front of the door contemplating the knob. When she reached out, she realized the digits of her paw were long enough to close around the handle, but her claws extended too far sinking into the wood of the door. "Ach!" She attempted to yank her claws out, but removed a chunk of the door including the knob in the process. She flailed around as if it were a mousetrap caught on her paw.

When Seth came up to the house two minutes later, she lay on her belly on the top step with her front leg covering her face and her paw extended out with the door chunk still attached. Her furry face was wet with tears and she felt her lower fangs extended out in a pout. In an attempt to be quieter, she only allowed herself short sobs. This technique started to make her feel light-headed.

"Lil?"

She held her breath as he approached so he wouldn't admonish her again for being too noisy.

"You're still a Shih Tzu. Why didn't you wait for me to explain?"

She stood up and turned around on the porch, knocking the porch swing into the window glass with the force of one wing, before settling back down with her backside to him.

"Nice." He walked up the steps and sat down next to her reaching out with his hand to stroke her ear. It felt great—almost as good as the wind in her face. It took the utmost control to prevent her hind leg from tapping. She would not give him the satisfaction. She felt his hand on the feathers of her left wing next as he explored her new appendages. "Dude these are the coolest wings I've ever seen. It's like you're under a black light all the time."

"Humph."

When he got to her paw, he discovered the doorknob. "Ya need some help with that?" He didn't wait for a response, but gingerly pried the wood off. "So I gather you haven't found the courage to look yet?"

"Screw you," she rumbled.

"Oh yeah. Quite the beast you are. Heart of a lion."

She popped her head up and stared at him. "What?" she asked. Suddenly she knew what she was without looking. Lily remembered the guardian lions chatter between Frank and Larry. *Shishi.* Seth jumped up with her.

"Easy, Lily. You have a crazy look on your face." He

eased his body in front of the door. She barked at him a deep primordial sound that broke the night's calm setting off coyotes to singing and dogs to howling four cabins over. "Guardian lion? You think you are a guardian lion?"

She nodded too revved up to worry about her mind leaking her thoughts.

"That explains a lot."

She tapped her front paw on the wood beneath her.

"Well, there's your noise that you make. Even as a pee wee, it's like a cross between a small roar and a bark." Lily knew he was proud of himself by the set of his shoulders. "You *roark*." Then he started to laugh. "Get it. Not you rock, but you roark. And then, see, I combined roar with bark so we have roarking."

Lily exhaled a loud stream of angst.

"You don't like it?"

"It sounds like something dirty. Now get your cat ass out of my way so I can see my scary self and have a good cry."

CHAPTER 🪶 41

SLIMY BOHUNK

CALDWELL PULLED INTO the driveway of the Miller's 1960's ranch home. Several tries at the doorbell earned him nothing. There wasn't a car in the driveway, but he peered into the garage to see that Phil Miller's Beamer was inside. Forensics released the vehicle once they had finished with it.

As he stepped down from the stoop, he heard a woman shriek. Caldwell ran toward the side of the house. A blonde woman in a red and white polka-dotted bikini bounced by as someone sprayed her with a garden hose. Caldwell sighed. As he started to turn, he heard a male voice, "Come here baby, I like it when you're all wet."

Caldwell watched the girl run back toward Phil Miller who had made a miraculous recovery with his speech and cognitive abilities. He froze when he saw the detective. Caldwell noted his bulky weightlifter's body. His short-cropped dark hair didn't hide the nasty gash healing on his forehead. Red-brown lines raked across his chest and down his abdominal muscles. *What the hell made those?*

Miller stood motionless in his Tommy Bahama-looking palm leaf swim trunks, the hose still gushing water on to the lawn. *Douchebag.* The woman next to him giggled. At most, she was eighteen.

"I have a few questions for you," Caldwell said, pointing to the house. It was a direct command. All the color drained from Miller's face. He took his time turning the hose off then headed toward the door. They both grabbed towels off rusty metal patio furniture before going through a worn door that led to a dated kitchen. Miller reached into a dark wood cabinet to retrieve a glass which he filled up from the tap. He didn't offer Caldwell or the young woman any water. In fact, he hadn't met Caldwell's eyes since he turned off the hose.

Miller sat down in a chair at a round oak table. Caldwell reached across and introduced himself to the woman who offered him a limp handshake. "Detective Caldwell Simms, Atlanta Homicide."

The woman's green eyes widened and she swallowed. "Amber Hayes." She turned her head and looked at Miller, perhaps to catch his eye, but he ignored her. "Ms. Hayes. I'd like a moment with Mr. Miller alone. Then I just have a few questions for you. Perhaps, you could wait in another room." She looked again to Miller like she needed his direction, but he didn't give any. With a slight huff, she turned to leave the room. "I'll be in the basement." Miller spanked her on the butt as she passed his chair.

Miller's dark eyes finally focused back on Caldwell.

"You look a lot better, except for the nasty scratch on your chest," Caldwell said while pulling his notebook out of his pocket.

Miller scratched the stubble on his chin. He looked to be growing a goatee.

"Where were you last Thursday night?"

His smile crept over his features slowly. "Most likely I

was with Amber."

"You have proof of that?" Caldwell asked.

"I'll see if I can scrounge up a receipt from the movies."

"What time was this?"

He shrugged which wasn't a particularly large movement with his thick neck. "Don't know. Maybe seven."

"How about that afternoon?"

He sat back in the chair. "I believe I had a doctor's appointment."

"I'd like receipts for that afternoon and evening."

"What's this about?"

"Someone broke into Seth Moore's apartment. I thought perhaps since you had it in for his sister, you spread the love to her brother."

He snorted. "I don't have any beef with the pretty boy."

"So you're just a misogynist. Is that it?"

Miller's hands fisted on the table as he leaned in. "You have no idea what you're talking about. That bitch attacked me."

Caldwell cocked an eyebrow. "Mr. Miller, you have at least a hundred pounds on her. And we found her DNA under your fingernails."

"She's a—" Miller paused, pressing his lips together. "It was self-defense." Caldwell sensed that he wanted to spill it all.

Play it cool. Caldwell pushed his true feelings aside and switched tactics. "There's something more here. Isn't there? And you're afraid to tell me or they'll send you back to the shrink."

Miller squinted.

"What made the scratches on your chest?"

Miller chuckled. "I bet you found similar claw, paw, whatever they are, prints at that retired cop's place."

Caldwell swallowed. "What do you know about Li Liu?"

"Nothing. Never heard of the guy until I saw the news." He folded his arms across his chest. "But I'd bet my wad that you found feathers at his place. Didn't you, detective?"

Caldwell looked down at the table. "We know about Dr. Hitomi and the steroids." He knew no such thing. They had no evidence of communication between the two. All they had were cryptic notes and some of the neighbors' reports of seeing a car in Hitomi's driveway that could have been Miller's.

"I don't do steroids. As for Hitomi, I took one class from her. So you're going nowhere with this questioning."

Caldwell waited a while. He took his time to respond. The fridge smelled like something had expired. The hen wallpaper and the linoleum floor could have been from when the house was first built.

"How well did you know Peter Marx?"

Miller's eyes darted to the side. "I ran across him on campus. We played on the same soccer team in junior high."

"What about Lily Moore's neighbor, Mona Sinclair?"

"Old lady who OD'ed?" he asked, wrinkling his nose. "Why would I know her?"

Caldwell nodded. "We're through." He slid notepaper across the table with the dates of Peter Marx's death and

Mona Sinclair's written upon it. "Please produce some evidence of where you were on these dates."

Miller scowled. "I don't know what you think I did, but you are barking up the wrong tree."

"Fine. It's just I wasn't able to rule you out earlier as a suspect because you had been rendered a lunatic. Remember?"

Miller left and Amber corroborated his whereabouts for the evening Seth Moore's place was ransacked. She didn't have a lot more to add. Most of the interview she spent looking at her hands or shrugging. She had only been out with Miller a few times since his attack.

They walked through the living room on the way out. At the door, Caldwell turned. "Your mom at work?"

Miller's forehead wrinkled a moment than relaxed. "Yeah."

Caldwell returned to the unmarked. He called Big Lots to check on Barbara Miller.

CHAPTER ✒ 42

LODESTONE

IN HER SHISHI form, Lily ran through the field chasing little white moths that came out at night and flitted just above the grass. She accidentally ate one, but wouldn't make that mistake again because it was quite bitter. Vigilant yet curious in this form, she found herself wanting to chase or roark at any noise. However, she also sensed the bird in her wanting to bathe in the hot tub or stare at shiny objects for a very long time.

Round items, or things circular in general, were fantastic. Balls fascinated her to the point of distraction. She just never noticed how many things in the world are round —rocks, tops of banisters, tires, the saucer under planters except they don't make great Frisbees because they shatter between fangs.

Shiny! She bounded through the hedges of the neighbor's yard before making her way back to the cabin so Seth wouldn't worry. She click-clicked up the steps and pried the screen door open with her claw.

Seth sat on the couch reading the neighbor's paper. He looked at her as she stopped just inside the doorway. She was beyond pleased with herself. Her claws sounded like cleats on the hardwood floor as she made her way over to him with her tail wagging.

"Whoa. Stop right there. Not in the house!"

She froze. *What?* she asked in his head.

"You're tracking mud all over the house. What...what do you have in your mouth?"

Ball. As he leaned in, she gave him a little growl. *Mine.*

"Drop it!"

She daintily placed it on the ground so that it wouldn't break—at least not any more than the four holes from her fangs.

He sighed. "Lily. That's the neighbor's gazing ball. It goes in their garden. Geez, you have to be careful. What if they had seen you?"

Killjoy.

"They're probably gonna find your massive paw print and tell the authorities there's a mountain lion loose up here."

She huffed.

"Whatever, I suppose you're ready to go?" Tonight she would attempt flying.

After wiping the mud off the floor, Seth walked out to a clearing in the woods with her. He clenched a Bud Light in his hand. He looked to her expectantly. "I think you should take a running start. You know, like a plane taking off. You have a bit of cargo to lift."

She ran and ran. She flapped and flapped. She was about as adept as a penguin at flying. After a while, she flopped down in the clover and sulked.

"I don't think you want to fly," he said.

She lifted her head and growled. "That's not it. I'm scared. Maybe I can't do it."

"You *can* do it!" he said, lifting his beer bottle in a toast. "Wait, Wait. I know what you need." He set his beer at the base of a white oak tree. A minute later, he was in cat form singing R. Kelly's "I Believe I Can Fly" in his deep baritone.

He was very good.

Her practice flight was not impressive. If you are aviophobic, it's not such a great idea to have wings. After two hours, they were exhausted, but she had managed to achieve a decent altitude twice without hurtling to the ground in order to puke. She also managed to shift into three forms: Shih Tzu, shishi, and her girl-bird form that Seth termed Bird Light, not to be confused with Bud Light. The last form was just as disturbing as the others were since she sported fangs in her human face, mutated feet, wings, and *sometimes* a soft down on her body. She looked like someone in a bad Halloween costume when covered in the down. Of course, the times she didn't produce the down she was butt-naked. *Choices, choices.*

Despite the nausea, Lily went to sleep feeling as if she had achieved something. For once, she had been in full control of herself and her shifting.

In the middle of the night, her control was gone. She awoke drawing rasping breaths. *Air.* After bounding out of bed and across the room, she threw open the window, tied her nightgown around her neck, and hopped on to the ledge.

Her body was throbbing and feverish. Flames of heat traveled from her eyes down her throat and swirled around her breasts. The path continued to her stomach, then lower. She'd never felt like this before.

Closing her eyes, Lily unfurled her wings in the soothing night air. A refreshing cool balm traveled down her shoulder blades and into the appendages on her back. Other parts remained tingling in an indescribable inferno. She ached.

The night sky was a cool river calling to her burning body. A spinning disorientation overtook her as all sight and sound disappeared from her world, and then she crashed. The cool earth was beneath her as she lay on her side, the wet loam attempting to extinguish the fire that had spread throughout her body.

Pushing up to a sitting position, she took in her surroundings. *I did it again—teleported.* Her arms and back ached. She looked around her to see broken tree branches, blooms and leaves. She had crashed through the canopy above and been lucky to land on the soft loam instead of rock. The Chattahochee River had a pungent smell. She was back in Atlanta. Her nostrils filled with indescribable decay.

She knew the river was polluted, but she was on fire and the water was an irrefutable temptation. Stretching her neck, legs, and arms, Lily determined that everything still worked. There was something else though, a sublime smell that beckoned her, pulling her up the bank, through the trees toward the lights of a building.

In the middle of the night, not all slept in the apartment complex.

Closing her eyes while subduing her breathing, she succeeded in retracting her wings. No one was around as she unrolled her nightgown to cover herself. But various pets growled a low rumble as she crept past windows. Not trusting herself, she repressed any thoughts of wings or travel. Instead, she used her clawed hands and feet to scale a post to the second story and gracefully leapt on to the balcony.

She didn't know what she had become, but with profound certainty, Lily knew she needed to be *here*. As she drew closer, she saw the vertical blinds partially open. Through the slits, she watched as a man paced a sparse living room strewn with papers and files. The clutter continued from a black leather couch to a tired wooden table that looked to function as a desk. He plopped down on the couch with a groan, his long legs extended. He wore navy running shorts and a Lupus Run for a Cure t-shirt. His disheveled hair curled from the humidity.

Trembling, Lily placed her bare cheek against the cool veil of screen that separated them. His head turned to the door. The scent incapacitated her. She synced in to his breaths, heartbeats, and every subtle movement. She remained bound by his scent; apparently living one of her dreams.

RUBBING HIS ACHING eyes, Caldwell wished that sleep were no longer a stranger. Her hair, her legs, her tortured eyes...the blood. It all haunted him. He knew she must be alive somewhere. He had to find her.

Shaking his head, he laughed at himself. *Damn I'm one obsessed bastard.* He had scoured through his notes, returned to the stupid high school parking lot, and trudged through Piedmont Park. Alone, he jogged the streets around her house at night. He drove by Seth's place and the Ansley Park home. He was cracking up. He kept seeing the terror she wore on her face that day at Liu's and in his dreams.

Focus. Whatever the hell was going on—delusions, fantasies, early dementia, he needed to suck it up and get a fucking grip. *But the dreams...how could anyone be okay after those dreams?* Violent, haunting, erotic as hell.

He felt like a total head case and was physically ill from the conflict inside his body. Lake still questioned whether Lily Moore was one of their key suspects. *This is so screwed up.*

He turned toward a noise on the porch. A sound, almost like a trill, had come through the screen. Juiced with adrenaline, he walked to the sliding door and pushed the blinds aside.

Lily?

She stood on the thin railing, the moonbeams setting her skin aglow. Her eyes were illuminated.

Struggling to find his voice, he stepped on to the porch with his hand held up like he was trying to stop a jumper.

"Don't...move!" His voice hitched. He had meant to sound authoritative. She stood on the railing with her mouth open, panting. Caldwell reached for his gun and got nothing. *Great.* He had left it on the table. He just did not think clearly when it came to her.

She turned to look over her shoulder as if she might just drop backwards.

"Don't," he pleaded. He didn't blink or move. He attempted to focus on other things than the features revealed too explicitly by the thin nightgown.

Tears coursed down her cheeks.

Aw hell. "Just...stay there. Please." Her breathing had quieted, but her face remained wet with tears. She was as still as a statue, except for a slight tilting of her head as she studied him with her intense eyes. They burned into him.

"Seth would never intentionally hurt someone."

"It was a stupid move," he said.

"I know. He wasn't himself." She looked away as if ashamed.

"I want to help you Lily. Can...can you get down off of there; you're giving me a heart attack."

She met his eyes, her lips pressed tight.

Caldwell returned the stare. His eyes took everything in: the short blonde hair, her smooth uninjured skin, and her muscular legs. Then he noticed her feet. They were misshapen, like...claws. He looked back at her pretty face and pretended he hadn't noticed. "You need to trust me, Lil— Ms. Moore."

Something in her eyes flashed. "I thought I could trust you." Her face dropped.

"You can." He meant it, but doubt clutched at him. *What am I doing?* People were dying and he was standing on the balcony trying to catch a cornered, unpredictable woman, *creature*.

As if she sensed the change in him, the doubt, an ugly net he was extending, she turned her body sideways to look out again into the sky.

He was losing her. He decided to grab her.

Her eyes flashed again. Something struck his chin and he saw stars. That was the last thing he remembered.

CHAPTER 43

GBI

CALDWELL LEANED AGAINST the door frame of Tiny's office. Tiny reclined in his chair with his feet propped up on the desk talking to KPD's crime scene investigator over the phone. They were going round and round about tire tracks. When Tiny hung up, Caldwell felt someone behind him.

He watched as Tiny dropped his feet from his desk while attempting to sit up straighter in his chair. "May I help you?"

Caldwell turned around and came face-to-face with Georgia Bureau of Investigation Agent, Rebecca Scott. He recognized her. They had worked briefly on a homicide ten months ago that involved two juveniles. It had been an ugly case. Of course, what homicide case wasn't ugly? "Agent Scott?"

"Detective Simms. How are you?"

"Okay. You heading up to see the lieutenant?"

"Of course. Looks like we get to put our heads together about this Moore family," she said. She wore her dark hair pulled back, revealing a Slavic heritage in the bone structure of her face and the shape of her eyes. Her blue shirt matched her eyes. She wore dark slacks over legs that went on and on and on. Caldwell knew Tiny would notice.

"I'm Rebecca Scott," she said stepping into Tiny's office.

"Tiny."

"Pardon me?"

Tiny hopped down from the chair. She was wearing sensible low-heeled shoes, but Tiny still came to her bust line.

"My name is Tiny."

"Oh. I've spoken to you on the phone, briefly."

Tiny just stood there staring at her. Caldwell cleared his throat.

Scott raised her eyebrows.

"Uh, I'm going up to see the Boss man, now. I'll walk with you," Tiny said.

"Very good," she said with a smile.

"Did you see the *Lord of the Rings* movie?"

"Honestly, I fell asleep," she said.

"Oh no. Well I was in it." He led her down the hallway. "I was a hobbit extra."

"That's funny I don't remember seeing any black hobbits."

"Well, I've never seen any good-looking GBI agents, but it doesn't mean they don't exist."

Caldwell rolled his eyes up in his head as he followed behind them.

In any other situation, he would be glad for the input from the GBI, but he didn't want Scott's nose in the Moore family business. No matter how much he tried, he couldn't be objective. He had been so relieved to see Lily Moore alive last night, but then the guilt kicked in. He should have told Lake about her visit, but he couldn't bring himself to do it. Caldwell didn't want to believe that she had hurt anyone. *Had she?* His thoughts continued to circle back to the sight of her strange feet and his stomach churned.

He grabbed a Coke from the machine in the break-room. Katie Quinn would be arriving shortly for questioning. He needed to have a clear head.

CHAPTER ✒ 44

KATIE QUINN

CALDWELL FELT CLAMMY under the lieutenant's intense scrutiny. The lieutenant could read him like his mother could. "What happened to your chin?" he asked, scowling.

"Tree branch got me when I was jogging," Caldwell said. He was working hard to keep up with Lake who was plowing down the hall. Lake stopped in his tracks and narrowed his eyes.

"What?"

"Don't lie to me, Simms. I know all your tells," Lake said. He shook his head then continued to the observation room to look through the glass. Caldwell came up next to him. He couldn't tell Lake that he caught a toe nail/claw in the chin.

They studied Katie Quinn, Seth Moore's girlfriend. She was in a different interview room than the one they had used to question Mr. Moore five days ago. Maintenance still needed to patch the wall from the Seth Moore incident. The thought made Caldwell's stitches itch.

A jeweled clip secured Miss Quinn's swept-up golden blonde hair. Her pink blouse clung to ample breasts. Her amber eyes looked worried and she bit her plump bottom lip as she fidgeted with an amethyst pendant. It didn't surprise Caldwell that Seth's girl was a looker.

Lake wrinkled his nose as he studied the pretty woman on the other side of the glass. "You think she's involved in this shit?"

Caldwell just sighed. "Let's find out."

"Hi, Miss Quinn, I'm Detective Simms and this is Lieutenant Lake. We've spoken over the phone, but it's nice to meet in person."

She nodded.

After they recorded the preliminary identifying information, Caldwell leaned across the table toward her in a conspiratorial fashion, "I know this is difficult. Lily Moore is your best friend and you were close to her brother as well. We are just reviewing details; trying to find any gaps in the info we have so far."

Lake pulled his chair in closer, drawing Quinn's attention to him. "So have you heard anything from the Moores since Seth's stunt the other day?" Caldwell glanced at him sideways. *So much for easing into things.*

"I don't know what you mean by stunt—"

"This," Lake said, pointing to Caldwell's head.

Quinn's mouth hung open.

"Assaulting an officer, Miss Quinn."

She swallowed.

"Your boyfriend assaulted my detective, so you might want to reconsider protecting him in any way," Lake said.

Okay not the approach I was going for, but you're the boss.

"I spoke to Seth on the phone the day before his meeting with you," she said, looking back down at the table.

"How would you describe your relationship with

Seth?" Caldwell asked.

Quinn began to smile then seemed to catch herself. "We've been dating for a couple of months."

Caldwell scanned her face. There wasn't a glint of doubt in her eyes that Seth Moore was innocent.

"You see any changes in his behavior recently?" asked Lake.

"Of course."

Caldwell leaned in.

"He's sick about his sister, as am I," she said.

Lake nodded. "Was Seth taking any particular medications that you were aware of?"

"No."

"Do you know if he used any medications or drugs in the past?" asked Caldwell.

She manipulated her pendant. "Seth was not a drug user. I hardly ever saw him drink."

"No antidepressants after his father's death?" Lake asked.

"Oh, now he did mention that he took something for a while to address panic attacks."

"Inderal?" Caldwell asked.

"I don't remember the name of the medication. I'm sorry." Her brow furrowed like something just struck home.

Caldwell nodded. "Do you know a woman by the name of Tashi?"

"Tashi?"

"Seth's been exchanging emails and phone calls with a woman named Tashi," Caldwell explained. They knew from Larry Jones that the Shih Tzu's name was Tashi, but he wanted to see Quinn's reaction.

Katie's eyes narrowed. "He's never mentioned anyone by that name." He could see by her confused expression that they had blind-sided her.

"I know you care about Seth," Lake said. "But sometimes people have several sides to them. There may be a side that you don't know. Think very carefully about any emotional outbursts or odd behavior you may have noted in him."

"I don't understand. Seth was a pussy cat."

Caldwell snuck a glance at the lieutenant.

"What do you mean by pussy cat?" Lake asked.

She looked at him, curiously. "Gentle."

"You ever see a big, white cat hanging around?" Lake asked.

"What?"

"White cat, two different colored ears, bobbed tail," barked Lake, his own ears red.

Quinn's brows drew down in confusion.

Lake continued to stare at her.

"Seth rescues a lot of cats. I've seen black ones, grey ones, white ones. In fact, he spoke with me the day after Mr. Liu went missing. He had been up late at the vet rescuing a pregnant cat."

"Which vet?" Caldwell asked. He started to feel lightheaded again and he knew it wasn't the pea green walls of the eight by ten foot room.

She hesitated. "Some vet up in Marietta."

"A name would be helpful," Caldwell said, softening his voice, attempting to calm her.

She looked at her hands in her lap and worried her bottom lip again. "Dr. Gladwell? Something like that."

"He mention that he had been in contact with his sister?"

"No. He mentioned how worried he was about her."

Lake tapped his pen in a staccato rhythm on the table while staring at her. "How long have you known the Moores?"

"Since grade school." She lifted her chin as if to challenge Lake. "I've been praying that Lily's alive. We've lost touch a bit since Pete's death, but we've been best friends. She spent a lot of time with my family during the summers, especially after her parent's divorce."

"You haven't heard a thing from either of them?"

"No. Seth hasn't answered any phone calls, texts, or emails. I even tried calling his mom, but she's been in China—something about her mother being ill." A tear escaped the corner of her eye. She brushed it away with her hand.

"We've talked about Dr. Hitomi—"

"Yeah, she's crazy."

Caldwell held his tongue. "What about Li Liu. Did either of them talk about him?"

"Neither of them had talked about him for some time. But then Seth mentioned that he had contacted him to sort some things out about his father's death."

Lake shut the folder in front of him. Quinn sat up in her chair, "Are we finished?"

"For now," Lake grumbled. "You need to notify us if either of them makes contact with you. They're in great danger. Keep in mind that aiding and abetting is a major criminal offense," he added as he escorted her out.

Her face flushed red and her lips pressed tight, but she

didn't respond.

When the elevator doors closed, Caldwell turned to Lake. "That GBI agent making you cranky?"

"Quinn's gotta have some inkling of where they may hole up. Check back with her later and see if you can pick her brain." Caldwell followed behind him.

"You all right?" Caldwell asked.

"No, Simms, I'm edgy," he said glaring. "Too many secrets. People protecting people because they have feelings for them."

"Okay—"

"I don't want to find another dead body. I'm worried it's gonna be Li or one of the Moores."

Caldwell burped up his breakfast burrito.

"I'll see if I can track down the vet. You follow up on our other leads," Lake said. His gray shirt was already wrinkled. "I gotta go see what the hell Tiny told Agent Scott. I feel like I just left Red Riding Hood with the wolf."

Caldwell chuckled. He was *pretty* sure he meant Scott was the wolf, which left Tiny as Red Riding Hood.

CHAPTER ✒ 45

RENEGADE

CALDWELL HAD LEFT early around 4:00 p.m. after putting a call in to Sax Ad Agency where Quinn worked. He had planned to catch Katie Quinn off-guard at her condo in Buckhead. She wasn't home, but her retired neighbor was. They spoke for a while about the Quinn family. She let him know that they went to Sedona every year at this time and she mentioned a cabin in Helen.

That was the spark Caldwell needed. He searched properties under the Quinn name. He hadn't turned up anything. Then he looked at the marriage certificate and found the stepmother's maiden name, Hughes.

Several hours later, he paced back and forth in his small living room thinking about the paper work that he found on the Hughes's cabin. At 8:30 p.m. he dressed in all black, climbed into his blue Ford Explorer and headed north on Highway 19. His Journey CD blared from the speakers as he drove fifteen miles over the speed limit. He worked his Juicy Fruit gum until his jaw ached and caught himself singing off-key to "Don't Stop Believin'."

He sweet-talked his GPS, but she still got him lost in the dark. One and a half hours later, he stopped at a Shell gas station to confirm with a local the country road that he needed. On Alternate 75, he passed Hootenany Hills Drive.

After going back and forth several times, he eventually figured out Horton Creek was the road with the sign that read "Pat's Place."

He turned off his radio and drove with his parking lights on, attempting to read the addresses. Several times, he caught himself singing the banjo music from *Deliverance*, particularly when he flashed his lights and they illuminated ancient dilapidated school buses stranded in an overgrown lot.

When he came to a fork of two driveways, he stopped while the engine idled. He needed to do the rest on foot. Backing up about five houses, he drove on to the side of a grassy strip next to a high, chain-link fence. It looked like people had parked here before. Once he was satisfied he was far enough off the road, he turned off the engine.

His heart pounded rapidly as the all too familiar rush of adrenaline hit him. A cold sweat broke out on his forehead. It was pitch black out his window. He pulled on his hat before exiting the vehicle.

He switched on his small Mag flashlight as his Timberland boots crunched on the gravel road. Night creatures scurried through the foliage on both sides of him. An owl hooted in the distance. It was a muggy eighty-degree night. Sweat ran down the sides of his face. He'd take city noise to this woodsy quietness any day. Drawing his gun, Caldwell slowly made his way to the two driveways. There was no indication which one was 349, but he followed his instincts, heading left.

The house wasn't visible from the road. He headed up the gravel driveway without the help of his light. Covered in pine needles, the side of the driveway offered quieter terrain. Three hundred feet in, he got his first view of the A-frame cedar cabin. To the side was a garage fronted by an old jeep Wrangler. Gun drawn, he approached the side of the cabin. Lights were on upstairs and down.

Caldwell stood still for several minutes while he scanned the upstairs, then the downstairs, detecting no movement. No prosaic household noise broke the silence of the night as he crept closer. He crouched beneath the window. The sharp cedar scent mixed with pine, and he barely stifled a sneeze. Caldwell couldn't find anything to stand on. He'd have to go around back or walk right up on the front porch to peer inside.

Hugging the foundation of the cabin, Caldwell made his way to the backyard. Light spilled from sliding glass doors on to the deck, revealing a hot tub. He slowly made his way up each step until his head cleared the top of the banister. Overhead track lighting revealed the great room and kitchen of a cozy cabin. The main floor appeared unoccupied. So much for a hideout. The damn place was a fish bowl. For the hell of it, he tried the back door before the front door and windows. He flipped over the plaque by the front door. "The Quinns."

Caldwell returned to the rear deck, settling into a dark corner with his back against the hot tub. It provided the perfect vantage point for seeing anyone who came into the great room or kitchen. It was 10:00 p.m. Surely they hadn't gone to sleep yet. As he listened and waited, he thought back to the day he had walked into Larry Jones's house to discover Lily Moore as a Shih Tzu. His thoughts drifted to her face at the Liu property after she had been beaten and shot. Seth Moore popped into his head, causing him to grit his teeth. His stitches itched under his solid black cap.

He was used to stakeouts. Hunkering down, he prepared to wait until the wee hours of the morning.

"THIS IS A very bad idea. This is the worst plan you've ever had. This ranks up there with your 'let's put a roman candle in dad's grill' scheme."

Lily rolled her eyes.

"Just so you know that membrane comes across your eyes when you do that," Seth said.

She stopped. The avian eyes disturbed her. In all her shapeshifting forms, she had a third eyelid.

"When it comes to this guy, you're not rational. Just because he didn't shoot you once, doesn't mean he won't shoot you, given a second chance," Seth said.

"You make a valid point. Let's send you in. You're the one that gave the poor man a concussion and made him the laughing stock of his department. I'm up for some entertainment. Go on kitty. See if he's a cat lover."

They sat twenty feet up in a pine tree where they had watched Detective Simms's surveillance of the cabin. Thankfully, Lily's animal instincts had overridden her human fear of heights. She could fly and jump from high places without a problem now.

It was just after midnight. Caldwell Simms had been propped against the hot tub waiting on them for over two hours. Seth thought they should run because he assumed that Simms wanted to "put a cap in his ass." Lily argued Detective Simms was there to help them. Why else would he be there without back-up?

Seth was convinced he was up to some nefarious act, possibly one in conjunction with the masked Watcher. Neither of them could be sure, but Lily was not running or hiding any more. She wanted it all to be over. In her mind, she flirted with the idea that her trip the previous night may have been the impetus for this visit. No way in hell was she telling Seth that she teleported to Atlanta.

"Again, Lily. How did he find us? And, if he's a good guy, why the hell is he sneaking around with his gun in the dark?"

"Zzzzzzzzzzzz." With their heightened senses, they heard Detective Simms's snores. They looked at each other.

"Since when do bad guys fall asleep on a stakeout?" Lily asked. "Evil people are too crazy to sleep. Now an overworked, underpaid civil servant would be more likely to succumb in this weather and at this time of night."

"This isn't going to work." Seth started to move toward their backpacks, which hung from a nearby branch. Lily glared at him. He knew she was stronger than he was otherwise he would have already tackled her.

"You need to trust me." Before he could argue, she grabbed her backpack and flew down to the ground, landing in a crouch. She had Mr. Quinn's Glock 36 in the back of her pink cut-off sweatpants. She felt the warm breeze on her bare chest. Sprouting wings had shredded her tank top, but she managed to keep her bottoms on so she considered this progress. She would have needed to transform fully to Bird Light for the soft down to cover her body.

"Not looking," Seth hissed from his perch.

She grabbed the backpack while retracting her wings. After throwing another tank top over her head, she took off running before Seth tried to catch her.

Her plan was for him to stay in the trees since his presence could be incendiary. She leapt over the railing to land precisely in front of the sleeping detective. She was shocked to find his eyes open, gun drawn. That's when she jumped on his lap in a panicked bird state, pinning his arms to the hot tub with her claws. The gunshot exploded in her ear.

The loud report had her ears ringing. Simms had rolled his hips and started to flip her off his lap when the gun discharged. Lily's head throbbed where she had bashed it on the hot tub.

Feathers rained down, coming to rest on every wet surface. Detective Simms was on his side, her legs wrapped around his waist. They stared into each other's eyes. Everything was in slow motion. His lips moved, but she couldn't hear what he was saying to her.

The hot tub gushed water all over the deck. Her left hip hurt where he had slammed her down. Her hearing returned suddenly.

"You bird brain! Mary Mother of...Lily. What did you do?" Seth stood on the railing. His now dyed black hair stood completely on end. Lily watched as his eyes followed the flowing water. She knew his feline side didn't like getting his feet wet.

Her cheek rested against the side of the hot tub. Detective Simms slouched low, the top of his head touching the fiberglass.

"Lily?" Simms asked.

Looking down, she noted that she was naked from the waist up and there was blood in the water.

Seth pulled his shirt off in order to cover her. Then he ran inside to turn on the back floodlights. He returned within three seconds.

"Who's hurt?" Seth leaned over them. Simms glared up at him.

"I don't think you're helping, Seth. Go inside." She brought her right arm up to keep the shirt to her chest while unhooking her leg from the detective's waist.

Seth backed up two feet and fretted. "I told you that guns are bad!" He must have been reliving the night he found her in Larry's backyard.

Simms looked green. Lily feared he was going into shock. She didn't know if it was from fear or physical pain. Seth had told her when she got mad her eyes could make a grown man piss himself. With Seth raving in the background, the detective turned to look at her.

She gazed back at him. "Are you hurt?" She noticed the wound at his temple had re-opened and oozed.

He shifted, then winced. Simms looked down. Despite his black pants, Lily could see the blood in the dark. The hot tub wasn't the only victim. She was terrified.

"Never, ever listening to you...we are so fu..." Seth rambled.

"Shut up, Seth!" Simms yelled.

Lily and Seth both froze.

Seth's mouth hung open.

Lily looked at him. "Towels, now, hurry." While Seth ran inside, she sat up and pulled his shirt over her head. When she turned back, Simms had drawn his gun.

Why didn't I listen to my brother? Her weapon had slid further into her underwear when she was wrestling the officer and now it felt like she had a load weighing down the back of her drawers.

Her eyes watered. She gulped for air and hiccupped. "Please don't."

Simms looked at her, then at his hand. She noticed it was trembling. His face showed surprise. Of course it did. He just had some winged demon woman jump him. Shit she would have shot her own mutant ass. He raised his left hand to grip the gun tighter. She shut her eyes and held her breath. She wasn't some fierce guardian; she was a chicken. Her impulsiveness was finally going to be her undoing.

There was a click.

"I have no idea why I'm trusting you," Simms said. She opened her eyes to see that he had engaged the safety and no longer had the gun pointed at her.

That's when she lunged at him.

She hugged his chest and cried, overwhelmed with relief.

"Thank you," she gushed.

He awkwardly patted her back.

"I didn't recognize you. You weren't a, uh, dog."

"Sorry, I can't imagine what you thought was coming at you!" Lily looked down at his hip. "We need to get you off this wet deck."

Seth burst through the door with blankets as well as every piece of linen from the Quinn storage closet. He came to an abrupt stop when he saw her hugging the detective's neck.

"Oh, for Christ's sake, Lily. Get off the man already.

Isn't it bad enough you shot him?"

"I didn't shoot him. He shot himself," she insisted.

"She tackled me. My gun was in my hand. Thankfully, I didn't hit her. The bullet just grazed my hip." He apparently was not happy with her version of the story.

"You should have shot her," Seth said. "Seriously, Lily, you don't just jump someone!" He completely missed the irony of his statement, forgetting he had jumped Simms in the interrogation room barely a week ago.

"I was trying to be quiet about it, but he woke up!" She stood.

"You're as stealthy as a bunch of drunken frat boys." Seth said.

Now toe to toe, they stared at each other. Simms gasped. Lily stepped away from her annoying brother, breathed, and retracted her claws.

"Let's get him inside," Seth said.

Without thinking, she reached down and scooped him up in her arms. She felt his body tense. Seth did his funny cat giggle. Lily blushed from her own strength. She didn't dare look at the officer. She didn't want to see his face that surely would confirm what he really thought about her.

She plopped him on the counter top, near the kitchen sink.

"Seth, get the first aid kit," she ordered. He dashed out the door to grab the backpack where she had dropped it on the wet deck.

The detective's pants smelled burnt where the bullet charred through them. She grabbed the hole to rip his pant leg open further. She did the same with his black boxer briefs. Then she grabbed his black shirt and lifted it up to inspect his stomach and chest to look for more wounds. Seth returned in time to give her a dirty look. She just shrugged. *What? I couldn't leave him in the wet shirt.* She accepted a towel from him to apply direct pressure to Simms's wound. The detective attempted to take care of things himself, but she wouldn't let him. He was all business as he gave them instructions in cleaning wounds. Seth kept eyeing her. So what if she was relishing her role as medic.

"Lily. Don't you think he needs to go to the hos-pi-tal?" Seth asked, drawing out the word like she was touched in the head.

She stopped her triage and looked at him. This hadn't occurred to her. She looked to Detective Simms. "Um. Seth can drive you to the hospital, but only if you promise not to tell anyone where we are."

Seth rolled his eyes. "Don't be stupid. Of course, he's going to call someone. He's a cop." Simms remained eerily quiet.

Lily looked down at his wound. *My God, what have I done?* Her eyes began to water.

"I really think I'll be okay. It just grazed me," he said.

Lily looked like she was going to hug his neck. He gave her a warning look.

"You need some ice," he said.

"Seth, get him some ice."

"I meant for *your* head."

She looked into his slate blue eyes, confused.

"Sorry about the bump on your head," he said.

"Well it's better than a bullet," she laughed.

He looked at her. This was the closest she had ever

been to him except for when she was at Larry's. He licked his lips. She closed her mouth before she drooled. He gave her a tight-lipped smile, no teeth. She noticed he was shaking and realized he had to be in a lot of pain, but he still didn't go for his gun. It rested next to him on the counter, safety engaged.

After they dressed his wounds, Seth gave him a spare pair of sweatpants and white t-shirt. Upstairs, Lily changed out of her wet clothes into a tank top and shorts. When she came back, Simms was on the couch with a blanket draped over him. As she was getting him some ginger ale, Seth grabbed her arm. "What are we going to do now?"

"I don't know," she rasped.

"Great planning," he said. His eyes travelled to her injured head. "Does it hurt badly?"

"Not awful, but I've got the crucible. Detective Simms doesn't." Seth let go of her arm. "The Vicadin and Extra Strength Tylenol are upstairs," she suggested.

He sighed as he went to retrieve them. Simms said no to the Vicadin even though she could tell he was tired and in pain.

"I need you both to sit down," he said. Lily sat down at his feet. Seth sat in the rocking chair directly across from them. Simms sat up straighter as if to appear stronger and more authoritative, "I expect your full cooperation from here on out."

Seth scowled. She smiled.

"I want an honest, direct answer," he ordered.

Seth squirmed in his chair. Lily forgot to breathe.

"What *are* you?"

CHAPTER 46

FROM THE LOST NOTES OF PETER MARX

August 5, 2010

I found her notes. The Vestiges are showing signs of aggression from the steroid injections. Shocking. Instead of backing off treatments or reducing dosage, Dr. H has increased the treatments. Subject V1, in particular, is 'harboring aggressive thoughts.' He didn't divulge his feelings to Dr. H. She learned this through reading his mind. That's right. She reads minds. She knows my thoughts, doubts, and grave concerns regarding this research. She didn't verbally threaten me. She didn't have to.

An interesting development occurred yesterday. Subject V2 expressed his wish to withdraw from treatments. We'll see what happens from here. The shapeshifter, Subject C, has withdrawn from treatments. I know that she hounds him mercilessly to resume. Tells him, he's a danger without his medicine.

At this point, I feel the responsible thing to do is learn the identity of the Vestiges and monitor them to see how bad their reaction is and if Subject VI is not only harboring aggressive thoughts, but acting on them.

   -Peter

CHAPTER 🪶 47

NEW ALLY?

LILY SAT UP in bed, screaming. The dawn's gray light filtered softly through the gauzy white curtains of the cabin. Across the room Detective Simms stood, motionless. His hair was on end from sleep mixed with panic.

He had been on the lumpy couch before she sounded the alarm. Maybe it was a dirty trick putting the Vicadin in his soda, but it had contained him enough that she had worked the handcuffs on him and moved him to the lumpy couch across the room from her in the master bedroom.

Feathers drifted in the air, but they weren't hers. Scanning the bed, she saw sliced down pillows and torn sheets.

"What the fuck?" Seth asked from the doorway. Balanced on all fours with her wings spread, she perched naked in the middle of the bed. Seth growled. The detective put his manacled hands out in a placating gesture.

"Night terrors," he suggested. His eyes were intense as he met Seth's. Lily watched as Seth assessed Simms's intact sweatpants and makeshift bed on the couch and...the handcuffs. The officer averted his eyes from her. Seth approached the bed, looking down at the floor. Lily sat back and drew her wings in front of her like a cloak.

"Lil?" cautioned Seth. "You need to close your mouth

then your eyes. Take a deep breath in through your nose."
She did as he instructed. "Take your time as you exhale out
through your mouth." The heat escaped her, spilling forth
into the room. The hot tears on her cheeks began to cool.

"Again," he said.

Her eyes popped open at the creak of the floorboards.
Simms was approaching, concerned.

"Stay back, Detective Simms," Seth said.

He didn't look like he liked taking orders from Seth,
but he backed up to stand in front of the sofa. The morning
light struck his face. Warmth spread down the back of
Lily's neck as she looked at him.

"Lily," Seth demanded her attention. She didn't want
to tear her eyes away from Simms, but Seth grasped the
sides of her head. With much effort, she closed her eyes.

"Get a hold of yourself," he whispered. She finally
understood what he meant. *Whose body is this anyway?*
She retracted her wings after Seth threw a warm blanket
over her. Opening her eyes, she clutched the blue blanket to
her as she scooted back to rest against the headboard. She
studied the patterns of the blanket, her face warm with
shame.

When she looked up, Seth sat scowling at the foot of
the bed. "I thought you were going to tie him up with the
rope downstairs." He folded his arms across his bare chest.

"Well," she squeaked. "He's injured and we gave him
medication. I needed to monitor him and make sure he
stayed breathing."

"Where'd you get the handcuffs?"

"From the Quinn's bedside table."

"Ewww." Seth said. They both looked over at the

detective who was eyeing the cuffs in a whole new light.

Lily didn't tell Seth about shifting to Shih Tzu mode and curling up next to Detective Simms after licking his wounds. The deep gash on the officer's head was now a blotch of pale pink with a sliver of a brown scab starting. Her crazy saliva in conjunction with the crucible had worked some kind of magic. Now what were they going to do with him?

Seth shook his head. "Lily, next time you handcuff someone, I suggest you handcuff him *to* something. If he wasn't drugged he could have just walked out of the house!"

"Give me a break. You've taken my phone, my gun, and my keys. Don't yell at her."

Seth approached him. "Please sit down."

The cop didn't move. Lily admired the way his chest filled out her brother's white Hanes undershirt.

Seth turned his head toward her, his lip curled in disgust.

"What?" she asked.

She glanced at the detective who pressed his lips down as if to suppress a smile.

"Geez, did ya both hear my thoughts?" The detective wore a crooked grin.

CALDWELL THOUGHT BACK to the night before. The room had smelled like cool mountain air. He realized it was her scent. Her thrashing had woken him several times, but he was too drugged to stay conscious for long. He watched from the couch, albeit half-drugged, to witness her body change in her sleep. At one point, he had looked across to see her tiny porcelain feet peeking out from a cocoon of wings that she wrapped around herself in sleep. The feathers were brilliant. She looked like a little angel wrapped in the iridescent wings with her bleached blonde hair framing her round face. Then he noticed fangs. *More like a killer angel who could render him in two with her claws.*

Caldwell's healed hip perplexed him. His head hurt from trying to make sense of things. Perhaps he was lying in a coma somewhere in a hospital and these were his crazy head-injured thoughts.

He had seen them in their animal forms. Now what was he going to do? Were they telling the truth? It sure seemed like it. He also knew that Dr. Gladson knew about them and didn't tell the police. Lily would be dead if he hadn't helped them. Now Caldwell understood why Lily had avoided the police. She was a new shifter with little control. No telling what some of his colleagues would have done if she had flashed *those* eyes at them; not call animal control, that's for sure.

Caldwell tried to make his head stop spinning. He wished he had spoken to Lieutenant Lake first. He wouldn't be trapped in the Moores' lair, defenseless if he had waited. Actually, the more he thought about it, he was relieved. If Lake was here, he would have shot one of the Moores last night. They would definitely take his badge. Unless, he could persuade the Moores to trust him. Trust the police.

It would be a bit easier convincing the Moores to come in if the APD had a solid suspect, but they didn't. However, they did have a lead—a set of tire tracks. Tiny didn't have those results back yet. There were too many things Caldwell needed to sort out. He knew there was no coaxing the Moores to return to Atlanta with him. The adoption paper work from the Department of Vital Statistics was stuck in some government black box. That plane went down in the Sea of Red Tape and was yet to be recovered.

Light spilled through the skylights promising another beautiful day. Too bad he couldn't enjoy it. He gritted his teeth. The Moores had slunk outside on the front porch to talk.

"Hey! You can't keep me locked here forever!" Caldwell knew they could hear him. He'd noticed how they could talk to each from different floors of the cabin. He sat on the steps midway down, handcuffed to one of the metal balusters of the railing. He wanted his phone, his keys...*his gun!*

CHAPTER ✒ 48

POWER STRUGGLE

LILY SAT ON the natural wood porch swing sipping on coffee from a Savannah College of Art and Design mug. It made her think of her friend Katie and the fact that they had broken into her cabin. *God, what must she think right now? Does she think we're dead...or killers?* Seth rested his butt against the front porch railing in front of her.

"We can't worry about that right now," he said. He wore cargo shorts, Reggie's Nike Air Hoops and an army green shirt so he would be somewhat camouflaged in the woods.

"I wasn't talking, *thinking*, to you," she snarked. She adjusted her t-shirt. It was Seth's idea after she appeared topless one too many times. They cut a vertical rectangle out of the back of a brown shirt, leaving a strip at the bottom that they halved. She then could tie it to tighten the shirt at her low, low back. If she shifted to Bird Light, this allowed room for her wings, but kept her covered. If she shifted to her other forms she was pretty much SOL. Black cargo shorts and lace-less tennis shoes completed her outfit.

It was 7:00 a.m. The weather report suggested record-breaking temperatures for early June along with humidity at eighty percent. Lily was sweating, but more from nerves. They had a cop drugged and tied up. What the hell would their father think? This brought tears to her eyes and she pinched herself. *Get a fucking grip.*

She inhaled deeply the scents of the grass, pine, jasmine before exhaling slowly while scanning the woods. Perched in the low branches of a Dogwood tree, a Cardinal sang his *whoit, whoit, whoit, whoit.* Followed by his *what-cheer, what-cheer.* Her ears continued to attempt to localize a low frequency buzzing sound close to them.

"We need to leave here. We'll go hide in the woods," Seth said. Lily watched as morning fog rolled across the foot of the pines. Seth ran his hands through his spiky black hair. The pink splotches on his cheeks betrayed his emotions. He was coming down off Inderal. More sensitive than usual, his anxiety swelled while he continued to plead with her about their plan.

It had been almost a week since he started his withdrawal. He spent several sleepless nights stalking the woods. Sometimes it was downright painful for him. She could hear his caterwauling from miles away. He had rebuffed her attempts to ease him with the crucible. His eyes made it clear that he would rather she threw a live grenade at him.

"Seth. What's that low tapping, almost buzzing sound?" She wanted to enjoy the birds' song and this, this was not natural to the woods around them. Seth set his coffee on the railing; his eyes suddenly cat—almost aqua with deeper clouds of color surrounding his slit pupil. They both jumped down the steps and stopped in front of Detective Simms's Explorer.

Seth dropped to his hands and knees at the back bumper and searched the undercarriage. Hair on end, he stood up holding a gray and white device smaller than a cell phone.

"Geez Seth, that could be a bomb," Lily growled.

His nostrils flared as he pulled the device closer to his face. Lily drew closer. "It's a tracking device. See. It says security on it."

Lily stood next to Seth. She smelled the sunny meadow scent she came to recognize as him, but mixed in was the scent of animal and sweat and gun oil—her nightmare, the Dark Watcher. *More like assassin.*

In disgust, Seth threw the device violently against the cabin. The force caused it to shatter into tiny pieces. No human could have done that much damage. The buzzing stopped.

They heard yelling from the house. *Detective Simms.* "What the hell's going on out there?"

Seth sprang up the stairs. Lily ran after him. "Seth. Wait. You don't know—"

When he turned around at the screen door, every muscle in his body quivered, ready to pounce. "He brought them straight to us."

Lily tried to breathe as she followed Seth into the front hall. On the oak stairs, Detective Simms sat sweating. He obviously had been trying to kick at the metal balustrade with his bare foot. His slate blue eyes looked deeper blue when he was angry.

"Why didn't you just shoot us? Or are you getting some money or bonus if you turn us over alive for some sick fucking government agency to experiment with us?" Seth crouched in front of the cop, his face in the detective's.

Lily stood behind Seth. Her chest hurt. Why did she trust a complete stranger? And why had she expected him to trust them? They'd run from him, drugged him, and kept him hostage. Why would he be on their side? She tried to ignore his scent of musk, citrus, spice, and sweat. The more nervous he got, the stronger it was to her.

She gained her voice, then. "We found the tracking device." She bit the inside of her cheek so she wouldn't cry and appear weak.

Detective Simms's alarm showed in his eyes. "What tracking device?" Seth studied the detective's face with his cat eyes aglow while Lily locked eyes with the cop.

"The one on your Explorer," she spat.

He struggled to stand. "Let me see it."

"Seth took care of it," she said.

"Jesus Christ. Do you understand what this means? You gotta unlock me. I need my gun, my phone. I need to call the lieutenant. Someone may have followed me here!" The tendons down the sides of his neck bulged. He was pissed.

They all stood on the steps at an impasse. Detective Simms maintained his awkward position, slightly bent over from where his hands attached to the railing.

"I don't have a tracking device on my personal car. You turned off my cell phone so no one could track me that way, either. No one knows where I am." He looked down then, as the realization of that statement appeared to wash over him.

Lily took a step backward. When Seth turned to her, he looked frightened. "We need to get out of here," she said. He grabbed her upper arm and proceeded to push her to walk down the stairs. She pushed back. "No! We need to take him, too."

"Don't be stupid, Lily."

"Lily?" The detective said her *first* name, his voice pleading.

"Don't look at him," Seth hissed.

She looked around her brother's shoulder and knew she couldn't leave the cop. "We don't have time for this. They may already be in the woods watching. Would you leave Dad here?" she asked her brother.

He growled at her under his breath.

Both their heads turned at once. Someone was coming down the gravel driveway. In a blur, they ran for their weapons and packs positioned at the back door.

The front window shattered. Rifle shots pinged through the air. Lily dove to the ground. On her hands and knees, she scrambled now with the Remington youth rifle in her hands and her pack on her back. Detective Simms had flattened himself on the steps. She wiggled up the stairs as what sounded like firecrackers went off behind her. With trembling fingers, she reached out with the key and unlocked his cuffs. Once free, he grabbed her wrists.

CHAPTER 49

MOORE ARMAGEDDON

SETH WAS SHOOTING out the front of the house. Then he drew inside to reload. She continued to stare into Caldwell Simms's eyes attempting to read what they were telling her. She had his gun shoved in the back of her pants. He released her right wrist, cocked an eyebrow and reached around to feel her butt. He pulled out his gun and released her other wrist. Then he pushed her to the side and ran down the stairs. Seth had his back against the front wall when a woman began to shout outside.

The cop slunk to the other side of the open door across from Seth. "I know you can hear me, Lily Moore!" Lily flinched involuntarily. "Listen carefully. We have your China man. He may be alive or we may have carved him up with his fancy Kung Fu knife. Or maybe we've kicked him, like old dog Tray."

A car door slammed and she heard gravel churning as the woman backed the vehicle out of the driveway. What did that last line mean? *Old Dog Tray* was a poem by Stephen Foster. She didn't recognize the woman's scent or voice.

As soon as the car engine faded in the distance, she ran for the jeep. "Lily!" Seth screamed from behind her. Detective Simms stood in the doorway, his gun trained on

Seth.

Lily saw his clenched jaw as he stared at her, then Seth. "Where are my shoes, keys, and phone?"

Lily didn't dare move her eyes from the cop and the gun. "They're under the bed in my room."

Seth's mouth dropped open. Yeah hindsight, it was a stupid hiding place.

"Drop your weapon and go get it," he spat.

Lily placed the rifle on the gravel drive and eased toward the house. She scooted past him, then ran up the stairs to retrieve his items. Her brain whirled and whirled as she attempted to process the information. When she got back, Seth sat on the porch swing, the cop perched on the railing across from him. She placed the items on the ground in front of him. "Sit next to him." She moved to the swing.

Hey Seth, we can take him.

The cop huffed and Seth snorted despite the tense situation. "Damn mind diarrhea," she said.

"Don't move!" He squatted down to put his shoes on, keeping a watchful eye on each of them. Before they knew it, he was at the SUV's door, shouting on the phone to his lieutenant. They sat in the backseat; their weapons were on the front floorboard under the cop's watchful eye. *Where's the trust, the love?*

Seth and Lily looked at each other. She wanted to know if he had a plan and she could read from the expression on his face he had the same question. The answer was no. Without hurting the cop in some way, they didn't know how to get away from him.

Lily had suggested to Detective Hottie that they work together and had reached for her rifle in the driveway, but he had stepped on her hand. He then ranted that he was sick and tired of their antics. He sounded just like her dad, which sucked all the rebellion out of her at the time. She created a new name for him as he slapped cuffs from the back of his car on her and Seth, Detective Hothead.

As he tore down Alternate 75 in pursuit of the black suburban, Journey blared from the radio. She realized he didn't know it was on.

"She got at least a five minute jump on us because I was tied up," he yelled into the phone. When he hung up, he took the time to glare at them in the rearview mirror. "Li Liu's life is at stake here. Do you understand that's why I can't arm you and say 'hey let's go shootin' like some red-neck?"

His impression of a southern accent was terrible. If Lily wasn't so devastated, she would have laughed.

"Because of your stalling, we may never catch her," he screamed over the sound of the siren and Steve Perry. He reached forward and clicked off the stereo.

Lily barely registered the greenery that sped by the window. Her brain worked over time chewing on the fat of this disaster. "Did you ever find the shooter in the woods at Li Liu's?" That earned her another glare from the cop. He didn't answer. "Because this whole set up feels like déjà vu." In the mirror, she saw his forehead wrinkle. "You know, the whole gun-toting person who acts as a diversion?" Her voice trembled, because right now, Detective Simms looked like a trained killer and she wasn't on his good side.

Seth reached across and squeezed her hand. "Sorry I called you a bird brain last night." She shrugged. Jumping a cop in the dark wasn't her finest moment. Now they were chasing after a black SUV. She didn't know the person inside; she just knew they were going the wrong way.

Detective Simms slammed on the brakes as another unmarked performed a Tokyo drift in front of them and cut them off. Lily rubbed her chest where the seatbelt dug into her.

"No, no, no. Shanghai shithouses!" Caldwell Simms face flushed crimson. "Not the Cowboy. This is not happening."

A very large man stepped out of the Crown Vic. *Is it a man or a tank?* He wore navy fatigue pants, boots, and a protective vest with GBI in yellow. His wraparound sunglasses and spiky blond hair screamed quintessential Bad Ass.

"Geez, it's like the Terminator and GI Joe had a child," Lily whispered. She swore the Cowboy looked up at her.

"Don't move," the cop growled to them before he shoved open his door and got out.

They could hear their entire exchange. "Simmmmm-ulator."

"Agent Mercer."

"Nice duds, man. The APD doing the whole casual Friday thing?" Lily bit back a chuckle. Detective Simms still wore Seth's ratty gray sweatpants, and undershirt with his black dress shoes, no socks. "Listen, Harding's dead. Scuba divers found him at the Philadelphia quarry in Tennessee. Found an abandoned black Suburban a mile up the road here. Helen PD is combing the fields to track the shooter."

"Any sign of Li Liu in the car?"

"Nothing so far. Scott and Lake want you to meet them at Helen PD headquarters. We've set up a command station. I'm to transport your prisoners."

Lily growled under her breath. She darted her eyes to her brother.

One eyebrow raised, Seth whispered, "Fuck this."

Lily reached through the bucket seats of the Explorer with her cuffed hands. It took two tries to get the pack and the rifle. "Shift now Seth and hang on to me."

She wiggled her leg, coiling the strap of the pack around her ankle before sliding the rifle strap around her neck. *Damn handcuffs*, but she didn't have time to shift to Shih Tzu and remove them. Seth clung to the front of her shirt, cat claws digging into the material and some skin.

"Lil, I'm not sure I want to do this."

"There's no way I'm going with the Cowboy."

She closed her eyes and drew on the pulsing from the crucible as the world around her started to spin, her stomach dropped out and then she plummeted down the hole in time and space.

"YEOW. YEOW."

Lily lay flat on her back on a very hard surface. Above her loomed a diverse canopy of hickory, oak, and sycamore leaves. The hickory leaves, shaped like so many hands, framed an overcast sky. The humidity-soaked air felt suffocating.

The distinctive sound of a cat retching caught her attention. She turned her head to see her Bobtail brother draped over a branch of a Dr. Seuss tree. That's what they had called Mimosa trees as kids because of their fluffy pink pom-pom blooms and feathery fern-like leaves.

She shook her head as she sat up. Her backpack lay in the tumbled gravel road ten feet ahead of her. When she turned to her brother, she noted her rifle hanging by its strap on a branch just below him along with his cargo shorts.

Lily kind of wished she could throw up. Teleporting always made her nauseous. Several deep cleansing breaths helped steady her nerves, stomach and woozy head.

"Yeeehaaawwww, what a ride." Seth gasped in his deep baritone. The woozy cat wore a silly grin.

"You liked that, did you?" Lily stood up. The handcuffs had disappeared. *Cool trick.* She had no idea how she did it. She retrieved the pack from the road as Seth scrambled down the tree, cargo shorts in his jaw. She turned her back while he shifted to human.

"We had to do it," he said coming up alongside her.

"I know."

"Who the hell was that woman?"

"I didn't recognize her scent or voice," Lily said.

"I smelled the Watcher too. Like she had been around him recently," he said in a hushed voice. "I smelled his scent at Liu's crime scene. He was there, watching them work."

"Or working *with* them." They stood on Tray Mountain Road, Forest Road 79. It was roughly an eight-mile stretch of curving tumbled gravel road that led to the Appalachian trails. From there, hikers trudged toward Tennessee, the summit, *or their doom if they found the*

Watcher.

Lily and Seth had been on this mountain as kids. The woman had said old dog Tray. Lily figured it was a hint. Tray Mountain was less than a twenty minute ride from the Quinn cabin.

They looked at the lush Georgia foliage surrounding the path. The dark canopy of trees juxtaposed with cheerful black-eyed Susans as they started their ascent. Lily had landed them about two miles from a gravel lot that led to the apex.

"You don't think they are at the bottom, do you?" she asked.

"No. This was a good call. The sick bastard wants us to hike to the top."

The forest felt lush and tropical like a jungle with its dense variegated flora and fauna. It contrasted drastically with the touristy town of Helen just six miles to the south. Although given the current situation, Lily much preferred walking down the cobblestone streets of the Alpine-like village...*and stopping for an ice cream at Scoop-to-Scoop Ice Cream Parlour.*

Seth's eyes widened. "You're thinking of food right now. Really?"

Lily adjusted the rifle she carried. Seth had the Glock as they hiked the road. They both used their heightened olfactory skills to scent the area. The path finally opened into a graveled round lot. A blue SUV was the sole car. Two paths diverged: one marked by a white blaze, the other by blue.

The car was empty, at least of anything living. She turned to look at Seth, fear and rage melding into a hateful knot in her stomach. "What the fuck does he want from us?"

"Apparently he's not an animal lover," smirked Seth.

"This guy could be waiting in the trees for us with a sniper rifle," she gasped.

"Ya think?" Seth asked, his blue cat eyes gleaming aquamarine in his human face.

"Kinda wish I hadn't rebelled against the gun training Dad kept trying with us," she said.

Seth sighed. "Oh how sweet. He left us a note." He walked toward a piece of paper lodged under the windshield wiper.

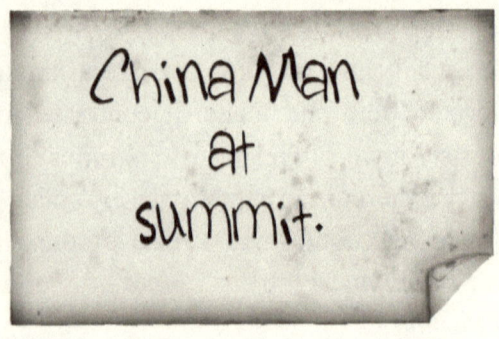

"Well, good thing he spelled that out for us," Lily said. "The lady that tried to bash my head in with a halberd is here too."

According to the signboard, they started their trek up the white blaze trail at 3,850 feet. The path angled uphill with oak, hickory, and locust trees serving as sentry.

Seth carried her pack. She left her back bare in case she needed to spread her wings. A half mile in, they came upon an outcropping and boulder that looked out to the

Hiawassee River basin. She stopped a moment to catch her breath. Lily wasn't out of shape, but her nerves were making respiration difficult. "This is crazy," she said.

"I know."

"Maybe we should have told Detective Simms," she said.

"So he could use the radio and notify his buddy who wants to slice and dice us?" He wiped the sweat off his face with the front of his shirt.

They turned south to continue their ascent. Tree roots provided stairs as they trekked around a left curve. To the right the ledge dropped off into woods so thick they could swallow a person whole.

Lily focused up ahead. Rosebay rhododendron bloomed light pink, creating romantic archways for their walk toward doom. As the sun struggled to break through the haze of the morning, it created a ghostly feel. Her thoughts went to Mr. Liu and if he was still alive. Seth had the Glock in hand, she the rifle. A scent filled her sinus cavities evoking a rage from within her, which made the crucible glow a demonic red. She detected a whisper, the slightest disturbance of air.

She lifted her rifle and stepped to Seth's side to fire at the dark shape about twenty-five yards up the trail. She fired again and considered shifting to Bird Light, but then Seth stumbled. Lily almost tripped over him as he fell to his knees. She noticed the bright orange tassel first. Her head muddled, she looked up, but was unable to locate the Watcher again. She knelt next to Seth, placing her rifle close to her on the ground. A dart almost three inches long stuck out of his neck.

"Lily?" He attempted to move which was making things worse. *Stubborn mule.*

He glowered as he registered her thought.

"Sorry," she whispered. "God, Seth. Stay with me." But his eyelids began to droop as she pulled at the dart. She tore some of his flesh as the end had barbs. "Crap. I'm sorry." The situation had her more confused than ever. Some lady fired real bullets at the Quinn cabin, but the Watcher was using tranquilizer darts? Why?

She looked up again through the sunny haze, scanning the path and the surrounding woods. It was quiet. Lily tried to swallow, but her mouth was bone dry.

"Seth, you need to shift," she pleaded. She wanted to fly and she wasn't sure she could carry him. His eyes fixed on her. They were barely slits now. He was too out of it to shift. That's when she started to talk in his head about the raunchiest things she could imagine. She used words she had never spoken to anyone as she described parts of women. Images went through her head that would make Hugh Hefner blush.

Seth opened a bleary eye and looked at her. He appeared too sedated to express shock. Lily watched as her words took effect and prompted Seth's shift to feline form. The cat lay limp as a rag doll in the dirt. Well now she knew at least one of Seth's triggers. Hadn't he insinuated as much in his college shifting story about his "first time?"

Lily ducked her head under the strap of the rifle so it hung around her neck. She put the Glock in her cargo shorts pocket. Then, she scooped up the limp cat's body. The tranquilizer dart had pushed her to the edge. Flashes of color swirled behind her eyelids. Her stomach dropped as they plunged down a now familiar spiraling hole. Branches flew around them, but she didn't notice.

In just two weeks, she had been attacked three times. She didn't recognize the men and women involved, but she realized there were at least two individuals working in tandem to destroy the Moores. Lily had tasted their deep hate tinged with an unyielding fear. Mr. Liu's presence throbbed in her brain. Instead of fading in the distance, it became a strong crescendo filling her ears. Hindsight is always 20-20. She'd have to do this alone. She needed to get her brother to safety.

CHAPTER 50

UNDER THE GUN

LIEUTENANT LAKE SCRUTINIZED him with a scowl. His breath smelled of Mountain Dew and pork rinds. Apparently, he had fallen off the health food wagon. "Another diversion?" Lake asked.

"Absolutely," Caldwell said. He now wore a pair of too tight jeans, work boots, and a black APD polo shirt he'd rounded up from their small group. Caldwell's car had all the windows shattered when the Moores disappeared into thin air.

When Caldwell had called Lake from the Quinn driveway, the lieutenant had been just twenty-five minutes away. When Caldwell didn't' check in the previous night and his cell phone rolled to voicemail in the morning, Lake had taken action. Actually, Tiny had. With his cell off, they couldn't use the GPS locator. Since Caldwell had taken his personal car, there was no tracking him.

Tiny broke into his apartment early in the morning and saw his notes left on the kitchen counter. *Good ole Tiny.*

Lake didn't have the whole story so he hadn't bawled him out yet. The tracking device Seth Moore obliterated against the cabin wall was not theirs and Agent Scott denied it was one of the Bureau's.

Scott and Agent Drew Mercer, aka the Cowboy to

Caldwell, combed through things downstairs while Lake and Caldwell spoke in hushed voices in the master bedroom of the Quinn cabin. The Helen Police Department's techs would be arriving soon and Caldwell was considering adjusting a few things. A thought he'd never entertained in his whole career.

Lieutenant Lake's eyes scanned the room. Lily's torn red tank top and sleep shorts rested upon the rumpled linens of the bed. Caldwell stood up and walked closer. He noted a pattern to the chaos of sheets and comforters. She had arranged the linens in a circle, built up like a bunker with a hole in the middle. *A nest.* Lieutenant Lake reached across and plucked a large, shiny feather from the sheets. "You wanna explain this?"

Caldwell stayed by the bed. He looked into the lieutenant's hazel eyes bracketed by crow's feet. He glanced at the open door then back at his boss. Caldwell crossed the room and shut the door. "Okay. Don't get mad—"

"Shit. That's my ex-wife's favorite line," Lake said, shaking his head.

"I followed a lead to the cabin, conducted surveillance —"

"Failed to call in for back up," added Lake. He shoved his hands in his black Dockers pants most likely so he wouldn't throttle Caldwell.

"I didn't have confirmation on any of my hunches." Caldwell held his hands up like a traffic cop so he could continue his story. "Waited for two hours on their back deck. Lily Moore returned and popped out of nowhere, startling me. I accidentally fired my gun. It grazed my hip."

Lake looked down at his hip, confused. "I noticed you

had a slight limp, but—"

"It was a flesh wound. They provided first aid...well more than first aid." Caldwell stopped. If he told the truth, would they take his badge now? "Lily Moore is a shape-shifter. She turned into a bird creature scaring the crap out of me in the dark, causing me to discharge my weapon. She has some healing abilities." He wasn't about to tell him that he laid on the couch last night half-baked while a Shih Tzu licked his wounds. Or that Lily Moore used a voodoo necklace lit up like a light saber to make all the pain go away.

"I thought she was a dog," Lake said.

"Um. Apparently, she can be several things. Hence, the reason they have avoided law enforcement. There's nothing normal about them. They're terrified. The suspect shot Ms. Moore and kidnapped Liu. Dr. Gladson treated Lily the night of the attack or she would have died. He used to treat Mr. Moore, a.k.a., Barney the dog.

"Koko Hitomi is a shifter. She's a bit unstable. We already know she supplied Ms. Sinclair and Seth Moore with Inderal. She used them as human guinea pigs," Caldwell said.

Lake's mouth hung open. His hands went to his short-cropped hair. "Sinclair?"

"Was a shapeshifter. The Inderal helped to suppress some of her animal instincts. Some shifters are more in control of themselves than others. Ms. Sinclair apparently had a really bad situation."

The lieutenant began to pace the oak floors while spinning his index finger in the air for Caldwell to wrap it up.

Like an auctioneer, Caldwell spit it out, "Miller attacked Moore that night and attempted to rape her. She shifted for the first time and defended herself as a bird, dog— creature."

Lake didn't blink.

"She stayed at the Jones/Harding residence as a Shih Tzu. The two men had no idea it was her."

"Well we already let Jones go. Harding is dead. Where are the Moores now?"

Caldwell sighed. "Well, after I shot myself, they attended to my wound. Then they took my phone, keys, and weapon from me and handcuffed me to the banister. Of course, they let me go when some shrieking woman opened fire on the place this morning. When I was calling you, I had them in the back of my car."

"Unrestrained?" gritted Lake.

"No. They were cuffed. We were fine until the Cowboy skidded out in front of us." Caldwell felt a throbbing at his right temple and his eye twitched.

Lake closed his eyes and shook his head. He held his index finger motionless as he re-engaged. "What woman?"

"I don't know."

Lake looked like he needed a shot of Wild Turkey, but Caldwell knew those habits were behind him. The lieutenant stared at him. Silence was not golden. Caldwell flashed him a nervous grin.

The lieutenant's hand shot to his hip to pick up his buzzing cell phone. "Lake."

Caldwell breathed deeply then backed up to sit on the lumpy couch.

"Shit. Shit. Fuck!" Lake backed up and sat on the bed, smashing the nest. He hung up. "That was Tiny. We got the name and we got the tire tread results."

"Who?"

Lake's scrunched up his beet red face. He looked distraught enough to cry. Caldwell gave him a moment. The lieutenant ran downstairs. After the screen door slammed shut, Caldwell looked around the room again. He wanted to be driving, pursuing someone at 95 miles per hour, but he had no direction so the point was moot. He had to wait for someone to report a sighting of the shooter or the Moores.

Caldwell reached across to pick up the ripped tank top on the bed. As he grasped the fabric in his hand, his head exploded with a blinding pain. He called out while dropping to his knees. Disoriented, he grabbed his head as he heard Lily's screams in his head. Lily's rage transcended any other thoughts or feelings in Caldwell's brain. *Hibacker Farm. Shot. Paint horse.*

Caldwell shook his head while sucking in air. He was kneeling on the floor with his arms on the bed, the red tank in his right hand, his head lolling forward. In the background, he heard the pounding of feet on the stairs.

He stood up, dropping the shirt.

"Everything all right up here," Scott asked, followed by Agent Mercer.

"Sure."

"What the hell were you shouting about?" the Cowboy asked.

Licking his lips, he tried out his tongue. "Hibacker Farm."

Scott hesitated. Lake came back in the room. "What's going on?"

"I think Lily Moore's been shot at Hibacker Farm."

"How the hell do you know that?" Agent Mercer asked. Scott placed a hand on her hip.

"She's been in my head before. You can question me if you want, but look around. Obviously, they've been here. I was right about the cabin. I know I'm right about this."

Lake looked at him intensely. His signature antenna was sticking up in the back of his otherwise perfectly combed hair. "Vest up. We've got a bead on our shooter."

"What?" they all asked.

"I'll explain, but let's move people."

As they burst from the cabin, he heard Lake on the cell phone. "I need a warrant..."

CHAPTER 51

HIBACKER FARM

IN THE UNMARKED Caldwell and Lake raced down Alternate 75 with sirens going. Lake slowed only upon sight of the enormous billboard:

The lieutenant missed the gravel driveway the first time because they were both too busy looking at the sign, which was in the middle of the field rather than marking the entrance. Lake glanced in the rearview mirror before skidding to a stop and driving on to the shoulder of the road to back track to their destination.

Jesus, and he makes fun of my driving.

Once in the driveway, the car rocked to a halt and Caldwell jumped out, gun drawn. Scott had returned to the command post at the Helen PD headquarters and Agent Mercer had headed to the airport to see about a chopper.

Lake took the unmarked slowly down the rest of the driveway with the intent of checking out the house. No one answered at the farmhouse when they had called on the phone.

Caldwell scanned the perfect rows of green cornstalks that stood with their yellow silk painting a line to the vanishing point. At their convergence, the old white farmhouse ghosted against a cerulean sky.

He viewed the vast acreage, feeling overwhelmed. When he spotted the faded gray barn, he took off at a run. At the fence, a beautiful Paint horse stood stock-still. On the ground, a bare foot poked out from the last row of corn. *Such an idyllic scene spoiled by the stark naked human body.*

He approached with caution, looking from side to side and behind him. She had dumped the body here and left, but he wasn't taking any chances. The man wore a peaceful expression. The sound that reached Caldwell next brought him to a halt.

"Zzzzzzzzzz."

"Mr. Moore?" Caldwell said as he drew closer.

"Mmm?" Seth's eyes fluttered. He was nude except for the backpack placed strategically across his pelvic area.

Caldwell walked to him and nudged his shoulder with his foot.

"Seth!" Caldwell said.

Seth jumped straight up in the air before searching the ground. His eyes were wide, his hair on end.

"Easy!" Caldwell's heartbeats thudded in his temples. He could see the terror in Seth's eyes.

"Lily?" he asked, spinning around before facing

Caldwell.

"Take it easy." Caldwell looked at the dried blood on his neck. "You shot?"

"Darted." Moore rubbed his head as if to comfort himself. He reached into the backpack, drew out a pair of shorts and slipped them on. Caldwell pretended to be preoccupied with the horses.

"We need to go!" Moore urged.

"Where?" Caldwell reached out to steady him, but he swatted him away. Moore's eyes were bright blue and glowing, his mouth hung open, like...a cat flehming the air.

"Tray Mountain. Tray Gap—the Summit." Moore adjusted his backpack and took off down the row of corn. Caldwell was amazed that a second ago, he had been passed out cold. His shoulder radio squawked as he ran after him.

"House is clear," Lake said.

Caldwell felt nauseous. *Dammit.* Lily had purposefully led him to her brother. And now, the perp had her on the mountain exactly how he wanted her.

Alone.

CHAPTER ✒ 52

LILY

HER MOUTH FELT like sand. The heat rose off the rock in vertical waves. While she had taken care of Seth, her fan club had made their way to the summit of Tray Mountain and then beyond. Lily stood alone on the rocky floor of the summit. Like a stage cue, a spray-painted white arrow pointed to the center of the surface. She remembered the portent of the vulture triumvirate as she looked at another triad. This time they were benchmarks—three round geodetic survey markers punched into the rock. Two had arrows, the main one, a triangle.

Lily felt a cold sweat break out across her upper lip. The triangle, the ancient symbol of a spiritual gateway—a possible geographic area of demonic activity and influence on earth. *Lovely.* Straight ahead was a blue blaze trail composed of a tunnel of trees with stone steps leading down. She knew they had gone this way. With each step, she wondered what the hell they had in store for her. But she continued because she knew they had Li Liu.

Once through the tunnel of trees, the path opened up. She continued past a campsite on the right and halted in the shadows of tulip poplars and oak trees. They towered over a field of pink phlox, orange mushrooms, and lime green ferns—for some reason she thought of Lucky Charms cereal and her stomach grumbled.

Her eyes followed the curve of the trail. She'd been here once before, with her father. Lily knew that just past the field, the path wound through trees another twenty yards then opened up at a campsite with the Montray Shelter, a gray Adirondack-style refuge for Appalachian trail hikers. Without hesitation, she took to the air.

If they hadn't been arguing, they may have heard her stellar landing as Bird Light in a tree nearby. Lily thrashed to untangle her wings from some branches. They both carried assault rifles. The woman must have been in her late fifties. Her voice carried through the air as she admonished Mr. Liu's kidnapper. They were by the fire circle, in front of the raised shelter.

Next to the woman's foot lie Li Liu curled up on his side. Manacles bound his ankles and wrists. He mumbled under his breath with his eyes squeezed shut.

"Shoot to wound, then I'll dart her," the Watcher said.

"The police are on their way. I'm not taking any chances. I'm just gonna kill the bitch and we can get out of here. You saw what she did to my son!"

Lily waited. The silver ball of the roulette wheel rolled around her head, finally coming to rest in its slot. Nothing made sense. Yet, everything made sense. Life was a game of chance. It had spun her round and round. One of her attackers was Phil Miller's *mother*? Was Phil the Croupier who had started the wheel turning? *Had he started with Peter? What are my odds?*

The man she recognized from somewhere.

"I need some information from her. Don't kill her."

"Ernie, I don't know why you didn't bring the hounds.

They would have flushed her out by now," said Mrs. Miller. She pronounced "why" in the traditional southern way, cutting it short to "Whah."

Ernie?

The mention of dogs triggered a remote memory of meeting Ernie what's-his-face at a company picnic. He was the Atlanta PD's tracker. Was Ernie working with anyone else on the force?

She remembered Seth had suspected it was a member of law enforcement. He recognized the scent from Liu's property.

She had the advantage. The logical thing to do was shoot them. The problem? She had lost the rifle when teleporting Seth. She left the pack with him as well. However, she did have the Glock resting in the back of her waistband. The cargo pockets just hadn't seemed as secure as the back of her granny panties.

She needed to pull it together for Mr. Liu. At that moment, she realized his eyes weren't closed all the way. Touching the crucible for strength, she spoke to him. *I'm here, Mr. Liu.* His lids fluttered as if he were struggling to open them. He shook his head.

As quietly as she could, she clawed her way down the tree and drew the Glock. Lily retracted her wings so that her back rested firmly against the knotty bark of an old oak. She took one more breath. Counting seemed like a good strategy. One...two...three—she made it to the next tree. One...two...three...and to the next one. It was just like doing the waltz. *No problem.*

Mud and debris covered her brown shirt that remained incredibly intact. Scratches decorated her arms from twigs, branches, and flying debris during her cyclonic rage storm that had *teleported* her and Seth. She couldn't think about Seth right now. Her head already throbbed from exertion and stress.

"Let's just shoot him and leave!" Miller said, pointing down at Li Liu like he was damaged goods. Lily's heart hammered wildly against her ribcage. She was within twenty feet now. She needed to get closer. Once she fired, she'd need to follow up with fangs and claws.

A prodigious amount of acid swirled in her stomach. Her legs felt like noodles as she crouched low, placed her gun on the ground and shifted to a Shih Tzu. With the gun in her teeth, she crawled on her belly through the long grass until she was ten feet away and hugged the base of one of the aged oaks with its twisted limbs that had survived the crucible that was Tray Mountain.

Swallowing vomit, she shifted back and raised the gun assuming the stance her father had taught her. The shot rang out echoing across the expanse of trees into the valley below. She missed her target. *No!* Ernie dropped to his belly in response to the blast, gun in hand. Screeching filled Lily's sensitive ears. She had missed the dog handler, but struck the woman. Miller writhed around on the ground yelling obscenities while blood spurted from her upper arm.

Lily dropped and rolled behind a rock to avoid his bullets. *Note to self: must learn how to aim gun.* She peered around the rock to see Mr. Liu scooting on elbows and knees away from Ernie. Again, he shook his head in an emphatic "no" at her.

The overwhelming compulsion to protect overrode any sense of reason. Fangs filled her mouth, her legs and arms expanded, and her back ached as wings released. She had thick furry legs like a Saint Bernard with the claws of a mountain cat. Something wet soaked her paw. *Eesh, drool.*

With a roark, she launched herself at Ernie Gates intending to pin him and tear out his throat. She heard a snap and felt wire tangle around her as she thrashed around on the ground. The more she clawed and bit at the trap, the more tangled she became. The net consisted of a chain mail material like the kind used for shark diving.

Desperate, she looked for Mr. Liu. His energy pulsed around him in a waning, green layer. Lily focused on Ernie Gates, whose energy field was an angry red as he stalked toward her. He was a good tracker and *trapper*. Too focused on Mr. Liu's face and planning her stealth approach, she hadn't noticed anything in the tall grass.

"I saw you at the football field. A monster, just like my mother," he said, the gun trained between her eyes. Lily's head buzzed like it was full of a thousand bees. "I started to feel something after our fight at Liu's studio. At first, I thought it was your scratch that precipitated the change. That you infected me. All the steroid treatments Hitomi had given me started to strengthen me, but it was after the studio that I was able to block Hitomi from invading my mind. Then I thought of Phillip who was a Vestige too and had gotten treatments. You bit and clawed him, but nothing happened."

Lily struggled with the net some more. She actually was making some headway with her teeth, breaking the chinks in the chain mail. She stopped when he leaned down. "It was difficult with your friends of the Atlanta Homicide division swarming the place, but I managed to procure your grandmother's letter and get it translated. You need to tell me about the crucible and how it works. Otherwise, I'll shoot different parts of Mr. Liu until he bleeds out."

Lily growled.

He laughed. "With your grandmother's necklace, I can finally be who I was meant to be—the First Born."

Lily refused to meet his eyes. She looked off toward Barbara Miller. Miller's keening from the bullet wound had given way to whimpers, but now she was silent, curled in the fetal position against a rock of the fire circle, still clutching her rifle. Lily' heart lurched when she saw Mr. Liu worming his way toward the woman's leg.

Lily looked at Gates, but it was too late. He sensed the movement behind him and turned to shoot. Lily wrapped her paw, net and all, around his ankle as rage and pain coalesced into her vortex and drew the evil into the spinning hole with her.

CHAPTER ✒ 53

THE SUMMIT

AT 10:30 A.M., THE temperature hit ninety-two degrees. Sweat rolled down Caldwell's neck, tracing the path of his spine. Not a twinge of Lily had hit him since the cabin. They had notified Helen PD that they were apprehending suspects in the park. The local police were not part of the team going in much to Caldwell's relief. He had no idea how to explain to anyone else what they might see. However, local officers were assisting in blocking off the area to traffic and another team was on standby if they required back up. Agent Mercer was in the chopper making passes of the area overhead. Scott had rejoined them and stood by their side holding a sniper rifle, her huge eyes intense.

"Shoot to wound," Lake said.

Caldwell bit the inside of his cheek. "Lieutenant?"

"If it's Ernie, know he's a good shot."

Scott nodded. "Barbara Miller's not a bad shot either. She won the Dixie National Rifle contest three years in a row as a teenager." Scott's brows rose. "'Course, she's fifty now, but that doesn't mean she's lost it."

Caldwell looked to her in question.

"I mean lost her skills. Can't speak about her mental stability."

"I know she's real pissed off about her son," Caldwell

said, shifting his weight. They stood around the hood of Lake's unmarked. They had a short, but steep hike to the summit. Visitors at the Bison View Lodge reported shots fired close to thirty minutes ago. He looked at Scott then at the Lieutenant. He wanted to trust them, but he knew they were considering the circumstances of Lily Moore's disappearance and the fact that technically she had been on the run.

Lake knew the details of Caldwell being captive inside the Quinn cabin, Scott didn't. Caldwell didn't want to wait a second more, but he wanted Scott to understand. "Lily Moore has some special abilities."

Scott turned to him. "Simms, you think I'm a complete dumbass. I can put things together. I've seen some freaky shit. Don't patronize me. I watch *Fringe*. I've studied the forensic reports including the ones from the wildlife lab."

He nodded once and took the lead, gun drawn. He turned around once more and looked at both of them. "Don't hurt her."

Lake rolled his eyes. "Simms, cut the shit or I'm leaving you in the car—handcuffed, windows up, no air."

Caldwell charged toward the summit with Lieutenant Lake. Scott brought up the rear, stopping and scanning the area with her scope. Caldwell arrived first, pulling up short. Lake almost ran into him. Greenery encircled the apex that was no more than a ten by twelve foot stepped rock floor. The only thing visible was the sky. Without communicating, the three performed an awkward side-step, searching the space and the dense surrounding shrubs.

Nothing.

"Shit!" Caldwell said.

Scott took off for a break in the foliage, a rocky path descending the back of the mountain. Caldwell didn't let her get far before taking the lead. They walked single file down the narrow path lined by dwarfed and gnarled oaks. Eight minutes later, they came upon a campsite with a raised wooden shelter. A slumped figure in jeans, boots, and a blood-soaked camouflage shirt lay against a rock.

Lake and Scott scanned the trees, looking into the shadows as Caldwell crept closer, his adrenaline shooting through his veins like a speedball.

They drew up to her calling out their credentials.

When Caldwell reached the rock, he squatted down to check her pulse. Sweat and mud matted a mess of blonde hair. Smoker's lines radiated out from her mouth in a sunburst pattern. Someone had used a sock for a tourniquet to staunch the bleeding. Lake radioed for emergency personnel.

Barbara Miller opened one eye.

"Mrs. Miller, you're going to be okay. Paramedics are on their way," Caldwell said. When he looked up, Scott was vigilant, scanning up and down in the trees and shrubs.

"Shot me," Miller said, voice hoarse.

"Who?" Caldwell asked. Lake and Scott stood with their backs to him facing the trees.

"The demon freak," spat Miller. She scrunched her face into one tan wrinkle. Caldwell waited. "Lily Moore."

"Where is she?" he asked.

"I have no idea," she retorted, resting her head back down against the rock.

"Hang in there, Mrs. Miller. We need your help," Caldwell pleaded. "Is Ernie here?"

She lifted her head slightly and glared at him. "She took him away through the air. You believe that shit?"

Caldwell heard Scott shouting behind him. "Drop your weapon."

He turned and stood up. A man stumbled; his slight build wavered drunkenly, holding the side of the shelter to steady himself.

"Li?" called the lieutenant as he took off toward him. The man sat down hard on his behind, finally surrendering to his body's will. Bending over, Lake surveyed his condition. Caldwell pulled up next to him while Scott attended to Miller. Bruises bloomed all over his face and arms. His left eye closed to a slit.

"She's gone," he rasped. "He's got her!" Tears streaked down Li Liu's battered face.

CHAPTER 54

FROM THE LOST NOTES OF PETER MARX

August 20, 2010

Something has gone incredibly wrong. When I came into Dr. H's lab this morning, the place was trashed. I read in her notes that Subject VI has homicidal thoughts and the doc is concerned he is planning to hurt someone. She's refusing to issue any more steroids to him. I'm sure he can find anabolic steroids from another source.

I waited outside Dr. H's home tonight. Subject VI showed up and they argued. He left around 9:30 p.m. and got into a blue Suburban. I couldn't see his face—he wore a baseball cap.

I followed him so I could figure out who he is.

He pulled up in front of MY house and waited

outside for an hour. I didn't think he saw me, but he must have. When he finally left, I tried to follow. He ran a red light and sped off, but I got his license plate number.

As I returned to the house, it occurred to me that I might not be his target. Perhaps, the target is my neighbor, Subject T.

I'm worried about my safety, my neighbor's, and Lily's. Tomorrow, I'll confront Dr. H so I can learn his identity. Maybe then I'll have some idea what to do.

–Peter

CHAPTER ✐ 55

MURDER

A BACKWASH OF pigment spread across the water forming thick tentacles that probed the lake's surface then sank down seeking the silty bottom.

Her head throbbed from pressure mixed with pain. Lily's eyes trained on the tentacles following their path until she hit the wide-eyed stare of Ernie Gates. Memories came flooding back. Bile burned up into her nose as she retched into the water.

Gates lay shipwrecked on a rock—his lower torso still in the water. Blood oozed from his head, trickled to the stone, then dispersed into the water creating the bloody oil slick. Head wounds bleed a lot. She knew that first hand.

Panic jolted her as she detected his faint heartbeat and shallow breaths. She scanned the brush, trees, and footpaths as a rush of human sounds assaulted her ears. Lily thrashed toward Gates. A series of convulsions rather than swim strokes carried her across the inlet. Her side felt like someone had taken a soldering iron to it. Shot. Again. By the man she dragged under the wooden footbridge with her.

A child's high-pitched voice carried through the still air. A family walked and babbled as their feet pounded on the wooden slats overhead. She held her breath hoping she had stirred up enough mud from the bottom to mix up the blood. When they were out of range, she released her breath and looked into the eyes of a killer.

He blinked. His mouth moved. She tilted her head as he whispered into her ear.

Ten minutes later, Lily still hid under the bridge. She recognized her surroundings—Unicoi Lake where Smith Creek came into the body of water. The pain in her side caused her to examine her wound. The bullet had traveled clean through and her preternatural body was using the powers of the crucible to begin healing. The locket's power couldn't quell the queasy feeling overwhelming her though. She gathered that had more to do with the now dead man next to her.

Judging by the height of the sun in the sky, it had to be early afternoon. She considered curling up with the corpse and waiting until dark before moving. She doubted police helicopters and search teams would spread out from Tray Mountain to this location for some time. However, someone's friendly canine could easily root her out. Them out.

She hadn't intended to mortally injure Gates, just stop him from hurting Li Liu anymore. Relief mixed with the cesspool of fear swirling in her gut. At least it happened naturally, with a rock and all. If that's considered natural—crashing down to earth like a meteor. She had only teleported a few times and always with a strong intent in her head. This time she just leapt thinking of water. It's a wonder she didn't wind up in the middle of the Atlantic.

The stench of fish, mold, algae, and blood permeated her senses as Lily considered what she must do to survive the rest of the day and night. She did the only thing she could—she turned into a ShihTzu.

CHAPTER ✒ 56

FIRST BORN

SARAH CLEMENS SAT at her vanity brushing her soft, white hair. Lily watched through the swing-hinged window that hung open to the milder temperatures. Clemens stopped her grooming and turned her attention to the 10:00 nightly news. Lily followed her gaze to the TV screen.

Detective Caldwell Simms looked mighty fine in a navy blue suit as a reporter interviewed him about the discovery of a body at Unicoi Lake. Lily sighed through the screen as she rested in the branches of a mimosa tree just a week after her encounter on Tray Mountain. The mosquitoes didn't dare come near her.

"Yes Ma'am, that's what I said. At 6:30 yesterday morning, a fisherman discovered the body that has been identified as that of Ernie Gates. Next of kin have been notified," Simms said.

The reporter shoved the microphone back into his face. "But wasn't Gates an employee of the APD?"

"He was a Search and Rescue handler who contracted with various organizations including ours."

"What was the cause of death?"

"The Medical Examiner has yet to make the final determination. Authorities retrieved a vehicle from the water as well. There's a possibility Mr. Gates was driving at a high rate of speed and crashed through the guardrail on Georgia 356."

Lily grinned. Genius, really. Staging it to look like he crashed with her in the car. She planned to resurface in a week or so claiming amnesia.

"There are reports that he is responsible for the kidnapping of a retired officer, Li Liu and is also tied to the murders of Peter Marx and Gates's biological mother, Mona Sinclair."

"This is an ongoing investigation. I can't comment further at this time."

"What about the Moore girl?"

Clemens huffed and strode across the room in her white cotton nightgown to turn off the TV. "Liars," she hissed.

Lily protracted a claw to slice the screen so she could slip in with ease. She really had wanted to hear what Detective Hottie had to say about her. She wore a lovely new green sundress she'd found on someone's clothesline. A pink pom-pom from the Dr. Seuss tree perched behind her right ear. Other than the skunky roots she had, she thought she looked darn fine for a presumed dead girl.

Clemens turned and shrieked. "Jesus Christ!"

"Not even close, lady."

Clemens scrunched her nose in disgust. "I'm calling the police."

"Go for it. They would love to hear this story." Lily said.

Clemens backed up and sat at the vanity. Her hand travelled back toward the grooming paraphernalia and a gaudy broach on the surface.

"Uh,uh," Lily said. The woman pressed her lips together in a tight line as she released the sharp pin.

"What do you want?"

"Retribution for Peter and Mona." *And even Frank.* He may have been racketeering, but he didn't deserve to die. Lily's anger kept the tears at bay.

Clemens cocked an eyebrow, setting off the fine wrinkles of her face.

"Your nephew and I had a heart-to-heart. I know that you told him about his biological mother when you discovered the true story about Mona's twins. I know you were aware of Dr. Hitomi working with shapeshifters and you steered him to her—thinking she could help him. I know you hated your sister because she was beautiful and powerful even though she wasn't the First Born. But you *are*. Yet, you're not able to shapeshift. Are you?"

Clemens clasped her delicate hands in her lap as she glared at Lily.

"And I know you pulled all the strings including paying off Frank Harding to hide Peter's notebook in a safety deposit box after Ernie killed him since Peter had discovered Ernie's plans to murder Mona." Lily took a breath and smoothed down the creases in the front of her dress.

"You are really troubled like they said. I thought your brother had issues. But you definitely need some jolts to the synapses."

"Or possibly a few bullets would help me. Huh, Bonnie? Nice shooting at the Quinn cabin. Next time don't ditch the car. I'm sure they'll find some trace evidence when they finish processing Ernie's car."

"Miss Moore. I knew your father. Your grandfather knocked up my sister and created this mess in the first place." Her brow wrinkled as she looked down at her nails. "Actually I believe your mother's family started the trouble. But your grandmother's dead now, isn't she?"

Sarah Clemens turned back to the vanity and began to brush her hair again.

Lily clutched the fenghuang locket and averted her eyes as she thought of Waipo. It became impossible to swallow. She reminded herself to breathe as tears filled her eyes. The crucible glowed red sending its reassuring waves to wash over her. Lily welcomed the tremendous freedom of her stomach dropping before she teleported. She had said her piece.

CHAPTER ✒ 57

AFTERMATH

CALDWELL RESTED AGAINST an overturned rain barrel at Li Liu's ranch. Liu sat on a shoeing stool next to him, his bruised temple exhibiting a yellow starburst pattern. His haunted eyes remained on his mare, Rosie. Caldwell swallowed a lump in his throat as he watched early morning haze circle the base of the white pine trees in the distance.

"Nothing?" he asked Li as he looked across to a hobble containing Rosie's saddle and an enormous white cat with bobbed tail. The cat didn't blink, but stayed seated in the saddle as if taunting him.

Liu answered, his voice devoid of emotion. "She's out there. Considering the injuries she's suffered over the last month, my guess is she's trying to remember who she is and what happened." Liu rested his chin atop his hands propped up by a cane.

"Sarah Clemens is in custody. We found trace evidence on the car she drove to Helen. We also found Peter Marx's notebook in her possession." Caldwell sighed as he looked to the cat. In the dirt beneath the hobble rested an ankle monitor. Caldwell didn't make an effort to keep the annoyance out of his voice. "Really? Can't you even pretend while I'm here that it's effectively keeping you in state until the hearing?"

Seth the cat leapt down, leaned back and put his back leg through the device before shifting into human form. Caldwell averted his eyes as Moore slipped into a pair of shorts he retrieved from the ground.

"Sorry," he said softly.

Caldwell shook his head. Seth had apologized quite a bit, but it didn't change the circumstances. The captain had placed Caldwell on administrative leave while the department investigated and decided his fate.

Seth was cooperating with the authorities. The judge had released him with the ankle monitor into Li Liu's supervision until the next hearing. The DA was working a plea bargain for Seth. He most likely would get community service as long as he testified regarding Dr. Hitomi and her research.

Caldwell didn't really care about anything else right now. Sure, he worried his career was in the crapper, but until he saw Lily again, he knew he wouldn't be able to sleep or rest or concentrate on anything else. She was out there somewhere.

CHAPTER ✒ 58

AND SHE FLEW

LILY STARED AT Waipo's head stone. With trembling fingers, she traced the outline of fucanglong, the dragon of hidden treasure engraved upon the surface. The figure assumed to undulate and pulse, but it was just her grief bringing him to life deceiving her mind and heart.

She placed a single red rose upon the earth, "Shangdi baoyou," she whispered. God blesses.

The crucible pulsed red, blue, yellow, white, and black against her chest. Lily held her breath as the most exquisite singing reached her ears. Off in the emerald hills of the Nanhua Mountains the fenghuang sang to her its soothing songs.

After three days in her grandmother's village, Lily still felt 7,000 miles away from the truth, but closer to Waipo. While tempted to remain cloistered in the remote village, Lily knew she couldn't hide from life. With longing, she searched the landscape again for the colorful bird, but it had disappeared leaving an empty place in her heart. She hadn't found all the answers here, but managed to garner some peace and strength, taking the first step towards healing.

Time to face issues back home.

She couldn't procrastinate any longer. She planned to

visit a certain Atlanta homicide detective. *Will he be Detective Hottie or Hothead when he sees me?* She clutched the crucible as her stomach lurched and she took a chance, plunging down the spinning roulette wheel of life.

ACKNOWLEDGMENTS

To Rosemary Hill, widow of poet Christopher Logue, thank you for permission to use "Come to the Edge." A special thanks to Editor, Brittiany Koren of Written Dreams for her guidance.

To my critique partners and beta readers—you have my deepest appreciation and respect: Karen Chamberlain, Amanda Haas, Catherine O'Brien, Lin Llamazales, Cheryl Puetz, Byron and Bronwyn Robinson, Heather Smith, and Neil Wilkinson. To Tammy, thanks for discussing diabetes with me. Shout out to V.A.M.P. Book Club whose members have cheered me along the way.

To beta reader and incredible friend, Stacy Bailey Darnell, thanks for always championing me and listening. To fellow author, M.E. May (Michele)—this book would still just be a thought without you! Your constant encouragement, guidance, and strength have been my inspiration.

Other wonderful sources of knowledge: Chinese language —Dr. Liuxi Meng, Kennesaw State University; Circe Tsui, and Lily Li. Police Procedure—Dr. Stan Crowder, Kennesaw State University; Lee Lofland and Derek Pacifico via Yahoo Groups Crimescenewriter; Retired Officer Ted Richardson. Ballistics— GA Firing Line; fellow writer, Claire Burke. Medication questions—Kim and Nattaya as well as the rest of the Walgreens Pharmacy staff in Marietta, GA. General medical questions—Pat Higgins.

For all those experts who helped me along the way, thank you for sharing your knowledge. I take full responsibility if I still didn't get it right.

Finally, thank you to the Georgia Writers Association for being an amazing resource for authors.

ABOUT THE AUTHOR

Tricia lives in Marietta, Georgia with her husband, Lou, her little yappy dog, Lola Belle, and her big orange mutant cat, George. Her two stepsons, Joseph and Robert, make stopovers as well, making sure to keep life an adventure.

Tricia earned a B.A. in Journalism and Anthropology from Indiana University in Bloomington. After moving to Atlanta in 1992, she obtained her Masters of Education in Communication Disorders from Georgia State University and spent a decade working as a Speech-Language Pathologist, most recently in the pediatric field treating children on the Autism Spectrum.

Writing has always been a part of her life—like breathing and chocolate. For more information about Tricia and her books, please visit www.triciazoeller.com.